Praise for
Patric...

CAROLINA GIRL
"*Carolina Girl* is full of the warmth, humor and poignancy that make Rice's books very special."
—*Romantic Times*

McCLOUD'S WOMAN
"Intriguing and passionate."
—*Booklist*

ALMOST PERFECT
"Brilliant and riveting, edgy and funny."
—MARY JO PUTNEY

IMPOSSIBLE DREAMS
"Patricia Rice shows her diverse talent as a writer in *Impossible Dreams*. . . . [It] will leave readers with a smile on their faces."
—Kentucky *Murray Ledger & Times*

BLUE CLOUDS
"Totally engrossing! Fast-moving, great characters, suspense, and love—a must-read!"
—*The Literary Times*

Also by Patricia Rice

GARDEN OF DREAMS
VOLCANO
IMPOSSIBLE DREAMS
BLUE CLOUDS
NOBODY'S ANGEL
ALMOST PERFECT
McCLOUD'S WOMAN
CAROLINA GIRL

CALIFORNIA GIRL

A NOVEL

PATRICIA RICE

BALLANTINE BOOKS • NEW YORK

California Girl is a work of fiction. Names, characters, places, and incidents are the products of the author's imagination or are used fictitiously. Any resemblance to actual events, locales, or persons, living or dead, is entirely coincidental.

An Ivy Books Mass Market Original

Published in the United States by Ivy Books, an imprint of The Random House Publishing Group, a division of Random House, Inc., New York.

Ivy Books and colophon are trademarks of Random House, Inc.

The excerpt from the forthcoming title *Much Ado About Magic* is reprinted by permission of Signet Books, a division of Penguin Group (USA), Inc.

ISBN 0-8041-1984-8

Printed in the United States of America

Ballantine Books website address: www.ballantinebooks.com

OPM 9 8 7 6 5 4 3 2 1

ACKNOWLEDGMENTS

I am immensely grateful to my brainstorming buddies who not only understand when I demand hot air balloons but willingly go along for the ride. Without you guys, I'd be up in the air without a way down.

As always, I bow before the expertise of Connie Rinehold. If there are gaping holes in this book, I put them there despite Connie's warnings.

And for the first time, I thank Renee Halverson for her excellent perception just when I thought I was so mired in the mud I might never crawl out.

Bless Pat Nagle for providing crucial Santa Fe details after I had to bypass the town because of a snowstorm!

For those readers who may be interested in learning more about diseases of the heart, I recommend beginning with the American Heart Association at www.americanheart.org.

The resources of the National Historic Route 66 Federation (www.national66.org) have been invaluable in researching this book. Thanks to them, the highway may be gone in places, but not forgotten.

I have strayed from the beaten path occasionally and created places where I needed them, but if I name a building, place, or thing, it's still there, or was last time I checked.

❧ ONE ❧

"It's my life and I'll live it my way!"

At this clearly recognizable battle cry from behind the hospital room door, Alys Seagraves almost cracked up. Blown away in relief, she slid down the wall of the corridor and tried not to laugh—or she might end up crying.

Mame was alive and kicking. Not only kicking, but butchering Frank Sinatra songs.

Alys had spent these last few hours terrified that her best friend may have died like everyone else in her small universe.

Assuming a lotus position on the corridor floor, she sought her center as she'd learned to do in Mame's School of Alternative Life Lessons. Palms turned up and resting on her knees, she took a deep breath.

Deliberately wiping out negativity, she concentrated on the here and now, seeking the good times as Mame had taught her to do. Head up, eyes closed, Alys focused on the long-ago morning when her six-year-old self complained about writing the "ys" in "Alys" instead of the easier "Alice."

Her conservative, gray-haired mother got a faraway look in her eyes and smiled. "I thought if I could have a

1

beautiful miracle like you at forty, we should celebrate with a special name, one all your own."

It wasn't until later that Alys realized what a break in tradition that bit of whimsy was for her conventional parents. She treasured that memory. She loved them for trying to give her the freedom they'd never experienced in their hardworking lives.

"Life can't be vacuum-packed and preserved like meat in a freezer!" Mame's familiar voice bellowed from the hospital room across the corridor. "Don't put that thing on me."

Groaning at Mame's cockeyed argument, Alys leaned her head against the concrete block wall.

If the hospital personnel and visitors scurrying past her thought it odd to see a twenty-seven-year-old woman assume the lotus position in a hospital corridor, they offered no indication of it. Alys was rather proud that she'd made it this far into the bowels of her personal hell.

Love is the power that heals. She repeated her mantra, seeking her energy balance. She would think positive thoughts and look to the bright, gleaming future. Mame would not die. Not like her father. And mother.

And Fred. Orphaned and widowed within two years.

Angrily fighting back tears, she scooted up the wall, using the cold concrete as a brace for her backbone. Shoving away, she marched the few feet into Mame's room.

"Thank goodness, there you are!" Disregarding the nurse attempting to take her pulse, Mame cranked the head of her bed into a sitting position at the sight of Alys. "Get me out of here. I have entirely too much to do to lie about any longer while these people poke and prod me."

Mame's naturally thin build gave her lined face an almost ascetic appearance of skin and sharp bones, but the vivid red of her hair bespoke her vibrancy. She'd had her roots touched up for the trip.

"What did the doctor say?" Alys hoped her voice wasn't as hoarse as it sounded as she tried to ignore the dripping IV and clicking heart monitors.

Suppressing her fear fed the bubbling panic. In her head, the room diminished to throbbing tubes, blinking lights, and the pounding thrum of heartbeats. Her breath caught in her lungs.

"Sit down," Mame ordered. "You're turning whiter than I am."

The nurse chuckled and dropped Mame's bony wrist to note her chart. "The doctor said she has a myocardial infarction, and he wants to run more tests. Are you family?"

"They've called Elliot," Mame said with disapproval, not giving Alys time to reply, much less to run away or even sit down. "We'll have to make a break for it before he gets here. Sign me out."

"Unless you're family, you can't do that." The nurse pulled the curtains across the window, shutting out the sunshine. "You shouldn't even be in here. Mrs. Emerson needs her rest."

"I have all eternity to rest," Mame protested.

"Mame, it's all right." Why did Mame not want to see her famous nephew? Alys thought Doc Nice might be very handy to have around in a hospital. He'd always seemed immensely intelligent and amusing on the radio. "You scared the bejeebers out of me back there," she said to change the subject.

"Miss, you really need to leave." The nurse hung up the chart and cranked the bed down.

"I won't rest unless she stays," Mame announced, not with the querulousness of age but the imperiousness of a queen. "Does she look capable of smuggling me out?"

The five-ten, two-hundred-pound nurse looked at Alys in her childish smocked dress with the skirt falling at mid-thigh and snorted. "She doesn't look big enough to be out of school." The nurse flipped off the overhead light, immersing them in darkness before padding out and closing the door.

Alys wrinkled her nose and sank to the tile floor, resting her head against her crossed legs. If she could find her center, she might stay without freaking out.

"How's Beulah? I didn't wreck her, did I?" Mame whispered eagerly, snapping on the bed light.

Alys sought her friend's expression in the pale glow of the lamp. Mame was fine. Mame had to be fine.

Alys's rusted-out Nissan was not fine. It had been totaled when Mame passed out at the wheel of her Cadillac—Beulah—crashing it into the Nissan's rear end, thereby transforming her rusty little car into an accordion against the garage wall.

"Beulah just has a dented bumper," she replied reassuringly. "I drove her over here."

"Then help me out of here. We need to be gone before Elliot arrives." Mame fiddled with the wires hooking her to the monitor in an apparent attempt to remove them.

"Mame! You've had a heart attack." At least, that's what she guessed an *infarction* was. "You can't just get up and walk out." Although she certainly sympathized with Mame's determination to escape. How could anyone get well in the chilly dark with machines beeping off heartbeats as if they were minutes on a parking meter?

"I know how much you hate being here." Mame frowned when the monitor apparently didn't detach as easily as she expected. "There is no reason to keep me here except doctors are afraid of being sued."

"My dislike of hospitals is irrational," Alys protested halfheartedly. "Doctors did everything they could for Fred. It's unfortunate that cures for cancer haven't developed beyond the witch doctor stage, but that doesn't apply to you. You should listen to them."

"They nuked Fred and stuffed him with pills until he wanted to die, which made his last years hell for both of you," Mame said vehemently, examining the IV attachment. "I refuse to die like that. When I'm ready to go, I want to go with a big bang."

Alys bit back a semi-hysterical giggle. "You almost did. The neighbors thought they'd been bombed. Beulah packs a wallop."

Mame beamed. "There, see, you can smile. Now get up off that floor and unchain me."

Alys took another deep breath and stubbornly maintained her yoga position.

Undeterred by her young friend's refusal to comply with orders, Mame noted with delight that Alys had finally shed her depressing blacks.

Mame wasn't certain she understood Alys's choice of coming-out clothes, but she heartily approved the thought behind them. The pink cotton dress printed with tiny blue hearts and flowers belonged on a child, but the scooped neckline revealed womanly cleavage, and the elasticized smocking showed off the slender waistline of youth. Alys still looked like a teenager untouched by life.

Other than the creamy skin of a child, Alys possessed no one remarkable feature. She was of average height and weight, with sleek, mink-colored hair—currently cut with wisps that stuck out at stray angles—unremarkable gray eyes, and even features. But Mame had watched the men at the school swivel to follow Alys's progress through the halls. Even in dull black, her attire had emphasized her womanly attributes.

Mame liked to think she was responsible for Alys's transformation, but she knew she'd only coaxed out what had been lost for a while. She suspected that provocative baby-doll dress had come from Alys's college wardrobe.

At the sound of a familiar determined stride down the hall, Mame sighed in exasperation. She should have known Elliot would run from the ends of the earth to be here.

Elliot would insist on batteries of tests, forcing her to stay in here for days. She *couldn't* stay. She was on a mission, but Elliot would never understand that. She loved her brilliant nephew, but his focused lifestyle limited his options—and hers.

Mame glanced down at Alys, who had apparently entered a meditative trance, and the germ of an idea blossomed.

She'd been on her way over to Alys's to explain about the student who needed their help. It wouldn't have required a great deal of change to their travel plans, but she didn't dare tell her now with Elliot about to walk in.

Mame fully intended to help Dulce save her niece, but Elliot would never approve of the risk. She thought Alys might.

She began to smile as her idea flowered into full bloom.

Maybe her fainting spell was for the best if it brought her nephew home. She knew Elliot's habits well. He would need someone to pull him out of orbit once he realized she had escaped.

Alys was strong enough to ground him.

Looking at Alys's cap of dark hair and ripe figure, she chuckled. Alys would definitely divert her nephew.

Mame cranked the bed back up and tucked her hair behind her ears.

Undisturbed, Alys remained on the floor, the fabric of her full skirt falling short of her bare knees. Hearing Elliot open the door to the darkened room, Mame recognized the elements of a perfect distraction, and pure mischief replaced the last vestige of her apprehension. Watching Elliot and Alys together could rival a good Doris Day movie.

She snapped off the bed light, and Alys disappeared in a pool of darkness.

A pair of size thirteen polished wingtips emerged from the darkness to connect with Alys's hip, and a soft leather computer bag just missed her head. She leaned over to dodge the blow, while their owner stumbled in the opposite direction, grabbed Mame's IV, and did a wicked samba with the pole until it rolled into the bed.

Mame snapped the bed light on.

Gazing up a long trousered leg as the visitor righted himself, Alys saw the difficulty of balancing all that masculine length against a spindly aluminum pole. From her position on the floor, she thought surely his head brushed the ceiling.

Or maybe that was just the effect of the intruder's badly rumpled curls. If his barber had meant to style that hair, he'd failed badly. Or else the wearer hadn't combed it in days.

"Elliot!" Mame called cheerfully. "You really didn't have to come. I'm fine. I was just asking Alys to drive me home."

"Which is why she's staging a sit-down strike in the middle of the floor?" he asked, eyeing her with dubious interest.

It wasn't as if he were bulky, Alys decided, studying him in the dim light from the bed as he dropped his bag behind a chair. If this was Mame's nephew, she'd always wondered what the man behind the voice looked like. Magazine photos couldn't begin to do justice to his air of confidence.

Like Mame, her nephew possessed a lean elegance, but unlike Mame, his height seemed to go on forever. Of course, it might help if she stood up. She hadn't decided if she was capable of it yet.

Despite the dryness of his words, the newcomer's rich voice conveyed reassurance. He'd carried in a breath of fresh fall air that drove out the smell of hospital disinfectant, creating a safety zone around him that let her breathe freely for the first time since Mame's accident.

In the light of the bed lamp, his dark, compassionate eyes could hypnotize. She had to concentrate on the subtle hook at the end of his narrow nose and his long Jeff Goldblum face with the curl hanging in the middle of his forehead to keep from falling under the spell of his gaze.

"Alys, this is my nephew Elliot, the one the radio calls Doc Nice. Elliot, this is Alys Seagraves. Turn on the light and then find a nurse to check me out. I want to get dressed."

"Miss Seagraves." The heartthrob nodded acknowledgment of Mame's introduction before picking up his aunt's wrist to test her pulse.

Alys hesitated, brushing her bangs out of her face to study the situation. For some inexplicable reason, Mame hadn't wanted her famous nephew here. Should she stay for Mame's sake? Did the nephew exude positive or negative energy? With those eyes, how could she doubt he exuded anything but kindness?

"I'm perfectly well, Elliot," Mame said. "I have too much to do to lie here trussed up like a helpless babe. It was simply a little spell." Mame attempted to jerk her arm away, but Elliot held her firmly.

"You crashed your car," he retorted. "It was not a little spell. You had a heart attack."

"A spell," she insisted. "And Beulah only has a little dent in her bumper. It's Alys's car that's wrecked."

"Mame, you have a personal and genetic history of congestive heart failure. We have to run tests to check for damage and adjust your medication to prevent further impairment and relieve the fluids. You know that."

Alys eased to her feet and backed toward the door. Her heart still beat irregularly and her palms were sweating. Mame seemed to be in better hands than hers. Her nephew was a doctor who wrote books all about diet and exercise and had a radio show more renowned than Dr. Laura's. She supposed he specialized in nutrition and not heart medicine, but surely he knew what was best for Mame. She could flee the confines of the hospital in all good conscience.

"Alys, you can't leave," Mame shouted. "She's having a panic attack, Elliot. Calm her!"

"Mame won't 'shuffle off this mortal coil' anytime soon," Elliot said with dry reassurance. "And I don't bite. Your leaving is raising her pulse rate. Stay."

Alys blinked, feeling as if a warm, rich blanket had been thrown over her, shutting out the deathly cold of the air-conditioning. He had the most amazing voice. It resonated deep down inside of her. No wonder he had a radio show.

He could quote Shakespeare. When was the last time anyone had quoted Shakespeare to her? And he did it without a script in front of him.

"I know you hate being in here, hon," Mame interrupted Alys's stunned reverie, "but we need to make plans. Elliot, Alys and I have our trip all worked out, and there's no time to waste."

"Aunt Mame, you've just had a heart attack. You're not going anywhere." Elliot picked up Mame's chart and fished his reading glasses out of his pocket. "Thank you for looking after my aunt, Miss Seagraves. I'm sorry about your travel plans, but you'll have to go on without her."

"Mrs.," she corrected, watching him with fascination. He must be giving off positive energy. Her panic was lessening without having to concentrate on lotus blossoms. She'd much rather concentrate on Doc Nice.

Ever since she'd met Mame, she'd heard all about her wonderful nephew, seen his pictures, heard the stories Mame loved to tell about his dedication and hard work. She'd even listened to his radio show. His reputation was well deserved, because on the air he was *funny*. And understanding. He didn't talk politics or personal accountability, but *listened* to his callers, thus earning him the appellation of Doc Nice.

She didn't see that side of him now. He behaved like every impersonal, scary doctor she'd ever known.

He perched his black-rimmed reading glasses on the end of his nose and scanned the chart, angling it under the bed lamp. "The stress of planning this trip was evidently too much for you, Mame. We have to find the extent of the damage." He glanced at Alys. "Tell her that her life is more important than gallivanting about the countryside."

"Maybe to Mame, life *is* gallivanting about the countryside." Alys didn't know where those rebellious words had come from, but Mame looked at her with approval, so she stuck to them.

Elliot set his mouth in a stern reprimand that had probably sent interns fleeing. "Life is about responsibility, and mine is to see to my aunt's health. Her heart muscles are weak. She needs rest and medication."

"Stuff it, Elliot. You sound just like your late, lamented father." Mame sat up higher to peer around him. "Alys, take Beulah and go on without me. This is something you really must do, and I will be miserable if I think I'm the one preventing it."

"Mame, I can't go without you," Alys protested her friend's generosity, although the gleam in Mame's eye caused her to hesitate. She recognized Mame's mischief when she saw it, but couldn't imagine what she was up to. "Maybe we can do it next year. I can cancel the reservations."

"Nonsense. I have a copy of the itinerary. I'll catch up with you. I wouldn't miss this vacation for the world." Sitting almost straight up as if she weren't attached to half a dozen tubes and wires, Mame waved her thin hand in dismissal.

"Miss Seagraves, please go on without my aunt," Elliot said patiently. "I doubt she'll be able to join you, but there is no reason you shouldn't go. I'll see to Mame. She'll be fine, although that Cadillac has to be a hundred years old," he warned. "I recommend renting a car."

"Beulah has only sixty thousand on her," Mame protested. "You have the keys, Alys. Go. Enjoy."

Gulping, trying to read Mame's expression, Alys nodded. "I'll think about it. Mame has my number, Dr. . . ?" Alys stammered, backing toward the door. She knew his name; she just couldn't seem to grasp anything except "Doc Nice" at the moment.

"Roth, Elliot Roth," he finished for her. "I'll call you if there's any change. You have a cell phone, don't you?"

"I'll find you!" Mame called cheerfully.

Watching the fey creature edging toward the door, Elliot recalled reading to his younger brothers from books containing pictures of fairies posed for flight. With her overlong bangs curving into short, dark hair that framed her pointed chin and wide eyes, Alys Seagraves only needed a mushroom to perch on. He had the ridiculous urge to capture her in the palm of his hand and tell her not to go. "You'll need a cell phone if you're driving, Miss Seagraves."

"Mrs.," she murmured. "I'll think about it."

She fled, probably on butterfly wings, Elliot decided.

"Pretty, isn't she?" Mame asked with all the innocence of a child with her hand in the cookie jar.

"Married," Elliot replied, feeling inexplicably depressed at the thought. It wasn't as if he had time for a life, much less a wife, so he didn't know why it mattered. He hadn't noticed the ring on her finger until her insistence on "Mrs." had forced him to look.

"Widowed," Mame countered with triumph. "Husband died of cancer over a year ago. She's been grieving too long. She needs this vacation."

Widowed? She didn't look older than Eric, and his youngest brother was still in grad school.

"She has a thing about doctors and medicines," Mame continued, waving away his offer of a water glass. "Doesn't believe in them," she finished gleefully, watching his reaction.

Elliot refused to fall for his aunt's incessant meddling. "Watching the suffering of someone you love can be traumatic," he said with the dispassion he'd learned to use in med school. "That's no reason for you to agree with her fears, or to encourage them."

"I'm not ill, Elliot," Mame warned. Her long, thin face resembled his in many ways, but hers could go from laughter to sternness in a blink of an eye, while he'd trained his to composure. "I bet I feel better than you do. Heartburn plaguing you again?"

"Plaguing" was too mild a word. The burning pain had started with the phone call informing him of Mame's hospitalization, and her argument now raised the flames to furnace proportions. If he'd been alone, he would have doubled over and groaned. He had regular checkups, so he suspected it was just old-fashioned stress trying to give birth to an ulcer.

A good chug of Mylanta would relieve him, but he'd hastily ended his book tour to fly home to St. Louis and broken speed records driving over from the airport rather than hunt down a bottle. "If you'd just behave,

I'd be fine," he gently chided. "Now lie down and rest. I want to talk to your doctor."

"Ask the nurse for some Pepto-Bismol," Mame urged as he lowered the bed. "You ought to carry a bottle."

"In my back pocket," he agreed without cracking a smile.

She slapped at him the way she always did when he was being smart-mouthed, never hurting but merely warning him that she understood his sarcasm.

"I love you, Elliot, but you're a pain in the ass sometimes."

"I love you, too, and you're a pain all the time," he said with a smile. He didn't know where he would be without his aunt. He owed her so much, he couldn't hope to repay her in a thousand lifetimes. Taking care of her was the least he could do.

She studied him with a stern look that always meant a lecture. "I've had a full life to show for my years. What do you have to show for yours?"

"Three books and a radio program?" he asked teasingly, attempting to defuse the gloom Mame's topic cast. They'd had this argument before, mostly when he told her that his research might save people from dying, and that's why he didn't have time to come to dinner. Or for a visit.

"Which shows how very little you know about life," she complained pertly. "If you would quit running away from it, you might find an existence beyond the material."

Stubbornly, Elliot refused to discuss life philosophies. "Rest, Mame, and I'll be right back."

"No, you won't," she said with more pride than irritation. "They'll all want to talk with Doc Nice. Go, enjoy, relax a little. You're too thin. Eat. Have some nice warm milk."

Laughing silently at the idea of his rattlebrained aunt telling her health-conscious nephew how to eat, Elliot tucked her in and headed for the nurse's station.

He wasn't running away from anything. Quite the contrary. He fought death every minute of the day. He jogged regularly, followed his own diet advice, and was far healthier than most thirty-five-year-old men.

His father had died at thirty-five. Of a heart attack. While driving with his entire family in the car.

The pain in Elliot's chest burned hotter.

✤TWO✤

"Mame!" Staring through the early-autumn twilight at the empty space in the parking lot where his Range Rover had been, Elliot groaned in dismay. Until a minute ago, he'd been grateful the car had been parked at the airport in St. Louis when he ran off the plane to rush down to Springfield to look after Mame.

He should never have believed even for an instant that his aunt had defiantly gone to visit friends on another floor as he'd assumed when he'd discovered her absence. As the eldest of three orphaned brothers, he'd been the responsible one, the one who had to learn and counteract Mame's unpredictable, often rebellious habits. He just hadn't thought she'd ever go so far as to risk her *life*. What in hell was she up to?

Mame had not only escaped the hospital—she'd stolen his car.

Resisting pounding his head against a lamppost, he called himself three kinds of fool. Exhaustion was his only excuse. He knew Mame was knowledgeable enough to pull out all her monitor connections without help. He'd been delusional to think she wouldn't want to worry him by running away—just as she'd accused *him* of doing, dammit.

If Mame didn't want to be found, even the police would have difficulty tracking her. She might be on the flaky side, but she was wilier than a coyote.

Remembering Mame's earlier arguments about her travel plans, he kicked himself for not asking for the sprite's number. He knew why he hadn't done that. Asking a woman for her number meant interest, and he didn't have time to keep up his end of even the most meaningless of relationships.

But if anyone would have a clue of where to find his aunt, he'd bet *Mrs.* Alys Seagraves would be the one. He only prayed she hadn't agreed to any of Mame's half-baked schemes.

Using his cell phone, he called the New Age school his aunt worked with. Over the years, "Doc Nice" had built a reputation that opened doors. Most of the time, Elliot merely tolerated the recognition, but at moments like this, he welcomed it. Within minutes, he had the phone number of a yoga student named Alys. With a "y."

No one answered when he dialed the number.

His car and his aunt were gone. So was Alys. They'd left him no choice.

He called the police.

Sitting on the low roof of the sixties-era ranch-style duplex that had provided her major source of income these last few years, Alys admired the red and gold of the maple leaves at eye level rather than watch the movers below haul the remains of her old life away. The renters on the other side of the house had already moved out. Now it was her turn.

The place had been mortgaged to the hilt, and the consignment store wouldn't pay much for her meager belongings. These last eight years of her life had been a roller coaster of highs and lows. She'd had the breath knocked out of her when she'd hit bottom with that last plummet, but it was time to experience the thrills again. No more self-pity. Full speed ahead, into the future. All she had to do was figure out what that future was.

She couldn't even plan tomorrow without worrying about Mame.

Which led directly to thoughts of Mame's nephew.

She'd spent these last years in a state of suspended animation. She hadn't thought any man would ever turn her on again. But Elliot's obvious concern for Mame stirred more interest than she cared to admit. She wanted to believe Mame's stories about her nephew's dedication to healing, but just because a kid doctored hurt birds and dogs didn't mean he couldn't be a Type A jerk now.

The old Alys had an irrational thing for Type A personalities. The person she wanted to be preferred the illusion of Doc Nice. She'd like to think the warm, understanding radio persona would believe his aunt was intelligent enough to make her own decisions. Maybe he would recommend that Mame return to the comfort of her home if all she needed was bed rest and medication. She'd much rather be sitting with Mame at home right now than sitting up here, wondering what to do next.

The roof was still warm from the day's sun, but the fading light had brought an autumn nip to the air. With her toes tucked in the crease between thigh and hip, her palms upturned, she breathed deeply and attempted a meditative trance, but too many images bombarded her, and she lost her center.

She'd lost her center the day Fred had given up fighting the cancer. She recalled the day with crystal clarity, sitting in the doctor's waiting room, anxiously awaiting the results of his lab test, praying the drastic radiation and chemo treatment had worked and the cancer was still in remission. She'd just buried her parents. She was still mourning their loss. She couldn't believe God could be so cruel as to take her husband, too.

They'd made so many plans for the future, believing the treatment would work. Fred had planned an itinerary for Paris and Rome. He'd wanted to explore Mayan ruins next, and snorkel in the South Pacific, all the things they hadn't done because they'd been too busy building careers. They'd even talked of children.

She desperately wanted him to have all that and more. Sitting in the waiting room, she'd prayed and prayed until tears had run down her cheeks.

The instant Fred had walked out of the doctor's office, she'd known her prayers hadn't been answered.

"It's back," he told her with resignation when she ran to hold his frail hand.

"We can fight it again," she assured him. Unable to accept defeat, she whipped out her calendar book to write down the next appointment, even though the days that had once been packed with activities now stretched out without a mark on them. "I heard of a new treatment I can call and find out about."

"No." This time, his voice was flat.

Fred had been a trial lawyer, with a rich, evocative voice that could sway juries and tempt Satan. She'd heard his voice rage in fury and murmur in love. She'd never heard it go flat.

"Dr. Thompson has a better suggestion?" she asked hopefully, searching Fred's beloved face. He had never been a handsome man, but always a compelling one.

Today, with his hair thinning from the radiation and his weight down from the chemo, he appeared decades older.

"No." Carrying himself as proudly as he could after a year of painful treatments had drained him of every ounce of energy, he walked out without making the next appointment.

He had never gone back. Rather than repeat the hell he'd been through, he quit, just like that. At first, she had tried to persuade him to travel in hopes that would improve his frame of mind, but no matter how she tempted him with brochures and plans, he claimed he didn't have the energy, sank into his pillows, and flipped television channels.

He'd given up hope. She hadn't. Where there was love, there was always hope. She understood his reluctance to return to the indignity of the hospital and their painful treatments, but she was incapable of giving up on the man she loved with all her heart. So she'd searched the Internet for alternatives, combed the library, looked for every available cure that might appeal to him, offering each with such hope in her heart that it should have cured him with the power of her love.

Fred had humored her by taking herbs and letting her bring in spiritual healers who promised to open his mind and improve his mood. Books swore that laughter made the best medicine. She would have hired clowns if he'd let her. On the days she made him laugh and he could sit up like his old self, she'd be certain her positive thinking was helping. And then the next day, he'd be back in bed, refusing to go to the hospital.

Her hopes swung wildly back and forth with each new treatment the doctors recommended. With the oncologist's suggestion of a new drug, she'd sold her engagement ring and filled a prescription that made the last of Fred's hair fall out and his once bronzed skin turn yellow.

But he'd given up long before that treatment failed. She'd read about it in the books. If he hadn't quit the radiation, if he'd kept up his spirits, believed in something, *anything,* he could have lived longer.

He was a strong-willed man, and he'd decided to die. So he did.

Leaving her numb and shattered and drifting.

Tears welled up from that core of grief inside her, and Alys let them spill down her face. She'd spent years holding them back, maintaining a cheerful smile, pretending for Fred's sake that everything would be better. The tears had frozen inside her, so that when he'd died, she'd simply gone through the motions of grieving.

They fell easily now. In this past year since his death, she'd slowly let go of her anger and heartache. Mame had been a friend of Fred's family, and the day Alys had walked through the grocery store with tears streaming down her cheeks, Mame had introduced Alys to the School of Alternative Life Lessons, and gradually brought her back into the world.

At first, Alys had obliged for lack of anything better to do. She couldn't sit in the house forever. So she signed up for every class the school offered, and later found others that they hadn't. It had taken time, but she had finally accepted that, no matter how much she hated his choice, Fred had every right to choose death. His decision wasn't prompted by anything she had done or not done. She couldn't direct the lives or wishes of others.

Gradually, her energy returned, her outlook improved, until now she was ready to make some decisions.

Her first decision had been to sell the duplex and most of her worldly goods. Fred's life insurance had paid the bills and bought her a little time, but she would have to return to work soon.

This little jaunt with Mame was to have been a journey of self-discovery, a road to plan her future. Or had been, until Mame's setback. Now she had to decide whether to go on or linger.

Giving up on meditation, Alys toyed with the Superball she'd found in the gutter. She remembered the day one of the neighbor's kids had thrown the extra-bouncy ball into the yard. It had been one of Fred's good days, and he'd enjoyed playing catch with the boy, watching the tiny hard ball bounce higher than the house. Had he lived, Fred would have been a good father.

Then the ball had landed in the gutter, and he didn't have the strength to fetch it. He hadn't gone back outside again.

Memories like that were the reason she had to leave.

She leaned over to watch the last of her furniture being carried into the consignment-store truck. Liberation from the material was an exciting concept. She could feel the freedom already. She wouldn't miss her furniture, but she did miss her Nissan. She needed a car if she wanted to see the world.

Alys eyed the enormous pink Cadillac in her driveway. Mame had told her to take it, that she would catch up with her later. If she believed Mame was as healthy as she declared, did she dare?

Except for the buckled bumper, Beulah gleamed with years of loving care. Mame had earned the car decades ago for selling cosmetics, and it was as much a trophy as a means of transportation. Alys didn't want to imagine how Mame would feel if anything happened to it.

Of course, if she didn't take it, she couldn't set out on her journey. She had no home, no car, and no place to go.

The police car pulling up behind the Caddy's tail fins diverted that train of thought, thank goodness.

She spun the Superball in her palm and watched with interest as Mame's imposing nephew unfolded from the backseat. From this distance, Elliot Roth appeared cool, collected, and sophisticated—the kind of man who snapped his fingers and the world laid down at his feet.

The two uniformed police officers stepping out of the front of the car consulted with the good doctor. She'd lived a quiet life. The only child of elderly parents, she'd been a relatively obedient teenager. She'd never had officers of the law in her home. Was Mame's nephew about to sic them on her? For what? Stealing Beulah? Maybe her journey of self-discovery would start behind bars. She could become a career criminal.

Unaware he stood in the path of the movers, Doc Nice stared at the SOLD sign on her front lawn. He wasn't paying any more attention to the movers than they were to him. The burly truck driver backed down the stairs carrying a heavy oak cabinet, and Alys debated watching the play unfold without interference.

Mame must have had a reason for wanting to escape the hospital before Doc Nice arrived. That gleam in her eye had meant something. Alys just hoped it wasn't something dangerous.

Deciding the doc probably had only good intentions and shouldn't be blamed for Mame's mischief, Alys cried out a warning. An alert policeman grabbed Elliot's shirt and jerked him out of the mover's path, narrowly averting the collision.

All three newcomers turned their attention to the roof. Alys waved. As if they'd seen countless women perched on rooftops, the policemen shrugged and returned to examining the vintage Cadillac.

The doc's upturned face looked oddly agitated at the sight of her, as if he'd lost his best friend. Alys appreciated his long-legged stride across her brown lawn, but she didn't think all that concern was for her.

What if Mame had taken a turn for the worse? Knowing she wouldn't be able to breathe until she knew, Alys flung her Superball at him just to see how a renowned author played ball. "Catch!"

Unfortunately, he didn't wrap his fingers around the small ball fast enough, and it bounced hard, ricocheting off his hand into the Cadillac's window. It was Alys's turn to wince at the resulting cracking noise.

Unconcerned with the window, the good doctor absently rubbed the center of his expensive knit shirt while he watched her scoot toward the gutter. His hair fell forward in untidy curls that made him more human than famous, but casualness didn't disguise his tension.

As she eased down the rotting trellis, Elliot stepped over a dead holly, caught her by the waist, and helped her to the ground.

The intimacy of a man's heat burning through the cotton of her dress shocked her into remembering how long it had been since any man had held or touched her. She missed that closeness.

Lowering her to the grass, the doc didn't release her waist. The intensity of his deep brown eyes held her spellbound. Or maybe it was the subtle scent of his shaving lotion making her a little light-headed.

"Have you seen Mame?" he demanded without preamble.

She stared up at him, too shocked to speak. Or think.

Apparently recognizing his forwardness, Elliot dropped his hands and backed away. "I apologize, but this really could be a life-or-death situation. Mame left the hospital. If you know where she is, please tell me."

Mame left the hospital. For a brief moment, she felt exultation. Mame was fine.

Then the doc's urgency sank in. Mame wasn't fine. Alys took a deep breath to calm her spinning thoughts.

Doc Nice had a radio-show voice—moderated and melodious and—Alys wrinkled her nose and gave it some consideration—nice, she concluded. Doc Nice spoke nicely, even under obvious stress.

"If she's run away, she must have been feeling better." Alys had spent the last few years speaking in a voice as modulated as his, attempting to hide her heartbreak behind pleasant reassurance for Fred's sake. She didn't have to do that anymore. The knowledge that she could yell and scream and be sarcastic again was liberating. "Mame's a grown woman and knows her own mind. You shouldn't have bothered the police." She wanted to believe Mame was feeling fine and was just off running a few errands to prove it.

Elliot's look of disbelief made her uncomfortably aware that she wasn't exactly a testimony to reliability. She was hot and sweaty and her hair was probably standing on end. She'd only had the haircut to please Mame and never remembered to keep it up. Once it had started growing out, she'd whacked at the parts that annoyed her. Fred's illness had eliminated any pretense that looks mattered. She crossed her arms defiantly.

"Mame disconnected all her monitors and stole my car. She has no cell phone or any way of reaching me. I don't consider that a rational act on the part of someone in ill health." He glanced in the direction of her house and nodded at the two officers crossing the yard to join them.

"May we look inside, Miss?" one asked politely at Elliot's signal.

Alys admired the officer's very stern, very young face. "If you think she's hiding beneath my dust bunnies, be my guest. Mame may be skinny, but she's not that small."

When Elliot started to follow them, she poked him in his taut abdomen. Abs of steel, she noted. "How did she take off her monitors without everyone in the hospital running into her room?"

He didn't touch her again, although she might have liked it if he had. Despite her annoyance with the man's behavior, he awakened sensations she'd thought long dead. Self-discovery included exploring sensations, didn't it? It was a pity she and the good doc appeared to be at odds regarding Mame's health. Obviously, he thought his aunt hadn't the brains to take care of herself.

Maybe it was time she learned to accept being at odds with medical authorities. They certainly had proved they weren't infallible gods. Perhaps Elliot was part of the learning process the Universe had in mind for her.

"My father and my grandfather were doctors, and Mame worked in their offices," Elliot replied. "She knows as much about medical equipment as I do. It's urgent that I find her."

"Is she going to be okay?" She didn't want to ask, but cold tentacles of fear wrapped around her heart. Mame epitomized the vibrancy of life that Alys wanted to return to, and she would do *anything* for her.

Remembering the gleam in Mame's eye, Alys had the sudden suspicion Mame was counting on that. Which meant—She studied Mame's nephew speculatively as he spoke.

"The few tests they took indicate congestion and arrhythmia." Elliot's mouth tightened. "Without further testing, I can't predict the result, but she's already passed out once. It could easily happen again. She might not get treatment quickly enough next time."

Alys swallowed hard and stared into the canopy of colorful maple leaves over Doc Nice's shoulder. "She's had these spells before, hasn't she? And lived to tell about them?" She countered his fear with her hope, understanding better than he that neither of them had a choice in Mame's decision.

"The more often she has these attacks, the more her heart tissue is damaged. We have to adjust her medication, and she has to rest. We may need to put her in an assisted-care facility."

She could almost hear her friend's belligerent response to that: *It's my life and I'll die if I want to.*

She didn't want Mame to die, but she didn't want her to spend the rest of her life in a nursing home either.

Torn, she glanced over at the pink Cadillac, half expecting Mame to step out and demand that she be allowed to live her life her way. "I can't believe she'd leave without me," she murmured, more to herself than to Elliot. "She never drives farther than the grocery store or school. I was amazed when she drove over here."

"Mame is capable of anything when she puts her mind to it," Elliot said with conviction. "I have to find her before she does something foolish."

As the policemen emerged, dustier but empty-handed, Alys had a thought. "Her suitcases? Were they still in the house? Did you look?"

"What suitcases?" And then his eyes widened. "She always packs and leaves them by the door. There weren't any."

"We were planning on leaving first thing in the morning. I told her I'd carry them for her. Maybe they're still in her room?"

He shook his head in certainty. "I had an electric lift installed on the stairway so she didn't have to walk up and down. She refuses to move to a smaller place, but she hates the lift. She sends things up and down in the chair and she walks. She would have sent the suitcases down just to prove she could."

She remembered Mame's disdain for the lift.

Hope faded. Alys bit the tip of a finger and tried to think where else Mame could have gone, but she knew there was only one conclusion. Mame had her suitcases and her nephew's car. She had a copy of the itinerary, and an old boyfriend waiting at the end of her journey. Alys didn't think Elliot would appreciate the significance of that.

"She's driving to New Mexico," Alys said with a sigh. Mame had left without her.

"New Mexico?" Doc Nice's eyes lit with hope, and the policemen arrived in time to jot notes.

"Where in New Mexico?" the younger officer asked.

"Albuquerque, for the Balloon Fiesta." Before they could run off and call in the news, she added, "She wanted to revisit her honeymoon journey. The Balloon Fiesta was only incidental. She's driving old Route 66 to see the sights she saw with her husband in the sixties."

Alys had the uneasy feeling that there might be a little more to Mame's escape than that. She couldn't believe Mame would risk her life for a sentimental journey.

"Route 66? It doesn't exist anymore," the older officer said.

"The Route 66 Association has the old road mapped out," Alys explained. "It gives directions on how to find the Americana that interstates have gone around. We modified the route and made an itinerary to suit Mame."

Elliot still looked concerned, but he held out his hand. "Where is the itinerary? I doubt she'll follow it, but we can have the police looking for her along the road."

"And what will the police do when they catch her?" Alys demanded. If Mame was determined to drive to New Mexico, then Alys owed her friend enough to respect her wishes. "Throw her in jail? Chase her down with sirens blaring? That's enough to give most people a heart attack. The idea is to help her, not terrorize her."

At her argument, Elliot strode toward the Caddy. "If I follow the route she's taking, I can be there when they find her and have her taken to the nearest hospital." He opened the car door, but the keys Mame usually kept in the ignition weren't there.

They were in Alys's pocket.

She had been uncertain about borrowing Beulah, but now that Elliot was threatening to go after his aunt, she knew what she had to do. That gleam in Mame's eye meant more than mischief, and she owed it to Mame to protect her. "What do you mean, *you*?" she called after him.

He bent over to examine the cracked Caddy window, then turned to the officers. "Can you put out an APB on the Rover? I'll take my cell phone. When they find her, I can be there to pick her up."

Alys watched in dismay as the policemen returned to their radio to report Mame's direction. Without further ado, they backed the patrol car out of the drive, leaving her alone with Elliot. "You don't have the itinerary," she reminded him. Where had she packed the itinerary? Probably in the suitcases in the garage. She'd had to remove them from the Nissan before it was towed.

"If you'll give it to me, I will," he said, standing beside the Caddy's driver's-side door as the police drove off. "Just give me the keys and I'll follow her."

"So you can put her in a nursing home?" Outrage roared to life, and it felt good. "Mame is a grown woman and has a right to a choice. If she's this determined to make the trip, I won't let you bully her out of it."

"She could be dying!" He didn't shout, but his knuckles turned white where he gripped the door as his fear finally broke through his reserve.

"She could be *living*," she screamed at him, shocking even herself. "You go back to your happy, healthy world while I catch up with her and talk her into seeing a doctor."

Was that a flash of guilt in his eyes? If so, he recovered quickly.

"Mame needs me, and I'm going after her." Crossing the small lawn, he snatched the keys she'd pulled from her pocket.

The brush of his hand on hers shot electrifying shock waves up her arm, but undeterred, Alys followed him back to the car.

"Fine, then see if you can find her without the itinerary." Triumphantly, she propped her hands on her hips as he climbed into the driver's seat. His scowl proved she'd had the last word.

The movers walked over with a clipboard and invoice. "Signature, ma'am?"

As Alys scribbled on the line indicated, she heard the roar of a powerful engine. Glancing up, she watched Doc Nice backing the pink Caddy out of the drive.

He was leaving her there with no car, no phone, and no furniture. And no way to find Mame.

≋ THREE ≋

Racing down the driveway, Alys smacked the driver's window of the Caddy before Doc Not-So-Nice could back into the street. Unfortunately, that was the window the ball had hit.

She winced as the glass splintered in a dozen zigzag cracks. Mame's nephew hit the brake and stared through the destroyed window in astonishment.

He turned off the ignition and threw open the car door, climbing out to tower over her. Holding her stinging hand, she jumped out of his way. Before she could decide whether to continue asserting her rights or run, he took her hand to examine it.

"Did you cut yourself?" He turned her hand back and forth in the fading light, checking for damage.

He had the most amazing touch. If she'd mutilated her hand, she swore he could heal her with just that touch. She didn't want her hand back. She wanted him to hold it forever.

Satisfied she hadn't been injured, he released her. She almost sighed in regret.

"Are you out of your mind?" he demanded, staring at her in incredulity. "What did you hit the window for?"

"I have no car, remember? And no place to stay."

He continued staring at her as if she were speaking in an alien tongue.

"You're taking my only means of transportation," she explained patiently, "and they're about to haul off my furniture."

The consignment-store truck roared to life to emphasize her point.

Without waiting for his response, Alys stalked past the Caddy's mile-long pink hood, back to the garage where her bags waited.

Apparently having managed to translate what sounded to her like a perfectly clear explanation, Elliot jogged up beside her and picked up the heavy bags as if they were grocery sacks. They were old bags without roller wheels, containing every piece of clothing Alys thought she'd need until she landed somewhere. They were so heavy, she had to haul the bags out in a wheelbarrow.

She tried not to gape as Elliot easily tucked one under his arm and lifted the other.

"I've decided to take Mame up on her offer of the car," she said, initiating a conversation since he did not. She hadn't really decided to keep the car until he'd started to drive off with it, but it sounded like a plan now. "I'll be happy to drop you off," she offered.

He shot her another are-you-from-outer-space look and kept going. She supposed from the point of view of a harried professional in search of a misplaced aunt, he had a right to think her deeply weird.

Dismissing his attitude, Alys returned to the house to lock up. She had no idea what she was doing, but whatever it was, it had to be better than sitting in the driveway on her suitcases like a homeless waif.

With wistfulness, she took one last look around at the

lovely wood floors she'd kept waxed and polished to a high shine. Empty now, they simply looked barren and old. With a prayer that the new owner would find more happiness here than she had, she shut and locked the door on her life with Fred.

While Elliot arranged her luggage in the Caddy's cavernous trunk, Alys usurped the driver's seat. Like Mame, he'd left the keys in the ignition. In discovering those keys, she knew her mission.

"What are you doing?" he asked warily, shutting the trunk to discover her seat appropriation.

"Taking us to Mame's," she answered, staring out over the long pink hood in a moment's trepidation at the task she'd just appointed to herself. "Her place is big enough for a small army. I won't molest you. And if we're traveling together, you might as well get used to having me around."

"We're traveling together?" he asked, his expression cautious as he tucked his long legs into the passenger side.

At least he didn't run screaming from the car at the suggestion. Most men would be raising the roof, but he just sat there absorbing her assertions as if they were symptoms he had to diagnose.

Like insanity.

She wasn't sure that was too far off the mark. Going after Mame had some basis in logic, but she'd just suggested she ought to travel with a man she'd never met before today, even if she'd known *of* him for months.

Her whole purpose in traveling with Mame had been to find out who she was and who she wanted to be. She was on a limited time frame here. She couldn't afford too big a distraction.

In just the attentive way Elliot Roth studied her, he gave her thoughts she shouldn't be thinking.

His masculine proximity was overwhelming even in a car this big. His short-sleeved shirt revealed sinewy forearms overlaid with dark hairs and accented by an expensive gold watch. His shoulders loomed over the seat and his dark curls brushed the sagging cloth of the car roof. Maybe she *was* insane to suggest this, but her new life waited out there, and Mame was part of it. If he wanted to tag along, fine.

Adjusting to the newly awakened hum of hormones, she backed the car onto the quiet street. Driving off, she watched in the rearview mirror as her home faded into the distance. Blinking back tears, she set her chin. The time for looking back had ended. *Forward, ho!*

"Do I get a chance to express my opinion?" he finally asked.

"As long as it includes us finding Mame." With the shattered window open, the wind blowing through her hair, and the wheel beneath her hands, Alys inhaled a deep breath of freedom. She had to believe that Mame was blazing a trail to a new life, and both their futures shimmered with limitless possibilities.

She refused to consider the alternative.

"I'd planned on setting out tonight . . . if you would give me the itinerary," he added politely as she steered the yacht-length car through her shabby-genteel neighborhood, in the wrong direction for the interstate.

"Mame won't drive at night. My bet is that she's looking for a driver. We're better off spending our time checking with some of the students at the school. Maybe someone will call you and let you know they've seen her. Besides, we both need some rest before we set out."

"We?" Intense dark eyes studied her with an air of skepticism.

"You're the one she ran away from," Alys pointed out. "I was supposed to travel with her. She's more likely to let me find her than you."

He shot her an annoyed glance that probably meant she was right but he wouldn't admit it. Still, he didn't question further, sensible man that he was. He crossed his arms and his fingers beat a little tattoo on his biceps.

She disregarded his irritation. She needed space, a time to let go, and Mame had offered it. Alys didn't know if traveling with Mame's nephew was the smart thing to do, but she was feeling more defiant than smart right now.

Springfield wasn't a major city, but a sensible town of quiet residences. Since moving here to Fred's childhood home, she'd developed a liking for the slower pace and the small-town friendliness.

But she'd been trapped by circumstances for years and had no desire to be trapped again. She didn't have much money, but she wanted to experience a little bit of the world before deciding her fate.

"How does one become a travel writer?" she wondered aloud, trying on the first interesting occupation coming to mind as she turned Beulah down Mame's street lined with towering oaks and mansions.

"By being a journalist?" he guessed, apparently willing to humor her.

"You're a doctor, not a journalist, and you write books," she argued, not ready to give up on the first exciting idea she'd had in a long time.

"I had a friend in college who told me I ought to write a book about my nutrition research. He got a job in publishing after school. I had a draft manuscript just as the diet craze started. Networking and timing."

She remembered from her old career how networking and timing worked. She couldn't get excited about real estate, but writing sounded good. "I could start by writing a column for the local paper, I suppose."

"If you're independently wealthy." The chuckle in his voice indicated his opinion of a columnist's salary.

At least his sense of humor wasn't scripted.

Seeing Mame's old Victorian mansion, Alys steered the Caddy into the shaded drive. As a former Realtor, she had a good eye for houses, and she loved Mame's gracious old Victorian. Mame had let the siding weather too long without new paint, and the gingerbread trim on the wraparound porch needed work, but the shaded front lawn with its jungle of azaleas and neat wrought-iron fence spoke of generations of love and family that no modern suburban residence could duplicate.

But it was entirely too large and impractical for Mame. An albatross. Perhaps Mame was finally ready to relinquish all the old memories it held and start on a new path. Maybe that's what this was all about.

Swinging her legs out of the car, Alys took the familiar gravel path to the kitchen without waiting for Elliot to open the car door.

Watching the poetry in motion of Alys's hips beneath her flirty skirt as she strode down the walk almost knocked Elliot's concern for Mame into a tailspin.

He tried to ignore his companion's nearness while he unlocked the back door, but she stood a step higher, and a flyaway lock of her hair brushed his nose. A light, summery fragrance wafted around her, and Elliot gritted his molars at the familiar tightening in his groin. Traveling with Alys Seagraves would be a trial unless he got a grip.

He couldn't remember agreeing to travel with her. She'd just sauntered into his life and made hash of his mind. It had been a long time since a woman had done that—if ever.

He concentrated on locking up behind them while Alys swept into Mame's kitchen as if it were her own. Her blithe forwardness fascinated him. She opened the refrigerator and helped herself to the few eggs Mame had left behind. He'd grown up in this house, still had a room here, and he wasn't as familiar with the kitchen as she was.

"Come here often?" he asked when she located a skillet and a spatula.

"Mame likes company. She's had half the students at the school here at one time or another." She cracked the eggs into the pan and glanced at him through a shiny lock of hair falling across her high-boned cheek. "Want some?"

She probably had no idea how his testosterone-drenched brain translated that suggestion.

He didn't know how to act with this fey female who had walked in and taken over Mame's kitchen. Elliot had a suspicion if he wasn't careful, she might usurp his life in the same way. "No, thanks. Cholesterol can kill you."

"So can trucks, kids, and cell phones."

Ignoring the quip, he hit Mame's ancient answering machine to pick up messages from people he'd missed in his earlier search. Not one of them had seen Mame today.

"She spent the morning at the hairdresser's." Alys flipped her eggs. "She probably had lunch at the cafeteria. Mame took a leave of absence from her classes at the school for this trip, so she may not have seen anyone else unless she asked them to drive. If she stopped for her suitcase, maybe one of the neighbors saw her."

She knew his aunt's activities better than he did. Elliot started calling the neighbors, just in case they'd noticed a car parked in the drive.

The eggs smelled mouthwateringly delicious, but he'd never be able to eat them. Worrying about Mame had twisted his intestines into knots.

She fixed toast and slathered it with butter and jam, obviously not suffering from the same anxiety as he. Or any sense of health-consciousness. Elliot ground his teeth and listened to one neighbor after the other deny they'd seen his aunt.

"She never missed a day of classes. I had no idea she was ill. I thought only fat people had heart attacks. Or stressed-out people," his uninvited guest added in a voice laden with meaning.

He took a deep breath and tried to accept that his aunt could take care of herself. He'd been relying on her strength for years. There was no reason for going off the deep end just because he was no longer in command of the situation.

He wandered around the kitchen opening cabinets, looking for something healthy to munch on. "We have a family predisposition for heart failure," he said, trying not to lecture. "It's not the kind of thing doctors can test for until it happens. Obesity, poor diet, smoking, or lack of exercise would aggravate or hasten the condition but not cause it."

Innocently licking the jam off her lip, Alys followed him around the room with clear gray eyes that seemed to see right through him. Crystal-ball eyes, he decided. She ought to be a gypsy.

"As would stress," she added. "Do you know yoga?"

"I run every morning, work out at the gym when I have time." He thought yoga and meditation a New Age waste of time for bored housewives, but he politely refrained from offering his opinion.

"And I suppose you compete with yourself in those workouts?" Cleaning up her plate, she carried it and her utensils to the sink to wash. "Run an extra quarter mile, beat your time by a few seconds?"

"Keeps it interesting." Unable to tolerate further exposure to her long, tanned legs beneath that short skirt, Elliot headed for the door. "I need to finish some work. Do you know which room is yours? I'll carry your bags up."

He could swear something otherworldly watched him through her dark-fringed eyes, eyes that contained wells of wisdom far older than her years. How old was she? Nineteen?

"The pink room. Are you an early riser?"

"I can finish my run by five-thirty, if you'll be ready then."

She nodded, and her hair bounced. "The first hotel on the itinerary is only about six hours away."

"She could be halfway there by now." He hesitated in the doorway. He was dead on his feet, but if they left tonight . . .

She shook her head as if she heard his thoughts.

"Mame hates driving. She'll either take it very easy and stop early, or she's out hunting a new driver."

"Or she could be flying to Alaska." Not wanting to think of Mame picking up hitchhikers or believe that he was heading out on a wild-goose chase, Elliot walked away. Maybe the police would find her first.

"Mame, what is this?" Dulce asked in incredulity at the sight of the Range Rover.

Turning off the ignition on Elliot's great throbbing beast of a vehicle as Dulce opened the passenger door, Mame clung to the steering wheel a while longer, letting her heart slow down. Thank heaven it wasn't dark yet. She could have backed over a regiment of Cub Scouts and never known it in this monster.

On the sidewalk, Dulce guarded all her worldly possessions: two cardboard boxes tied with string, a battered brown valise, and a kitten in a basket. The girl looked more frail than Mame felt, and she suffered a pang of guilt at dumping the burden of her ill health on her.

But then Dulce lifted age-old black eyes, and Mame breathed easier. Like Alys, Dulce's few years had packed a lifetime of experience. Unlike Alys, Dulce had struggled most of her life. She was stronger than she looked.

"My nephew didn't think Beulah was safe, so I borrowed his car." *Not one word of untruth,* Mame thought righteously. If Elliot hadn't been so pigheaded, she wouldn't have to litter her stairway to heaven with evasions.

"And where is Mrs. Seagraves?" Dulce asked, not immediately heaving her belongings into the Rover. "You should not be driving alone."

Although she gave lip service to the school's beliefs about spiritual connections, in emergencies Mame preferred the old-fashioned direct route of speaking to the Head Honcho. She offered up a silent prayer asking for forgiveness for what she was about to do.

If she missed her guess and Elliot didn't seek out Alys, prayers wouldn't help, because she'd never forgive herself. She'd promised Alys this trip.

But even if her independent nephew didn't find Alys, Mame had every confidence that Alys would hunt down Elliot the second she heard Mame had escaped the hospital. Mame was counting on them far more than she wished to reveal, even to herself. She had a feeling she and Dulce might need backup for what they intended.

"I'm doing a little matchmaking," Mame replied with a confidence she was too tired to feel. "We've had a change of plans. Can you drive this thing?"

Dulce leaned inside to check out the Range Rover's huge seats, leather interior, and array of blinking dials. "I have never even seen the inside of something like this, Mrs. Emerson."

Opening the driver's door, Mame gingerly climbed down. She'd taken the car out on a dirt road and driven it back and forth through the biggest mud puddles she could find. Elliot's shiny new car now possessed a thick coat of dust and mud that made it look as if it had been driven up mountains and through rivers. She'd covered the license plate in the same way. She had no illusions about her nephew's caretaking tendencies. He would call the police to find her, and she didn't want to be found. Not yet.

She felt every bit her age right now, but with a little

sleep, she'd be fine. The thrill of being on the road again would rejuvenate her.

The seriousness of her purpose would revitalize her energy. Sitting in the passenger seat was restful, wasn't it? She'd be fine.

"You can practice driving a little this evening," she told Dulce, "and we'll set out first thing in the morning. I need to rearrange a few things, so we're staying at a friend's house tonight. She's not home, but she left me the keys." She could hide the car in the garage. "And I've told you, you must call me Mame."

Ignoring her student's expression of concern, Mame climbed into the passenger seat while the girl loaded her boxes into the back.

"Mame, we do not have to do this," Dulce said in a low voice. "I can take the bus to Amarillo."

"You cannot kidnap your niece and expect to escape on a bus. You will need help. Alys and Elliot will be right behind us, and my friend Jock is waiting in Albuquerque. It's safer this way."

Dulce brightened. "You have explained to Mrs. Seagraves, then? And she approves?"

Mame had no idea how Alys would react to kidnapping, even a legal and justified kidnapping. She was fairly certain Alys would object to Mame's involvement, though. Whether or not she realized it, she had the same caretaking instincts as Elliot.

But there wasn't any way Mame was leaving a child in hell when she could do something about it. Men with more power than sense didn't frighten her. Dulce's niece belonged with Dulce's family. If Alys and Elliot didn't fall in with her plans, then Jock would just have to leave his damned hot air balloon and come help. He was the one who had invited her on this trip—for old times' sake.

Jock had always been the reliable sort. A pity she hadn't realized that forty years ago. But back then, reliable had been the last thing she'd wanted.

Mame smiled patiently. "Alys understands. Now climb in and let's see what this monster can do. I'm thinking of calling it Cerberus."

Dulce didn't know mythology. With the enthusiasm of youth for all things mechanical, she climbed willingly into the jaws of the guardian to the gates of hell.

Lying in Mame's pink-and-white guest room in the early-morning dark, Alys heard Elliot leave the house for his run. She hoped the exercise would reduce the electric field around him, or he would short out all her fuses before day's end.

He could short out her fuses by existing.

She'd imagined this journey as one of self-discovery, not sexual reawakening, but her body buzzed with her mental conjuring of Elliot joining her in this bed. She liked his lean elegance and thoughtful eyes and the strength in his hands. If she stuck with the physical, she liked him very much.

It was the know-it-all physician's attitude that riled all her defiant instincts. From experience, she knew doctors weren't the gods they pretended to be. In fact, they were pretty clueless when it came to recognizing the importance of the mind-body-spirit connection.

Still, he was a hunk. She'd only known one man in her bed. Did Elliot's long fingers and big feet give evidence of the length of his—

Laughing, Alys shoved off her covers and climbed out. She should have bought a new nightie if she meant to entertain those kinds of ideas.

She hadn't bought new clothes in eons. It wasn't as if their budget had allowed for them.

Rummaging through her suitcase, realizing how shabby her wardrobe had become, Alys shrugged it off. Her goal in life wasn't to impress Elliot Roth. Her old business suits and evening dresses had gone with her books and personal items into storage. She'd worn a lot of black after Fred got sick, and Mame had made her pack it all away. That pretty much left her old college clothes. She pulled out a pair of gold leggings, a bronze body shirt, and a gauzy multihued shirt of autumn colors to dress it up. She'd packed for travel and comfort.

Glancing down at the shiny band of gold on her left ring finger, she pursed her lips, made a decision, and slipped it off. Had she been thinking clearly, she should have buried it with Fred, but at the time, she'd thought she'd been burying her heart with him.

Mame had forced her to realize she had only one life to live, and it wasn't in eternity. If she meant to make the world a better place, she had to go forward from here.

Not quite ready to completely give up the symbol of her old life, she tucked the ring into her purse.

By the time Elliot returned and jogged up the stairs to shower, Alys had investigated Mame's freezer, located packages of frozen strawberries and waffles, and prepared breakfast. The fruit was a concession to Elliot's diet preferences. As far as she was aware, all diets called for fruit. The sausages were hers.

By the time he appeared, he entered a kitchen redolent

with the aroma of rich Colombian and frying meat. "Coffee?" he asked in a disapproving tone. "I didn't think Mame drank coffee."

"She keeps it for guests," Alys assured him, although she knew Mame loved a good cup of coffee. Maybe she should quit reassuring people and just let reality hit them. It wasn't as if she was his keeper.

In the early light of dawn, after a good night's sleep, he'd lost some of his drawn, anxious look. Today, he favored a successful executive in complete charge of his life. He'd slicked his natural curls back from his high brow, had donned professorial black-rimmed glasses to read the newspaper tucked under his arm, and wore a starched white shirt with his silky, pleated trousers. He carried a sports coat over his arm—apparently his one concession to informality. He must still keep clothes in his childhood room. She bet he usually wore three-piece suits.

Eyeing the neatly set kitchen table with its place for two, he threw down the newspaper but didn't sit. "I'm capable of fixing my own breakfast."

"I'm certain you are." She set the pretty cut-glass bowls of fruit on the ruffled place mats she'd laid out. "But I'm in a hurry to hit the road."

That seemed to be an acceptable excuse for waiting on him. She noticed his shoulders were wider than she'd realized, as he stretched them uneasily beneath his fitted shirt. His glance roamed from the table, to the toaster, to anywhere but her. Finally focusing on the refrigerator, he crossed the room and opened it.

"The milk's all gone," she called to him without looking over her shoulder. She set out Mame's green-flecked coffee mugs, admiring the design by one of the school's more successful potters. "I hope you like your coffee black." The waffles popped from the toaster. She transferred them to plates that matched the cups and sat down. She hadn't enjoyed setting out a nice meal in a long time.

"I don't drink coffee." Taking the remaining seat, he didn't reach for the brew she poured for him but checked the plate she laid out. "This looks wonderful, thank you."

Polite, if it killed him. "Last chance for home-cooked food," she said with irony, cutting into cardboard waffles decorated with bottled syrup. Once upon a time, she used to mix up made-from-scratch waffles on lazy Sunday mornings, covering them in fresh strawberries and real whipped cream. Doc Nice would have a heart attack if she told him that.

"There are ice chests in the garage. We could stop at the store and buy some fruit and yogurt to take with us. Fast food is suicidal." Savoring the waffle, he unconsciously picked up the coffee cup, then realizing what he'd done, set it back again.

"I saved my money so I could pig out at every decadent hamburger joint on the route. *You* can eat yogurt and tofu. I'm in search of the best homemade pie in the country." She only bought into *some* of the school's New Age philosophies. Eating granola wasn't one of them.

Instead of looking appalled, Elliot narrowed his eyes over his forkful of waffle. "Once we find Mame, we bring her home. This is not a vacation."

She loved Mame. She wanted to help her if she needed help. But Alys had a suspicion that—for whatever reason—Mame needed help in eluding her overprotective nephew more than she needed a hospital room. She had to place her confidence in Mame doing what was best for herself.

Despite his tame appearance, Elliot Roth looked as if he might growl and bite if she didn't agree with him. Who was she to shatter his illusions?

She tilted her mug in salute. "To Mame."

❧ FOUR ❧

"If you give me the itinerary, I can plan a route that might save us time." Elliot hauled his companion's bags down the porch stairs and contemplated buying her an overnight case if they had to do this too many times.

Too many times? They ought to find Mame by tonight. He should only have to haul the bags wherever Alys Seagraves was going and call it a day. If he spent any more time in the company of legs like hers, he wouldn't be responsible for his behavior. Today they were molded into gold spandex, and he could see every tempting curve through her gauzy shirt.

"I won't give you the Caddy's keys, so you don't need the itinerary," Alys chirped.

She looked like one of the autumn leaves floating from the maples in the yard. Bizarre, but colorful. Elliot ignored the twinge beneath his rib cage. He shouldn't have eaten the waffles.

"What kind of car did Mame steal?"

Her provocatively light eyes gazed up at him from beneath a thick fringe of dark lashes and untrimmed bangs. It looked as if she'd let her hair grow too long, then hacked it straight at the collar, leaving the irrepressible locks of her former hairdo to turn up or stick out haphazardly.

"I drive a Range Rover. Or did."

He threw their bags into the trunk—her two huge heavy ones and his overnight bag—while she gathered a bouquet of leaves and tucked a yellow rose behind her ear. He waited for her to break out in a rousing chorus of *Oklahoma!* or something equally uplifting. She had the unreal effect of a staged drama in his prosaic life.

They both halted at the driver's door, and he could see the impertinence in her eyes, laughing at him. Only Mame ever laughed at him like that, and she wasn't Mame. "You navigate, I drive," he said, holding out his hand for the keys she'd appropriated.

"You Tarzan, me Jane." She slid behind the wheel, leaving him empty-handed. "Jane drives. You look for Rover."

Under normal circumstances, he might have smiled at her foolishness, but finding Mame was serious business. He wouldn't let her pretend this was a joyride. He walked around the hood to take the passenger seat while she turned on the ignition. "How do I know you won't head for Chicago?"

"Because I love Mame, too," she said simply.

He refrained from commenting. Love had its downside. Chasing incorrigible aunts was a case in point.

"Doc Nice is grumpy in the mornings," she chanted cheerfully, looking over her shoulder and backing out while he buckled up. "Maybe I could write a book— *Traveling with Doc Nice.*"

"You do that." He'd hoped to be out of here by six,

but it was already going on seven. Mame could be half-way to anywhere. "Where's our first stop?" he asked.

Waiting for her to reply, he made the mistake of glancing in her direction.

Was she wearing anything under that shirt? Her breasts moved fluidly as she turned the Caddy's big steering wheel. Surely natural breasts weren't so high and round. Not that he had a ton of experience for comparison. He'd been trained to look past the sexual.

A silken lock of dark hair fell forward over her cheekbone, distracting him, as she consulted the odometer and set the mileage gauge. "Mame booked a hotel in Tulsa for the first night," she finally admitted.

Relief flooded through him. Tulsa had excellent medical facilities. "We can do that in three hours." He'd thought about renting a car, but the local rental agency had been closed last night, and he hadn't wanted to waste time waiting for it to open this morning. The Caddy could carry them to Tulsa with no problem.

"Not if we go through Kansas," she said, blasting his relief to pieces. "We can take the interstate out of town, but Mame has Highway 96 marked to Carthage as our first stop."

Elliot had the urge to reach over and grab the steering wheel out of her hands, but he maintained his outward calm. "We don't have to go through Kansas to get to Tulsa. The interstate takes us straight through. Mame needs to be in a hospital."

She turned into the stream of traffic, releasing a cloud of disapproval into the air. How the *hell* did she do that without saying a single word?

"Mame was married in a church in Carthage before

setting out on her journey," she said frostily. "That will be her first stop. How soon do you want to find her? Tonight, or now?"

Elliot crossed his arms and let her aim for Highway 96.

"Mame, why do we stop at these places?"

Eyes closed, leaning back on the Rover's wide leather seat, listening to her heart, Mame smiled at the lilting accent of Dulce's question. "You said Lucia's grandfather brings her home only on weekends and holidays, didn't you?"

Already, Dulce had learned to look warily at Mame's diversionary tactics. "But she is in that dreadful boarding school! She has quit speaking to everyone after Salvador told her she could not to speak to me again."

"Do you know where the school is?"

Mutely, Dulce shook her head and choked the leather-covered steering wheel.

"Then we must wait until Wednesday when her grandfather brings her home for her birthday. Amarillo is only a day's drive and this is Monday. Until then, I'm visiting a few fond memories. I was married back there, to a man who dreamed so big, he thought he could save the world if he put his mind to it."

Dulce remained silent. Mame didn't know if she was thinking or just concentrating on navigating the unwieldy SUV around a tractor hauling hay.

Safely back in the right lane, Dulce spoke. "You loved your husband very much?"

"When you're young, you're in love with love, in love with the world, in love with yourself. It's all one. The lucky ones hang on to all that love and make it work."

She'd had decades to think about the paths not taken. She couldn't explain them all in a few hours.

With the steady patience of her nature, Dulce thought about this, then nodded. "My sister mistook sex for love, too."

Mame shouted in laughter. She was going to enjoy this trip. She already felt a world younger.

Lying on the back bench of the small Precious Moments sanctuary, her hands folded over her chest, Alys contemplated the mural on the ceiling. "Why do you think they put that up there where no one can really see it?"

"So heaven can? Come on, Mame's not here. The car isn't in the lot, unless she parked over at the amusement park. Let's get moving." Elliot paced up and down the nearly empty chapel.

Doc Nice had focus down to a science. Earlier, in hopes of lightening his mood, she had turned the radio dial to cheerful music, but he'd insisted on National Public Radio—as if Mame's whereabouts might be broadcast on the news.

She'd pointed out the beautiful autumn colors and the fascinating rusty artwork decorating poles along the highway, advertising an art gallery. He looked over his shoulder to check traffic behind them to see if she could pass a tractor hauling bales of hay.

She supposed that kind of intense concern for an elderly aunt showed a great deal of love and respect, but not a lot of understanding of human nature.

She'd hoped to show him spiritual peace in the chapel so he might open up, relax, and let the world happen. Instead, he'd made fun of the saccharine murals of big-eyed children. She'd insisted it was a spiritual calling that had driven the artist to erect the temple, but privately, she agreed with his laughter. She would cross off working in tacky tourist traps from her possible-jobs list.

"The chapel Mame married in isn't here anymore," Alys informed him, swinging up from the bench to follow him into the next room. "She thought she ought to see what this one was about."

Elliot studied the stained glass and quit his mockery. She hoped he was doing as she was, picturing Mame as a young woman, marrying a man about to go off to war. Had Mame and her husband thought they had their entire lives ahead of them? Was her young husband's death the reason Mame lived each moment as if it were her last? Was she trying to teach Alys something?

She'd have to reward Elliot for his patience by pointing out the interesting notation in the guest book as they left. Of course then he'd realize she'd been stalling, giving Mame time to think out whatever she had in mind. She figured Mame could call Elliot's cell phone whenever she was ready to turn herself in. Should be interesting to see how Doc Nice reacted to insubordination.

"Do you think children are still sweet and charming like the ones in the murals, or do they pop out of the womb screaming 'I want' these days?" she asked, studying the wall. The Precious Moments children were piercingly lovely, content at their prayers. She'd thought to have a pair of children of her own by now. But she'd have to have a husband to have one, and that wasn't going to happen. Maybe she should be a schoolteacher.

"Children learn from the adults around them. If you're planning on having any, they'll probably dally in churches and sing in rest rooms." For a change, he didn't sound sarcastic, just pragmatic and accepting.

He apparently hadn't entirely forgiven her for the earlier episode when they'd stopped at a gas station to fill up. NPR had been playing Judy Collins's "Amazing Grace" when she'd climbed out of the car. The rest room had lovely acoustics, and she'd tested them with the lyrics. The mechanics had clapped when she'd emerged, and Elliot had gone all male and huffy, ushering her out as if she were an addled adolescent.

It had been kind of nice having his strength between her and the world, but Doc Nice needed to loosen up. He'd obviously lived alone too long.

"Song and laughter heal the spirit." She sighed blissfully at the morning sunshine through the colored glass. "I wish Mame were here. She'd have some lovely stories to tell."

Now that she was on her feet and walking, Elliot hurried toward the door. "And I want to keep her telling stories for a long, long time. Hurry up."

"Slow down." She lingered on the autumn garden path leading back to the gift shop, but Elliot's long legs carried him ahead of her. Trotting to keep up, she balked at the pedestal near the entrance where the big guest book lay open for visitors to sign. Elliot had stalked right past it when they'd entered. She'd signed it and dated her name. Just as Mame had.

With a look of patient resignation, Elliot halted with his hand on the door. She had to give him credit for being quick on the uptake. Instead of yelling at her for dawdling or telling her she'd already signed the book, he registered her location and her tenacious stance as if struck by a bolt from the blue. In a few quick strides, he was in front of the book, examining the entry she pointed out.

"Damn," he muttered under his breath. "I'm surprised she didn't note the time she was here."

"It's today's date and it's only ten. How far behind can we be?" Delighted that he hadn't exploded all over her for dallying, Alys dashed out the doors, into the sunshine.

"What's the next stop?" Elliot demanded, his long strides swallowing the distance to the car.

"According to the guide, U.S. 71 was Route 66 in the fifties. It takes us into Joplin, where we can find the original Route 66 into Baxter Springs, Kansas. There's a restaurant there with a safe once robbed by Jesse James. We can have lunch. Wouldn't it be fun to go horseback riding and pretend we were outlaws?"

Alys raced ahead of Elliot, loving the feeling of moving on, getting ahead, seeing what the world was all about. She wanted to dance in the sunshine, climb the trees, and laugh with the children in the school bus in the parking lot.

She was free! She'd forgotten how fabulous it was to be herself, without any responsibility to anyone or anything.

She leaped to grab a yellow leaf dangling from a tree branch, and Elliot gave her the patient look an adult does a child. He was worried about his aunt, so she excused him. For now.

His cell phone rang as they reached the car, and Elliot unconsciously rubbed at his chest throughout the conversation. Sitting on the car hood, swinging her feet, Alys tried to pretend this was 1969 and that she'd just been married and was heading out on her honeymoon.

Of course, they didn't have cell phones back then, and she didn't think Mame's husband would have been talking into one if they had. But she could imagine the excitement of admiring her new husband, of setting out on a journey to the future, of anticipating a wedding night.

She eyed Elliot as he snapped the phone closed and stuck it in his pocket. If he weren't quite so restrained, she could imagine him in her bed. He'd tousled his hair into curls again. She liked the sexy way they softened his lean features. He looked real, not like some unobtainable movie star or muscle-bound oaf.

But she had a hard time imagining a famous physician falling into any of her plans. He was obviously goal-oriented, and she liked bouncing where life took her, thank you very much. "Any news?" she called, leaping from the hood.

"No. I left the cell phone number with the neighbors in case they heard from her. They're just checking in."

He really did look anxious. Despite the reassuring tone of his voice, the little scar beside his mouth had deepened to match the dimple in his chin. She wished she could ease the concern in his luscious brown eyes, but he had to reach that plateau on his own. She'd spent countless hours worrying herself into ulcers over Fred, and not one minute of that worrying had cured him. Telling Elliot that wouldn't help.

"I can drive anytime you get tired," he offered.

"And end up in Tulsa for lunch? No, thank you." She hopped into the driver's seat and watched him arrange his long legs on the passenger side. She thought he was behaving quite decently, considering the extent of his concern for Mame.

He'd rolled up the sleeves of his white shirt in the

growing heat. As they drove toward the highway, he draped one bare arm out the open window and angled his position to study her. "Are you even old enough to drive a car?"

Wow, where had that come from? Wide-eyed, she admired the unruly curl hanging in the middle of his forehead, then offered him a beaming smile.

Momentarily thunderstruck, he jerked his gaze back to the map he'd found in the glove box.

Tickled that he was as caught by this weird electricity between them as she was, she obliged him with the truth. "I'm twenty-seven. How about you?" Twenty-seven, and she'd never even crossed the state line. All but bouncing in the seat, she watched the road signs for miles to Kansas.

"Do you have a driver's license to prove that?" he asked with a distinct air of testiness.

"Yup. Are you going to tell me to act my age now?" She pushed back in the seat and stretched, which pulled her leggings taut. Sitting still wasn't one of her better traits. She caught him sneaking a peek but didn't call him on it.

"I have a younger brother who's twenty-eight and still in school," he answered, as if it were relevant. "He rides a motor scooter and lives in a circus. You'd have a lot in common."

"A circus?" She didn't think she and his brother would have much in common. She was much too old for scooters and circuses, but she was interested in knowing more about Elliot Roth, and she finally had him talking.

He shrugged. "Circus. Or a zoo. People coming and going. Animals everywhere. Weird music, strange décor, incense burning. Typical college atmosphere."

"I never went to college." Well, she'd commuted from her parents' home in St. Louis to the university freshmen year, but Fred had swept her off her feet that year, and she hadn't spent much time thinking about classes.

"Are you planning on going to college now?" he asked.

Ignoring his question, she sat forward to watch the road signs on the four-lane road as they drove through Joplin. "Look at the old car sitting on that pole. I wonder what it represents?" She slowed down to stare at a car's hood sticking out of a building, apparently an advertisement for a Route 66 body shop. "Interstates are never this much fun. Is this where old cars come to die?"

"This is not about fun. This is about finding Mame before she has another attack." But this time, he swiveled to stare at the signpost and not the traffic behind them.

"I'll wager anything that Mame is out here having fun," she insisted at his contrariness. "We can't wave a magic wand or look in a crystal ball and find her, so we might as well enjoy the journey. Maybe it will heal what ails you. Worrying certainly won't get us there faster."

"Someone has to worry or nothing gets done."

He said it without resentment, and she thought there might even be a hint of humor behind the thought. The man was subtle. She'd have to start listening closer.

Alys pulled to the right, neatly circumventing an ancient Cavalier creeping along in the fast lane. A pickup hitting the gas as they left town jammed his squealing brakes to avoid her. She felt Elliot grab for the door handle.

"Are you trying to get us killed?" he growled. "Slow down."

"I'm doing the limit. Don't be such a worrywart. They really like their antique cars here, don't they?" Eagerly, she scanned the ancient rock buildings and cotton-littered fields of the old road, lapping up every new sight.

"We don't need to see Jesse James's safe," he argued. "We could be in Tulsa before Mame if you'd get on the interstate."

"The interstate doesn't go through Kansas." Thank goodness she had kept the keys or they'd be roaring for Tulsa right now. "And if you want to find Mame, you have to follow her route. Take a shortcut, and you might miss her.

"I've never been to Kansas," she said into the silence that followed her logic. "That's about the only stretch of the old Route 66 still existing. Mame was adamant about following this route."

He gave her a sleepy-puppy-dog stare as if he didn't quite know what to make of her. Briefly, the sun caught in the dark hairs of his muscled arm. She directed her gaze back to the road.

"Kansas is not a place many people are eager to see," he informed her.

"I am. I want to see everything. I've never been outside of Missouri." Happily, she watched the rolling countryside unfold around them. "Will there be a sign telling us when we enter Kansas? I wish I had a camera."

"There's one in my bag. If you're twenty-seven, why haven't you ever been out of Missouri?"

"My parents were set in their ways and didn't travel. Fred and I were building our careers and didn't take the time. And then the cancer happened, and life as we knew it stopped. I regret that." She set her mouth firmly. She wasn't much into impassioned speeches, so that was as much of one as he'd get.

"Cancer is not something one regrets. You fight it, hate it, despair of it, but I don't see 'regret' as the appropriate word."

She blinked in surprise at his fervency. "Okay, I regret that *life* stopped. I should have made Fred quit his job from the very first. We should have traveled, done all those things we'd promised ourselves we'd do one day. He never had a chance to see the Empire State Building or the Eiffel Tower. We never swam in the Gulf or saw Mayan ruins. There were so many things we never did . . ."

Tears spilled over, and she swiped at them furiously. "I don't want to go backward. I've been there. I want to move on."

"I'm sorry, I—"

With a loud *pop,* the Caddy fishtailed across the pavement. Alys grabbed the steering wheel with both hands and gently pumped the brake, trying to prevent the unruly car from spinning out.

Elliot leaned over and held the wheel, giving her the leverage she needed to hold the heavy car on the road while she slowed down.

A semi flew by, air horn bellowing, and the car swayed in the rush of wind. Horns honked behind them. Brakes squealed. The old road might be slower than the interstate, but it was well traveled. Sweat beaded on her forehead while she fought to bring the tires under control.

She held her breath as Beulah slowed, and she bumped the car off the side of the road. The Caddy listed to the right. Another semi flew past them, rattling the windows. She heard Elliot utter a soft curse, and out of the corner of her eye, caught him wiping his forehead with the back of his arm.

Shaken but unharmed, Alys leaned into the steering wheel, and took a relaxing breath. "Just like in the movies." She hadn't experienced an adrenaline rush like that in years. She didn't want to relive it again anytime soon, but it was good to know she was still alive enough to experience it. "I didn't think cars had flats anymore. Do you think there's a spare or do we hitch a ride back to Joplin?"

Elliot stared at her as if she'd sprouted wings. "People get killed hitching rides with strangers." He pulled out his cell phone.

"Spoilsport." The man couldn't take a joke. Flying high on life, she climbed onto the soft shoulder of the road and admired the autumn cornfield. Stretching, enjoying the tug of each muscle, she breathed in air thick with dust. The Caddy was far enough off the road for safety. She'd done good.

The back tire was a mess. Mame would be hours ahead of them. Alys suffered a twinge of guilt, then reminded herself that Mame was an adult and in full possession of her faculties. She hoped.

She gestured, and Elliot released the trunk latch from inside. Opening the lid, she rummaged around for the ice chests he'd insisted on bringing. She'd packed one with soft drinks. He'd packed one with water and yogurt and other disgusting oddities. She'd long ago concluded a healthy spirit and her stomach had nothing to do with each other unless it involved chocolate.

Popping the top of a Coke, she took a sip, then lifted the first of the ice chests out of the trunk so she could dig down to the tire.

Still on the phone—apparently holding for AAA—Elliot grabbed the chest from her and carried it to the side of the road. "I'll unload it just as soon as I'm off here," he told her. "We don't have any idea what kind of shape the spare is in. Or if there's even one in there."

Accustomed to doing for herself these past years, Alys shrugged and removed the second chest anyway.

A pickup slowed down to check out the Caddy's tail fins. This was car country and people noticed prime antiques like Mame's pink Cadillac. When Alys shaded her eyes to see who was looking, the truck pulled off in front of them.

A pair of good-looking teenage hunks climbed out. "Need some help, ma'am?"

Elliot instantly returned and planted himself between her and the boys. "No, we don't," he called back over the highway noise. "I've got it under control."

Alys gave him an incredulous look and elbowed him out of the way. "Isn't this great?" she murmured for his ears only. "It's just like living in the sixties. Haven't you ever watched those old shows on Nickelodeon?"

Of course he hadn't. Modern civilized man considered himself above good ole Andy Griffith. She'd had lots of time over the past few years to watch all the reruns from Mame's generation. There was a lot to be admired in the old ways.

Checking out the two burly young men, Alys concluded they looked safe. She cruised in their direction, leaving Elliot behind. "The tire blew up," she yelled over the traffic noise. "Would you like a Coke? We have a trunk full that we'll have to empty to get at the spare."

Both young men dragged their gazes from her to warily watch Elliot. With eyes in the back of her head, Alys could just about see his disapproving expression. He was probably worried they'd run into the gang from *Deliverance* or serial killers who wanted to steal their Cokes and thirty-year-old Cadillac.

"He doesn't bite," she said cheerfully as Elliot's shoes crunched the gravel behind her.

"Triple A says it will take an hour to get someone out here." Elliot dropped a heavy hand on her shoulder.

He may have meant it as a threat to tell her to shut up or as a proprietary gesture to tell the two young men to back off, but Alys felt a sensual shiver all the way to her bones at his touch. His sexy aftershave added flavor to the dusty air, and his protective attitude had her reverting to adolescence when she'd thought the big handsome men on the screen hauling their women around were the epitome of romance.

She glanced mischievously at the stern set of Elliot's square jaw, then back at the young men shifting uncertainly from foot to foot. "All the Cokes you can drink, boys. Let's see if we have a spare."

Without waiting for Elliot's permission, she led the way to the ice chest and handed out soft drinks. While she chattered, her two broad-shouldered Good Samaritans emptied the heavy bags from the trunk.

Elliot studied her with an enigmatic look in his eye. Proving his civility, he hefted the luggage the boys took out of the trunk without comment on her highhandedness. His shoulders strained the seams of his fancy dress shirt, but he didn't break a sweat carrying them to a safer distance from the rushing traffic.

With the luggage safely stowed, he leaned against the

guardrail and crossed his arms, keeping an eye on the proceedings but not interfering in her little fantasy trip to the sixties.

Maybe her purpose on this journey was to teach him to share the burden of life's stresses.

❧ FIVE ❧

Sipping the water Alys had carried over to him, Elliot contemplated the two yokels casting surreptitious glances at his companion as she admired their handiwork. Admittedly, she looked almost ethereal with her see-through shirt blowing in the breeze, but what the yokels didn't know, and he was just starting to suspect, was that there wasn't a damned thing fragile about Alys Seagraves.

When the boys removed the spare tire from the trunk, she smiled so proudly at them that they straightened their backs and worked harder to free the no doubt rusty jack. For that smile, Elliot had half a mind to elbow the clods out of the way and show her how a real man jacked cars and changed tires.

But he wasn't a teenager running on hormones. He took another swig and let the boys prove their masculinity.

Seeing the laughter peeking from beneath Alys's thick fringe of lashes as she walked toward him, Elliot crossed his arms and appreciated the view of her swaying hips and enticing curves. He supposed he'd been young and foolish enough to fall for a woman's wiles once. He just didn't remember when.

"Verifying you still have the old sex appeal?" he asked as she approached.

Instead of taking insult, she leaned next to him against the rail, crossing her arms over her breasts in imitation of him. "When I was a kid, I was plump and wore thick glasses. My parents knew nothing about the latest fashions, and I had no sister to teach me, so I looked like a geek. I was happily married before I had laser surgery and learned to make myself presentable. I never learned to flirt. Why shouldn't I start now?"

She said that without an ounce of whining and with such interest that he couldn't take offense that she was just toying with him. For the first time, he noticed her ring finger was bare. When had that happened?

"Because flirting is dangerous?" he asked wryly, unwilling to analyze the meaning of the missing ring. Before she demanded an explanation, he continued in his best radio talk-show manner, "Your husband must have been a man of rare good sense if he married a geek."

She turned her approving smile on him, and he felt it clear down to his metatarsals. Maybe it was a damned good thing he couldn't see his radio callers if they could spit and fry him with a single look.

"Fred was a geek, too. A brilliant one. We met in a movie theater showing a French film with subtitles. The theater was almost empty and we each had attended alone. We laughed in the same places and started arguing over cultural symbols before the movie ended. Afterward we spent half the night talking. I missed out on a lot by marrying young, but I'll never regret it."

Her sincerity stirred him. He understood gawkiness. He'd been a beanpole as a teenager. But he'd always been too dedicated to his cause to care about his dateless life. With two younger brothers and a huge responsibility on his shoulders, datelessness had been convenient. But lonely.

"A real-life love story, I guess." He wasn't certain if he believed in love at first sight and had to wonder what would have happened had Fred lived on as a geek while she'd turned into a butterfly.

He winced at the sadness filling her eyes.

"One love story a lifetime is about all I can manage," she said decisively.

Remembering she'd just lost her husband, he mentally kicked himself. He sought for something reassuring to say. "Mame was like that. She lost her husband in Vietnam and never remarried." Like that was helpful. Why didn't he just throw himself in front of moving traffic?

She crushed her empty Coke can and leaped up, casting him one of her laughing glances. "From the sound of it, she had three young boys to occupy her. Why on earth would she need a man?"

Knocked off his complacent block, Elliot remained seated while she danced off to thank the young men jacking the car down. The spare tire was a size too small and Beulah listed to one side.

He'd never thought of life from Mame's perspective. She must have been young and widowed just like Alys when his parents had died. He knew he owed his aunt far more than he could ever repay for taking in him and his brothers. He was doing everything within his power to make her life easy now that he had the opportunity to do so.

But he'd never really considered that Mame had given up her life for them. She was intelligent and vivacious and could easily have remarried. Instead, she'd devoted herself to raising children who weren't her own.

Had it been a case of one love story a lifetime? Or lost opportunities?

Rising, he followed Alys to the car, reaching for the wallet in his pocket to reimburse their friendly neighborhood tire changers. Before he could pull out a couple of twenties, Alys reached up to hug one grinning young man and kiss the cheek of the other.

Something very like jealousy gnawed at the vulnerable place beneath his ribs.

When Elliot offered the cash, the young men grinned, shook their heads, and wandered back to their truck, finishing off the cans of Coke Alys had handed them.

"Can't buy me lo-o-ve," Alys sang, patting him on the hand holding the money before dancing back to the driver's seat.

Trying not to gnash his teeth or laugh out loud, Elliot shoved the bills back into his wallet and vowed to find Mame at the very next stop—before he developed a split personality.

Alys parked in front of the sign welcoming them into Kansas so Elliot could take her picture. She didn't do anything so common as stand in front of the sign but clung to the top and smiled over it, nearly giving him heart failure when the post swayed.

She insisted on taking his picture as well. Fascinated with the digital camera, she held on to it afterward, aiming it at the scenery before returning to the car.

"Perhaps I could take up photography and illustrate my travel columns," she said with the perpetual enthusiasm that was starting to wear on him.

Or perhaps it was worry over Mame that gnawed at him. He kept a constant watch for his Rover along the side of the road as Alys wove around tractors and pickups. The incident with the tire had his nerves jumping, but at least he knew Alys could handle emergencies. Could Mame handle a blowout? How far behind her could they be?

"Maybe you'd better look for a real job and use travel writing as your hobby," he agreed absently.

"I could go back to selling real estate, I suppose. I had to let my license go when Fred got too sick for me to attend continuing education classes."

In a few short hours he'd learned her moods cast light and shadow with the swiftness of passing clouds. He didn't hear wistfulness or regret in her declaration. He glanced over to see her gazing pensively at the old arched concrete bridge covered in graffiti ahead of them.

He picked up the Route 66 guidebook he'd found in the glove box. The bridge was apparently another historic monument to the past. If they stopped, he bet he'd find Mame's name scribbled on it. He refrained from telling Alys that. "If you earned the license once, it shouldn't be difficult to obtain again. I bet you'd be excellent at real estate sales."

She shrugged. "I love houses. Maybe I could be an interior decorator." She turned back to him and her eyes were alive again. "Is that what you did? Full-time doctoring and writing as a hobby?"

"I earned my degree but never really practiced. I spend a lot of time in research. So, yeah, maybe the writing was a hobby at first." Or maybe his life was a hobby. When he wasn't researching, or taping his radio show, he devoted all his free time to writing up his findings and conclusions. His only other activity in life was sleep.

He was relieved she didn't have a crystal ball. She seemed to see right through him as it was. Fortunately, she didn't call him on it since the sign for Baxter came into view. He glanced through the guidebook's description. This might be the only town in the area where Jesse James *hadn't* robbed the bank. Maybe that uniqueness was what they should advertise.

"What does your Rover look like?" she asked as the first sign of the town appeared in the windshield.

"Black." *Idjit.* He should have told her that sooner, but he'd been worried about her concentrating on traffic. "Missouri plates, luggage rack, no distinctive markings." Elliot scanned the street for the big vehicle. On the narrow two-lane with parallel parking that comprised the few blocks of the business district, it should stand out like a sore thumb. He didn't see it anywhere.

"Does it have one of those computer navigation systems?" she asked with wide-eyed interest.

"Yeah, but I can't imagine Mame using it. I'd feel better if I knew she could. What if she's lost?"

"She'd ask directions." Laughter definitely tinted her voice. "Boys prefer toys."

"Why would Mame be interested in Jesse James?" he wondered aloud to divert her train of thought. Yeah, he liked toys. And no, he didn't like asking for directions. But she'd already guessed that.

"I believe it was her husband who liked outlaws. He was apparently a bit of a thrill-seeker, rode the rodeo, flew balloons, drove a Harley. Maybe he considered himself an outlaw."

"Mame married an idiot like that?" Elliot could have bit his tongue but it was too late.

She laughed and scanned a line of cars down a side road while they waited at an intersection. "Mame was quite proud that he'd done what he wanted to do before he died. I suspect he would have mellowed as he grew older, but he never had that chance."

It was amazing that Mame hadn't died, too, given the family curse. Elliot rubbed the ache developing in his midsection.

"Where's the restaurant?" He'd had enough psych courses to know fear of death led to life-paralysis. He didn't need to drive down that path.

"On the corner over there. There was a parking space down that side street. Why don't I circle around, park there, and we can walk and stretch our legs?" Apparently catching his resistance, she added, "We can look down side streets easier."

"And everyone in town can see us coming in this pink elephant," he admitted. "So would Mame."

He wasn't accustomed to anyone else driving, and it was all he could do not to press his foot against an imaginary brake or shout she was too close to the curb while she maneuvered the Caddy around the block and into a parallel-parking space.

Every head on the street turned as they climbed out of Beulah. The cracked window and listing trunk didn't add to the Caddy's pink charm. By the time he walked around the hood, Alys had already started down the sidewalk, oblivious to the stares they attracted.

"Oh, I haven't seen one of those since I was a kid!" She darted into a nearby store just as he caught up with her.

Wondering if he was expected to follow, Elliot realized he hadn't spent enough time in the company of others lately to remember how shopping together worked.

Figuring he'd lose her if he left her—not a bad idea, except she had the keys and the itinerary—he glanced up and down the street for any sign of Mame. Finding none, he stopped at the store window to see what had caught Alys's eye.

A display of old-fashioned toys.

Shoving his hands into his pockets, he studied the wooden lettered blocks, an old Tonka tractor, a whirligig, a hula hoop, and a baby doll in a christening gown. If she came out with the doll, he was heading for the hills. He didn't want to be anywhere in the vicinity of a female with a ticking biological clock. He smiled at the old plastic doctor's bag with a stethoscope. He'd had one of those.

Alys bounced out before he had time to worry that she'd escaped through a back door. He was actually looking forward to seeing what she'd purchased. Obviously, he'd been under too much stress lately.

She waved a colorful aluminum whirligig like a magic wand under his nose. "And they had bubbles!" She rummaged in her sack to produce a small red bottle. "They had a wand that blew *enormous* bubbles but I didn't think we had room for that." She dipped the wand into the bottle and produced a twinkling stream of fragile bubbles with the first wave.

"I don't suppose you'll tell me what you plan to do with those?" he asked. She was such a mixture of child and wisdom that pinning her into any one niche was equivalent to classifying bubbles.

Her arched eyebrows lifted in surprise. "Play with them, of course. Didn't you ever play with bubbles?"

"When my brothers were little, I guess." He strode down the block to the restaurant, darting glances down alleyways for the familiar sight of his Rover. He didn't need her analyzing the reasons he'd never learned to play.

Alys trailed behind him, leaving a string of bobbing bubbles, to the amusement of passersby.

Smiling, she stopped to chat with an elderly lady who admired the spinning gold-and-copper whirligig. The gnawing in Elliot's stomach demanded feeding. He ought to go ahead, grab a table, and let her catch up.

But he lingered, watching her throw her dark hair back in laughter. When was the last time he'd laughed like that? He wanted to smile just looking at Alys. She was like the whirligig, bright and shiny, spinning uselessly just for the fun of it.

He didn't have to approve. He could just enjoy.

He'd enjoy it a lot more if he knew Mame was safe. And that Alys wasn't deliberately dawdling to give Mame time to get farther ahead. He should never have mentioned the assisted-living home. He had a feeling that had pushed his travel companion over the edge to Mame's side.

She ran up to him a second later, catching his hand as if she did it every day, dragging him onward. "She thinks she saw Mame earlier. People notice strangers in small towns. The toy store clerk didn't remember her, but the owner was out to lunch. We could check back later."

Flabbergasted, not just by her observation but by the

electric shock waves of her slender hand in his, Elliot accompanied her into the Cafe on the Route.

Alys hadn't been spinning uselessly. She'd been more focused than he was. "Maybe you should be a detective," he muttered, probably to himself, since she was busy looking for a bank safe in a restaurant. If this crumbling structure had once been an old bank, outlaws *should* have robbed it.

Heads swiveled at their entrance. Still holding Alys's hand, Elliot felt as if he'd been caught robbing a cradle, but he didn't release her. The old high school, gangly awkwardness threatened to turn him into a hormone-fogged klutz as they threaded their way through chairs and tables. Thankfully, Alys released his hand so he could think again. There for a moment, he'd been blinded by shining gold and copper.

He remembered to scan the room for Mame and to ask the waitress if she'd seen her. He felt foolish asking. What difference would it make if Mame had come and gone? They couldn't catch her any faster. The uneasy possibility that this was a wild-goose chase lodged in his throat.

"You're fretting again," Alys said as Elliot slid into the seat across from her, wearing such a serious frown that he almost had her worrying. She loved Mame. She didn't want anything to happen to her. But after Elliot had explained the nature of Mame's problem, and she knew Mame had been taking medication and dealing with it for years, she honestly thought it was best if Mame came to them and not the other way around.

"I don't like the idea of Mame driving alone," he admitted. "I was hoping someone had seen her so I could ask if she had anyone with her."

His heart was in the right place, Alys decided, although he kept rubbing his chest as if he feared losing it. "We can stop at the collectible store later. Mame couldn't have resisted going in any more than I could."

When he relaxed, Elliot's whole face transformed. The frown beneath his dark curls disappeared, and his little boy smile twisted at her heart. The crescent scar beside his lips turned upward in a smiley face to match. When all that masculine attention was focused on her, she felt as if she were the only woman in the room.

She felt like a woman.

It had been a very long time since she'd remembered she was one. Not a busy wife. Not a caretaker. Not a zombie. But a woman in the eyes of a good-looking man. Her nipples sprang to attention beneath his appreciative gaze. He looked away before she could melt into a puddle.

She studied her companion speculatively over the top of her menu. Elliot pulled his reading glasses from his pocket and seemed engrossed in deciding what healthy item he should nibble on next. She couldn't really be interested in a man who ate like a rabbit, could she?

She'd been without sex for so long, she could be interested in a rabbit with the appropriate equipment. Elliot Roth definitely had what it took. The question was, did *she*?

She'd never really been shy. Reserved, maybe, but she'd outgrown that with her sales courses. She just didn't have a lot of experience with men.

Elliot Roth was a wealthy, famous man in his prime. He would have women hanging all over him. He had responsibility written all over him as well, so indiscriminate sex was probably out. He probably had a steady girlfriend. She would have done better with the boys who'd changed the tire if casual sex was all she wanted.

Casual was definitely all she could handle at this stage, just to see if the juices still functioned.

She would never see him again after they found Mame. Casual.

Elliot slipped his glasses back into his shirt pocket and glanced up at her from the depths of his intelligent eyes, and all her decision making flew out the window.

He was the one. If she intended to rediscover herself, and end years of abstinence, Elliot Roth was the man she wanted to do it with.

Mame, she prayed silently, *don't have a heart attack. Let your positive energy heal so I can borrow your nephew for lascivious purposes.* She had a strong hunch Mame would approve.

"The Caesar salad," Elliot told the waitress. "And could you grill the shrimp instead of frying them?"

The devil prompted Alys as she ordered, "French fries and chocolate cheesecake with whipped cream on top, please."

The waitress grinned and scribbled the order.

"Bring her some of those grilled shrimp, too," Elliot added. "And sliced tomatoes if you have them."

"Bring him some of the cheesecake," Alys countered, handing the menu to the waitress and meeting his gaze head-on. "And a big old glass of Coke."

"That stuff will kill you," he protested.

"Yeah, but I'll die happy. How about you?" she teased.

The waitress escaped before the war could escalate.

❧ SIX ❧

"You can't really mean to eat that stuff." In appalled fascination, Elliot watched Alys dip her spoon into a decadent bowl of whipped-cream-laden chocolate cheesecake. The only healthy thing on it was a strawberry.

He couldn't remember anyone over the age of ten eating like that.

"One bowl of dessert will not kill you." She dipped her spoon into the chocolate, and sampling the flavor, hummed in appreciation. "For all I know, the human body develops an immunity to cheesecake just as it does arsenic. Gad, this is incredible."

Her pink tongue flicked across the spoon to clean it. Elliot had to drop his gaze to his cheesecake. He squirmed in the chair, refusing to let libido overrule good sense. "A diet of arsenic has long-term debilitating effects."

Out of curiosity, he sampled the whipped cream on the dessert the waitress had set in front of him. Plastic. *Blech*. He could resist. She must have been deprived for a long time to consider this good eating.

"I'm not recommending a diet of cheesecake," she admonished, happily digging into both cream and pie now that she'd tasted them separately. "I'm just saying one slice won't kill you. It might even make you feel better."

"Finding Mame would make me feel better." He stabbed his fork into the dessert. Maybe he needed the antacid action of dairy.

"Mame spent her entire life raising you and your brothers." She shook her spoon at him. "Now she's free to do as she pleases. If this is what pleases her, you shouldn't interfere. You know as well as I do that she will let us know if she needs help. You have a phone and she has the number."

Distracted by her waving spoon, waiting for the dollop of cream to shoot across the table, Elliot glanced up to catch Alys licking a patch of chocolate on the corner of her lips. When he caught himself wanting to lick the spot clean for her, he swallowed his bite of cheesecake whole.

By the time he'd stopped choking, he'd prepared his argument. "The stress of the journey could worsen her heart condition. Her life is more important than a Balloon Fiesta."

"Her life *is* the Balloon Fiesta," she said serenely. "Life is a journey. Which would you rather do—spend your whole life in the fast lane fighting traffic, or stop to watch the balloons?"

"That's New Age baloney." He slapped down the fork, and ignoring the soft drink she'd ordered, sipped from his water glass.

"Not to Mame. She's doing what she believes in."

What was she trying to tell him? Probably nothing he wanted to hear. He rubbed at the heartburn this discussion—or the cheesecake—engendered.

"Are you okay?" Her huge eyes watched him with concern.

He liked having her watch him as if he were that

whipped cream she was inhaling, but he didn't like having anyone fret over him. "I'm not used to rich desserts," he replied, unwilling to tell her more.

She studied him briefly, then finished off her last bite with a sigh of pleasure. She patted her mouth with her napkin. "Little girl's room."

She flitted away in her butterfly mode. Heads turned to watch her pass by. She stopped to speak with the waitress, who glanced in his direction. Why did that scene make his chest burn more?

A moment later, he knew.

"Doc Nice!" the waitress chirruped, handing him the check. "I listen to you on the radio all the time. Could I get your autograph?"

Heads swiveled. This was a small room and the waitress hadn't exactly been quiet. He scribbled his autograph on a napkin and reached for his wallet.

A woman at a nearby table turned around and handed him a notebook. "Please, for my daughter? She swears by your books."

A small cluster of women surrounded the table before he could pay the check and escape.

Not until the waitress brought back his credit card and Alys still hadn't returned did he realize she'd stiffed him for the check and disappeared.

Escaping his admirers and hurrying outside, Elliot fumed. They hadn't seen a sign of Mame. For all he knew, Alys could be fleeing in the Caddy.

Striding down the street, he stumbled to a halt when he turned the corner and saw Alys sitting on Beulah's big pink hood, blowing bubbles. A weary mother pushing a stroller and clinging to the hand of a whining toddler stopped to let the child watch.

Oh no, she wasn't doing this to him again. No more dallying. Elliot opened the passenger door to indicate he was ready to leave. In no hurry, Alys leaned over to hand the whirligig to the enchanted child.

She slid off the car hood, leaving the mother to stroll away, smiling and listening to her toddler's excited chatter.

Oblivious to Elliot's observation, Alys slipped into the driver's seat and stretched her legs. She snapped on the seat belt, and handed Elliot a roll of Tums. "Mame was in the collectible store this morning. The owner didn't know for certain, but he thought she was with a young Hispanic girl. Short, long braid, wearing jeans. That's as much as he remembered, Sound like anyone you know?"

She'd have him spinning like the damned whirligig. He didn't know anyone in Mame's life these days. Frowning at the Tums, Elliot tore open the package and popped one into his mouth. "You're more likely to know her than I am." He hated admitting that. He wanted to be annoyed at her delaying tactics, but she kept unbalancing him.

He scooted the seat farther back so he could stretch out. He missed the Rover's head room but he was damned glad they had the Caddy and not one of those rolling eggs they called cars these days.

"I don't know everyone at the school," Alys said, switching on the ignition. "And I don't know your neighbors. I can't think of anyone fitting the description. Do we need to buy a spare before we leave here?" She steered the car from the parking space into traffic.

"It's a regular tire, not one of those disposable ones.

It'll hold. We can buy a new one in Tulsa after we find Mame."

Alys contemplated telling him that they wouldn't find Mame unless she wanted to be found but decided that defeated her purpose. She could keep Elliot entertained while Mame enjoyed her freedom, and she would see the USA as well. She mentally waved good-bye to Baxter as she drove into the unfolding fields of Kansas.

She really ought to be thinking about how she would travel on to California after they reached Albuquerque, but she was more interested in what she would do with the man beside her. How could she reach his positive energy and heal his spirit if he wouldn't relax?

"Can you sing?" she asked. At his look of inquiry, she shrugged and turned the radio dial. "My turn to choose."

"The passenger gets to choose." He dialed the radio back to the news.

"Then the passenger should go soak his head." She switched the dial back to a classic rock song and jumped in on "Jeremiah was a bullfrog."

It felt smashing to sing again. She'd always loved cruising down the highway with the windows open and the radio blaring. Maybe she needed to rediscover the things she loved. "I don't suppose travel writers can afford convertibles?" she asked as the song ended.

"Real estate might. Stick to what you know," he advised.

"I want to go forward, not backward."

"You think running away to New Mexico and becoming a travel writer is going forward?" he asked incredulously. "Are you sure you're not sixteen?"

"I am *not* sixteen." Grumpily, she glared out the window. Catching sight of the sign ahead, she cried, "Oklahoma!"

She veered suddenly out of traffic and onto the shoulder, causing Elliot to pop another Tums. Two states in one day!

She ran up to the WELCOME sign to have her picture taken and admired the lanky doctor adjusting the camera. He really was quite patient despite his pragmatic tendencies. He even sat on the ground in his fancy dress slacks to aim the photo upward for a different angle. He looked much more human sprawled on the ground.

And masculine. She had a bird's-eye view of his crotch.

As if catching her wavering interest, he rose hastily, brushing off grass. Realizing she had the ability to turn on the self-controlled doctor, Alys let exhilaration zing through her veins when they climbed into the car again.

She returned to their earlier conversation while the cow pastures and hay fields of Route 66 passed by. "I don't see any reason why I shouldn't explore new horizons."

"Because you haven't explored the old ones?" He didn't miss a beat.

Good man.

"Because you can't run from who you are," he finished complacently.

Bad man. That was about as asinine a piece of advice as she'd ever heard. How could she run from who she was if she didn't know who she was?

Singing along with the radio, she tuned out Elliot Roth and his sexy shoulders and sleepy eyes. No wonder Mame had run away. The man was infuriatingly predictable.

The two-lane carried them through flat farms, but to her disappointment, no oil wells. Instead, she spotted a longhorn and insisted on having her picture taken with the animal while she sat on the fence. She needed a cowboy hat.

They drove through small towns that might have been forgotten by time but not by McDonald's. A humongous coal and tractor-trailer train halted them on the main street of Vinita. Elliot leaned his seat back and closed his eyes—probably counting to ten before he blew a blood vessel. Alys was relieved he didn't demand that they return to the interstate.

The old road became a well-traveled four-lane outside Vinita. After Elliot read the guidebook aloud, Alys drove around downtown Foyil until she located the road's original pink concrete. He didn't read the book to her again after that.

By the time they reached Claremore, it was obvious they wouldn't be able to see Mame or the Range Rover unless it was directly in front of them. There were far too many cars. Since Mame had a solid head start, Alys didn't count on them catching up with her anytime soon.

Elliot turned the radio back to the news at the first road sign for the interstate into Tulsa.

"The interstate is a toll road," she informed him with a touch of frost. "Route 66 takes us directly to I-44. It's even a four-lane."

"How far is the hotel?" was all he asked.

"Other side of Tulsa. The place Mame stayed in for her wedding night isn't there anymore so we chose a Doubletree nearby."

"Swimming pools and screaming kids." He grimaced.

"If you're really Mame's friend, you'll convince her to come back with me to get some rest and have those tests run."

"And would you let her continue to Albuquerque if she's fine?" So far, Oklahoma didn't look much different from Kansas. Or Springfield, she decided, watching still another McDonald's pass by as Route 66 entered the interstate.

"Once we have her medication adjusted, I'll put her on a plane and send her straight out there," he promised. "Driving is too stressful at her age."

Alys rolled her eyes. "You are so *clueless*." She shifted lanes and pointed out a sign ahead. "Seventh Street is where the hotel is. We're not far from the Museum of Western Art that Mame wanted to visit. She was eager to see how much Tulsa had changed, though, so I don't know what she would do first."

Mame had old friends here she wanted to look up as well, but Alys decided to keep that bit of information to herself. It wasn't as if she knew who the friends were, much less how to reach them.

Elliot tensed as they exited the interstate merging into downtown traffic and found the hotel—a skyscraper towering over the Convention Center, a far cry from the old motels of the sixties. "Drive through the garage," he ordered. "Let's see if the Rover is there. I'm hoping she found a driver and isn't out there on city streets in rush hour."

"Mame has stayed alive for sixty years without your help. I imagine she knows what she's doing. I'm not entirely certain you do."

She shouldn't be insulting the man with the credit card. Mame had paid the travel agent in advance, but she had reserved only one room a night. Alys was supposed to drive to earn her half of the hotel cost. Before Fred died, the banks had canceled her credit cards after she'd exceeded her limit and fell behind on payments. How did she explain that? She didn't think he'd given an instant's consideration to the possibility that he wouldn't find Mame and head home today.

"Pull out on that side street," he commanded after they'd gone up and down the hotel parking garage ramps and back to the exit without seeing a single black Range Rover.

She stared at him incredulously. "Why? You want to pay for parking just for driving up and down ramps? Shouldn't we at least go into the hotel and ask?"

"We have to hide Beulah. If we're here before Mame, she'll probably run off if she sees the car and knows we're waiting."

"You think she doesn't know you'd follow her?"

She parked in a church parking lot several blocks away. Elliot jumped out, obviously in too much of a hurry to answer.

Enjoying the lovely autumn day, studying the city around her, Alys followed at a more leisurely pace. To her secret delight, Doc Nice slowed down so she could keep up. "Did you have other business you should be seeing to besides Mame?" she inquired.

"I was on a book-signing tour, which I canceled the minute I heard Mame was in the hospital. Mame knew I would."

Back in sync with him again, she took his arm. "She adores you, you know. She tries not to brag, but she talks about you all the time."

"Then why the hell is she putting me through this?"

he demanded with confusion, his long legs carrying him faster.

"I'm not Mame, so I can't speak for her, but is there ever a time when she isn't thinking of what's best for you?" She tugged his arm, slowing him down.

"I don't see how this can be good for either of us." Reverting to anger, he shoved open the door of the hotel lobby when they reached it.

Alys couldn't remember the last time she'd stayed in a hotel. Surely she and Fred had taken a vacation at some time. It had just been so long ago, the memory was buried under too much debris, and she couldn't recall it.

She didn't have time to admire the huge vase of incredible flowers in the center of the enormous lobby. Elliot strode directly to the desk to ask if Mame had checked in yet.

The desk clerk checked his computer. "Are you Mr. Seagraves?" he asked.

Alys stepped up. "I am Alys Seagraves. We reserved the room."

"Ah, yes, here we are." He reached in a drawer and removed a plastic key card. "Mrs. Emerson has already signed for the room. It's on the top floor with a view of the skyline."

Could finding Mame really be that easy? Exchanging a glance with Elliot, who looked both elated and skeptical, Alys accepted the key and followed the clerk's direction to the elevator.

"I smell something fishy," she said as they entered.

"Probably the swimming pool," he muttered, tensely shoving his hands in his pockets.

She tried to stay nonchalant, but her heart kicked up another notch with each floor the elevator climbed.

Elliot jiggled the coins in his pocket. "Mame's probably exhausted and napping. I hate to wake her," he said as the elevator arrived at their floor.

Alys cast him a look of incredulity. "When was the last time you saw Mame nap?"

He had the grace not to argue. Snatching the card key from her hand, he strode to the right as if he knew precisely where he was going. It took Alys a moment longer to figure out the directional signs and linger over the spectacular view from the window.

Oklahoma was *flat*. Well, so was a lot of Missouri.

She hurried to catch up as he opened the door. Admiring the size of the elegant suite they swept into, it took her a moment to notice Elliot's silence. Not until he stalked across the room in obvious fury and whipped out his phone at the window did she realize he'd really expected to find Mame here.

Surely he didn't believe Mame would drop dead just because she'd eluded them? That sounded like Mame had all pistons churning to her.

"Maybe she's out touring the museum?" she asked as a peace offering after he checked his voice mail and apparently had none. "It's right down the road."

Elliot shoved the phone back in his pocket and flung open the draperies, as if that might reveal Mame's hiding place.

Alys gave up attempting to interpret the wealth of emotions in her companion's silence. Mame was alive and up to her usual tricks. Elation welled in her knowing Mame was fine—while she was standing in a lovely hotel suite with a king-sized bed and the very appealing Elliot Roth, even if he did appear on the verge of explosion. *Relish the moment.*

Rocking back on her heels, Alys contemplated the meaning of Mame's change in game plan. She and Mame had reserved rooms with two double beds, not suites with king beds.

Obviously, Mame was using the situation to create mischief. That Mame felt healthy enough to indulge in her usual tricks reassured Alys no end.

Buzzing with anticipation while waiting for Elliot to work this out, Alys stroked a tall plant on the suite's coffee table. "I thought hotels left chocolates or cookies on pillows, not orchids."

Elliot was scanning a piece of hotel stationery he'd picked up off the desk. His explicit curse answered a lot. He popped another Tums and reread the missive.

Refusing to be deterred, Alys held the plant pot and bounced on the end of the bed. How did one make an orchid bloom? And what color would this one be? "I don't suppose you know if Mame wore an orchid at her wedding?"

"There's a picture in the photo album of her wearing a huge one." Elliot flung the stationery on the bed beside her. His expression was enigmatic. "I may have to wring her neck."

Dying of curiosity, Alys handed him the pot. "I don't know if the bloom on this one will be huge or not. We ought to buy her a corsage when we find her."

"If we don't find her, we can bring orchids to her funeral." He slapped the pot back on the table while Alys picked up the letter.

Her chuckles as she read Mame's insane note drove Elliot crazy. How did she turn off her anxiety and let go like that? He paced up and down the suite to keep from watching her expressive face too closely. He knew what it would take to make him forget Mame for a little while, and he didn't like knowing that about himself.

He'd stayed in fancier suites, with better views. He'd never stayed in one with a playful sprite who revved all his motors.

If he wanted to continue following Mame, they'd have to spend the night here.

He had his credit cards. He could get another room.

He didn't want to.

Pacing and trying not to analyze that reaction, he watched Alys read the letter again and chuckle. He didn't see what was so damned funny. Mame knew he was here. She had dodged him. On purpose.

"She's matchmaking!" Alys bounced back against the bland navy-and-beige cover and giggled.

Elliot didn't think grown women ought to giggle, but he was too aware of her slender figure splayed across the enormous bed to be reasonable. The image of what they could be doing together on that bed fried his brain. He was tired, worried, and ought to be picturing wringing Mame's neck instead of wondering what Alys Seagraves wore—or didn't wear—beneath her clingy knits.

Her breasts bobbed freely enough to believe they were unfettered.

"She says she's staying with friends," he pointed out with irritation. "She wants you to take care of the orchid and make it bloom. She has some idiot idea that you have a green thumb." Remembering the heat-blasted shrubs of Alys's brown front yard, he thought Mame had gone senile on him. Hell, one more thing to worry about.

"Her note says you like green tea before bedtime!"

Alys crowed with laughter, waving the paper as if it held the secrets to life. "Check the drawers to see if she left your favorite jammies."

Okay, that was pretty funny. Elliot bit back a reluctant grin. His aunt had her outrageous moments. He could appreciate that. "I quit wearing jammies after I outgrew the penguin ones."

Quaking with laughter, she grabbed a pillow and buried her face in it to stifle her roar. "Penguins!" The pillow muffled her shriek. She came up to ask, "Did you know that penguins have sex only once a year?" before burrowing into the pillow and roaring again.

Obviously, his childhood reminiscences contrasted a little too vividly with his adult identity to send her over the top like that. Did she think he was the kind of guy who had sex only once a year? He didn't know whether to laugh with her or strangle himself. Maybe he ought to see about getting another room. They still had time to check out that museum she'd mentioned.

Maybe he'd rather check out the king-sized bed with her in it.

King-sized bed.

Elliot dropped his head in his hands. Alys's laughter took on a whole new meaning. Mame had set up the suite for the two of them, complete with wedding corsage.

He had a bad feeling this trip was going to be a lot longer than he'd anticipated.

❦ SEVEN ❦

"I won't let her do this," Elliot muttered, the perfect image of outraged male as he headed for the door. Add some bull horns to go with the tousled curls and Alys figured she could wave a red cape at him.

"This room is already paid for," Alys called after him. "And if Mame needs to reach us, this is the room she'll call." So, he was a little tense. Under the stress, he really was a nice man. She shouldn't rattle his cage like that, but it was so much *fun*. She had felt helpless for so long that she simply couldn't resist wielding this tiny bit of power by tweaking his chains.

He halted abruptly, looking trapped, and she relented. "If I'll ruin your reputation, get your own room, and I'll let you know if she calls. But I have to tell you, I can't afford a room of my own."

"Ruin my reputation?" At his look of incredulity, she laughed.

"Well, you are Doc Nice. How am I supposed to know how your adoring public sees you? Or if you have a fiancée elsewhere who would be incensed at your sharing a room?" She gestured at the acres of bed. She'd been sleeping on a cot for years. First, to be close to Fred during his illness without disturbing him with her tossing and turning. And then, because she couldn't bear sleeping in the double bed he'd died in. "It's not as if there isn't enough room."

She thought she'd wiped him speechless with her invitation. Elliot's eyes widened with an interest that shot lightning bolts and sizzled through every fiber of her clothing. Uh-oh. She didn't know whether to roll under the bed or flaunt whatever it was he wanted to see.

"I think we better hit the Museum and look for Mame," he finally replied with desert dryness.

She might have felt insulted by his tone if he wasn't having such a difficult time tearing his gaze from her.

Almost relieved that they didn't have to have a showdown just yet, she swung off the bed. "I need my suitcase with the toiletry bag."

Elliot shoved his hands into his pockets, and his mouth turned up in a mocking smile. Even with his curls rumpled and his wrinkled white shirt rolled up his arms, he could pass for Mr. GQ. She didn't like the look of that smile, although she sure wouldn't mind kissing it.

"Give me the car keys, and I'll bring the car back here. I'm not carrying your bags for two blocks."

Well, heck. Neither was she. Nice shower, fluffy hotel robe—or hot walk to car and carry bags so she could keep the keys?

"Power requires sacrifices, doesn't it?" she asked grumpily, handing over the keys.

"You're not afraid I'll drive off and leave you here?" he asked, jingling the ring and not even trying to interpret her comment.

The itinerary was in her purse. He wouldn't be going anywhere without it. "Guess I could call and report the car stolen if you don't return."

"I'll be back." The look in his dark eyes was all male as he glanced from her to the bed, then let himself out.

Whoosh! Alys exhaled the breath she'd been holding. Doc Nice had some interesting facets hidden beneath that button-down appearance. Maybe she should turn up the air-conditioning, because the temperature had gone from zero to blazing in ten seconds.

Did she have any perfume left in her toiletry bag? If this was to be the first night of the rest of her life, she wanted to let out all the stops.

"You've shown your sister's will to Lucia's grandfather?" Mame swallowed her pill with a glass of water. She hated letting her body dictate what she could and could not do, but it was good they'd chopped this journey into small bits. If she wanted to look fresh and cheerful for dinner, she needed to rest. Her reunion with her old high school friend had been wonderful, but the hours of chatter had drained her. She hated to admit she was getting old.

"Salvador will not talk to any of us. He is a bigot, that man. He calls us 'peasants' and 'redskins.' He called my sister . . ." Dulce stared at the ceiling and gulped back a tear. "He called my sister ugly names and said her family would not get one cent from him. We do not want his money. We want Lucia. She is only five and should be with family, not strangers."

The guest room they'd been given had two narrow beds covered in matching blue-and-brown-checked covers. Mame reflected that her friend had obviously not changed her children's décor since they'd left home. Of course, neither had she.

"Your family should have hired a lawyer," Mame

said. "If your sister left a will appointing you as Lucia's guardian, and her husband left no will, then it seems to me the law is on your side." She lay back against the pillows and practiced deep breathing.

"We tried." Dulce clenched her fists. "Money talks and we have no money. His lawyer went to court to say our will is forged and that we must have torn up his son's will. Our lawyer said the court might place Lucia in a foster home until the dispute is satisfied. She is already traumatized from losing her parents. She used to chatter like a little parrot. Now she sits there like a lost mouse. It is this . . . this . . ." In frustration, she shook her fist at the window.

"She's lost both her parents. Violently. It will take her time." Mame tried to sound soothing, but Dulce's unspoken rage and grief filled the room. She remembered her own despair when she'd lost her brother and her best friend in a single night. If it hadn't been for the children . . .

She understood Dulce needed her niece as much as Lucia needed her. God had chosen Mame to help them through this, because she understood the anguish and frustration of loss. "Once we take Lucia home where she belongs, away from the school and a man who despises her, she will recover."

Dulce hung her head in acceptance. Wishing she were stronger, Mame closed her eyes again and sought sleep. She wouldn't let Elliot and the hospital be right. She would heal herself.

"Why did you leave the orchid?" Dulce asked quietly. "It has no flower."

"It has the promise of flowers." Mame smiled and relaxed, knowing she was right in this. "Someday, Alys will bloom like that flower."

"You are *loco*, Mame."

"That's what Jock always told me." Being crazy had its good sides as well as its bad. Remembering Jock, the sensible one of their inseparable trio of high school comrades, Mame drifted into dreams. He'd told her she'd never make a career of go-go dancing.

He'd been right, but she'd had fun trying.

"Remington was a realist. He sculpted what he saw." Elliot held the hotel room door for her after returning from their walk through the museum. The Western art had refueled Alys's excitement for the days ahead. She wanted to see Indians and deserts and cactus.

"Frederic Remington was a salesman." Alys flung her purse on top of the suitcase he'd lugged up earlier. She hadn't considered how difficult hauling those things around would have been for her if it hadn't been for Elliot. "He sculpted emotionally appealing images for the masses."

Now that they were finally alone, she was stalling. Elliot hadn't signed up for another room. He'd returned here without a word of expectation. She'd had hours in which to imagine how she would do this. She couldn't decide if she was nervous or eager or both.

As if he'd known what she had in mind, Elliot had gone out of his way to be accommodating. He'd toured the museum as if he'd actually been interested in Western art. He'd found Mame's name in the guest book before she did. Apparently reassured that his aunt was well and playing games, he'd agreed to Alys's choice of restaurants, although he'd refused the barbecue specialty.

He'd even picked up the tab.

And now he was checking his cell phone for messages

and pulling out his laptop computer as if he meant to settle down to business.

Damn, he was going to make her work for this, wasn't he?

Dropping to the bed, Alys sat cross-legged and flicked the remote control to the TV news. Elliot diligently typed away at his keyboard, ignoring her.

He'd showered and changed into a navy knit golf shirt that molded his chest. He wasn't a muscle-bound man, but she was quite certain he didn't have an ounce of fat on him. He had the wide shoulders of a jock and the trim abs of a runner. He had a curl hanging in the middle of his forehead.

Studying Elliot's narrow face eased the physical tension building inside her. If she didn't imagine how his body would fit against hers, she could watch those deep, intelligent eyes forever. Even when he studied her as if she were a flake in his coffee, his eyes reflected concern and a fascinating interest that had her thinking things she had no right to think.

She loved the strong jut of his nose with that bit of extra downturn on the end. It seemed to point out the sensual mobility of his mouth. He pulled a stern face too often, but she'd seen him laugh. Surely all the humor on his talk show wasn't scripted. Maybe Fate had assigned her the duty of teaching him to laugh more—as long as she could go her merry way afterward.

She sighed over the strong column of his throat above the open button of his shirt. He apparently did his jogging without a shirt. He had a lovely bronze tan. If she thought about that too much, she'd remember how white and frail Fred had been, and she would freeze up again.

She should have had two glasses of beer at dinner instead of one.

Elliot's absentminded rub at his midsection sealed the deal. He was too good a man to lose to ulcers at this early age. Mame would want her to take care of her favorite nephew. And Alys knew how to do it.

Recalling her sales lessons from years ago, she mentally repeated them while she flicked off the TV and removed her gauzy blouse. Be positive. Be aggressive. Make the first move.

She stood up to drop her blouse over her suitcase, and a corner of Elliot's eye twitched. She'd put on a fresh shirt after her shower, a short goldenrod knit that the gauzy blouse had mostly concealed. Without the blouse, he could see her nipples if he looked.

He was trying hard not to look.

"Do you think Mame will call tonight?" she asked, wanting his full attention.

"Only if she's ready to go to the hospital," he said, hitting a key on his laptop and glancing up.

Alys smiled and stripped off her shirt. She wasn't wearing a bra.

Elliot forgot Mame, his e-mail, and where he was.

Alys Seagraves had the perfect breasts of a *Playboy* model. Without the airbrushing. He could see a small mole just below her right breast. And maybe the left one was just a little larger than the right. He wanted to weigh them in his hands to find out. Bigger than peaches, smaller than cantaloupes, but just as round, their pointed pink tips begged to be plucked and tasted.

He tried to think beyond the physical but he'd lost control of his mind the instant she'd stripped off her shirt. He was standing up and didn't know how he'd got there.

"Life is meant to be lived, isn't it?" she was saying into the vacuum inside his head.

He wanted to ask her to define "life," but his tongue wasn't capable of coherent speech. Her delicate rosy nipples pointed upward as pertly as her nose. They were tight and hard and begging for attention.

"We can get a little of this tension out of our way and concentrate on Mame with more positive energy," she offered, a trifle nervously.

He was making her nervous. That wouldn't do. She'd offered herself up for his rejection, and he couldn't hurt her like that. She was newly widowed and needing release as much as he did.

"The body needs sex, doesn't it?" she asked, as if she'd heard his thought . . . and maybe sought some reassurance that she wasn't being foolish.

"It's a healthy, physical activity," he agreed, cursing himself for sounding like a radio talk-show host.

How in heck would he know how to talk at times like this? He'd never had a time like this in his life.

"I have no communicable diseases," she whispered when he stepped within touching distance of her.

"I haven't had the time or the opportunity to pick up any," he murmured. Did those lovely pink whorls just pucker and extend more?

"Condoms?" she asked brightly when he reached to touch.

Elliot halted in his tracks.

She winced at his hoarse expletive and looked as if she'd like to pull her shirt around her, had she been wearing one. Instead, she crossed her arms over her beautiful breasts.

Elliot drove his hand through his hair and forced himself to meet her gaze. "You deserve better than this." He couldn't believe that inane sentiment had tumbled from his mouth.

She had a heartbreakingly expressive face. Not glamorous or striking, and maybe not even pretty. Her big eyes were spaced too far apart, her nose was too short, and her luscious mouth was small to match her narrow chin. But together, her features were mobile and perfect. He read disappointment and relief and curiosity all at once in the way her lips curved and her dark lashes tilted over her disconcertingly light eyes.

Daringly, he brushed a silky strand of hair from her cheek and tucked it behind her perfectly formed ear. She ought to have pointy ears like a fairy sprite. She had a child's soft skin, and it colored as easily as a little girl's. Without thinking, Elliot dipped his head to taste an apricot-colored cheek.

She tilted her head, and his mouth encountered lips sweeter than wine.

Instinct routed civilized thought. Or maybe it was testosterone. He had to touch her.

Elliot wrapped his arm around her supple waist and lifted her against him so he could taste as well as touch. He almost staggered beneath the flood of sensation.

Her bare breasts crushed against his chest, and he would have stripped off his shirt to feel her skin to skin if she hadn't sunk so deep into his kiss that he couldn't bear to let her go. She clung to his neck and returned his kiss with a hungry urgency that elevated his body temperature in a flash.

She tasted so damn *good*. Like steak and chocolate and rich wine and all the things he'd denied himself for so long. She parted her lips and he probed deeper, needing to be so deep inside her that he couldn't come up for air.

Their tongues met and clashed, and they toppled backward onto the bed. Alys tugged at his shirt, until Elliot tore it off and flung it across the room. Finally, he had her beautiful breasts rubbing his chest, and he fastened his mouth hungrily to hers to keep from seeking lower.

Her hips bucked under his, but he wasn't ready to give her that yet. He wanted it all, every savoring minute and all night, if he could have it. A nagging reminder at the back of his mind warned him against something, but in full rut, he couldn't remember what.

He hadn't dared imagine this moment, but now that it was here, he couldn't think beyond it.

She had slender, smooth hands that curled enticingly around his back, exploring with the same sense of wonder that he felt. Sinking into the myriad sensations of her kiss, Elliot didn't think he could ever learn them all: the way her lips softened, and her tongue caressed, and her breath tasted of peppermint. He could spend the night just kissing her.

But like a child in a candy shop, he couldn't resist asking for more. Sliding his hand between them, he filled his palm with the weight of her breast and brushed the aroused tip with his thumb. He squeezed gently, his whole focus on the sensual give of womanly softness.

If he hadn't been on top of her, she would have levitated from the bed. Instead, she moaned and writhed against him.

Reaching for his fly—he remembered why he wasn't

supposed to be doing this. Hell of a time for his brain to kick in.

With every ounce of the willpower that had driven him to the peak of his career, Elliot rolled off and stared at the ceiling. His chest heaved and his groin screamed in stiff protest.

"No condoms," he reminded her gruffly before she could say anything.

She lay so still, he wondered if he'd hurt her. Fearing the worst, he propped himself on one elbow to study her. Crystal eyes stared up at him with wonder and admiration, and all of a sudden, he felt like Adonis. He dug his fingers into the bed to prevent them from straying to her breasts.

She closed her eyes, and he figured that was the signal for him to back off. Gingerly, he rearranged his too-tight underwear and rolled from the bed. She didn't move. They hadn't made it all the way onto the huge mattress. Her knees hung over the end. He could lift her hips from the mattress and . . .

Sighing, Elliot turned his back on her. He should have at least waited until he'd removed her leggings so he could have seen all of her. "I think I'll run around the block a few times. We'll leave early in the morning, so get some sleep."

"Better find some penguin pajamas while you're out," she muttered.

Some women considered his brains sexy, but Elliot couldn't remember any of them finding his body so irresistible that they wanted him to cover it. "I'll bring a pair for you while I'm at it."

Alys listened while Elliot pulled on a shirt and jogging shoes and let himself out. She didn't dare open her eyes until she heard the door close. Maybe she should have gone running with him.

Her entire body hummed. Heck, it sang out loud in a raucous chorus of "I want you, babe," complete with drum roll and crashing guitars. Maybe she should be a songwriter.

She didn't think she could attain a meditative position while remembering the silky feel of the dark line of curls down the middle of Elliot's impressive chest.

She didn't think she could sleep either. She lay there trying to relive the sensation of Elliot's hungry mouth devouring hers, the possessive urgency of his tongue sliding between her teeth, the exquisite pleasure of his thumb stroking her nipple, and she almost cried with the pain of unquenched desire.

At least she wasn't numb anymore.

All she had to do was figure out how to live without fulfilling desire. Neat trick.

Maybe Elliot would buy condoms instead of pajamas.

More likely, he was hunting a vibrator. Like he needed an airhead flake in his life right now. A lost waif in the woods of life. A woman determined to let his beloved aunt die if she so chose . . . at least to his way of thinking.

That doused her with the efficiency of a cold bucket of water.

There wasn't much future in a man who would hate her.

Not that she wanted a future with Elliot Roth, she told herself, rolling from the bed. A brief fling in the sack was all she needed. Tomorrow, maybe. They'd have all day. The next stop on the itinerary wasn't even two hours away.

⊰EIGHT⊱

Seek inner peace, Alys cautioned her rampaging libido, watching Elliot drape the shoulder strap of her heavy bag over his shoulder, rippling muscles she'd barely had time to explore last night. In his formfitting blue golf shirt and draped trousers, he was every woman's dream come true. She suspected a sleeping tiger might lurk beneath the Doc Niceness, but he'd proved his trustworthiness in her eyes.

She couldn't handle roaring tigers or alpha apes right now. To step out into the world, she needed the security of a purring cat. With the proper handling, Elliot fit the bill.

He'd come in from jogging last night after she'd fallen asleep, and he'd been up and jogging before she woke. If he'd slept in that acre-wide bed with her at all, she'd barely known it.

In packing this morning, he'd folded a fresh pair of blue pajamas into the overnight bag she was wheeling out of the room for him now. He'd done more than jog when he was out last night. What else had he bought while he was shopping? A shiver of anticipation brightened her day.

When he checked the room for anything they'd left

behind, he caught her staring. His gaze dropped to her mouth, and unconsciously, she licked her lips to see if she'd applied lipstick.

"Breakfast," he said, not lifting his gaze.

"Healthy," she agreed.

The electricity between them was so powerful, they were thinking each other's thoughts. *Dangerous,* her primal instincts screamed. *Necessary* overruled instinct.

He dangled the car keys he'd usurped last night. "You, or me?"

Clinging to the potted orchid, Alys let the warmth of appreciation fill her. He might occasionally seem stressed and remote, but he'd paid attention to her need to see everything. She could give him this little piece of the pie. "You. It's a short journey today. We have time to find a store where I can buy a book on orchids."

"We aren't going to catch Mame until she's ready to be caught, are we?" He closed the bedroom door behind him, and brushed a stray hair from her cheek as if he had some need to verify her reality. When she continued hugging the plant, he picked up the suitcases again.

"No. She needs to come to terms with her own mortality." She'd thought about that a lot. Deep down, she understood Mame's rebellion. Understanding didn't prevent her from panicking if she let herself think about Mame slumped over a steering wheel. To maintain her positivity, she'd rather stay in the moment and go with the flow.

"And while she's at it, she's teaching us a lesson about living?" he asked dryly. "When my brothers were little, they used to threaten to run away when Mame wouldn't let them do something foolish. She would hand them a backpack with lunch and a bottle of water and tell them to give her a call when they got where they were going."

"I take it you were too smart to run away?"

"Maybe, or maybe I lacked the courage. I was the oldest. I remembered too clearly the night my parents died. You could say I had abandonment issues."

He was showing her who he was. Along with satisfaction and wonder that Doc Nice had chosen to share himself with her, Alys discovered a burning hunger to know more. "I know you lost them in a car crash. Did they die instantly?"

The elevator let them out in the lobby, and she thought he'd forgotten the question by the time he'd handed in the key and progressed to the parking garage with their suitcases.

But he'd simply been biding his time. Opening the Caddy's trunk, he picked up where they'd left off. "I like to think they did. Dad had a heart attack and probably wasn't conscious. It was pouring rain and dark, and I don't remember hearing anything but my brothers crying. I'd been told it was important to get out of a broken car and get away from the road until help arrived, so I pried Eric out of his car seat and helped Ben out of his seat belt. We were lucky that the car landed as it did. We climbed out of the backseat on the side away from the road."

"How old were you?" she asked in amazement.

"Seven." He didn't seem to think that required comment. "Are we eating here?"

"I checked the telephone directory and there's an IHOP by the interstate," she said to take her mind off his story.

"Carbohydrates," he protested.

"They serve eggs. You need protein. It's cheaper than the hotel."

He opened the passenger door for her, then climbed in behind the wheel and steered the Caddy into early-morning traffic.

Elliot slanted a glance at her but drove back through the city in the direction she'd indicated. Alys sighed in contentment. It had been *years* since she'd indulged in sticky sweet crepes. Besides, if he was buying meals, she didn't want to cost him too much.

Holding the tall plant in her lap so it wouldn't fall over, Alys tried to imagine the terrified little boy he'd been, standing in the rain with his brothers protectively cuddled in his arms while he waited for his world to right itself again. Tears formed, and she wiped at them, knowing he'd hate to see her cry.

"How long was it before Mame came to get you?" she asked, continuing their conversation while they waited to be seated in the air-conditioned cold of the restaurant.

He didn't miss a beat. The connection between them was still there. "At the time, it felt like years. The police arrived, and the ambulances, and they took us to the hospital. By that time, my brothers were shaking and crying, and I had to try to comfort them. But I'll never forget the relief of hearing Mame's voice outshouting doctors and nurses and cops. It was the most welcome sound I've ever known. She walked all over them to get at us."

Alys nodded, too caught up in the tragedy to trust speech. How old would Mame have been that night? In her thirties? Widowed for years, with a life of her own, Mame had loved enough to sacrifice everything for her nephews.

She heard the love in Elliot's voice, and understood his need to take care of Mame as his aunt had taken care of him. Pointing out that Mame wasn't seven years old wouldn't alleviate his emotional need to rescue her. She couldn't deny his spiritual connection to Mame was far greater than hers.

Bowing before his greater need, she surrendered her own selfish concerns. "We can go right to the hotel she's reserved for tonight," she offered, taking his arm as the hostess led them to a table. She needed to absorb his strength while she sacrificed the trip of a lifetime. Her needs were irrelevant compared to his. "We'll hide Beulah, sit in the lobby, and wait for Mame to show up."

Sliding into the booth, Elliot looked momentarily grateful. Then, to her surprise, he shook his head. He had tamed his curls before he'd left the room, but the humidity had already worked its magic. He shoved on his glasses to scan the menu, and dark hair waved over the earpieces.

"We'd bore ourselves to death all day sitting there, and Mame would still elude us. She obviously knows how to find us. We can leave a message at the desk asking her to call, but otherwise, we might as well see the sights. What's on the agenda?"

"Why on earth hasn't some woman snapped you up?" she asked, marveling at his ability to read her mind.

He peered at her over the dark rim of his half-glasses. "Because I have more sense than to swallow bait?"

She grinned and ordered the strawberry crepes. That kind of charm could be even better than traveling with Mame.

And they had another night and another bed ahead of

them. Had he bought condoms when he'd bought those new pajamas?

She squirmed in her seat just thinking about it.

Elliot couldn't remember ever traveling with a woman for pleasure. He'd been on the road with publicists, at conferences with editors or medical researchers, spoken to all-women groups across the country. He'd taken women to concerts, to dinner, and to bed.

He'd never driven down a rolling country road in a pink Cadillac with a sexy pixie bouncing on the seat, singing "I Am Woman" at the top of her lungs. He hadn't a clue why they were hunting for a round barn— or why anyone would build one—but as long as she kept bouncing like that, he wouldn't complain.

Today, she wore a faded blue halter top and black hip-hugger jeans revealing a curving waist and flat belly. She didn't look a day older than sixteen, unless he happened to catch her eyes. Now he knew why they reminded him of crystal balls—they held age-old wisdom and a world of woe.

Her offer to sacrifice her trip for his sake had knocked him flat. How many other people in the world would have understood his anguish enough to give up their own pleasure for him?

He longed to make her laugh so she wouldn't regret her offer, and to erase the pain behind the unblinking crystal of her eyes.

Which was a pretty damned stupid thing for a man of his social ineptitude to think. Testosterone had apparently eaten his brain. Without a microphone in hand and a soundproof booth to shield him, he didn't know how to make people laugh, and he certainly had no idea how to erase her memories—or he would erase his own.

He pulled the Tums container from the ashtray and popped two. If he didn't find Mame soon, his heartburn would eat a hole through his esophagus, and he wouldn't have to worry about his shattered brain.

"I don't think a whole lot of those is a good thing," Alys informed him with concern. Since he was driving, she could fold her legs into the seat to balance the newly repotted orchid. "Maybe you should see a doctor."

"I *am* a doctor," he reminded her.

"Not a practicing one, you said. And doctors are the last ones to diagnose their own illnesses. It's foolish to diet and exercise and never have a checkup."

"You sound just like Mame. I get regular checkups." He swerved off the road into a gas station. "We need gas. You didn't tell me that driving Route 66 instead of the toll road would mean we wouldn't have service stations."

"This is a service station. It just hasn't been torn down and replaced with plastic." Setting the pot on the floor, she leaped out of the car the instant he turned off the ignition. "I'm going to see if they have ice-cream bars."

"Try not to incite any riots while you're at it." He might as well have talked to Beulah. Alys raced off, hair and breasts bouncing, to the admiration of every male in sight.

From the collection of Harleys at the side of the station, Elliot figured there were plenty of males inside enjoying the view. It was ridiculous to worry about a twenty-seven-year-old woman who should know how to take care of herself by now.

A woman who had never been outside of the state of

Missouri and looked as if she were sixteen might not be quite as experienced as she ought to be, though.

The antacid didn't help the roar of flame beneath Elliot's sternum. It took forever to fill the huge Caddy tank, and Alys hadn't returned by the time the nozzle clicked off. In keeping with the sixties' traditions of the old road, the ancient gas pump didn't have credit card capability. He had to go inside to pay. Route 66 might have been America's Main Street half a century ago, but it looked to him as if the rest of the country had picked up and moved to the suburbs in the decades since.

Idly wondering how many people drove off without paying, Elliot entered through the fly-specked glass door into smoke-filled air barely stirred by the wooden ceiling fan. The only man in the place seemed to be the attendant leaning on the counter, watching out the side window. Elliot followed the clerk's gaze, and his heart sank.

He could barely discern Alys's sleek hair over the heads of a dozen burly bikers sporting tattoos and heavy leather. He could see the end of a rotten picnic table and figured she was sitting cross-legged on the tabletop, eating her ice-cream bar. The bikers were shouting and jeering, but Elliot couldn't catch more than glimpses of a blue halter and bouncing hair past broad shoulders and beer bellies.

Slapping two twenties on the counter, Elliot loped out the side door. He wanted to curse fool women and innocent pixies and the laws of the universe, but his brain was too paralyzed for words. He wasn't a coward. He knew he had the strength for a good fight if necessary. But a dozen men . . . ? Think, Roth. Tell them their bikes are on fire? Did motorcycles burn?

Heart pounding, Elliot elbowed his way through the

crowd, hoping he could just lift Alys off the table and carry her out of here. The men crowding the table glanced at his face and eased from his path, apparently recognizing murderous rage when they saw it. He'd wager his next royalty check that Alys wouldn't.

A sharp cry sounding like *Aii-e-e-e* followed by a loud crack stood his hair on end. The bikers at the front of the crowd roared in approval. With one last vigorous elbow punch, Elliot shoved to the front—just in time to watch Alys offer the two halves of a split board to a bearded old guy with a graying ponytail. Had she just broken the board with her hand?

Seeing Elliot arrive, she grinned and leaped to the ground. "The ice cream was messy," she explained.

Stunned enough for that almost to make sense, Elliot staggered beneath a pounding blow to his back.

"Don't need to tote hardware with an old lady like her along, right, son?"

Tote hardware? Mental images of tire jacks leaped to mind, but Elliot had his arm firmly around Alys's shoulders now, all but shoving her toward the car, and he didn't care what the hell they were talking about.

"We'll see you at the barn!" one of the bikers behind them yelled.

Alys turned and waved. "Put some lotion on your nose or it's gonna fall off!"

Elliot winced, but when no one came after them with that tire jack, he opened the Caddy door and without finesse shoved her inside.

He pondered the possibility that terror and fury were the flip sides of the same coin while he drove down the road, battling incoherence. Alys didn't appear fazed. As expected, she didn't even recognize the rampaging emotions with which he struggled.

After depositing the orchid in a less heated spot on the back floorboard, she curled up in the seat, found a moist wipe in her overlarge handbag, and cleaned the ice cream off her fingers. She sang along with the radio, something about rolling down the river and toot, toot. Somehow, that seemed fitting.

"You can break boards?" he finally asked, deciding that was a neutral subject and didn't involve yelling his head off.

"They have a karate class at Mame's school." She wadded up the wipe and deposited it in the plastic bag she'd hung over the headrest for trash. "If I'm going to be a woman alone, I thought self-defense classes were called for. Control of one's life promotes positive energy."

He didn't care. He shouldn't care. It was none of his business. She was her own person and not his responsibility.

The refrain sounded hollow, even to him. "Karate does not work on men wearing heavy leather," he all but growled. "They had us outnumbered by six to one. If you make it a habit to entertain bikers, you'll need a better weapon than karate."

He caught her surprise without even looking.

"Were you *worried* about me?"

"You were surrounded by a dozen men and it didn't even occur to you that it might be dangerous?" Okay, he was almost shouting. *Chill, Elliot.*

"I have lived the last few years in terror," she announced coolly and succinctly. "I'm not doing that to myself anymore. *No fear* is my motto these days."

"No brains," he muttered, clutching the wheel. "You won't survive long that way." He wanted to wring her neck and talk some sense into her at the same time. Better yet, he wanted to get the hell away from her. She was a disaster waiting to happen, and he didn't need any more disasters in his life.

"Then I'll have enjoyed what's left of my life," she said serenely, staring ahead out the windshield. "Arcadia isn't far. I wonder if the round barn has a guest book?"

Biting his tongue, Elliot followed the narrow two-lane to Arcadia and the round barn. As he drove, Alys exclaimed over longhorns and oil wells, insisting on stopping for more pictures. The Harleys roared by, their riders waving in passing.

"They're traveling the same route?" he asked, returning to the car and stowing the camera in the backseat.

"Yup, Triple A members all," she said cheerfully.

"Are all the sights on our itinerary on theirs?"

Alys took pity on him. He was reaching for the Tums and looking as if he'd rip the wheel off Beulah if he could. Apparently that tame exterior of his cost a lot of energy. He'd looked so cool and casual sauntering through the crowd of bikers earlier that her heart had nearly stopped in appreciation, but his laid-back attitude had taken a toll. "Mame had her own agenda. I added the barn. We can drive on, if you prefer. Mame says most of the Route 66 things are just nostalgic and tacky."

"We can stop if you really want to see it."

"I'd much rather see the butterfly garden and go to the zoo. I adore butterfly gardens."

Arcadia and the round barn appeared in the windshield, and Elliot slowed the car. He caught a gleam of chrome from the Harleys in the parking lot. "There it is, last chance."

"It doesn't look like a place that will have a guest book. Mame would have gone on into Oklahoma City."

He hesitated, then drove on. Alys wanted to pat his jaw and tell him it was quite all right if she died tomorrow because she'd had today, but she figured he wouldn't appreciate the sentiment. Maybe she wouldn't either. What she really wanted was tonight.

He'd looked like a gladiator striding to her rescue when he'd waded through that crowd of bikers. Or a martyr, perhaps. She grinned. Either way, it had been nice of him to be concerned about her welfare. She'd been looking out for herself for so long now that she'd forgotten what it felt like to have someone care enough to look after her.

And she'd better get the notion out of her head that she needed any such person now. She'd gone down that road once, looking to others for love and security. She didn't intend to travel it again. It hurt too much.

Freedom was the life for her.

❦ NINE ❦

"Mame's not been here yet. I left a message with the desk clerk. We can't check in until three."

Elliot crossed the hotel parking lot in long strides, and Alys sighed in appreciation of his athletic grace and sculpted, tanned arms. Leaning against the car, she drank in the Oklahoma City sun and sights, and Elliot was a sight to behold. If all she had to do was look, she wouldn't hesitate for a minute. Those long fingers of his had been bliss last night. His kiss had been a revelation. The sleepy-eyed look he sent her now said he was reading her mind, and a delicious chill shivered down her spine.

So she might not want men in her future, but they sure could be handy to have in the present.

"Too bad about the room," she said cleverly, admiring the way his eyes smoked when his thoughts turned to lust. Maybe she ought to keep his mind on sex. He was a lot easier to handle that way.

"We could always find another." He opened the car door for her.

"Not until we've seen all the sights on Mame's agenda so you can rest assured that she's alive and kicking." Understanding Elliot's neuroses helped. It would be more beneficial if she understood her own. She didn't have to fall in love with a man to go to bed with him. She simply wanted to know if all her parts still functioned, and Elliot was an attractive opportunity. Once satisfied, she could merrily go her way.

"Why did Mame pick a Marriott this time? It couldn't have been here in the sixties."

"Most of the stuff here now was just in the planning stage when Mame came through. They had some big-deal city designer lay out the downtown back in the sixties. Mame said not much had been built back then, but her husband rode a bull in the stockyards, and she knew I'd like to see the fancy new stuff. We talked about staying at the Howard Johnson's on 39th, on the old road, but it wasn't in Triple A, and Mame likes her comforts. So we opted for a hotel near the museum."

"What's first, then? We don't even know if Mame is here yet."

Alys wrinkled her nose. "Do we need to replace the small tire?"

"Okay, tire store first. And then?"

"I guess then we ought to see the stockyards and look around for a likely restaurant for lunch. Maybe we'll luck out and hit it at the same time as Mame." She glanced at Elliot's grim expression. "Or we can call all the hospitals and make certain she's not in one."

His glare told her she'd overstepped, but he was way too serious about this. "If she needs you, she has—"

"My cell phone number, I know," he said with resignation.

"Let me ask the desk clerk if I can leave the orchid inside. It will cook in the car."

After imposing upon the hotel clerk to keep an eye on her orchid, she took her place in the passenger seat, and played with Elliot's digital camera while he drove south on the interstate. She loved framing a view in its little monitor, running the telescoping thing in and out until she had the picture just the way she wanted it. She hoped he'd give her copies of the photos when they were done. She didn't have a computer to put them on, but she thought there was some way of making print ones.

"I'd have to brush up on my computer skills to be a journalist, wouldn't I? Are the programs for photos difficult?"

"Not particularly, which is why there are ten thousand other people with more experience in that job line ahead of you. You might as well say you want to be a cowgirl when you grow up."

He said it in that same pragmatic voice that she recognized now as concern mixed with a touch of teasing. The man didn't know how to communicate without giving advice.

They found a tire store an exit away from the stockyards. The clerk took one look at the pink Caddy's enormous whitewalls and cackled. "Those are special order, man. I can have 'em tomorrow, or maybe next day. Ain't seen them beauties in a long, long time."

Looking grim, Elliot jammed his hands in his pockets. "We'll get back to you, then. Thanks."

Alys trotted out of the store on his heels. "Is the small one safe?"

"Yeah, but it's probably tearing up the transmission and brakes and wreaking havoc on the other three tires. Let's just hope Mame comes to her senses before tonight."

Alys was ambivalent about that, but she didn't mention it aloud.

Elliot drove to the next exit, circled the block, and parked the car near the historic district of the stockyards.

"Writing books is out, too, huh?" Picking up on her earlier topic of careers, she climbed out beneath his withering look. "There ought to be some *fun* job I can do."

"Like sing in a rock-and-roll band? You're showing your age again. C'mon, this way." He led her down the main street of the district.

Passing a Western-wear store sporting ten-gallon hats in the window, Alys tried to picture Elliot in cowboy boots and a Stetson and liked the idea so well, she grabbed his elbow and steered him inside. "You have to play the part right. You're not even wearing *jeans*. What kind of cowboy are you?"

"A comfortable one? What part am I playing?" Entering the enormous old building with its warped pine floors and battered wood counters, he stared around at saddles on the wall, cubbyholes filled with jeans, and an entire corner devoted to felt cowboy hats.

"Exploring the Old West, of course. Hats, first. We can't walk around in the sun without hats." She pounced on a small black hat with delight, balancing it on the back of her head and heading for a mirror.

"It seems to me black would be hot in the sun," he commented, looking over her shoulder.

He stood so close, she could feel the heat rolling off of him in waves, and a longing so strong welled up inside her that she had to step away. "Black matches my jeans," she said firmly, hoping he didn't notice her avoidance. "You can buy a white one."

"I'm not wearing a cowboy hat," he protested. "I'd look like an idiot."

"Wearing that knit shirt, you would. But try a hat with one of these Western shirts." She pulled a red-and-black number off the rack, complete with ivory snap buttons on the cuffs.

Not satisfied with just a shirt, she waltzed down the aisles gathering the necessary elements for her latest fantasy, and Elliot cringed. On a slow weekday, the cowboy-hatted clerks were more than happy to assist, and she had a wizened old man dancing to her tune. Before Elliot could explain that he was only humoring an idiot, the old man ushered him into the dressing room with jeans and shirts, and when he came out, the clerk was holding up boots for his approval.

"James Garner!" Alys cried, eyeing the cream-colored shirt with a top-stitched yoke that he'd chosen as the least horrifying of the lot. "You need a fancy Western vest and you could look like a gambler instead of a cowboy."

"I don't want to look like a gambler *or* a cowboy." But Alys looked at him as if he were James Garner and Clint Eastwood rolled into one, and with resignation, Elliot tried on a pair of brown stitched boots.

They were remarkably comfortable. Standing, testing the heels and toes, wearing the faded jeans she'd chosen, tucking his fingers into the belt loops in imitation of some old cowboy movie he must have seen, he *felt* like a cowboy. He even gave in and let Alys pound a flattish brown Stetson on his head. He hated his curly hair anyway. Might as well cover it up. At least the hat wasn't one of those ten-foot-tall jobs, or one with a turquoise-and-silver headband like the one she was trying on.

She looked cute with the broad brim shading her light eyes. She tilted it at a rakish angle, and his heart picked up a beat. She still wore her faded blue halter and black jeans, but the black hat with its sparkly headband suited her.

He was disappointed when she hung it back on its hook and turned to smile in approval at him.

"Perfect. Now we can go riding in the canyon tomorrow, and you'll look as if you belong there."

She spun around to investigate a rack of leather belts, leaving him reeling in her wake. Riding in the canyon? Horseback? Tomorrow? He hadn't even planned how to get through today. He had deadlines to meet, work to finish. He hadn't planned on a roller-coaster ride with a lunatic in a pink Cadillac from which there didn't seem to be any getting off.

When she handed him the hand-tooled belt she'd chosen, Elliot refused to put it on. "Does this mean you packed riding clothes in those enormous suitcases of yours?"

She blinked in surprise. "I'm wearing jeans. I have a baseball cap to shade my eyes. And a scarf for my neck!" She beamed as if she'd told him she had silver and gold.

Elliot caught her shoulder before she could spin away again. "The hat you had on looked good. Get that, and I'll agree to wear the rest of this ridiculous gear."

"Do you have any idea how much this stuff costs?" she asked in incredulity. "You don't have to buy any of it. I just wanted to see how you looked in it. Cool, isn't it?"

She darted off, leaving Elliot to stare at the startled clerk who'd overheard. She just wanted to see how he *looked* in it? No way. He wasn't buying that for an instant. Women did not simply look at clothes and walk away. He might be out of touch, but he wasn't comatose.

"I'll take these," he told the clerk, who looked more than relieved. "And add the hat she was looking at."

Elliot caught up with Alys in the bolero-tie section. There wasn't any way she was getting him into one of those string nooses, but that wasn't on his mind when he caught her shoulder again.

"Boots," he ordered, steering her toward the shoe department. "If I'm wearing them, you're wearing them."

"My suitcases are already too heavy," she argued, resisting his push. "I ought to be looking for cheap luggage. Or at least a backpack."

"Boots." He sat her down in the women's boot department and gestured at the clerk following him around. "Black ones. With some kind of silver things on them to go with the hat."

"They cost hundreds of dollars," she whispered. "I had no idea they cost so much. Let's get out of here before they start toting up all this stuff."

"Clothes cost money. These jeans were cheap. A hundred bucks for a hat is no big deal. When was the last time you looked at prices?"

At her wounded look, it dawned on him. Maybe he ought to just go bang his head against the plate-glass window a few times. *Dumb, Elliot.* Her husband had died after years of illness. She had no job. She'd sold her damned *house.* Mame had been paying her way. He'd been hanging around with the comfortable crowd too long.

"I'll write it off as research," he said with an edge of

desperation. "I can probably get a show out of it, and a chapter in the next book."

"Yeah, how to shop your way to fitness in two easy days," she scoffed.

She started to rise, but he stood in front of her chair, blocking her egress as the short clerk tottered over bearing a swaying tower of boot boxes.

"Out of my way, Elliot," she said between clenched teeth. "You forget, I know karate and a few other more useful martial arts."

"It won't kill you to try the boots on." He refused to budge.

"I can break bones in your foot," she warned.

"Not while I'm wearing cowboy boots," he taunted.

Grasping his shirtfront, she planted her feet on his booted toes, and he rocked backward—into the clerk with the tower of boxes.

Hats and boxes and boots flew everywhere, bouncing off narrow shelves of more boxes, and toppling the stacks.

Wrapping his arm around Alys's waist, Elliot hauled her off his feet, but he couldn't swivel fast enough to catch anything.

Hanging on to Alys, gazing at the chaos they'd created together, he had the amazing urge to laugh out loud, only he figured he'd end up rolling on the floor with some of the loose hats if he really let go.

"After this, we're spending a lot of money here," he told her, before setting her down and hurrying to help the traumatized clerk.

Alys dropped to her knees to scramble after boots and boxes while the clerk insisted it was no problem at all. She was trembling and didn't quite know why. She should laugh this off. It was no big deal. They were just a bunch of boots. She'd done stupider things in her lifetime. Mame would be singing about rounding up dogies right now.

She wasn't Mame.

Had she thought she was?

She sure didn't want to be, not after Elliot had held her like that. He wasn't even mad. He'd held her as if he'd done it all his life, as if she belonged in his arms, as if they fitted together like two pieces of a puzzle. It had seemed so natural, it had scared her half to death.

She didn't even know if he knew he was doing it. She'd given him one glimpse of sex, and he'd adopted a decidedly proprietary attitude. She didn't think their little power struggle was in any way similar to his manner toward Mame. It had felt like raw sex.

Hiding her flushed cheeks, she dug under a chair for a runaway boot. Broad hands captured her waist and hauled her upright.

He was doing it again. She stared up into Elliot's short-lashed dark eyes and caught her breath. His gaze dipped when she filled her lungs, reminding her that she was wearing a halter with nothing under it. The smolder developing in his eyes warned he'd noticed.

"We'll buy them all if you don't sit down and try them on," he growled.

"What happened to Doc Nice?" she asked in low tones as he released her in front of a chair.

"He met up with Alys Oakley. I may have to buy leather gloves and pack a pistol. Sit."

She sat. She wanted to argue. She wanted to wriggle away just to assert her rights. But he'd been cooperative with all her whims until now, and she kind of liked the way he'd just asserted *his* rights. If he had any. She hadn't decided about that yet.

"Remember, I know karate," she reminded him as Elliot pointed out a pair of boots to the clerk.

"You can break boards. Can you hit a moving target?" He lifted his expressive dark eyebrows.

The boots he'd chosen for her had gorgeous stitching all across the toe, a dainty silver-and-turquoise chain at the ankle, and heels that would really let her look him in the eye. They fit her feet as if they'd been tailored for her. Sighing with regret, Alys stood. Well, she could almost look him in the eye. Her nose reached his chin.

"Want to find out if I can hit a moving target?" she asked.

In answer, he leaned over and kissed her.

Fifteen minutes later, Alys wore her sparkly new boots and hat into the morning sunshine, and her head still spun from that kiss.

She didn't know what he was doing to her, but she liked it too much to believe it was safe. On the other hand, the air was charged with positive vibrations and Elliot wasn't rubbing his chest.

She halted to admire the jaunty tilt of her hat in a window, and admired Elliot's long, lean reflection in the process. With his flat Stetson and boots, he only needed a holster on his hip to complete the image. In the window, they presented the appearance of a perfect couple.

She didn't want to be part of a couple. She wanted to be herself.

"I'll pay you back for these," she insisted, for the umpteenth time.

"Find Mame for me, and we'll call it even." He caught her elbow and steered her onward.

"You can't buy my loyalty," she protested. "Just because you look like a cowboy doesn't mean you have to behave like one." But she liked it when he held her arm. It was kind of like being chosen by the most popular boy in class. She'd had that feeling with Fred, too.

Dangerous.

For these last few years she'd thought of Fred only in terms of his illness and death. She'd nearly forgotten the love they'd shared. He'd given her good times, years of laughter and love. She ought to remember them more and let go of the pain.

Elliot was reawakening emotions that might better be left alone, but he was giving her happy memories, too.

Unwilling to give up more happiness than she'd known in a long time, she swung along at his side, delighting in watching heads turn to follow Elliot's long-legged stride as they walked by. Hers, for a day. That could work.

Other than attracting attention, they accomplished nothing at the stockyard. If Mame had been there that day, they had no way of finding out. Wandering the old street of run-down buildings, looking for a suitable restaurant, Alys tried to think like Mame.

"She'd choose a steak place," she decided. "She'd figure you'd eat vegetarian."

"Every place in Oklahoma is a steak place, if you haven't noticed," he said wryly. "That's why we're in a stockyard. It's cow country."

"Then let's choose one with homemade pies."

"Because Mame likes pies or because she figures I don't eat them?"

"Because I like pies." Reading the menu outside what

appeared to be a popular restaurant, she checked the dessert offerings first. "Black-bottom pie," she said in satisfaction.

"I'm not even going to ask." He escorted her into the crowded, dim lobby, where a miniskirted cowgirl led them to a booth. "You will eat a real meal, first, won't you?"

He sounded so pained, she had to laugh. "I'll have to read your diet books pretty soon if I don't start eating right. You don't understand what a joy it is to eat real food instead of the frozen cardboard I've been surviving on. Cooking for one is depressing."

"That's how I've always eaten," he admitted. "I never thought of it as depressing. Just necessary."

"Isn't this more fun? Did you have any idea there were so many ways to fix a steak?" She scanned the menu, trying to decide how much real food she could eat and still leave room for pie.

"Miss Seagraves?" A bow-tied waiter in a vest and carrying a box stopped by the booth, disconcerting both of them with his knowledge of her name.

"Mame." Elliot was out of the booth before Alys could open her mouth.

She watched him disappear toward the lobby while she smiled at the startled waiter. "He's the restless sort. I'm Alys Seagraves. How did you know my name?"

"The red-haired lady said to give you this." He handed over the box with a card taped on top. The box moved.

Alys rummaged through her purse for a dollar, handed it to the boy, and with skepticism, eyed the box he deposited on the table. Maybe she ought to wait for Elliot to return before opening it. A box that moved and—

purred?—might need two hands. Mame wouldn't give her a cougar or anything, would she?

She slit the envelope attached and read Mame's spidery handwriting on the card inside. *I promised a friend that a doctor would look at Purple's paw. You and Elliot looked real cute in your cowboy clothes. Have someone take a picture.*

Elliot was about to go ballistic. Fanning herself with the card and chuckling softly, Alys watched for his return. Mame had been somewhere close by, and just recently. She was fine.

Alys wasn't so certain about the creature inside the box. It whimpered and sniffed along the box walls. *Purple?* Who called an animal Purple?

She couldn't leave the poor thing in there forever. Elliot must be out canvassing the street. Or maybe he'd even found Mame. She ought to be out there refereeing the fight if he had. She couldn't leave the box here.

Cautiously, she slipped a string loose. The box lid jostled and the occupant cried louder. If a baby mountain lion jumped out of this thing, she wouldn't be responsible for the consequences.

She worked at another string, sliding it over a corner until it fell on the table. The cross-tie remained, but it was loose.

Before she could figure out how to open it without letting the creature out, one side of the box lid pushed up, the string slid off, and a furry gray-and-white ball leaped for freedom.

Diving from the table, the animal flew under the bench of the next booth. Alys almost tumbled out of her seat trying to catch it. Knocking her water glass off, she fell down on her hands and knees to search for the creature.

Poking her head into the darkness and thanking the heavens that no one was sitting on the bench, Alys cornered the hissing kitten. Kitten, not cougar.

"This is another one of those things I don't want to ask about, isn't it?" Somewhere behind her upturned rear, Elliot's voice was dryer than the dust-covered roads they'd driven in on.

❧TEN❧

Alys's jeans fit her nicely rounded buttocks in a way that had every man in the place staring. Elliot was tempted to grab her slender waist and haul her out from under the table. He'd thoroughly enjoyed the last time he'd lifted her, even if he'd had to leave an extra-large tip for the clerk who'd had to scurry for boots and boxes in the resultant crash.

But he wasn't a dumb brute. He had to figure she was under the table for a reason and that reason had something to do with the now empty box sitting on their table. If she backed out carrying a rat, he was drawing the line.

She wriggled from beneath the table carrying a bundle of protesting fur.

"Did you find Mame?" she gasped as she stood up, attempting to calm the clawing animal.

She didn't seem the least fazed by sharp claws or shrieking howls. Did nothing freak her out? Every person in the restaurant was staring at them as if they were an entertaining circus, and she seemed intent only on Mame. And she thought *he* was focused?

"No," he answered in disgust. "I didn't see the Rover either. I looked everywhere. How does she do that?"

"Mame is a great believer in walking." With a wry lift of her eyebrow, she looked from the screaming kitten, to the box on the table, to the waiter hurrying toward them, and asked, "Do you think we ought to leave?"

"I don't think we can stay here with a pet unless it's a seeing-eye kitten." Pulling the waiter aside, Elliot explained their dilemma while Alys tucked the protesting kitten back in the box and held the lid tight.

"They'll pack us some salads to go. Let's go outside before we attract any more attention." He took her elbow and led her past the staring patrons. "What did Mame's note say?"

"That she promised someone that a doctor would look at Purple's paw. Honestly, do you think she looks purple?" Stepping back into the heat, Alys peeked beneath the lid and the kitten spit and roared again.

"Is she expecting me to look at a *cat's* paw?" Leaning against the restaurant wall, Elliot rolled his eyes. "Does she want me to become a vet?"

"Well, it would keep you home more often." Now that they were outside, she removed the kitten from the box and held it up for his inspection.

In guilty silence, he examined the kitten, finding the sore paw and probing until he discovered a thorn. "Mame has my first-aid kit in the Rover. How am I supposed to pull this out?"

"Tweezers. I have some in my suitcase. I have a small first-aid kit. Can we use human antiseptics on kittens?"

"Like I know?" Seeing their waiter appear in the entrance, Elliot walked over to sign away his life on the credit card, including another large tip to cover the service of boxing up the lunches. He could see where having Alys around could become an expensive proposi-

tion, but he had to admit it was the best entertainment
he'd had in years.

He was actually hungry.

Handing over the receipt, he accepted their doggie
bags. Or maybe they were kitty bags. The smell of food
calmed the creature instantly.

"We can eat in the parking lot. It's almost empty."
Carrying the kitten in one hand and the box in the other,
Alys swung down the street in her high-heeled boots and
sparkly hat.

All they needed was Mame to complete the parade.
Elliot glanced over his shoulder in hopes of catching his
aunt peering out at them from a doorway. No such luck.

Straddling a bench near the car, Alys divided her attention between the cat box on the ground and the lunch
Elliot set out from the bags. He was gratified by her cry
of delight when she discovered the small container of
tuna for the kitten and the black-bottom pie he'd ordered for her.

Almost wishing for a juicy steak instead of the salad
he'd ordered, he watched Alys feed the kitten in between
bites of pie.

She ate her dessert first.

"Didn't you say you were plump as a child?" He had
a hard time reconciling it with her current slenderness.
"If you always eat like this, how did you ever lose an
ounce?"

"Lifestyle change. I was sedentary at home. After
marrying Fred, I wanted to do everything. Went to real
estate school, worked, studied, tried to be the perfect wife
and produce balanced meals. We only had one car, and
I walked between work and classes. When he was first
starting out in practice, money was tight, so I couldn't

buy snack foods." She sent him a mischievous glance. "Didn't read your books either."

"Balanced meals?" He was always open to new methods of eating properly. Different metabolisms required different diets, although Alys had to be the only person in creation who could survive on a diet of pies.

"We need a leash. How will I let her out in the grass?" Ignoring his question, she climbed off the bench and sat on the ground with the box, lifting the kitten out to sniff around in the area outlined by Alys's legs.

The kitten lifted its hurt paw and meowed and Elliot winced. With a sigh, he threw away the remains of his salad and sat on the ground with Alys, touching his boots to hers to give the kitten more wandering room between their legs. He felt like a little kid again.

Alys smiled in approval and answered his question. "Fred liked steak and potatoes, and waffles with cream. He was skinny and ate like a horse. So a balanced meal was meat, lots of starch, maybe a veggie, and dessert." Her smile disappeared. "He didn't live long enough to develop colon cancer from his bad diet. He had a malignant melanoma that went to his lymph glands before it was detected."

He was a doctor, but he didn't know what to say. Sadness lingered behind the crystal clarity of her eyes, but she sounded matter-of-fact, as if she'd come to terms with what had happened. "So now you eat your dessert first because the world could end before the meal is done?" he asked.

She beamed at him. "Exactly. Want some?" She handed over her unfinished pie and licked a piece of chocolate from the corner of her lips.

He wanted some all right. Pie wasn't what he had in

mind. He took her offering anyway, licking the Styrofoam plate clean of chocolate. The stuff was sinful. So
was Alys. His gaze drifted to the shadow between her
breasts as she leaned over to play with the cat, and he
wanted the right to touch.

Maybe he needed a little sin in his life right now. It
wasn't as if he had anything better to do while he waited
for Mame to turn herself in.

The kitten meowed ear-scraping protests while Elliot
dabbed its thorn-free paw with antiseptic.

Purple's sandpaper tongue licked Alys's hand the instant Elliot released her. Liquid warmth flooded through
Alys at the affectionate caress. She held the creature up
so she could meet its green eyes, then kissed its perfect
little nose. "You're adorable, baby. Now, how do we
find your mama?"

"I suspect Mame means for you to be its mama." Elliot closed up the first-aid kit and returned it to the suitcase in Beulah's trunk.

Alys froze. She had no intention of being anyone's
mama. She didn't ever want to be put in the position of
losing someone—or something—she loved again. Foot-
loose and fancy free, that was her.

The kitten wriggled to be put down, and she was half
tempted to set it loose in the parking lot. She couldn't, of
course. That would be the same as putting it to death.

"I can't keep a kitten. What in the world would I do
with it?"

"What does anyone do with cats? Feed them, give
them a bed to sleep in, that sort of thing. They're not demanding." He slammed the trunk closed.

"Here, then, you take care of it. You have a place to take it." She handed the kitten to Elliot.

He crossed his arms in refusal, looking like a stone statue of Hercules dressed in cowboy gear. "I travel too much. Hang on to her, and we can give her to Mame, if you like, but it looks to me like Purple wants to be friends."

The cat purred and bumped Alys's jaw with its little head. She cuddled the kitten over her shoulder and glared at Elliot. "I don't want to get attached. Let me drive. You hold Purple."

He raised skeptical eyebrows. "Are you planning on going through the rest of your life without any attachments? Is that why you want to be a travel writer?"

She hadn't thought about it. She preferred *doing* to thinking. Grumpily, she headed for the passenger seat. "We'll need kitty litter and a box if we're keeping her."

"Yes, ma'am. And a water mister for the orchid. I remember."

She thought he was laughing at her as he slid behind the wheel to go in search of a discount store.

"Pets are like children," she said defensively. "They need loving care and attention. I don't have it in me any longer."

He shot her another of his disbelieving looks but didn't argue. Once they found a store, he helped her tie Purple in her box so they could leave her in the car. Inside, he threw a kitten-sized travel carrier into a shopping basket. While she looked for a book on cats, Elliot checked the ingredients of cat foods to choose the one with the most nutrition. Alys found a purple cat leash. Elliot chose the litter box and paid for it all.

"I'll need to start a list of how much I owe you," she muttered as they lugged their purchases back to Beulah.

"The kitten and orchid are my aunt's fault, not yours. And I bought the hat and boots for me, because I like looking at you wearing them." He opened the car door for her so she could dump her packages on the backseat.

Startled by the warmth in his voice, Alys jerked her head back so fast, she clipped Elliot's chin. He caught her shoulders to steady her, or attempt to steady her. Her whole world whirled when he held her like that.

He liked looking at her?

Finding her center again, Alys retreated from his hold to release Purple. The kitten writhed in her hands and licked her cheek, her furry tail wagging like a dog's. She would not get attached. *Would not.* Gently, she set the disappointed cat into its new carrier. "I bet you say that to all the girls."

"I give out diet advice to girls," he said dryly, handing her the rest of the packages, "not flattery."

That was an interesting aspect of Elliot Roth that she hadn't considered. "I suppose some women might consider diet advice a seductive topic," she murmured, hiding her smile.

"We do not want to go there," he warned. "I have had women standing at the back door of the radio station when I'm done taping a show. Suffice it to say that women who think diet advice is seductive are not high on my list of potential dates."

"You emit such negative energy." She shook her head in sympathy. "No wonder you suffer indigestion. Diet and exercise are only *part* of the formula for healthy living. Cheerfulness and positive thinking ease stress and open the channel for spiritual healing."

"Heart failure is caused by the very physical buildup of plaque in blood vessels leading to and from the heart," he corrected. "Lack of adequate blood supplies weaken the heart muscle. An electrical derangement of the heartbeat triggered by strenuous or stressful activity causes cardiac arrest. Cheerfulness will not clean out the arteries or build a stronger heart. Diet and exercise will."

"You really don't let yourself feel the energy, do you?" Poking a cat treat between the bars of the cage for the protesting kitten, Alys tried not to let disappointment shadow her interest in Elliot. Men simply didn't open their hearts and senses as women did. She'd hoped he was different, but he was a doctor. They were the least likely creatures on earth to look past their narrow physical view of the world, proving once again that she was better off without a man in her life.

Not that she wanted one, she reminded herself. She would just like to think Mame had a nephew who was a little more sensitive.

Eliot didn't need to understand her to have sex with her.

"I have tons of energy," he said meaningfully, opening the front car door.

She hid another smile as he took the driver's seat. "Stamina is not what I had in mind."

"It's almost three. Should we head back to the hotel?" Undeterred, he watched her through eyes gone dark with desire.

"To check in." Refusing to give in to his sexy gaze—although it activated all her long-frozen hormones—Alys stared straight ahead. "I still haven't seen the zoo or the butterflies." If he was anticipating the evening half as much as she was, he'd be salivating by day's end.

That should give him some incentive to ignore her inadequacies.

"Are we likely to see Mame at the zoo?"

"We're not likely to see her, but I'll bet she was there. She'll want to compare notes when we catch up with her."

"Will we catch up with her?" he asked, as if she had some special knowledge unavailable to him.

"At the Balloon Fiesta, I'm sure. This really is what's best for her, Elliot. She's running scared right now." Mame had given no indication that she was involved in anything except a few days of freedom, so Alys didn't mention her suspicion that his aunt was up to something besides matchmaking. Mame was quirky, but this trip had gone a little far beyond just quirky.

Not that a dense male who didn't open himself up to spiritual energy would notice.

"If Mame knows as much as you say she does," she continued, "she knows how to take care of herself. And she has one advantage that you don't—she understands the power of the spirit. She's generating positive energy, opening channels, and connecting with the spirit that flows through us. It would have been better if I was with her, but your negativity might counteract her well-being."

"I am not negative!" he argued. "I'm positive that she can live until she's ninety if she'd only follow the damned rules."

"Rules create stress, especially if they're rules created by others. Mame needs to feel in control of her destiny. That gives her strength and feeds into her energy. Hospitals take away that control and sap energy. Hospitals are jam-packed with stress and bad vibrations."

"We don't have medical phasers we can zap at people,

like in some *Star Trek* movie," he protested. "Hospitals are necessary."

"Maybe scientists ought to work on energy phasers." Stubbornly, she crossed her arms. Maybe she didn't want to go to bed with this man. He was even worse than Fred with his logical mind that required everything be proven. "No wonder men die young and widows populate the senior citizen centers."

"Could we go back to the part where I tell you that you look cute in the hat?" He parked Beulah in the hotel parking lot.

She slanted him a glance from the corner of her eye. He looked dead serious. He really had his heart set on a repeat performance of last night. Cheered that the eminently successful, attractive Doc Nice wanted her enough not to argue with her, she pretended to consider his request. "Only if you promise not to tell me that I'm cute when I'm mad."

"That was next on my list, but I'll refrain."

Laughing that he'd managed to say it without saying it, Alys followed him into the hotel lobby. The clerk had no messages and the room they checked into held no surprises.

"Does Mame have friends here, too?" Elliot asked warily, canvassing the room as if he expected his aunt to leap out at them from hidden corners.

"I don't know. We know she was here while we were shopping, but she may be trying to get ahead of us now. Tomorrow is a longer journey, although I'd rather explore here than Amarillo."

Until she'd said it, she hadn't realized how she'd exposed herself. Would he choose to race on to Amarillo tonight? It wasn't as if he had any interest in zoos and butterflies. She tried not to look too interested in his decision.

Elliot ran his hand through his rumpled curls and stared out at the Oklahoma City skyline. Absentmindedly transferring his hand from his head to rub at his solar plexus, he faced her. "I can't kidnap her and heave her into a hospital. If she's feeling well enough to keep going, the decision has to be hers. She has my cell phone number. It's a little late to go traipsing through canyons or whatever she has on the itinerary for tomorrow."

The question in his dark eyes when he turned to Alys cemented the evening's activities. He didn't push or demand or take control of the situation. He left the decision up to her, and happy wings of freedom fluttered in her chest. "The zoo. Let's release Purple so she doesn't grow too bored in her cage."

He nodded, relinquishing the reins of worry he'd attached to his aunt. Now if only she could get him to relax and enjoy himself, she would have channeled enough positive energy to keep Mame going a while longer.

She hoped. She lived in dread of the phone call saying Mame had been taken to the hospital again. Positive energy, she reminded herself. No negative vibrations.

"Seafood tonight," she promised. "We can bring some back for Purple."

Oops, she'd forgotten she wasn't supposed to become attached to the kitten. Well, a few nights of caretaking wouldn't hurt.

If she saved enough food money in this brief sojourn with Doc Nice, she could afford a bus ticket to her dream. She'd never seen the ocean. She thought she had what it took to be a California girl.

❧ ELEVEN ❧

"Elliot is in good hands." In satisfaction, Mame pushed away from her hiding place off the hotel lobby. If her nephew didn't recognize the value of a woman like Alys, she couldn't help him if she had a hundred lifetimes.

"He is a grown man. He has already healed *Púpura*. He can take care of himself." Dulce slipped out of the ice-machine niche. "It is yourself you must worry about."

"Now that your foolish Purple is in good hands, it's you and Lucia we must worry about. I'm feeling healthy as a horse." That was only a tiny lie. Her pulse rate was irregular, but that was because of Dulce's difficult situation. By tomorrow, matters would be under control. How difficult could rescuing a child from a cantankerous old bigot be?

Mame wasn't quite so certain about what waited on the other side of this adventure, but at least she would have settled all outstanding matters before she subjected her traitorous body to whatever depredations the doctors had in mind.

"I would never have agreed to this had I known about your health, Mame. You risk too much for us."

If Mame hadn't had another fainting spell, Dulce would

141

never have known. Maybe she should take two pills for safety's sake. She dismissed her companion's concerns with a wave of her hand. "I risk nothing but a few days and a bit of fun. We'll be out of Amarillo and into Albuquerque before Salvador knows what hit him."

Mame ignored Dulce's worried expression. Positive energy and blind luck had brought them this far. They couldn't fail so close to their goal. The Universe must have meant for her and Dulce to help each other, or they wouldn't have been heading in the same direction. It had been sheer coincidence that she'd mentioned going to Albuquerque to a student who'd known Dulce's desire to go there, too.

"You do not know Salvador," Dulce murmured, hurrying after Mame. "He is a big man in the community, in more ways than one. He was a truck driver, and he bought the truck company for which he worked. He despised my sister not just because she was a Navajo, but because she was a woman. He will not respect you any more than he respects me."

"That will be his downfall," Mame replied confidently. "God is on our side. Let us free Lucia and you will both be on your way to safety."

Mame trusted the words Dulce muttered under her breath were prayers. Their next task wouldn't be quite so easy or pleasant as bringing Alys and Elliot together.

A bundle of gray fur darted from beneath the sofa fringe, hopped to a cushion, and took a flying leap at a lamp shade. As the lamp toppled, the kitten sailed from the shade to the top of the entertainment center, where it peered over the edge in confidence that it had eluded capture by the humans who had just invaded her territory.

"Mighty Cat," Alys declared in admiration of the kitten's acrobatics. They'd put a DO NOT DISTURB sign on the door and left Purple to roam in the hotel room while they visited the zoo. She didn't seem to have done too much damage. Standing on tiptoes, Alys reached for the culprit.

"Wildcat," Elliot suggested, righting the lamp and shoving the sofa cushion back in place. "We should have left her in her box."

"Keeping the poor thing penned up would be cruel." Alys placed the purring kitten over her shoulder, absorbing its soft rumble with pleasure.

She wouldn't admit to nervousness as Elliot flung his Stetson on a table and reached for the phone. He'd been a complete gentleman all afternoon, patiently escorting her through the zoo and the butterfly garden, even expressing interest in the scientific displays of butterfly migration and propagation. He wasn't the kind of man given to public displays of affection, but he'd held her hand often enough for her to learn to like it. She'd enjoyed sharing his intellectual interest and discussion, enjoyed it far too much for her own good. She'd be better off becoming attached to the cat than the tiger awakening behind Doc Nice's laid-back façade.

What was wrong with her that she couldn't walk through the world alone without craving the company of others? How would she ever learn to stand on her own?

Elliot ordered a bottle of wine from room service, then sat on the edge of the bed to remove his boots. Unlike the prior night, there was assurance in his every move. He had no doubt how this day would end.

That knowledge shivered her timbers as much as the idea of a committed relationship. She didn't want him counting on her for *anything*.

"Would you like to shower first, or shall I?" he asked. He was always amazingly polite, even when on the verge of murder. Maybe she hadn't driven him quite that far yet, but she calculated she and Mame had skirted pretty close to his boiling point a time or two. Or maybe she was wrong, and he really was just a purring kitty-cat looking for a good time.

"Watch the news and Mighty Cat, and I'll be quick." Her heart suffered an erratic beat when Elliot fixed his smoldering gaze in her direction. She about had another attack when he rose to take the cat from her. Even without his boots, he towered over her. The brush of his big hand against her bare shoulder as he removed the cat stimulated far more than her starving libido.

"Take your time. I'm not going anywhere." Amusement and a sexy confidence laced his voice. Or was that her overheated imagination? He retrieved the cat but didn't immediately retreat to the bed.

Oh, gad. She'd wanted a bookish, harmless professorial type for her first lover, and what had she done? Turned him into Clint Eastwood. This close, she could even see the stubble of his beard. He was no longer a storybook fantasy but a real man, with very male expectations.

So what? She had some very female expectations of her own.

Still wearing her boots, she didn't have to stretch far to plant a kiss on his bristly jaw. "You smell like charcoal smoke." She darted into the bathroom before he could react.

She probably smelled like smoke, too. She'd persuaded Elliot into a steak-and-seafood restaurant, one that cooked the meat right in front of them. The steak had been scrumptious. Elliot had chosen grilled salmon, but he'd finished off her steak when she couldn't. She was corrupting him one food at a time.

She sang in the shower, washed her hair, and scrubbed with the last of her scented shower wash until her skin tingled, the scent of ylang-ylang filled the air, and steam fogged the mirror. She didn't really want to see what she was doing anyway. She simply wanted to let it happen. She stretched her arms skyward and her breasts lifted in anticipation.

This suite wasn't as impressive as the prior night's, but terry-cloth robes hung on the back of the door. Still moist from the shower, Alys wrapped up in the generous folds of a robe, then blew her hair dry. She doubted that she looked sexy, but then, she never had. Clean and available would have to do. And eager.

Elliot lay sprawled across the bed, his shoulders propped up on pillows while he watched the news with the cat sleeping curled on his flat belly. At Alys's appearance, his heavy-lidded eyes widened, and an appreciative smile settled on his lips.

"You look like one of those sexy ads in magazines. I wish I had showered first."

Caught off guard at the notion of her petite, unremarkable self as sexy, Alys didn't have a quick reply. She watched Elliot place the sleeping kitten on the covers and swing from the bed in a single easy movement. He'd unfastened the top snaps of his shirt, and she had a glimpse of bronzed skin and dark curls before he kissed the top of her head, eclipsing the view. He stepped into the steamy bathroom and closed the door.

Breathe, Alys. She took deep, cleansing breaths, and was almost steady by the time room service brought the wine.

Fred had introduced her to wine. She'd never developed much of a taste for it, and after he'd become ill, alcohol hadn't been part of their regimen. But she thought wine might be one of those things she needed to learn about, especially if she planned to live in California.

Besides, she needed the fortification right now, and wine seemed to be the sophisticated thing to do on her first foray into Sex and the Single Girl.

She had the waiter uncork the bottle. Pouring a glass, she wandered about the suite, trying to decide where she ought to be sitting when Elliot emerged from the shower. She brushed a leaf of the orchid, checking to see if any new life had emerged.

Should she disrobe and wait naked in the bed?

She might be assertive, but she wasn't that evolved yet.

Why was she so damned nervous? Women did this all the time on television and in books. Sex was a basic human process after all. Unless she intended to remain celibate the rest of her life, she had to overcome this— what? Fear? She wasn't afraid. She was just balking like a nervous bride on her wedding night.

Damn Mame for putting that wedding image into her head.

This first time, she would let Elliot lead the way. He had to be more experienced at it than she, and he was incredibly perceptive. She couldn't have chosen a better partner if she'd tried.

Sitting up against the bed headboard, wineglass in hand, she changed the TV channel and let Purple prowl over her legs.

Elliot finally emerged, his hair still damp and curling from the shower. His jaw glistened from a recent shave, and the fragrance of some expensive lotion entered with him. But it was his robe falling to mid-shin, revealing long, narrow feet and muscled calves, that was simply too intimate.

Alys panicked. Her wineglass froze at her lips, her heart threatened to leap through her chest, and she stopped breathing.

Elliot seemed blithely unaware of her paralysis. He poured a glass of wine, removed Purple from the covers, flicked off the TV, and settled down beside her, hip to hip. "You smell delicious."

It was apparently the right thing to say. Inhaling the intoxicating scent of clean male, she relaxed, and her lips unlocked. "Like a raspberry cream pastry?"

His chortle was low and incredibly sexy. "Contrary to popular belief, my fixation is not on food. The image I'm getting is of exotic incense and tropical flowers."

"I should change perfumes." She drained her glass and set it on the bed table. "I'm feeling more like Ivory soap and lavender."

Actually, she was feeling more like sex on fire. She'd been without sex *way* too long. With Elliot this close, she could feel the pressure of his hip, see the small scar beside his mouth begging to be kissed, and she longed to rub her toes against his bare leg. Her mind fogged before she could imagine further than that.

He set his glass aside, too. "We don't have to do this."

He brushed a strand of hair behind her ear and lowered his face close, so she didn't take him too seriously. She'd stopped thinking by the time his lips lingered over hers.

"I'm not sure we can stop." She wasn't a breathless kind of woman, but she'd almost stopped breathing again. She could see moisture still beading along his hairline, and if she got brave enough to meet his eyes—

She lifted her gaze to his and fell irrevocably into their dark, hungry depths.

"Anything is possible. Just not very probable." His lips closed firmly over hers.

Heat and moisture. Exotic scent and raw male musk. Wine and mouthwash and a vague flavor of charcoal. Alys sank beneath the pressure of Elliot's greater size, wallowing deeper in the pillows, into the soft, plush covers, letting his body blind her to everything except sensation.

His deft hand slipped beneath her robe to circle her breast. His uncalloused fingers rubbed the sensitive tip, and Alys moaned. She'd been parched for simple human contact. She wanted this to go on forever. She wanted *more*.

"You sound like Purple purring." He repeated the caress, adding extra attention to her aching nipple. "Let me know if I do something you don't like."

"What's not to like?" she murmured, unfastening the tie of his robe by instinct since her brain had left the building. With another purr of pleasure, she rubbed her hands over the hard planes of his chest. Elliot Roth had abs and pecs of steel.

He didn't use his mellow, mind-melting radio-show

voice to reply. Instead, he placed a knee on either side of her hips, trapping her beneath him, then leaned down to suckle her breast.

It was too much at once. Surrounded by his weight and size, imploding beneath waves of pleasure, Alys uttered a muffled scream.

Purple leaped to her defense.

"Ow. Ow. Ow." Swatting at the back of his neck, Elliot rolled away, grappling for the attack kitten.

The cool rush of air over warm skin warned that her robe was open, but Alys was more intent on rescuing Elliot. She'd rather get back to where they'd been than practice modesty. Purple leaped from her hands and dived for the table, knocking over Elliot's half-empty wineglass before diving for the floor and hiding under the sofa skirt.

Lying flat on his back, Elliot recovered quickly. He caught Alys's waist and held her posed over him. "Forget the cat," he growled. "I'm not done here." He cast her robe aside and pulled her down so his mouth could fasten over her breast again.

Not wanting to be cat-attacked, Alys bit back her scream this time, forcing it down until the scream turned to liquid pleasure spilling through her to pool between her legs—where Elliot's erection rubbed.

If he'd been a sailboat, she would be riding the main mast. He was definitely long everywhere.

"Oh, my, Elliot . . ." She tried to speak through gasps, but his mouth and tongue were doing things that she shouldn't even contemplate in the privacy of her bed at midnight, much less with all the lamps on and with a strange man beside her . . . beneath her, actually.

"Don't ask me to stop now." His voice rumbled deep in his chest as he moved from one breast to the other.

She didn't think she could stop. Wine and sex had usurped her wits. She thought her ovaries might actually be throbbing in anticipation. A lot of other parts certainly were.

"Condom," she gasped through the haze of lust.

"Got it." He rolled her back to the bed and groped for the table drawer, shedding his robe at the same time.

Taking advantage, Alys stared. He was long and lean and—Alys gulped in admiration and excitement—well endowed. Hung, as the books said. Elliot Roth could grace *Playgirl* magazine without shame.

"I hope those are extra-large," she murmured while he opened the package.

He looked startled, then a lazy smile spread across his face. "Supers," he assured her, returning to his appointed task by kissing her.

And so he was—super. Extra-super-duper. Magnificent. Leaving no stone unturned, no erogenous zone untouched. He must have researched sex as thoroughly as hearts and nutrition. Alys clenched her teeth to prevent crying out as his agile tongue licked her swollen clitoris. She definitely did not need Purple interrupting.

"To the moon, Alys," he murmured between her legs before applying one final, magical tongue stroke.

And she flew. Over the moon, into the stars.

She hadn't found her way back before he entered her, thrusting high and deep and sending her into orbit all over again.

Engulfed by feminine scents, pillowy breasts, and tight, massaging muscles, Elliot delayed his pleasure as long as he could, but it wasn't nearly long enough. Everything about Alys welcomed him. For the first time in his life, he'd found a home. Soft arms clung to his back, enticing cries beckoned, and feminine heat and moisture rose to greet him in such a way that every primal instinct in him clamored to claim her.

Uncomfortable with an uncivilized side he hadn't known he possessed, Elliot tried to curb his urges and slow down, but nature held the reins. With Alys's sweet heat urging him on, he thrust harder, faster, and spun out of control, taking her with more force than he'd known was in him. She writhed and bit back cries, heightening his need to go harder, faster. When he pushed her over the edge a third time, he couldn't hold back, and he almost collapsed from the sudden rush of his release.

Instead of rolling off to prevent crushing her slender body with his weight as he would normally do, Elliot sprawled across her, relishing the soft mattress of Alys's breasts while he gasped for breath. Losing control like that should have frightened him back to civilized behavior. Instead, it was akin to flooding him up with adrenaline. He craved a repeat of the experience, and his body was already gearing up for more.

She wound her fingers through his hair and murmured incoherent phrases against his ear. He must have dozed off because he woke to the damned cat kneading his buttocks with its paws.

"I think I'll kill Mame," he muttered ruthlessly, rolling over in hopes of smothering the animal.

No such luck. The kitten leaped free and curled up between them, licking its furry, evil smile.

Alys's startled look melted into one of understanding

as she followed his wrathful gaze. She scratched behind the kitten's ears, and gently lifted it to the floor. "I don't think it's possible to train cats like dogs."

He didn't want to hear about cats or dogs. He wanted to luxuriate in the ecstasy of her arms again, sink into oblivion, admire her charms, take her to the heights. He wanted her.

And he couldn't have her. She was headed to New Mexico and he was headed back to his looming deadline and multitude of responsibilities.

A dull, throbbing pain washed up his chest and settled under his ribs, and he fell back against the pillows.

On top of all she'd suffered, Alys Seagraves didn't deserve to be tied to another man with a fatal flaw. His father had died at thirty-five of hereditary heart disease. How much longer could diet and exercise prolong his life?

Not long enough.

⚹ TWELVE ⚹

Elliot woke to an empty bed and a tent of covers over his hips. Given his solitary life, this wasn't an unusual occurrence. But the tantalizing fragrance of woman and sex lingered on the sheets, and the sound of the shower running and a soft voice singing reminded him that this morning, he wasn't alone. A surprising surge of satisfaction rushed through him.

He didn't devote a lot of thought to his motives but threw off the covers and climbed out of bed. He supposed if he really thought about it, his own mortality drove him onward. If he had only months or a few years to live, why shouldn't he enjoy what was freely offered?

He grabbed a condom from the stand. Responsibility was his middle name.

Alys gaped at him in surprise when he stepped into the shower with her. Short hair clung in dark curls to her cheeks and forehead, and her huge eyes widened to silver pools of appreciation as her gaze dropped to the present he brought her. He grew harder at her smile.

"I never thought—" she started to say.

"I've noticed that about you. You don't think often enough. I like that." He cut off any protest by covering her open mouth with his.

She braced herself, but as their tongues collided and stroked and her hands circled his neck, he could feel her melting in his arms. He'd always thought of himself as the epitome of modern civilized man, but the Neanderthal lurking in his soul roared in triumph at her surrender. She was wet and naked, and her full breasts crushed wonderfully against his chest.

Leaning his shoulders against the tiled wall, he lifted her, and she wrapped her legs around his hips without hesitation, taking him in as if they hadn't parted at all last night. With a shudder of pleasure, Elliot rocked in place until she cried out in release. Only then did he give in to the urgency of his need, taking her with all the force pent up inside him.

She bit his shoulder to muffle her cries and climaxed again. This time, her cries and pleasure took him to the brink and over.

The hot shower plastered his hair in his eyes and ran down his face like tears of joy. Gasping, he snuggled Alys close, letting her pull away enough to find her feet but keeping his hold on her buttocks. They fit his palms as if made for him.

Always sensitive to the beat of his heart, he knew it pounded against his chest, but no more so than if he'd been running. This was far better than a good run. He wanted to explode with the joy of holding Alys. He'd had no idea how good this simple human contact could feel.

"We can't do this again," she said breathlessly, startling him.

Prying open one eye beneath the pounding water, Elliot looked quizzically at the dark wet head resting against his shoulder. "If we didn't kill ourselves this time, I'm sure we'll survive another."

She pulled from his arms, turned off the shower, and climbed out, reaching for a towel. "Nope. Sex is way too addictive."

He ought to be consoled that she liked their lovemaking so much that she considered him addictive, but rationalizing had no effect on irrational anger. "So is *food*. That doesn't stop you from eating it."

Rather than turn the shower on again, Elliot stepped from the tub to fight this out. At the moment, he felt as if she'd stuck her fingers into his chest and ripped his heart out.

"I don't get personal with food. If I did, I'd have to give up eating." She wrapped a robe around her, completely engulfing the view he'd been appreciating. "We're only a few days from Albuquerque. Neither of us is in search of a relationship. Why fool ourselves into pretending we have one?"

"Because the sex is good?" he growled, although he took her point. He might be interested in a relationship, but he couldn't be cruel enough to coax her into one. Despite his intent to consider her a flake, he liked Alys. She had good reason to be skittish about permanent attachments. She didn't deserve the pain of a family genetically programmed to die young. "What if I treat you rotten all day, and we just have mind-blowing sex at night?"

The musical chimes of her laughter didn't salve his frustration. He'd waited all his damned life for a woman as enchanting as this one, and when he finally found her, she wasn't meant to be his.

He'd better stop thinking like that damned quick, but he was having a hard time remembering deadlines and

radio shows when faced with a handful of radiant woman. Not just any woman, but one who stimulated him
on levels he could scarcely comprehend. Without even
trying, she challenged him. Most people simply capitulated to his determination, or got out of his way before
he noticed their existence.

There wasn't any way he wouldn't notice Alys. Or
that she'd let him ignore her.

"I'd rather you treated me nicely all day and ignored
me at night, thank you." She slipped from the bathroom.

Proving his theories about her independence and leaving him alone to glare at the foggy mirror. *You're a dead
man,* he told the ghostly image in the mirror.

He probably ought to be checking himself into the
hospital right now. Indigestion didn't last this long or
hurt this much. He rubbed the place above his rib cage
where the ache had taken root. One of the many reasons
he'd never practiced medicine was because he empathized
too strongly with his patients' pain. He'd hoped his research could produce the miracles his lack of practice
wouldn't.

It hadn't. With careful monitoring, he might live longer
than his father, but nothing would ever counteract ge-
netics. And if he didn't find Mame soon, sheer anxiety
would kill him.

Grimly, he returned to the main room to find Alys
feeding the cat from her hand. She wore her new boots,
a pair of snug blue jeans, and a black halter-neck ribbed
shirt with no cloth to cover her white, nicely rounded,
shoulders. He had to fight the memory of how she'd
earned that love bite on her right shoulder.

"Do you think we can put Purple in the saddlebags when we go riding?"

She'd erased the night as if it had never happened. Narrowing his eyes, Elliot threw his robe over the bed and stark naked, reached for his suitcase. He'd be damned if he would behave as if they'd never shared a bed.

Admiring the muscular expanse of shoulders and tight butt of the angry man rooting through his suitcase, Alys sighed in regret. Elliot Roth might dress like Mr. Conservative, but underneath that polish he hid raw male—the kind one admired in the movies and never met in real life. Or at least, she hadn't, though admittedly her life was pretty limited.

Maybe she'd been too hasty in writing him off. She just knew she'd woke up this morning feeling better than she had in her entire life, and she'd panicked. She wasn't supposed to feel this way.

"I moved straight from my parents house into marriage," she tried explaining while he hunted through his clothes, taunting her with his nakedness. "I don't know how to live on my own."

"I've got a surprise for you. It isn't all that great." He pulled on knit boxers that clung like a second skin, discarded the wrinkled white dress shirt he'd worn the first day, and donned the cowboy shirt from yesterday. He hadn't packed for a lengthy trip.

"But most people use the single life to figure out what they want to be," she argued. "I never did. I wanted to be Fred's wife, and that's all I was. I got my Realtor's license because he suggested I'd be good at it."

He jerked on yesterday's blue jeans. "I'm sure you'll

be good at anything you decide to do. What's first on today's itinerary?"

Okay, he wasn't buying her explanation. Neither was she, not when faced with what she was throwing away. Of course, she couldn't throw away something she didn't have in the first place. Her survival instincts were still good, even if her reasoning wasn't.

"The Route 66 Museum in Clinton, Oklahoma. We could just check the guest book to see if Mame stopped in."

"Fine, let's go." He pulled a belt through his belt loops, slammed shut the suitcase, and zipped it.

She could cave in to his anger or ignore it. Passive resistance was her specialty. She rubbed her nose against Purple's. "It's you and me, babe, and the sooner I find you a home, the better off we'll both be."

Never let it be said that she was wishy-washy. She'd plotted her course, and she meant to stick with it.

"We need to speed up this search." Elliot grabbed her heavy bag while Alys slipped the kitten into its travel cage. "I have a deadline to meet, and a radio show on Sunday."

Alys bit her lip against disappointment. "I can't imagine how you'll speed up Mame, but you're welcome to try."

As they'd loaded the car, she regretted caving in to his demands so easily. This was her one chance to see a small piece of the world before she settled in to waiting tables or whatever she'd have to do to survive. Just because Elliot had a life didn't mean he had to interfere with hers. Or Mame's. She had a suspicion Elliot had been in the driver's seat too long. He needed to learn how to go along for the ride.

While he arranged suitcases in the trunk, she strapped the kitten's cage into the backseat, secured her orchid, and stole the Caddy's keys from the trunk lock where he'd left them.

He shot her a black look when she slid into the driver's seat. "I'm paying for this trip. I ought to have some say in where we go," he said.

"Fine. Mackie D's or Braun's?" She revved up the engine. "Most of today's journey is on I-40, and you'll be lucky to get plastic food. If you want to munch acorns and raisins for breakfast, we can find a grocery store, and you can snack in the aisles."

"Whatever," he answered in resignation.

October in Oklahoma offered weather as changeable as her wardrobe, Alys decided, watching black clouds scuttle over the once blue sky. "Cold front moving in," she said in disappointment, bumping the car into a Braun's lot and parking. "No horseback riding today."

He climbed out and headed for the dinerlike ice-cream specialty store that populated this area more frequently than McDonald's. "Maybe some other time."

There might not be another time. She'd never rode on a horse, and she'd been anticipating it with glee for months. "The man hasn't learned to enjoy what he's been given," she told Purple. At least the kitten would be comfortable in the car in the cooler weather. She wouldn't have to give her up yet. She let the cat free to explore the car and filled her bowl with food.

Elliot was already standing in line and looking at the menu before she caught up with him. So much for the gentlemanly treatment he'd been practicing. The real Elliot Roth was wearing through.

He finished his meal first and walked outside to make

his daily call to the police from his cell phone while she dallied, debating whether she ought to go back for some of the restaurant's famous ice cream.

Deciding against it, she hung on to the keys. Elliot's grim frown said there had been no sign of Mame, so she didn't bother asking.

No sunlit cornfields today. In a fog of rain and clouds, they crept through traffic along the remainder of four-lane Route 66. It narrowed to two lanes and the traffic cleared outside Yukon, but eventually the old road disappeared, and they returned to the interstate. Mile after mile of desolate flat land stretched before them, unbroken by even a single golden arch.

The odd-sized spare caused the Caddy to tilt, but it was manageable. Puddles of water thrown up by semi tires splashed the cracked driver's window and seeped through to roll down the door, forming a damp spot on the carpet.

They stopped at the Route 66 Museum in the small town of Clinton, but it wasn't open yet. Alys advocated waiting to see if Mame showed up. Tapping away at his laptop, Elliot insisted on heading for the next stop on the itinerary.

Determined not to let his sour mood ruin the day, Alys handed him the packet of Tums, located a country station on the radio, and sang along with a new arrangement of "Ring of Fire" that had Elliot finishing off the Tums.

She drove through rain until Amarillo, stopping only to take a picture of the towering WELCOME TO TEXAS sign before dashing back into the warmth of the car. She was certain Oklahoma was a very nice state, but all she saw of the western half was windshield wipers and taillights. Her excitement at visiting new places had paled slightly since leaving Springfield.

Elliot glanced up from his work at her exclamation over the tilted water tower in Britten, but even she didn't have the heart to make him get out and take a picture in the downpour.

The clouds relented before they reached Amarillo. Alys laughed at her first sight of tumbleweed and stopped the car for a picture of a windmill. The rays of sun beaming from beneath the heavy clouds threw an orange light over the gullies and hills, and with a sigh of bliss, she figured out the wide-angle mode on the camera and snapped more pictures. This was what she'd come to see.

Entering Amarillo, she blithely decided to bypass their motel on the right to take the Highway 335 loop Mame had indicated as a shortcut to the Panhandle Plains Historical Museum down in Canyon. She thought they could find lunch easier outside the heavy traffic of the city, but realized her error as Amarillo disappeared behind them, and they passed miles of open field without encountering a single fast-food restaurant.

Elliot snapped off the radio and glanced around. "I thought Amarillo was our next stop."

"For tonight. But we're supposed to see the museum and the canyon this afternoon. Or maybe one today and the other tomorrow. Mame's itinerary is pretty loose."

"I think we ought to find the hotel and wait for her there."

"Like that would have worked well yesterday," she scoffed. "Mame isn't predictable. She could be riding down the canyon right now."

Stopping in a traffic backup, she glanced at Elliot to

see how he was taking that news. He didn't look happy. In fact, he didn't look well at all. "If you want to go back to the hotel first, we can." She didn't want to be totally selfish if he wasn't feeling well.

All right, maybe she *wanted* to be selfish, but she couldn't be. Scratch up one more piece of knowledge about herself—she couldn't ignore others. Probably went hand in hand with her need to be with people. Maybe she could be a sales clerk. They talked to people all day.

"How far is the museum?" he asked without looking at her.

"Just down the road from the state park. I thought it might have a nice place for lunch."

"I'm ready to stretch my legs, and the hotel won't let us check in until this afternoon. Let's go on."

She darted him an uncertain look but the traffic began moving. If only she could turn off her worry gene and her caring gene, she might progress a little better on this journey to find herself.

But she couldn't, so she took deep breaths, cleared her pathways, and did her best to send Elliot positive vibrations. They had days of travel ahead. She might as well do what she could to make them pleasant. It had never occurred to her that one night of mind-bending pleasure could ruin their trip.

It was a pity Elliot was another narrow-minded man who preferred physical connections over the metaphysical. She could help him much better if he would open up to the healing power of the spirit.

She didn't turn on the music station again but let him listen to NPR. It didn't seem to make him any happier, but at least he wasn't growling by the time they reached the flat town of Canyon. The museum area was on the main highway, and Alys pulled into the parking lot.

"Let's check the guest book first." He unsnapped his seat belt before she found a space.

"It's probably not a good idea to travel with a cat," she said with some concern after they'd parked and released Purple from her cage. The kitten crawled up Alys's arm and took a flying leap into Elliot's lap. "But I hate to leave her at a shelter."

Elliot absently scratched behind the kitten's ears before it darted off to attack a bug on the windshield. "Maybe we can persuade Mame to go home if we tell her the kitten is unhappy traveling."

"You live in a dream world, don't you?" Alys checked to be certain the cage had food and water. "Denial does not change the facts. We'll catch Mame when she's ready, and she'll go home when she wants to."

"I'm not in a state of denial." He slammed out of the car and waited for her to gather her purse and lock the car. "Mame is."

Leaving the window cracked to let in air for the kitten, Alys tucked her hand around Elliot's elbow and sent more positive vibrations. He definitely needed some calming energy. He was coiled so tightly he could generate electricity. Had she done that by declaring sex off limits?

He squeezed her hand between his chest and muscled arm and all but hauled her across the street into the museum.

"Mame has decided this is something she wants to do before she's faced with her mortality." Alys tried to force Elliot to understand the spiritual universe Mame inhabited.

"We can't always have what we want," he grumbled.

"We can, if we're willing to pay the price." She patted his shoulder.

She could tell he didn't like that answer but stewed over it while they pored over the guest book's latest entries.

Mame's name wasn't on it.

"We left early," she consoled him, "and we didn't stop in Clinton. We're probably ahead of her."

Without investigating the museum further, Elliot headed back out. Alys had to run to keep up with him.

"Maybe she's at the park already." He strode briskly toward the car.

"You can't mean to head for the park now!" She caught his elbow and tried to slow him down. "We haven't eaten. It could take hours to figure out where they might have a guest book in a *park*. We're supposed to take our time, enjoy the marvelous scenery." She had only one life to live, and she didn't want to barrel through it like he did.

"How am I supposed to enjoy canyons when Mame could be having a heart attack and falling off a cliff?" he yelled, stopping at the car and rubbing his chest with one hand while holding out his other for the keys. "You want me to enjoy horseback riding while wondering if my aunt is at the bottom of a canyon somewhere? I'm tired of playing these games!"

He'd never raised his voice to her before. Had she and Mame finally driven him to his breaking point?

"You know perfectly well that Mame is not in the bottom of a canyon, even if we haven't heard from her today. Odds are, she's having the time of her life." She paused for breath but didn't give him time to get a word in. A good tirade should never be wasted. "It's time you figured out there are some things in life you can't control. If you intend to spend your life worrying, you need to use your book royalties to buy a shrink."

Keeping the keys, she strode off in search of lunch.

≋THIRTEEN≋

It was nearly noon by the time Mame and Dulce fought through the downpours and reached the area just outside of Amarillo where Dulce's sister had lived. Mame noticed that her companion tensed as they took the side road off the interstate. They'd exchanged enough conversation over the last few days for her to realize Dulce had run as far and as fast from her roots as she could, earning a college scholarship rather than suffer her late sister's fate of marrying to survive. Mame suspected the self-defense classes Dulce was taking said a lot about her background.

Dulce had abandoned college and her dreams to come on this journey to take on a burden that wasn't hers. Mame saw something of herself in Dulce. The girl was no doubt wondering if she was crazy to throw her life away for her sister's child. There had been days when Mame had wondered that, too. But over the long run, she knew Elliot and his brothers were the best thing that could have happened to her. They'd ended a decade of selfish mourning and given her purpose.

Dulce drove past abandoned storefronts and empty parking lots, aging neighborhoods of deteriorating two-room houses, into an area of expensive shopping centers and golf courses. Taking the turnoff into a gated community with no security guard, she slowed to a crawl.

Houses adorned with Jaguars, swimming pools, and water-sprinkled lawns in this desert-dry country screamed excessive wealth. Mame had second thoughts about this expedition while watching a nanny push a plush twin stroller to a pretty neighborhood park. "Are you certain Lucia is unhappy here? It looks to me as if her grandfather can give her everything she could want."

"Salvador did not fight his way to wealth by being a nice man. He is cruel, calculating, and cold, and when he drinks, he is worse. He gave his son everything money could buy. Henrique shot himself after my sister died. Does this sound like a stable, happy family man? Lucia no longer speaks. Salvador won't let us—her family—near her. He has told the court he has put her in a school for *dysfunctional* children, and then wonders why she's dysfunctional."

"Money can't buy happiness, got it." Still, Mame warily watched the million-dollar mansions they passed by. A man with this kind of wealth could afford to go to the end of the earth to have his way. No wonder Dulce felt forced to kidnap her niece even though she had legal guardianship. It might take the entire Navajo nation to stop Lucia's grandfather.

"Do you have some kind of plan?" Mame asked worriedly as Dulce found the house and steered the Range Rover up the curving driveway. She'd been envisioning some pleasant ranch house where they could stop and find Lucia playing in the yard. Did children play in these yards?

"My cousin works for the utility company. He has parked his truck here and watched when Lucia comes home on weekends. He says there is a maid and the old man and no one else."

"This isn't a weekend," Mame reminded her.

"Then maybe he won't even be here." Dulce looked determined as she threw open the car door.

"You can't just walk into a place like this," Mame protested when it became apparent Dulce intended to do just that. "There are alarm systems. Someone will recognize you."

"Even if they don't recognize me, they'll know who did it." Dulce shrugged and climbed out.

"Wait a minute! Stop right there." Mame struggled with her seat belt while Dulce stood beside the driver's door in puzzlement. "If the maid answers the door, I can say I'm a social worker appointed by the court. You stay in the car. In fact, duck down so no one can see you."

Dulce's eyes widened, but she understood at once. Dulce was brown-skinned and young. Mame was white and older. The maid would listen to Mame.

Thinking Elliot's expensive SUV might add to the impression of respectability, Mame girded herself for battle, ignoring her erratic heartbeat. If possession was nine-tenths of the law, she was about to have the law on her side, where it belonged.

Clasping her big black purse in front of her as if she were as ancient as she felt, Mame rang the doorbell. It took several moments of waiting before the door creaked open. A small Hispanic woman peered around the partially open door.

"I'm Margaret Emerson, from the federal court in Amarillo." She opened her purse to display her identity badge from school. "I've come to have a few words with Lucia, if that is convenient."

"I will have to ask Mr. Mendoza," the maid said hesitantly. "Wait right here." She shut the door in Mame's face.

So much for hoping Salvador wouldn't be here. Turning around, Mame gestured at Dulce, but the girl was extremely bright. She was already racing around the side of the house.

Praying Lucia was somewhere easily accessible, Mame stood on the doorstep doing her best to look like a nonplussed court official, tapping her foot and glancing at her watch. She hoped the maid took a while. Locating Lucia in a mansion this size—even if Dulce circumvented security—could take time. Of course, if Dulce set off alarms, they'd be arrested before they drove a mile. Good thing she had Elliot's cell phone number.

Her next nightmare was that Mendoza would come to the door and demand court papers, but she should have known a wealthy man couldn't be bothered dealing with government lackeys. The maid returned to peer around the door again.

"Mr. Mendoza says you must make an appointment," she whispered. "And you must have papers from the court."

Keep the maid occupied was the only thought Mame allowed in her head. "I have papers from the court and don't need an appointment," she said coldly. "If Mr. Mendoza does not present Lucia this instant, I shall be forced to call the district attorney."

She wished she had a legal background instead of a medical one so she could sound more official, but she'd evidently frightened the maid sufficiently. Probably an illegal immigrant, Mame decided as the poor thing scurried off.

Still no alarms. Was Dulce inside yet?

Did she imagine it, or did she hear the roar of an angry man? Had he been watching her from the window? She would have been if she were in his place. Or had he just discovered Dulce?

Fighting for breath past the constriction in her chest, she anxiously watched the path Dulce had taken earlier. The instant her companion dashed down the drive carrying a weeping child in her arms, Mame ran for the car.

While Dulce threw Lucia's school backpack into the backseat and jumped in with her niece, Mame climbed into the driver's seat and threw the car into gear. In the rearview mirror, she caught sight of a short, barrel-chested man rushing out the front door—carrying a shotgun.

She hit the gas at the first explosion of gunfire.

Elliot ground his teeth and furiously gripped the Caddy's roof with fingers that should have dented the metal as Alys sashayed down the street toward the restaurant. His chest burned, increasing his alarm, but without his medical equipment he had no way of determining if he was in trouble. He had to find Mame before he checked himself into a hospital.

He rested his arm on the car hood and leaned his head against it, waiting for the pain to subside.

He had no reason to take his frustrations out on Alys. Losing his temper would not find Mame or solve his problems. He knew how to practice calming techniques to avoid the complications of his Type A lifestyle.

He still wanted to bash in the car's hood.

Sitting on the dashboard, the kitten watched him through the windshield. Alys had tied a red ribbon around its neck but the cat had mangled it and was in the process of shredding the ends with its teeth.

She'd told him he needed a shrink. *She* was homeless, penniless, and heading nowhere because she didn't know what else to do with her life, and *he* needed the shrink?

Uh-uh, he didn't think so.

He could see Alys's slim figure, crowned by the black cowboy hat, marching down the sidewalk-lined highway, her blue-jean-clad hips swaying in indignation. He wasn't used to accommodating anyone else's wishes in his life. Maybe he'd been a bachelor too long to fit well into a relationship.

So who the hell needed a relationship anyway? He'd been doing fine without one all these years.

No he hadn't. He had no knack for casual sex, no time to pursue it, and he wanted Alys in his bed again. And again. And again.

If he thought about it, he knew that wasn't all he wanted. He liked waking to her laughter. He enjoyed how her strange mind worked around his. And dammit, her *vibrations* did often ease his tension. The sex sure as hell did more than that.

And he didn't want her walking into more Harley-riding thugs or whatever other trouble she could collect in her naive belief in her invulnerability.

Knocking her over and stealing the car keys back wouldn't help him get where he wanted to be. Throwing a temper tantrum wouldn't either. If he thought it would help him find Mame, he might attempt both, but logic had returned. He'd just momentarily given in to the illusion that he might have some command of the situation. Stupid of him. He was starting to understand that the only person he had any command over was himself, and that was becoming increasingly tenuous.

Stalking after Alys, he caught up with her just as she turned into the doorway of another diner advertising barbecue and Texas-fried steak.

"What if we passed the Rover in the rain?" he demanded. "It was too dark to see far alongside the road." He caught her elbow to steer her through the diner crowded with college students.

"The police investigate cars alongside the road. If your cop friends filed an APB, they should be calling shortly." Jerking her elbow from his hold, she took the vinyl dinette booth and opened the menu so he couldn't see her face.

Elliot pulled the menu out of her hands and turned to the waitress. "Two iced teas, unsweetened, and two Cobb salads."

"I can fix salads at home. I want something I can't cook on my own."

"You need vegetables. Eat the salad and you can have pie."

Alys slapped her palms on the table and leaned over until they were nearly nose to nose. "I am not the one with the problem here. People *die*. Accept it, Elliot. You are not dictator of the universe. Face facts and get over it."

He thought about it. Then he leaned across the table, planted his lips on hers, and said, "No."

He liked the way she shut up and fell right into the kiss. He liked the way she thought for herself and stood up to him. He liked a whale of a lot of things about Alys Seagraves, and he wouldn't let her harm herself any more than he would let Mame.

He didn't like being stared at, however, so after shutting her up with a satisfying tongue tango, he sat back and let her do the same. If his expression was anywhere near as shocked as hers, they were already a sight to see without groping each other in public.

"What do you mean, *no*?" she asked, recovering rapidly. "I don't think you have an option here, Elliot. You cannot put Mame in a cage with Purple."

"But if I find her, I can reason with her. And as long as you're with me, I can see that you eat properly. You may get hit by a truck tomorrow, and I can't stop that, but I can try to see you live as long as possible."

"You're not God," she muttered, adding sugar to the iced tea the waitress delivered to the table.

But he noticed she ate every bite of the salad, even if she did slather it with dressing and ask for more.

When the waitress asked about dessert, Elliot told her no and pulled out a twenty-dollar bill before Alys could override him. It was time he took back the reins.

"We'll pick up cookies next door," he told her, dragging her to her feet. "We can take them to the park with us."

That got her moving. "Chocolate chip," she crowed. "I haven't had fresh-baked chocolate chip cookies since I was a kid."

"You're still a kid. Actually, I know *kids* with more sense." Leading the way next door, he ordered two oatmeal raisin cookies.

"Sometimes, kids understand things better than adults. You're way too adult, Elliot. Try being a kid again."

Pulling out her meager wallet, Alys ordered four chocolate chocolate chip. She slapped his hand when he tried to shove back her money, then stood on her toes to kiss his cheek to distract him as the clerk handed over their sacks.

"Not God," she murmured, opening the sack and removing a still-warm cookie.

"Not sane," he muttered back. "Have you even tried oatmeal raisin?"

"Not while in reach of chocolate chip."

She shoved a cookie between his lips and Elliot nibbled it. It was luscious and warm and packed with artery-choking butter and chocolate. He shoved oatmeal raisin into her mouth in retaliation.

She chewed a bite and nodded. "Not bad, but not chocolate."

"The difference between great sex and mediocre sex?" he asked, swiping the key from her hand as they marched back down the highway, opening the passenger door for her when they reached the car. He was still ticked that she thought they could forget sex after one night.

She caught Purple and slid into the seat without kicking his shins in retaliation. She kept him off balance, never knowing when she would blow up at him and when she would accept his dictates.

She didn't answer immediately, so he didn't know if she was stewing and furious or considering the answer or ignoring him. He started the car and followed the signs in the direction of Palo Duro Canyon State Park.

"Maybe," she finally said. "But then, what if sinfully delicious chocolate chip sex is actually *good* for you?"

They hadn't seen a sign of Mame since noon yesterday, and he was going insane worrying over her, but he had to laugh at Alys's reasoning. "You don't want oatmeal cookie sex?"

"Ha, big shot Doc Nice thinks he's chocolate chip sex."

"If you want to live dangerously, it might as well be fun." Content that he'd got her head screwed back on right and that he had some chance of looking forward to the evening ahead, he relaxed for the first time that day.

Which ought to worry the hell out of him but didn't.

"My word." Alys exhaled in reverence. The canyon opening below the scenic viewpoint in the visitor's center was far more than her imagination could ever have conjured from old cowboy movies. "It's a lunar landscape painted in colors."

"And Mame will want to see it by horse," Elliot said in resignation. "There was a sign for a stable at the entrance."

Alys couldn't conceal her eagerness. "You mean it? We can ride horses down there? Even if I don't know how to ride?"

"They'll be trail-broken nags, safe enough for Mame. If we're really lucky, maybe we've actually caught up with her this time."

So far, they'd not located Mame's name anywhere in Texas. The park's visitor center had a guest book, but it hadn't been very visible. Perhaps Mame hadn't seen it.

Since Elliot hadn't received any calls from the police, Alys had to assume all was well. She'd lived with worry far too long and had no intention of repeating the experience, not with the wonders of the earth spread out before her. As long as Mame was leaving a trail of orchids and kittens, Alys knew she was all right.

She offered Elliot her last chocolate chip cookie in gratitude. He broke it in half and returned the bigger piece to her.

She could never live with his high-intensity worry gene, but she liked his gentlemanly politeness. Of course, what he really wanted was more sex. If she wanted to be a risk-taker, shouldn't she go for it?

The stable didn't show Mame's name on their roster as having gone out that morning, and she wasn't signed up for later in the day.

"Maybe she's doing museums today," Alys suggested, trying to reassure Elliot and erase his frown. She could have bit her tongue after she said it. Now he'd want to go to the museum.

He looked torn, and she tried to hide her longing. She wanted to grab every opportunity offered, knowing life had a way of hitting people with buses when they weren't watching. Still, she understood his concern for Mame was deeper than her need to ride a horse through a canyon.

He shook his head and handed his credit card to the person taking reservations. "For all we know, Mame is right behind us, watching our every move. Or she found another stable. Let's see the canyon."

Alys flung her arms around his neck and kissed him. She'd never thought of herself as a demonstrative person, but then, her whole problem was that she didn't know who she really was. She could easily learn to be demonstrative in the company of a man who granted her every wish.

"Umm, hold that thought," he murmured against her mouth, holding her so tight against him that her feet left the floor. "I'm thinking of writing a chapter on a diet of chocolate chips."

"I'll read that one." She shoved away and dashed outside to examine the horses in the corral.

≋ FOURTEEN ≋

"We can't ditch the car. We need it to reach your mother." Mame watched worriedly out the hotel window.

When she'd first planned this expedition, she'd made the mistake of reserving a room in the Big Texan Motel in Amarillo, hoping for a touch of whimsy. At the time, she hadn't realized she would need a room protected by security guards and interior corridors. The Texan was designed as a cross between a frontier film set and the old-fashioned Route 66 motels that had only two floors and an exterior walkway. If Salvador was following them, he could smash in a window and be inside instantly. Unless he wanted to instigate a court fight over Lucia's guardianship, he wouldn't bother calling the police. A man with a gun didn't need a court order. He could go anywhere he liked.

"Surely he wouldn't hurt Lucia, would he? He was just shooting the tires, right?" Mame asked, trying to reassure herself as much as Dulce. She couldn't believe anyone would deliberately harm the innocent child sleeping in the middle of the bed.

The huge Range Rover sitting outside the motel room loomed like a billboard shouting "We are here!" She'd felt like a rolling target driving down the interstate after Dulce had explained that the purple semi cabs they passed belonged to Lucia's grandfather.

A policeman might not look twice at an elderly lady and a young woman driving down the highway in a muddy SUV unless they were violating traffic laws, but Salvador could tell his drivers exactly who to look for. As far as Mame was aware, the hotel could be seen from the interstate. Trucks flew across the bridge a few hundred yards from the door. It was only a matter of time before Salvador radioed them to be on the lookout for a Range Rover.

But the child had been terrified and all either of them could think to do was find the room Mame had reserved so they could let Lucia settle down while they plotted their next move. Secretly, Mame hoped Elliot would be there to help them, but he wasn't.

That was probably a good thing because he was likely to send them back to Salvador if he knew the truth. *Talk about mixed emotions.*

"He shot at the tires. And missed." Dulce stroked the hair of the sleeping child in the bed before rifling through Lucia's backpack. "I think Salvador hates giving up what he thinks of as his. He worked hard and pinched pennies until he owned that trucking company. It is his nature. I do not know what he will do if his drivers find us."

Mame had no answer to Dulce's fear. "He'll know we're heading for the reservation. If we turn around and go the other way, do you think we can lead them astray?"

Dulce considered this. "There is no place for us back east. We could look for a truck with 'Mendoza Trucking' on its side, let the driver see us, and head east as if I was taking her back to Springfield with me. But I don't know if we will be able to lose them long enough to turn and go the other way."

"What if Elliot and Alys take her to the reservation?" Mame asked. "We could make certain Salvador or his drivers see us head east, and lead them on a wild-goose chase until Lucia is safely with your mother."

Dulce looked doubtful. "Why would they do such a thing for us?"

"Albuquerque is only a few hours away. Why wouldn't they? They've already taken in the cat and the orchid, haven't they? That's the kind of people they are," Mame said with assurance, crossing her fingers behind her back.

"How soon will your nephew arrive?" Glancing nervously at the door, Dulce stashed Lucia's bright pink camera and assorted precious possessions into the backpack she had grabbed on the run. "There is no clothing in here, just what she takes to school with her. I need to run over to that Wal-Mart we saw and buy her some pajamas and things."

"If they went to the canyon, it could be hours before they return. Or they could just be waiting until check-in time." Mame glanced at her watch. It was past four. Fortunately for them, the room had been ready early.

"We should go on," Dulce said uncertainly. "Lucia does not know your nephew or Mrs. Seagraves. If we hurry, perhaps we will reach Albuquerque before Salvador can notify all his drivers."

"If they're looking, they'll be looking for *us*. They won't be looking for Elliot and Alys." Now that the idea had formed, Mame wouldn't let go of it.

She didn't want to admit she feared frightening either child even more if she should have another spell. Dulce had too many burdens already.

"Lucia is not a kitten. We cannot just leave her," Dulce protested.

That Dulce had agreed to come to the hotel said she knew as well as Mame that going on alone was dangerous. They needed help fighting an angry man with a gun and a fleet of trucks.

Although legally speaking, the law was probably on their side, it could still be messy if they were caught before they reached the reservation.

"We won't just leave her here." Mame sat down at the desk and fished out a piece of hotel stationery. "I'll write Elliot a note and explain where he needs to take her."

"I can't just leave Lucia with strangers without explanation." Frightened, uncertain, Dulce took up watch at the window.

"Once you pick up the things you need at the store, I'll take the car and hide it where it can't be seen. You can explain to Lucia what's happening and stay here until they arrive. They don't know you. Pretend to be a maid or something. We'll find a cleaning cart. As soon as they come in, you run. I'll wait for you at the Pizza Hut down the road."

Heart in her eyes, Dulce glanced at her sleeping niece. "It's not as if she hasn't been cared for by strangers before. It's just—"

"I know." Mame scratched the pen quickly across the paper. "You'll give her a safe home soon, one where she'll feel like talking. The Navajo court won't allow Salvador to touch her once we reach the reservation."

Dulce closed her eyes in prayer. Mame applied all her persuasive abilities to the note, hoping to convince her stubborn nephew to do what was best—and not necessarily what was right.

*   *   *

"Arghh! I'm not certain I'll ever walk straight again."
After spending the afternoon riding up and down canyon
trails, Alys massaged her aching thighs and tried to
straighten her knees before climbing out of the Caddy.
With interest, she eyed the fake representation of a colorful frontier town that Mame had chosen as their motel
for the night. "This isn't exactly how I pictured Texas."

Elliot carried their luggage from the trunk, looked up
at the pink porch of the section they'd been assigned,
and shrugged. "You expected to stay at J.R.'s palace?
You haven't seen enough rocks and oil wells?" His jog-
ger's stride didn't appear in the least harmed by hours in
the saddle.

They'd stopped at a men's clothing store on their way
back to the hotel so Elliot could pick up clean shirts and
accoutrements. Apparently after their argument today,
he'd committed to the remainder of the trip. Alys wanted
to feel jubilant, but she was just the tiniest bit scared of
continued involvement with him.

"Well, at least this isn't a Holiday Inn clone." Picking
up the orchid and Purple's travel cage, she limped after
Elliot toward their assigned room. Rush-hour traffic
roared past on the interstate behind them.

There had been no cryptic messages from Mame waiting for them at the desk when they checked in, not even
an upgrade to a king-sized suite.

She knew Elliot was worried and trying hard not to
show it, but he'd checked with the police twice today,
and there had been no sign of her. It wasn't as if Mame
were a criminal on the loose. The police weren't likely to
notice her unless she somehow caught their attention—
like crashing the car after a fainting spell.

Alys had to admit she wasn't as blasé as she pretended. They'd not gone an entire day without finding some reassurance from Mame that she was alive and well. Maybe she was waiting to surprise them inside.

A maid wearing jeans and pushing a cart stepped out on the porch of their room just as Elliot reached to put a key in the lock. Apologizing in Spanish, she scurried out of their way.

"I assume that means we have clean towels. I feel like I'm covered in grime from head to toe," Elliot said, waiting for Alys to catch up. He gave her one of his heavy-lidded looks that sent her blood racing. "If this place had a spa, we could work out a lot of kinks. Want to find another hotel?"

Oh, yes, she definitely would. Just thinking about what they could do in a whirlpool of water wiped away aches. Afraid she would come to rely on the pleasures he offered, she shook her head. "Mame would look for us here." She half hoped he would counter her objection.

Accepting it with a frown but no argument, Elliot lifted the heavy suitcase, opened the door, and froze.

Alys stumbled to a halt, nearly planting her nose in his spine. Hearing him growl something like *I'm going to kill her,* she thought it expedient to peek around Elliot's shoulder.

A small girl sat cross-legged in the center of one of the room's two double beds, emptying a red backpack on the covers. Wearing bright red overalls over a lace-trimmed white blouse, her shoulder-length black hair forming a fringe over big brown eyes, she gazed up from the bag in her lap to stare back at them.

"Oh, dear." Pushing past Elliot, Alys set her orchid down on the dresser and put Purple's cage beside it. "Close the door, Elliot. There's a note on the desk."

The child didn't appear to blink, although she gazed at the cat cage with interest. While Elliot hauled in the suitcases, Alys removed Purple from her cage and walked slowly toward the bed. The child showed no fear when Alys sat cross-legged on the end of the mattress, facing her.

"Hi, I'm Alys. What's your name?" Crouched in Alys's lap to examine the competition, even Purple momentarily behaved.

The child didn't speak but reached out a tentative hand to the kitten. Purple sniffed and butted her head against small fingers.

"Her name is Lucia." Elliot scanned Mame's note. "We're supposed to deliver her to a reservation in New Mexico."

Purple fled from Alys's lap, stalked regally past Lucia, and settled on a pillow to lick her healing paw. Lucia's head swiveled to watch. Still she said nothing.

Remaining on the bed's edge, facing the child, Alys took the note Elliot handed her and read Mame's erratic handwriting.

I need the two of you to trust me on this, Mame wrote. *Lucia has just lost her parents. Her grandmother has no transportation. She is waiting for her in New Mexico. I am fine but I can't be in two places at once. Lucia's aunt is in trouble and needs my help. Both of you know what it's like to lose parents. Take her to her family, please.*

At the bottom of the note she included directions to the reservation.

"I don't like this," Alys murmured, handing the note over her shoulder to Elliot.

He stood so close, she could lean back and rest her head against his torso if she wanted. She very much wanted, but she resisted. Elliot was more a temptation than chocolate chip cookies and black-bottom pie all rolled into one. Against her better judgment, she wanted to share her thoughts with him, wanted to lean on him for comfort and support, wanted to go to bed with him, even when she knew she shouldn't.

It looked like the question of bed had been answered. Privacy was now a thing of the past. She admired the hot pink camera Lucia held out to her.

"This is weird, even for Mame," Elliot said worriedly, placing his hands on her shoulders and massaging as naturally as if he did this every day.

It felt so good, Alys refrained from reminding him that she wasn't his to toy with. She checked the camera, but couldn't decide if the film had been used up. She aimed the lens at Lucia and snapped. The flash worked. "I wish she'd call. There aren't any messages on your cell phone, are there?" That was a stupid thing to say, and Alys cursed herself for it immediately. Reminding him of duty always distracted him from pleasure.

Elliot stopped his marvelous massage to check the phone. "No, nothing."

Watching the silent child attempting to attract Purple's attention, Alys thought about it, then shook her head. "I prefer to believe Mame knows what she's doing. She doesn't always do things like normal people, but she's far from senile. I think she's just rescuing another orphan." The how and why were valid questions

Alys couldn't answer. She simply knew Mame's heart and trusted it.

Elliot whistled softly and stuck Mame's note in his pocket. "I think there are better authorities to do that than us."

"There were probably proper authorities when your parents died, too, but Mame didn't bother with them, did she? She took you right home, gave you a bed, and let the authorities deal with themselves."

"Yeah, no matter what happened, we always came first," Elliot admitted, shoving his hands into his pockets as if to keep them from straying. "I didn't know it at the time, but the court tried to say a single woman of limited means was an unsuitable guardian for three young boys. Even though my father left us the house and life insurance, his practice closed after his death, and Mame lost her job there. I don't know what she did, but to this day there are still a few members of the judicial system who steer warily around her."

"Then we have to trust her now," Alys said firmly. A woman who could hold off the judicial establishment to protect her nephews was a woman to be admired, not argued with.

The small child attempting to attract the kitten's attention melted Alys's heart into a puddle. How dreadful it must be to lose parents so young and be thrust into a world of strangers. She should be eternally grateful her parents had lived long enough to see her grown and out in the world on her own. No more self-pity for her.

She wanted to hold this poor little girl, promise her everything would be all right, and make it happen— dangerous to think like that. She could never be a mother if she wasn't prepared for attachments.

"Albuquerque can't be more than three or four hours from here, can it?" she asked, deliberately breaking her concentration on Lucia and standing up to examine—what? Anything. She just couldn't watch the child anymore.

She'd been an only child. When she married Fred, she'd dreamed of a houseful of laughing, loving children. That dream had died with Fred.

"I don't think trying to find a house on the reservation in the dark is a wise idea," Elliot decided. "It would be midnight. And I haven't fed you."

"I wonder if Lucia has eaten? What do kids this age eat?" Fretting, Alys searched the desk for a room-service menu. "Hamburger?"

"You can't feed a kid on a diet of red meat." He swiped the menu from her hand.

The familiar argument reassured her. Elliot would know what foods were best for children. She didn't want to be the one relied on anymore.

"Where do you think Mame is hiding?" she whispered, using the excuse of preventing Lucia from hearing to linger close to Elliot.

"Wherever it is, when I find her, I'll wring her neck." Absently, he ran his fingers through her hair while glancing up from the menu to watch Lucia and the kitten check each other out.

"At least we know she's all right." She was becoming as uneasy as Elliot about the state of Mame's health. They'd been on the road for three days, and even these short hops could be exhausting.

Refusing to pick up Elliot's negative vibrations, Alys escaped his tempting presence and sat down on the bed again. Lucia shyly looked at her as Alys opened the backpack to check its contents.

"How old are you?" Alys asked in some hope of encouraging the child to speak.

Lucia held up five fingers, then ducked her head down to examine the book Alys handed to her.

"Five! You're a big girl. Do you like that book?"

Lucia nodded emphatically.

Well, the child could hear just fine, at least. "Do you know your grandmama's name?" Alys wondered how many kids could say their grandmother's name, but she didn't know how else to find out more.

Lucia sent her a heartbroken look, pulled the edge of the bedcover from the pillow, and rolled up in it. Only her head emerged, and she was looking at the kitten, not Alys. Purple seemed to understand that Lucia needed her and curled in a ball close by.

"Maybe we should call the police." Rubbing his ribs, Elliot frowned and looked uncertain.

"Mame might come back and explain everything." Alys knew that was overly optimistic, even for her, but she didn't want to turn the child over to the police. Lucia could be lost in the system and never seen again. And her grandmother was waiting for her on the reservation.

Trying not to worry about the child hiding in the bedcovers, she remembered Elliot had eaten the last of his Tums, and grabbed at the excuse to escape. "I saw a Wal-Mart up the road. I'll stretch the kinks out and walk over there while we're waiting for room service. Wal-Mart should have children's books. And she'll need a toothbrush. While I'm at it, I can ask the pharmacist if he has any recommendations for your heartburn. Will you be all right here with her?"

"I'm a doctor," he said with a tone of resignation. "I know the remedies for heartburn. I don't need anything, thank you."

"Physician, heal thyself. Maybe they have some sulphuricum. Bet you haven't tried natural remedies." Picking up her purse, Alys remembered Lucia's camera and grabbed it, too. "I'll get her some film."

He didn't look pleased, but he didn't object at being left with a child and a kitten, so Alys all but ran out of the room. She didn't know what Mame was trying to prove, but she wasn't going to prove it by her. She wanted her freedom, and she wouldn't be tricked into falling for biological clocks and sad dark eyes and playful kittens.

Or by a sexy man who had the idiotic notion he could take care of himself and everyone around him.

She'd set out on this journey to learn who she was and what she wanted. That was hard to do when sheltered by Elliot and worrying about Purple and Lucia. She needed to experience life face-on, on her own.

Determined to enjoy this moment of independence, she looked around with fascination. Following Route 66 had taken them down byways the interstates would never touch, but this particular stretch of the old road was right next to the interstate. Apparently a favorite for truck drivers, there were truck stops on either side, and the parking lot between the hotel and its restaurant was large enough for the big rigs. There were semis all around her.

Even though the hotel was on the new interstate and surrounded by fast-food joints and Wal-Marts, this was

Texas. She'd never seen trucks wearing longhorns, or tumbleweed rolling down city streets. Using Lucia's camera, she snapped a picture of the weirdly colorful motel, the tumbleweed, and the bright yellow restaurant, then started down the highway.

The street was jammed with rush-hour traffic, so she was glad Wal-Mart was within walking distance. It would take her longer to drive than to walk. She took a picture of some evil-looking men at the gas station who reminded her of pictures of Pancho Villa. They just needed to wear serapes instead of ribbed undershirts and gold necklaces. She thought maybe the beautiful woman on the corner was Native American, so she snapped her picture, too. Having lived in Missouri all her life, she'd not had the opportunity to meet many people of other cultures. It might be interesting to live here. What occupation could keep her here?

She wished she could build a career on taking pictures, but she didn't know how any of those she'd taken would turn out. Elliot had said he could show her the pictures from his digital camera on his laptop. She would have to remember to remind him.

He would tell her photography was another hobby and that she couldn't make a career of it. He was probably right.

Sighing in exasperation that she couldn't keep her thoughts away from Elliot long enough to figure out her path in life, she walked into the air-conditioned cold of Wal-Mart. Shopping might straighten out her brain.

She located some adorable picture books in both Spanish and English, a child's toothbrush, and a pretty bow for Lucia's hair. Deciding to find out more about Lucia's camera, she asked the man behind the film desk what kind of film it took. He told her he could have the current roll developed by morning, so she bought a new roll and left the old one. Maybe something on the film could tell them more about the silent little girl.

She had a long discussion about heartburn with the pharmacist before deciding on a packet of antacids. Maybe room service had delivered their supper by now. If she dallied long enough, Elliot could feed Lucia. He was the food expert. She didn't want to get involved.

A siren screamed somewhere down the street as she stepped outside, and she flinched until she realized it was in the opposite direction of the motel. She knew the hard way that caring for people meant worrying about fires and ambulances.

She didn't have the strength in her to do that again. She'd bravely told Elliot that people die, but that didn't mean she could tolerate losing someone she loved any more than he could.

So she wouldn't think about it. She wanted to enjoy the world around her without ever worrying again.

Passing by the truck stop, she noticed several of the drivers standing by their trucks staring at her. Driving must be a lonely profession. She didn't think she wanted to learn trucking, even if it meant she could travel. Smiling, she waved at the men, then aiming the hot pink camera down the street, she started snapping more pictures. She'd give Lucia a record of her journey.

❧ FIFTEEN ❧

"Jell-O tastes good, but green beans will make your eyes prettier."

Mame had told his brothers that vegetables would make them stronger and put hair on their chests, but Elliot didn't think that trick would work so well with a little girl. Lucia seemed to be studying the matter while she picked at her plate.

He'd pulled the hotel's small table over to the bed so she could reach her food, but her chin barely extended above it. She eyed him skeptically, picked up a bean, and pushed it into her mouth.

The door opened and Alys blew in. The sound of sirens racing by caused Lucia to glance up in alarm. Staying on a major highway had its drawbacks. Alys hastily shut the door.

Elliot couldn't tear his gaze away from her. She was so slight she ought to blow away in a good wind, but she'd broken a board with her bare hand and rode a huge horse down a difficult trail without faltering. And he'd spent a night in her bed. She wasn't frail.

She had curves in all the right places, but it was her expressive face he watched now. He'd seen her smile of pleasure when she entered. She'd been bouncing and happy—her natural state, he suspected. But as soon as she'd walked into the room, a light inside her had turned off, and he didn't know what had flipped the switch. Or who. She set her package down on the dresser and checked her flyaway hair in the mirror.

One thing Alys did not do was primp. She was avoiding him. Or Lucia.

She hurt his heart in ways no physical pain could. He wanted her to look at him with the joy he'd seen in her eyes last night. He needed her laughter and teasing to lift him from the rut he'd dug for himself.

He needed her to teach him how to enjoy life, but he couldn't ruin *her* life in the process.

"What did you find?" he asked, helping Lucia spoon up Jell-O.

"Books. No herbal remedies, just antacids. I used Lucia's camera to take some pictures and left her film there. We need to pick up her photos before we leave. Maybe they can tell us something about her."

He could hear the avoidance in her voice. She was distancing herself already.

He thought she'd been ready to share his bed again when they'd arrived at the motel. The only thing that had changed was the presence of the dark-eyed child.

Elliot studied Lucia. She was sturdy and wholesome, not in danger of departing the world soon. Her silence was heartbreaking but not a reason to deny her existence.

So maybe it was children in general Alys ran from. She didn't have any. Couldn't? That would be a tragedy for someone so specifically designed to bring joy and love into lives.

"What kind of books?" He cut another piece of chicken

for Lucia to chew and took the children's books Alys handed him. "Spanish and English? Do you think she speaks Spanish and that's why she doesn't talk?"

"She understands English. I just thought it might be interesting to try. How good is your Spanish?" She dropped down at the end of the mattress and flipped through the pages.

More sirens sounded outside and Lucia apprehensively watched the door, but Alys leaned on her elbow to show her the picture book, effectively distracting her.

"My Spanish is pretty much limited to *buenos días* and *gracias*," Elliot admitted.

Alys pointed at the picture of the pig, then the word *puerco* for Lucia. Lucia didn't repeat the word, but her eyes lit with fascination. "She understands Spanish, too."

Elliot gave up on feeding Lucia to start on his own dinner, now cold. He damned the images dancing in his head of Alys sitting beside a roaring fire, reading to shorter versions of himself. "Maybe you ought to be a teacher."

"You think?" She looked up at him eagerly, her crystalline eyes bright with interest. Her whole face lit with joy at the idea. "It takes years of education, but it's a real career, not a hobby."

That he'd generated her excitement stirred a ribbon of pride, but she made it sound as if she were asking for his approval. He wasn't going to be Fred, telling her what to do. "It's hard work for lousy pay. You have to do it because you love it."

"How do I know if I'll love it until I do it?" she countered. "Maybe I should just be a teaching assistant. Do schools have those?"

"They do, but you've got the brains and perseverance

to handle more than that." He stabbed his chicken a little too hard, and it slithered off his plate. "If you don't want to commit time and money to a career, then become a waitress in an expensive restaurant."

"Maybe I will. Then I could work anywhere." She bounced up from the bed to uncover the third plate on the table. "A hamburger! Thank you." She bent and kissed his head, then settled into her chair to munch contentedly.

He was too on edge to appreciate a peck on the head but too aware of the child watching them to act on his urges. Gritting his teeth, Elliot returned to eating the unpalatable mess on his plate. Why was he having a hard time thinking of Alys as a waitress in some greasy spoon?

After dinner had been consumed in a haphazard manner, they let Lucia watch a children's show on television. When she started to yawn, Alys showed her the new toothbrush, and she nodded her head. To their surprise, Lucia uncovered a pair of baby-doll pajamas from beneath the pillow when she emerged from the bathroom. Solemnly, she began to undress.

"Someone loved her and knew how to make her feel at home," Alys murmured to Elliot while he checked his voice mail one more time for messages.

"And someone hurt her," he muttered back. "She's terrified of sirens and isn't silent because she's deaf."

"Mame rescued her for a reason," she agreed. "Maybe we'll find her when we reach the reservation."

After reading one of the new books to Lucia, Alys tucked her into bed. Purple leaped from the dresser to curl up on the pillow beside Lucia. Elliot checked his e-mail in hopes of messages about Mame, then switched on the news to see if there was any mention of a missing child.

Pretending not to pay attention, he listened as Alys showered and changed into her long nightshirt. Did she intend to sleep with Lucia or him? His id argued with his superego over talking her into his bed. Even if they couldn't do anything with a child in the room, he wanted her beside him. All he accomplished was a burning pain in his side.

If the pain moved down his arm, he'd have to act on it. That was almost a certain sign of a heart attack. He hated frightening Alys, but he wasn't prepared to die yet. For now, he'd eat antacid and pray a lot.

Without fanfare, Alys slipped into the vacant bed. Elliot offered a silent prayer of thanksgiving and shut down his computer. Checking to see that the child slept, he unpacked his new pajamas, and went to take his shower.

He hated pajamas, but he'd never had to share a room with a five-year-old, and didn't know the proper protocol. He wasn't entirely certain of his reception when he crawled in beside Alys, either. He switched off the bedside light.

"Don't get any ideas," she whispered in a tight voice. "I just didn't want to frighten Lucia. Maybe we should have asked for a cot."

Fire burned in the hollow around his heart, but Elliot accepted her judgment in this. The uninhibited sex they'd shared earlier hadn't exactly been quiet. He was having difficulty explaining that to the tent in his pajamas, though.

"How do parents manage this?" he whispered back.

"With quiet passion," she murmured with a hint of laughter indicating she was aware of his predicament.

"Or quiet desperation." He was willing to do it with quiet passion, joyous noise, or in a house with a mouse. He didn't care so long as he had his hands full of Alys's joy and life and her vibrant body eagerly sheathing his sex. Even if they both avoided commitment, they could enjoy lovemaking. Unfortunately, she didn't appear interested in cooperating.

"I've already led the life of quiet desperation," she whispered back, all trace of laughter gone. "I'm not doing it again."

Well, he guessed that told him. Lying there stiffly, sensing she was as tense as he was, Elliot ground his molars in frustration and sought sleep.

They could be in Albuquerque tomorrow, Thursday. If Mame was waiting for them, he could be back to his normal life by Friday.

He tried thinking of a topic for his Sunday radio show. That should bore him to sleep.

The knob rattling on the chain-locked door startled both of them. Elliot could feel Alys freezing up beside him. Silently, they waited to see if the noise would go away.

The knob rattled again.

Throwing back the covers, Elliot pushed Alys down when she would have jumped up. "Call the front desk," he whispered. "It may just be a drunk."

"It may be Mame," she whispered back.

It wasn't Mame sliding a card into the lock, then slamming a heavy foot against it when it wouldn't budge.

"Down between the beds. Under them, if you can."
Elliot leaped out of bed to grab Lucia while Alys slid to
the floor, pulling the phone from the bed stand with her.
The child woke with a cry but hushed instantly when
Alys held out her arms for her. The kitten woke and in-
dignantly leaped to the top of the entertainment center.

The foot slammed again, and the wood door splintered. Elliot had taken his share of self-defense courses
in the past, but the one that had stuck with him most
was the practical one. He jammed the sturdiest chair in
the room under the doorknob. Then grabbing the heavy
table lamp, he ripped it out by the cord and waited behind the door. Alys and Lucia were completely hidden
between the double beds.

He heard Alys murmuring into the phone, and he
prayed the door held until security arrived. The only
other way out was the window beside the door—where
the thief stood.

His heart pounded so loudly he thought it ought to be
heard across the room while he waited for the thug to
kick in the lock. Elliot prayed that meant the intruder
had no gun or was afraid to use it. He couldn't imagine
why a thief would choose this room to burgle, but many
thieves were addicts and not the brightest bulbs in the
marquee.

A shoulder thudded against the splintered door. He
didn't hear shouts or pounding feet, so security wasn't
on the scene. The hotel probably had a retired security
guard sleeping in the back somewhere.

The lock gave, but the chain held. Outside, he could
hear the quiet rumble of an idling semi. Surely some
trucker in the parking lot could see what was happening

and would call the police. The parking lot was jam-packed with big rigs.

The door lurched open and caught on the chair and the chain. Elliot clamped down on his fury, raising the lamp in readiness. The two-bit creep outside the door would have to come through him before reaching the two innocents hidden between the beds. When he was a kid, he'd broken a baseball bat hitting a hard ball. He could connect with more strength and better accuracy now—with the power of fury behind the blow.

The chain tore from its mooring after another body slam against the door. Whoever was on the other side shoved again, and the chair toppled. It wasn't heavy. One more shove on the door and the chair would move. Tightening his shoulder muscles, Elliot waited for his chance.

The intruder pushed and the chair shifted across the opening doorway. Behind him, Elliot heard Alys scrambling about, but he didn't turn to see what she was up to. He focused all his rage on the fool just outside the door. From this angle, he couldn't use the intruder's head for a baseball, but he could come damned close.

In the darkness, his hearing was acute. Over the rumble of several semis he heard a muttered curse. A boot kicked at the obstructing chair through the partial crack, and the door swung wide. Bunching his muscles, Elliot held his fury in until a shaggy head peered around the door. The intruder was taller and bulkier than he was. Elliot adjusted his position to compensate, waited until the door swung open, and targeted the broad side of the man's head.

With a vicious swing, he slammed the heavy lamp into

a thick skull. The thief staggered, groaned, and stumbled over the chair, falling to his knees.

Before Elliot could adjust and grasp his weapon firmly again, another intruder rushed forward, hurling the door against the wall, just missing Elliot's nose. Caught off guard, Elliott stumbled backward. Unbalanced, he attempted to swing at the next thief's head but missed, smashing the lamp into his shoulder instead.

A curse splintered the silence, and after that, confusion reigned. With pain shooting up his chest and down his arm, Elliot threw himself at the second thief, bringing him down to the floor and pummeling him. The first intruder staggered upward, but Alys in nightshirt and cowboy boots, flew out of the darkness, kicking hard and accurately at a delicate area. Elliot winced when the man screamed and bent double.

Someone outside the door shouted a warning. A rough fist flew out of nowhere to connect with Elliot's jaw, and he staggered backward. Pain shot through his head and shattered his chest. He attempted to hang on to the thug in his hands, but the thieves outside were getting away, and Alys seemed intent on following. Releasing his grip on the thief, he grabbed the door for support. The pain in his side escalated as she rushed past, heading for the street.

With one last tremendous effort, Elliot grabbed Alys's gown. He jerked her down with him, clasping her tight against his chest as it exploded.

❧ SIXTEEN ❧

"We're going with him."

Terrified so much that she shook in her boots, Alys jerked a dress over her nightshirt and gathered a sobbing Lucia into her arms while the medics efficiently completed their tasks.

She couldn't absorb everything that had happened here. The police had roared in with sirens screaming, the intruders had run off, and Elliot hadn't moved. Still wasn't moving. Fear clutched at her throat, cutting off the blood to her brain. She couldn't think, only react. And her reaction was to hang on to Elliot for dear life.

He lay still and pale against the stretcher. A small trickle of blood marred his lip, but otherwise, he appeared to be sleeping. His tousled curls revealed no gashes, although a bruise was forming along his unshaven jaw.

Several patrolmen were canvassing the parking lot, looking for witnesses. The one remaining behind had called the ambulance.

"They didn't have guns," she kept telling anyone who listened. Elliot couldn't be dead. He couldn't be shot. He had to be sleeping. They just needed to wake him.

Terrified out of her mind, she squeezed Lucia closer. The medics ignored her while they tested vital signs, shot a needle into Elliot's arm, and readied him to be carried out.

"We need you to give a report, Mrs. . . ." The officer waited expectantly.

"Seagraves. I'm going with him." Carrying Lucia, ignoring the policeman, she hurried after the stretcher. This was nuts. The whole world had gone insane. They'd just been horseback riding. He'd fought off the intruders with the effortlessness of Clint Eastwood. Elliot was as alive and well as she was.

But he wasn't moving. She would have to wake him up if no one else did. Over the protests of the medics, she climbed into the ambulance, settling Lucia on her lap and reaching for the long, skilled fingers of Elliot's hand. The thieves were gone now. Elliot would simply have to wake up and help her deal with this mess. She needed him.

In the back of her mind, a voice shouted that she was behaving irrationally, but she shut it out. She didn't want to hear rational right now.

Blithely ignoring all argument as if she were deaf, Alys clung to Elliot until the medics shrugged and capitulated.

"Let us belt your daughter into the front seat, ma'am," one said in his soft Texas drawl. "She'll be safer, and we need room to work back here."

When Lucia went without complaint, Alys nodded. With the child's departure, she had both hands free to clasp around one of Elliot's. He still didn't move. Perhaps the shot had put him to sleep. She would send him positive energy while he got a good rest. He'd played the part of hero magnificently. She could hold on until he was ready to wake.

The siren screamed as the ambulance pulled out of the motel lot, and she knew that would terrify Lucia. Over the noise, Alys caught the medic's attention, pointed overhead, and shook her head. The medic understood, snapped an order to the driver, and the siren stopped.

Elliot still didn't move.

She continued holding Elliot's hand between hers, sending positive vibrations with the part of her still functioning. His skin was tough but uncalloused, the nails short and neat. She'd seen the power he'd packed when he rolled his fingers into fists. He was strong. He was a fighter.

Calling up her lotus flower, looking deep inside herself, Alys chanted her mantra silently, concentrating as if her life depended on it. She let her energy flow from her center, down her arms and fingertips, and into Elliot. *Love is the power that heals.*

The chaos settled into peace. Blossoming with renewed strength, Alys recalled the tenderness of Elliot's caress, the way he'd stroked her jaw and looked at her as if she were the moon and stars. Happiness flowed outward, found pathways from her heart and soul, enveloping Elliot in a blanket of comfort.

She felt his fingers tighten around hers, and joy bloomed.

She had no idea how long the ride lasted. She was jarred from her trance when the medic threw open the ambulance doors, jumped down, and began removing the stretcher. She couldn't hold on to Elliot any longer. He slipped away.

Panic abruptly replaced her earlier peace. The ambulance lights flashed red against the hospital walls. Medics raced with the stretcher through the automatic glass maw to the cold, artificial light of the emergency room.

Alys lifted Lucia from the front seat to ground herself. She stood frozen outside the hated hospital, dreading entering. Trustingly, Lucia leaned her small head against Alys's shoulder and clung to her neck.

In an unsteady daze, Alys let someone usher her into the outer ring of hell that was the emergency room. A man moaned. A stench of urine mixed with the odor of ammonia. She cringed, forcing herself not to turn tail and run. The medical technicians led her to the admitting desk, where a nurse asked her a question, but blind panic lurked in the back of her mind, and she stuttered incoherently over the answer.

A policeman arrived to question her more, and she had to concentrate on not giving out any information about Lucia. He didn't seem too interested in anything but the robbery attempt, and Lucia quietly slipped behind a chair to play with a magazine.

Fighting the panic attack by keeping one eye on Lucia, she darted glances down the hall where they'd taken Elliot, and clung to sanity by the edge of her teeth. Interns inquired about medical history. Nurses wanted to know about insurance. She had no answers, couldn't speak them if she did. The policemen offered to return to the motel for Elliot's wallet, and she nodded stiffly in agreement.

This was even worse than her worst nightmare. Elliot could be dying, and she couldn't go to him. They could take Lucia away and she'd lose her in the maze of red tape. Where was Purple? Had he run away? She hadn't found Mame yet. Oh, God, how could she find her center with everyone tugging at her from every direction?

The astringent scent of disinfectant and the earthier stench of blood merged with the crying and the sirens creating sensory overload, and she fought the urge to flee. She couldn't leave yet. She needed to find Elliot, to know that he was well.

Panic formed a red haze across her mind. She started gasping for breath, and the policeman rushed off to find a nurse. Lucia climbed up in her lap, and Alys clung to her, rocking back and forth. She couldn't give in to hysteria. She had to take care of Lucia. She had to find Purple. She wanted to see the orchid bloom. She couldn't do it all.

Tears spilled down her face.

A nurse offered her a paper cup of water. Gasping for breath, Alys shook her head. She accepted a brown paper bag and breathed rhythmically into it as she'd learned to do back when Fred spent weeks in the hospital.

Overcoming the hyperventilation, she rocked Lucia and waited, concentrating on blocking out the suffering around her.

Eventually, a nurse led her and Lucia to a tiny cubicle where a doctor with a clipboard waited. Elliot was sitting, leaning up against the pillows, and Alys nearly collapsed in relief and tears.

She didn't hear a word the doctor said. She set Lucia down on the cot, grabbed Elliot's hand, and winged prayers of recovery to the heavens. His fingers wrapping around hers were strong. He tried to smile, but it wasn't his best effort. She let relief flood through her anyway.

"I'm fine," she heard him say. "I'll be out of here shortly."

She thought the doctor objected to that, but she didn't

listen to him. She just needed to know that Elliot was alive. That he would live.

Then she could be on her way. She didn't have to stay in the hospital this time. Elliot was a doctor and could take care of himself. She had no responsibility to him or anyone else. She was free. Independent, the way she wanted to be. She could breathe again.

"I gave you my energy," she told him, knowing it was senseless to anyone except her, needing to let him know she'd done everything she could. She should have learned CPR instead of spiritual healing. He would have understood that better.

"I know," he whispered. "I felt it."

She ought to be surprised, but she didn't have time to register his reply. The RN lifted Lucia from the cot, distracting her.

"You'll have to leave, Mrs. Roth." The nurses and the policemen apparently hadn't exchanged notes on whom was who. "We'll have to take Dr. Roth up to a room for the night. Do you have a means of transportation?"

Eager for the distraction of little arms around her neck, Alys reached for Lucia. Checking Elliot to be certain he was still breathing, reassured by his nod, she let the nurses hustle her out, and agreed to let them call a taxi.

In her head, she knew she'd helped Elliot. She had done her duty. The rest was up to him. She could leave with a clear conscience.

"Mrs. Roth." The doctor caught her in the waiting room while she was standing there blankly, trying to figure out where to go next.

She looked up at him, saw his tired eyes, silvered hair, and tried to block out his words, but she couldn't.

"Your husband has a heart condition," she heard him say.

"Like Mame's." She nodded as if she understood.

He looked startled, then continued. "The condition is often hereditary, yes."

"He's dying, isn't he?" Now that she could breathe again, she was starting to put two and two together. Damn, but she'd been so stupid. Elliot had told her how his father died. Explained about Mame's condition. Told her why he did heart research. She should have known why he ate as he did. It wasn't heartburn.

"With the proper treatment, people with this condition can live for years," the doctor assured her. "He just overexerted himself this evening. He needs rest and medication for the congestion. We'll have to monitor him to discover the extent of the damage."

She barely heard anything beyond that. The strong, vital man who'd made love to her and fought off burglars for her was ill. He could die. Not today maybe. Or tomorrow. But someday.

She wasn't living through that hell again. She wasn't giving her heart away to be buried another time. She wasn't. She wouldn't. Elliot would understand. He wouldn't expect anything less.

She'd find Mame for him. And deliver Lucia. And take care of Purple and the orchid if she must. He'd have to take care of himself. He could do that. He'd been doing that for a very long time. He'd been doing much better on his own than with her.

Someone helped her into the taxi. She didn't remember getting there herself. Once she was away from the hospital, the panic lessened. She held Lucia, rocked her, and the poor little thing fell asleep against her shoulder.

If she could just look at the child as a task that must be accomplished, she could do this. She'd survived the past year by giving herself assignments and carrying them out. She'd always been an overachiever.

At the motel, the management apologized profusely, giving them a new room where security had carried all their belongings. Even Purple, looking shaken and confused, had been captured and now stared out at her from the bars of her cage. The poor kitten couldn't keep traveling like this. She'd leave him with Lucia at the reservation. They'd both be happier there.

Maybe she'd keep the orchid. She didn't have a home to take it to, didn't know where she was going after she found Mame, but it was just a plant. She could keep it alive for a while. She hoped. Driving down life's highway with a plant by her side was just the right speed for her.

Alys laid the sleeping child in a bed and covered her up. She would wait until morning, call the hospital and check on Elliot, then pack up the car. While management was apologizing, she'd asked them to send Elliot's bag over to the hospital. She needn't go back there. Just the idea of having to find the hospital and go inside again caused her to hyperventilate.

She sat down on the edge of the bed and tried to breathe evenly. She sought her center, but visions of Elliot pale and unconscious on the stretcher took up all the space in her brain. She changed the vision to Elliot in his new cowboy shirt and jeans riding down the canyon, shouting and waving his new hat in delight as the horse broke into a gallop. That was a good image, a strong one, one that filled her with joy. It brought tears sliding down her cheeks, but she'd learned to live with tears.

He'd be fine for now. She understood that much. And look at how long Mame had lived. If Elliot took good care of himself, he could live that long as well. She didn't need to live with him. She'd send Mame back to him. Albuquerque was only a few hours away.

"Dr. Roth!" Entering the room in the early dawn, the nurse looked appropriately shocked. "We have you scheduled for an echogram at ten. You can't leave now."

"I know what the tests will show. It doesn't matter. I'll see my specialist when I get home." Or to Albuquerque. Or Los Angeles. Whatever. After he found Mame. After he kept Alys from running away. Elliot tucked in his shirt and fastened his belt.

He was feeling far better than he should for a man with congestive heart failure, and he knew who to thank for that.

"I'll have to call the doctor. We can't just let you check out—"

"I'm a doctor. I'll check myself out. I can tell you my diagnosis without reading the charts. I can tell you what medication I need, what tests I should run. I can also tell you I'll be much better off once I reach—" They'd called her his wife. He might wish, but it wasn't to be, as last night had certainly proved. He corrected himself and finished, "Alys. And my own doctors," he added for good measure, because the nurse would understand that better.

Even he didn't understand what Alys had done last night.

She'd healed him. His heart had stopped functioning. He knew the symptoms, knew the condition had been building up for a week. Knew his chest cavity must be filled with fluids and that he needed rest and medication. But he was up and moving as if all he'd needed was a good night's sleep.

He was no doubt fooling himself, but it didn't matter. He'd rather fall over dead than let Alys run off on her own, and he knew damned well that she would, and he'd never see her again if she did.

She finally had him thinking in terms of a future—of his personal future and not some scientific advance he could discover before he died. He could have years ahead, and he didn't want those years to be empty. Alys was probably the worst possible choice for him, but he couldn't let her go just yet.

The nurse ran off to make phone calls. Someone had brought over his suitcase. That's how he knew it was almost too late. He jerked on his boots, found his hat in the closet. He was striding down the hall to the nurse's station to check himself out before the doctor on duty could arrive. Elliot walked into an elevator just as a harried intern ran out of another.

He was out the door and hailing a cab before anyone could stop him.

Now he knew how Mame had felt.

He wanted to tell the cabdriver to hurry, to take the yellow lights, to push the limit, but he balled his fingers into fists and forced himself to be calm. He'd spent a lifetime pushing himself and it had almost killed him. He wouldn't do anyone any good if he keeled over.

While the taxi rolled through quiet city streets, Elliot listened to his heartbeat, tested his pulse. Both sounded strong. Even the heartburn was gone. He didn't believe in miracles. He'd be happier once he had time to order tests to prove he was fine.

But just knowing he was closer to Alys soothed a part of his soul that he hadn't known was restless, filled corners he hadn't known were empty. In many ways, Alys had been right and he'd been wrong. He could accomplish more if he lived longer. He could live longer if he slowed down and learned to enjoy the moment, as she did. He wanted to relish whatever time he had left—whether five years or fifty.

He almost panicked when the taxi pulled up at the motel and the pink Caddy wasn't parked in front of the pink saloon front. She couldn't have left already!

On another day, in an earlier time, his chest might have started burning, but it didn't now. Peeling off dollar bills to hand to the driver, he pictured Alys's smile, steadied his frantic thoughts, and realized the motel would have moved her out of the room with the broken door. Now that he was calmer, he could see the boards across the damaged panels.

Gathering his suitcase, he followed the sidewalk to the back of the motel, and there sat Beulah, trunk lid gaping open.

Elliot flung his suitcase in beside Alys's huge luggage. He didn't know how she'd lifted hers to get it in, but he'd give her credit for doing anything she put her mind to. He sure as hell wouldn't want to be a target of one of her deadly kicks.

She didn't need him. He needed her.

Purple sat forlornly in his cage on the backseat, beside Lucia's red backpack. Alys had strapped the orchid into the front passenger seat. Elliot scratched the kitten's head, then, going to the back of the Caddy to slam the trunk, he stalked toward the open motel room door.

❧ SEVENTEEN ❧

"I'm not Fred."

Walking in the door she'd left open while she carried out luggage, Elliot pitched his Stetson on the bed, and Alys nearly fell backward in surprise.

"You don't have to take care of me," he continued. "Do me a favor, though, and let me know when you're leaving next time."

He looked glorious standing there with the rising sun at his back throwing his face into shadow. He stood with booted feet akimbo, his shoulders filling the doorway, a picture postcard of health. It might be easier on her if he wore bandages and carried a cane, so she wouldn't be so easily deceived.

"What are you doing out of bed?" Shocked, she sat down on the mattress. She didn't think her knees would hold her up. Maybe last night had been a mistake? She'd dreamed it? She'd almost rather believe she was hallucinating than know last night was for real.

"You gave me your energy, remember? Where's Lucia?" He glanced around until Lucia peeked out from the other side of the dresser.

"I didn't cure you of heart failure," Alys scoffed. "They must have miracle drugs."

Elliot hefted Lucia into his arms as if he hadn't been lying pale and cold on a stretcher the night before. Now that he was inside, she could see his healthy tan and the glitter of his dark eyes. He was furious with her.

Good. She was furious with him. Jamming the bologna and cheese she'd bought into the ice chest, Alys turned her back on him. "What am I supposed to do when you die next time? Leave your body on the side of the road?"

"I didn't die. I'll take medication. We'll stop by Wal-Mart to pick up Lucia's pictures and fill a prescription. Give me credit for knowing what I can or can't do."

She admired Elliot's strength and courage far more than she wanted to, but making himself ill was a damned strange way of surviving.

Alys shoved the top on the ice chest, lifted it, and glared at him. "I should give credit to a man who thinks he can walk on water? Mame collapsed just like you did and you raised holy Cain when she walked out. What makes you think you're any different?"

"I'm not over sixty, for one thing." Scanning the room to be certain she hadn't left anything, Elliot scooped up his hat and put it on Lucia's head. "And I'm a doctor. I'd know if I were suffering any symptoms of imminent death."

He was doing his best to keep from shouting at her, Alys could tell, but his sarcasm stabbed just as deeply. She wanted to feel guilty for abandoning him, but she didn't. Life was about survival, and she damned well didn't intend to lose herself again.

"I did what I had to do," she informed him, following him out to the car. "I'm not a nurse. I don't even know CPR. I couldn't make you better. My priority was to find

Mame and send her back to you and to deliver Lucia. You would have done the same."

That shut him up. He didn't look any happier at acknowledging her accuracy. Now that they were out in the light of day, Alys could see lines of strain around Elliot's eyes, and read the shadows in his gaze. He was grappling with mortality as ferociously as she was. That didn't make her happy either.

"I'm sorry if I hurt you," she murmured. She couldn't imagine hurting a man as self-sufficient as Elliot, but she thought her apology eased some of his strain. She might not owe him anything, but his friendship was worth preserving.

"Have you eaten?" He changed the subject rather than argue further in front of a child who listened far too intently.

"I've been to the store. We had juice and cereal and milk. I'm not a complete airhead," she answered stiffly. She also didn't have much cash on her and knew how to conserve what she had. Guilt finally struck her when she realized he probably hadn't eaten. "There's more in the ice chest." She set it down and opened it. "And bananas in the backseat. I didn't know if Lucia was old enough to eat grapes without swallowing them whole, and I didn't have a knife sharp enough to cut up apples."

"She has a whole mouthful of teeth and can eat anything you give her." He settled Lucia into the backseat and fastened her seat belt. "Do we need a child seat for her?"

"I checked the guidebook. She's old enough for seat belts here."

"Fine. I'll munch some cereal dry and have one of those bananas. Give me the keys."

"You can't drive!" she cried. "I'll not have you passing out while we're driving down the road at seventy miles per hour."

Elliot grimaced, and Alys regretted her comment instantly. That was how his parents had died.

Not acknowledging any hint of weakness, he took a swig of juice straight from the carton. Then he stored the ice chest on the floor of the backseat. "As soon as we find Mame and deliver Lucia, I'll check into a hospital. Until then, I'm sorry, we can't do this last stretch slowly. The keys, Alys."

His gaze was implacable as he held out his hand.

She studied him warily, but he didn't look as if he was about to pass out. He looked stronger than he had this whole trip. He wasn't even rubbing his chest. If she trusted Mame to know what was best, shouldn't she trust Elliot? He was a doctor at least and ought to know what he was doing.

"I liked Doc Nice better," she muttered, slapping the keys on his palm. "At least he attempted to be reasonable."

"Doc Nice was attacked by thugs and abandoned in the hospital by a woman he thought was his friend. You'll have to live with Doc Roth." In his heeled boots and tight jeans, he strode around the Caddy to climb into the driver's seat.

"Wal-Mart," she reminded him curtly, crossing her arms and glaring out the windshield while he started the car.

Maybe she wouldn't like this side of him. Maybe she could despise the domineering, unreasonable Doc Roth. That would make it far easier to leave him. She could find a waitress job in Albuquerque, and he could go hang.

How the devil had he managed to get so completely under her skin in a few days?

They stopped at the shopping center, and Elliot climbed out. Lucia had released Purple from her cage, so Alys stayed in the car with the cat and child, nervously trying not to think. Denial was a nice state if she could pull it off.

But her protective instincts beat denial into submission and activated all her defense systems. Last night's intruders had robbed her of any sense of security.

She studied every person who wandered too close to the car. It was early. The lot wasn't crowded. Two police cars were parked in front of a nearby café. A semi hauling produce had followed them into the parking lot and now idled in front of the grocery store. Employees were parking at the far end of the lot, heading into work for the day. Traffic had picked up on the highway, and a few more cars rolled in before Elliot returned.

As he emerged from the store, she could see the bruise beneath the stubble of his beard. She hadn't left him time to shave. Last night, he'd savagely defended them against at least three intruders. Understanding the ferocity lurking beneath the Doc Nice image, she saw a man this morning who looked almost menacing in his open-necked cowboy shirt and unshaven jaw.

This man had glared at her and shouted. He still didn't look happy with her.

But he climbed in and handed a shopping sack to Lucia, and Alys knew Doc Nice hadn't gone away.

Lucia withdrew a doll with dark curls, a shimmering gown, and tiny accessories to match and emitted a cry of happiness. Purple sniffed the toy and leaped into the back window in disapproval. Alys wanted to weep at the pang of longing the child's happiness stirred. She swiftly turned back to face the windshield.

If she was really stupid, she could pretend they were a happy, healthy family on vacation. She had a good imagination. She could pretend Mame had left Lucia with them so she could go off and play, and that thieves hadn't oddly chosen to break into their motel room for no reason. Pretending Elliot hadn't almost died and that they could all live happily ever after was even easier, and more dangerous to her mental health.

"Did you get your medicine?" she asked, determined to be practical.

Elliot tapped a slight bulge in his shirt pocket. "Grab the steering wheel and poke a pill between my lips if I collapse before we get there."

She shot him a disapproving look at his unfunny joke. "You didn't want Mame to drive."

"Let's not start this again. Little pitchers, and all that." He jerked his head in the direction of Lucia, whose happy coos had halted the instant they'd started arguing.

"How do you propose we talk about what happened last night?" Doing her best to sound happy, Alys smiled over her shoulder to reassure Lucia.

"We could forget last night happened," he growled, not starting the ignition. "It could have been drunks or some scorned lover who picked the wrong room."

Alys watched the child root through the photographs Elliot had given her and pull out an envelope of photos. "May I see the pictures?" she asked, curiosity getting the better of her.

With a solemn expression, Lucia handed over the packet of photos. Alys flipped through them, handing each to Elliot after she was done with it. She studied a photo of a dark-haired young woman who bore a family resemblance to Lucia, but it was taken at an odd angle and didn't reveal much. Most of the pictures were obviously taken by a child who didn't know how to use the camera well. One seemed to be of a burly man with a bristling mustache and an unhappy expression, but Lucia had only caught his torso and the bottom half of his face. Another photo appeared to be the dirty back end of a semi.

"Nothing in there that will do us any good." Elliot started the car engine. "Although that one you took of the pack of thugs on the street corner is pretty good."

Maybe she had a talent for photography, but her next career wasn't on her mind so much today. She put the picture of the young woman on top and handed the photos back to Lucia. "Is this your mama?"

Lucia shook her head, and holding that photo in her hand, tucked the others back into the film envelope. Glad the child had someone she loved to cling to, Alys faced forward again.

It wasn't in her to be serious for long. Maybe Fred had exhausted her worry gene. The sun was shining, Lucia was playing with her new doll, and Elliot looked like every movie star she'd ever sighed over on the big screen. She'd never fallen for the pretty ones. She'd always loved the second bananas, the ones who never got the girl. The handsome ones were too slick and shallow. The tough ones and the semi-nerdy ones, though, they had character. Let a man don a pair of glasses, and she was a goner.

Elliot could easily be all of them rolled into one. And she couldn't love him. Wouldn't. Love hurt far too much.

"When we find Mame, will you take her to the hospital in Albuquerque?" She still hated the idea of hospitals, but she hated worse the idea of losing a friend.

"I'm not familiar with the facilities in Albuquerque. I know some specialists working on some experimental techniques in L.A. I may take her there." He threw her a swift, unreadable, look. "And myself."

Alys gulped and nodded. Unable to speak, she reached over and flipped on the radio, searching for the local news.

"Is the truck still back there?" Dulce asked, focusing on the empty highway ahead of them.

"There's a truck back there. I can't tell if it's purple. The traffic is light, so he's staying way back, out of our view."

"Driving through the night was a dangerous decision," Dulce said grimly. "What if they'd tried to drive us off the road?"

"I'm assuming Salvador has some sense. If he wants Lucia home safely, he can't let his men be too reckless. They'll probably wait for us to stop before attempting to snatch Lucia."

"Oh, fine." Dulce rolled her eyes. "Then we must never stop. It's not as if this little road is littered with places to pull over anyway."

"You're learning to speak for yourself, excellent," Mame said with a weak grin. She hadn't worked out the pulling over and stopping part yet. After leaving Lucia with Elliot, they'd driven into a truck stop in hopes one of Salvador's drivers would recognize them. They'd led some poor trucker on a merry chase all night, driving east as if they were returning to Missouri. They'd taken the first opportunity to lose their tail, turned around, and careered toward Albuquerque on the southern route to the reservation.

Somewhere, they'd picked up another tail. Now breakfast and bladder needed attending.

"Next town, we lose him," Mame said confidently. "That will put them into a tizzy."

Dulce nodded grimly and hit the gas. They were in New Mexico now, her home turf. She'd already told Mame about her family scattered over the dirt back roads. It was time to lose this guy.

Traffic flooding toward Amarillo was heavy, but still on the light side on the interstate out of town that they traveled. Only a few semis rumbled along in their lane, and Elliot passed them easily. The morning sun was behind them. At the speed they were traveling, they'd be in Albuquerque by noon.

They rode silently with the radio playing a soft violin concerto that seemed to appeal to Elliot. Alys watched him relax, and she breathed deeply, trying to find the harmony between them again. If they could only turn the clock back a day . . .

The panorama through the windshield abruptly changed from plowed fields to a desert landscape of tumbleweed, yucca, and mesquite, with dramatic buttes rising in the distance. Alys exclaimed in excitement—they'd finally reached the Old West of her imagination.

"There's a visitor's center down the road," she said when they came within view of the welcome sign at the New Mexico state line. "Why don't we pull in there instead of stopping beside the road? We have a long empty highway ahead. We'd better take advantage of the facilities." She nodded toward the backseat.

In apparent agreement, he steered into a line of cars and trucks taking the exit ramp. The big rigs rolled into their own lot while Elliot pulled up directly in front of the visitor's center.

As a reward for not stopping for a picture along the interstate, the visitor's center had an even better welcome sign than the one on the highway. They took turns snapping pictures of each other beneath the big letters. Lucia tried taking a picture of both Elliot and Alys leaning against the sign, although Alys figured it would show mostly their legs.

Alys led Lucia to the rest room while Elliot checked their drink supplies. Noticing several rough-looking men lingering near the women's rest room, Alys held Lucia's hand tightly and ran over a mental list of defensive moves. Scratch eyes, knee groin, kick shin, stomp foot, and scream bloody murder didn't seem quite so feasible with a five-year-old relying on her. To her relief, a security guard wandered out, and the men moved on.

She was getting paranoid. Just because someone had broken into their motel room didn't mean every man in sight had evil designs.

When she and Lucia returned to the main room, Elliot was watching the weather advisory on the television monitor.

"More rain moving in. We'd better get ahead of it while we can."

Piling back into the car, checking seat belts and cat and orchid, perusing the map, Alys didn't notice Elliot's taut silence until some miles down the road. Uncertain of his mood, she watched the traffic, attempting to discern the reason for the muscle jumping along his cheekbone. A light rain spattered the windshield, but not to the extent that it leaked through Beulah's cracked window.

Traffic had picked up but they were still traveling quickly. She tried to concentrate on the scenery rather than Elliot's foot growing heavier on the gas pedal. He weaved in and out of traffic at a disconcerting speed. She cast him an anxious glance. Was he feeling ill?

Stomach clenching, Alys stared straight ahead, but she sensed every nuance of Elliot's actions. From the corner of her eye she could see his knuckles whiten on the wheel. She knew him so well, she could envision his jaw tightening and his mouth thinning. In another minute, he would reach for the antacid in the ashtray.

Instead, he hit the gas again, slipping the Caddy into the passing lane between two semis. The trucker he cut off blew his horn in rage, but Elliot held his speed until directly in front of a tractor-trailer rig slowing down to exit. Then he jerked the car back to the right, in front of the exiting big rig, hit the gas, and flew up the ramp and off the interstate, horns blaring like curses behind them.

"I don't want to ask," Alys whispered, too terrified to look.

"Don't." He whipped the car off the main highway into a shopping center parking lot, barely slowing until they reached the barren area between Dumpsters and loading docks in the back.

A pink Cadillac would stick out like an eyesore anywhere in the civilized world. These flat open spaces looked impossible, but he maneuvered into a shadow between a tall Dumpster and an empty trailer, then backed around so the Caddy was invisible to anyone driving by.

They sat silently. No one drove by.

"What did you think you saw?" Alys finally whispered after Lucia unbuckled her seat belt and climbed over the seat to sit in her lap. The child buried her face against Alys's chest and clung.

Her own heart pounded at an uneven rate. Taking comfort in the child's warm arms, Alys gathered her closer, trying to be reassuring while assimilating an assortment of frightening puzzle pieces.

"Maybe I'm crazy," he muttered, still holding the wheel as if it might fly off on its own. "But I thought I saw the same semi following us since just outside Amarillo. I thought we'd lost him at the welcome center, but it looked like he caught up."

"Purple cab pulling a produce trailer?" Alys tried to speak calmly for Lucia's benefit.

"I couldn't read what was on the trailer." Elliot turned to stare at her. "Where did you see it?"

"When you were in Wal-Mart. It was idling in the parking lot. I thought I saw it several times along the road and wondered if there were a lot of trucks like that out here."

He returned to watching out the windshield. "Maybe there's a whole fleet of them, and we're both paranoid."

"I agree." Holding Lucia, feeling her little heart race, Alys stroked the child's cheek reassuringly. "We'd better call the police."

"And say what?" He reached for the cell phone anyway.

"I have no idea. Ask them if there were any purple trucks outside the motel last night?"

He stared at her, his eyes growing darker. "I heard a semi idling out there during the break-in, but the lot was full of them."

"That makes no sense," she said. "We've seen too many horror movies—'monster trucks gone mad' sort of things. We'll be looking for giant ants next."

"What if it's Lucia they're after?" he asked quietly, trying not to sound too concerned while the child listened. "We didn't have any problems until she appeared."

"You don't really believe Mame would kidnap a child?" Even as she asked it, Alys wondered. Mame had definitely been up to something, but kidnapping? Why?

"I'll call anyway." He dialed the operator, connected with Amarillo police, and handed the phone to Alys. "Ask for one of the officers you saw last night."

As if she remembered any of them. Frantically searching her memory, she recalled the badge of the one who'd stayed with her in the motel room while they waited for the ambulance. Speaking the name into the receiver, she waited, and was given to a desk clerk, who said the officer wouldn't be in until afternoon.

She gave the clerk the little bit of information she possessed and let Elliot give them his cell phone number and explain about being followed.

The clerk didn't sound too interested.

"They probably get anxious calls all the time." Elliot clicked off the phone and returned it to its holder. "People get paranoid after a robbery."

Alys licked her lips. "I'm paranoid. What do we do now?"

Elliot leaned over and brushed his mouth against hers. "Breathe."

His breath feathered across her lips. She tasted orange

juice before he sat up again. He'd just had a heart attack. Or an infarction. Or something. He ought to be resting. Maybe they should find a hospital instead of traveling uncertain highways.

"Even if we're paranoid, maybe we shouldn't take the open road?" she suggested, trying to ignore the tingling sensations stirred by Elliot's touch.

He lifted a quizzical eyebrow. "There's some other kind?"

Shifting Lucia to Elliot's lap, she dug on the floorboard for the maps. "Route 66 fizzles out and there isn't much out here." She opened the big map. "The directions Mame gave us show the reservation south of Albuquerque. If there's any chance the thieves last night are related to Lucia, they may know where we're headed. Would changing direction throw them off?"

"Provided there is a 'they' and that we're not crazy?" Elliot thought about it. "I can't imagine Lucia being a target, but if she is, I suppose they might know where we were headed. The interstate is the biggest road out here and it heads straight to Albuquerque. Is there some way we can get off this road and circle back without ending up in Colorado or Mexico?"

"Given the state of some of these roads, it might take us all day, but if this is the Tucumcari exit, then the closest road is the state road north. It's a long way around and could take us a while. The easier road looks like the southern route out of Santa Rosa, but that's another fifty or sixty miles down the highway."

"Does the northern route go through the mountains?"

"I don't know about mountains. The map is flat. But the northern road is a black line and not a nice fat red

line like the southern one, so I assume it's a small road."
Her attempt at humor sailed right past his head.

"Let's see if we've lost the guy and go for the safer southern route." Switching on the ignition again, he bounced Lucia up and down on his knee. "Honey bear, you need to climb back into your seat or Purple will come up here after you. She's lonely."

Purple was happily sunning herself in the back window, but Lucia seriously evaluated Elliot's expression. Finding reassurance there, she climbed back over the seat, snapped her seat belt on, and settled in with her doll again.

Swallowing, Alys clasped her hands in her lap. She didn't want to be a family anymore. Every reason why stared her in the face. It hurt much too much to lose the ones she loved. She'd have to give up both Elliot and Lucia shortly. It was best to resist loving them.

As if understanding her pain, Elliot reached over to brush a strand of hair off her cheek. "I'm here. You're not alone this time."

Miraculously, it took only his understanding to raise her spirits. She wasn't alone. Lucia had family she could go to. Elliot would go on with his life. She could live for today.

Crossing her legs in the seat and laying her palms face-out on her knees, Alys closed her eyes and basked in his positive vibrations.

Maybe positive energy could make Elliot well again.

Could positive energy drive away mysterious purple semis?

❧ EIGHTEEN ❧

The wide-open spaces felt less inviting as they drove the conspicuous Cadillac through the town's broad streets back to the interstate. Alys swiveled her head back and forth, searching for any sign of a purple truck, but there was barely any evidence of human existence. Maybe people didn't drive in the rain out here.

Elliot roared down the ramp into traffic and continued west. Alys couldn't find a radio station playing music. Restlessly, she crossed her legs on the seat, then straightened them again so she could turn around and check on Lucia and look out the back window.

"Purple to starboard," she murmured, attempting to sound nonchalant so as not to alarm Lucia.

"Yeah, I see it." The scar beside Elliot's mouth turned upside down as he tightened his lips and checked the rearview mirror.

"Do you think it's the same one?" Alys asked, picking up the map again.

"I'd have to see the trailer. Maybe it's just coincidence. Is there another exit we can take?"

"There's absolutely nothing out here. How far have we gone, do you know?" She studied the wide-open spaces on the map.

"We've been driving fifteen minutes or so. Check for mile markers on the side of the road, then look at the exit numbers on the map. That will tell you how far away we are."

The purple cab pulling an unmarked trailer roared past, and they both breathed easier. It wasn't the same one. Coincidence. Still, Alys studied the side of the road for mile markers, just in case.

"Maybe some driver took a fancy to you back in Amarillo," Elliot joked, but it fell flat even as he said it.

"It's not as if there are a lot of other roads to choose from. We're probably all driving in the same direction," Alys offered in explanation. "We could meet up with the Harley club at Santa Rosa. That's the next Route 66 turnoff."

Elliot continued to check the rearview mirror, but his hands didn't grip the wheel as tightly. "We'll take the southern route anyway. If it's a good road, it will be a nice change from the interstate."

"The northern route goes to Santa Fe," Alys said wistfully. "That's where we were supposed to spend the night."

"Maybe later, after we deliver Lucia. We'll make a few calls, see if Mame has shown up anywhere."

She should be delighted they were almost at the end of their journey. She'd intended to leave Elliot behind, travel on her own—by bus, if necessary.

But the realization that they had only a few more hours together didn't raise her spirits.

Elliot muttered beneath his breath what sounded distinctly like an inappropriate curse. Startled, Alys checked the windshield. A semi was slowing down in front of them, but she couldn't see the color of the cab.

She looked over her shoulder. A semi with a purple cab was right on their bumper. She could practically stare into the driver's face. She didn't recognize him, but her heart thumped in terror. "He's too close. That's dangerous," she whispered.

"They're trying to force us to the side of the road."

"Why?" she asked, but there wasn't time to think about it.

She checked the mile marker, double-checked the exit number, and did a quick calculation. "Two miles to the next exit. But it doesn't look like much of a town."

The semi behind them pulled into the passing lane, came abreast, and stayed there. The rig in front of them slowed down even more. Traffic began to build behind them.

"This makes absolutely no sense," Alys whispered. "Maybe we should see what they want."

"Not if last night was any indication." Elliot took his foot off the gas to fall farther behind, then cursed again.

"We don't know that it was truckers last night," she argued. Glancing over her shoulder, she knew her argument was wasted. A third semi had come up behind, boxing them in.

Her thoughts jumped to the memory of the photo of the back end of a semi in Lucia's camera. How many children took pictures of trucks?

Highway signs indicating the next exit rose into view. The semi on their left began easing over as if they didn't exist, forcing Elliot toward the shoulder of the ramp. The semi in front moved up the ramp to block them from escaping.

Rain slammed the windshield, fogging the interior

with the moisture from the leaking window. The truck tires threw up rivers, almost blinding them.

"All right, I can do this." Whistling a tune that suspiciously sounded like "Whistle While You Work," Elliot hit the brake, swerved Beulah to the side of the road, threw the car into reverse, and began backing down the shoulder.

Even at forty miles an hour, a semi couldn't stop and reverse that quickly. The remaining two trucks roared past and up the exit ramp. The lines of traffic behind them flew past, rocking the Caddy in their wind.

Amazed, shaken, Alys merely stared at Elliot as if the top of his head had just blown off. Still whistling, checking the rearview mirror, he found an opening in the traffic and pulled out.

"How far is the next exit?" he asked, easing into the passing lane and flying past the exit the trucks had taken.

"Maybe thirty miles. There's a rest stop." She needed a rest stop. If she hadn't wet her pants by now, she would by then. She checked the entrance ramp and spotted a purple semi idling there, hazard lights flashing. Could the driver see them in the rain?

"Good." Dodging in front of a cattle truck so he couldn't be seen, Elliot abruptly steered off the interstate on the left in a patently illegal maneuver. He held tight to the steering wheel as he drove Beulah over the rough divider between the parallel east and west lanes. Halting, he waited for an opening on the other side, and slipped into eastbound traffic, still whistling.

Alys had closed her eyes somewhere along the way. When no crash resulted, she peeked between her lashes.

Not even a police car roared out of the rain to arrest them for the U-turn.

"Next time, I'm driving," she muttered.

Elliot laughed. Laughed! She wanted to smack him with something, but she was shaking too hard.

"If the semis were waiting for us, they'll have a long wait, especially if they decide to continue west looking for us." Adjusting his seat, he flipped on the radio and found a country station. "You want to see Santa Fe, we'll see Santa Fe."

Alys checked on Lucia. Apparently oblivious to the drama playing around her, she'd fallen asleep holding her doll, with Purple on her lap.

"It's Lucia, isn't it?"

"If so, for once Mame knew what she was doing," Elliot admitted. "If someone is after her, I can handle it better than Mame."

"I think you lived with her too long." Surely he wasn't enjoying this?

Elliot chuckled. "It does give one a warped perspective. I'll trust Mame over dangerous truckers who force innocent people off the road. So we'll go to Albuquerque the long way around. Maybe rogue truckers only patrol the interstate."

Leaning her head back against the seat, Alys tried to believe that all was well. Except now she knew she was riding with a lunatic—a gorgeous, sexy, dangerous lunatic. Elliot seemed to be thriving on adventure, while she just wanted to survive.

No, she wanted to *live*. She'd been just surviving for far too long. And living was what Elliot was doing right now. She'd have to study the holes in her theory some other time. First, she had to make her heart start beating again.

"The first lighting at the Balloon Fiesta is Friday night. That's tomorrow, right? I'm losing track." She breathed deeply, saw no purple cabs, and decided to admire Elliot's profile instead of the scenery. He seemed serene. He wasn't even reaching for the Tums.

"Sounds good to me. I assume that means you and Mame intended to stay in Santa Fe tonight and check in at your Albuquerque hotel on Friday in time to get to the balloon park. So chances are Mame is sightseeing in Santa Fe as we speak," Elliot replied with confidence.

"Exactly." The way he said it returned the world to normal. Finally relaxing, Alys studied the words pouring from the radio so she could sing along the next time she heard the song. She could still find some way of traveling to Los Angeles later. Right now, she was heading for the historic town of Santa Fe with a gorgeous man at her side.

They took the exit at Tucumcari and traveled a nearly empty state road toward the mountains, without a semi in sight, but the rain turned to sharp pellets of ice by the time they passed Conchas State Park.

"It's snowing," Alys declared in astonishment, staring out the windshield at the desert landscape. "This is New Mexico. I was thinking heat and cactus."

They'd just passed a cluster of trailers and houses near the park, but beyond that sign of civilization, they seemed to be the only people out here. Only one or two cars passed going the other way—perhaps for good reason.

"The elevation has been climbing since we crossed the border. We're headed into the mountains." Elliot focused on a road nearly obscured by the sudden blustery weather. He would prefer offering Alys a snowball fight to driving through this if the stuff accumulated, but he was too busy cursing himself for not driving straight back to Amarillo and turning Lucia in to the police. "Maybe we ought to turn back and see if the park is open."

"It's not that bad yet." She checked over her shoulder, but Lucia was still sleeping. "Let's see if it won't let up. It's only October. It will probably melt right off in a little while."

He was listening to a woman who had never left the state of Missouri, who probably thought this was an *adventure*. Maybe he ought to have his head examined instead of his heart.

But if they turned back, they could meet head-on any truck who might have turned back in search of them. The road was too lonely for that scenario. He preferred hoping for the best and staying the course.

Alys unfolded the map to check their location after passing a road sign. "We're not even halfway to Las Vegas."

Elliot hoped that was in New Mexico. Although if they were headed for Nevada, the back end of Beulah wouldn't be sliding on icy patches. "What could we have done yesterday to tick off semi drivers?" he asked, still struggling with the mystery of the trucks.

She shrugged. "The only truck drivers I remember from yesterday were at the motel and truck stop, but they weren't doing anything interesting."

"Maybe it was just coincidence. Maybe some drunks saw you walking by yourself and thought you were alone last night, and that's why they broke in."

"Right, and there's no connection to purple semis?"

"Exactly." He liked that theory. Unfortunately, it didn't make much sense.

Of course, if the world made sense, he shouldn't be alive and feeling healthier than he had in a long time. They must have pumped him full of drugs.

"I saw you kick one of the jerks," he said, figuring to add a positive note. "He'll be fortunate to father children. You didn't learn that in karate."

She clasped her hands in her lap—not a good sign, he was learning.

"I've spent the last year taking classes. Self-defense was one of them. You were doing pretty well on your own, but I was afraid there might be more of them outside." She glanced sideways at him through the shield of her hair. "I never took you for a brawler."

He couldn't read her tone. Had he frightened her? He'd come close to frightening himself, but just thinking of those thugs harming her or Lucia raised his hackles all over again. "In pursuit of moderate exercise, I've tried wrestling and boxing. It's been a while."

"How are you feeling?"

This time, he heard the nervousness behind her words. "I promise not to lie to you, all right? I feel fine—angry, confused, and hungry, at the moment, but otherwise fine. Maybe last night was just some minor malfunction from a blood pressure spike."

That was hogwash, but she seemed to accept it. Elliot was glad she hadn't studied heart medicine along with everything else she'd taken this last year. He had no explanation of why he'd survived last night. He just knew that since he had, he wanted to celebrate whatever might be left of his life.

Mame was over sixty, so it followed that if he could avoid homicidal truckers, he might live that long. He still had time for a life. He just didn't think Alys would want to share it—rightfully so.

"Santa Fe is a fun place to visit. Maybe we should stay there for the night, wait for the weather to clear." He'd spent his entire life running against time. This morning he'd vowed to slow down and enjoy what he'd been given while he could. Why not start now?

Alys unclasped her hands, reaching out as if to catch snowflakes through the windows. Light played off the silver beads dancing from her bracelets, and he relaxed. He'd done the right thing by suggesting Santa Fe. She was unfurling again, radiating sunshine, coloring his dull gray world.

"I've never seen mountains," she replied in a voice filled with wonder. "Mame and I were planning on spending several days up here after the fiesta, with maybe a side trip to Taos. I'd love to stay for the night." She threw him an apprehensive gaze. "If you're feeling well. If you think whoever is waiting for Lucia won't mind. If you think Mame is all right."

Mame. He had to let go of his need to take charge of the world around him if he wanted to enjoy each minute as it happened. Alys had been right all along. Mame was an adult capable of making her own decisions. She had the right to choose her own life. As he did.

Elliot took a quick look at Alys again, at the silky short hair brushing her cheekbone, and the way her upturned nose and small chin gave her an elfin appearance. He didn't have the right to ruin her life. If she had been a more sophisticated woman, one who didn't form attachments simply because they enjoyed each other's company, he might not be so apprehensive. But she was and he was, so he'd better take this cautiously.

"Mame is in sunny Albuquerque, riding balloons," he concluded. "If she needed Lucia immediately, she shouldn't have left her with us. Or maybe like you said, she's in Santa Fe exploring."

"But I thought . . . a hospital?" Wide clear eyes watched him.

"I'm sure Santa Fe has one if we need it. One more night won't hurt, and this weather isn't fit for driving. How far until Las Vegas? Can we stop for lunch?"

She eagerly started flipping through guidebooks. "It should be only about forty-five miles away. They have a bunch of hotels, so there are bound to be places to eat. We booked the El Rey Inn for this evening in Santa Fe. It's supposed to be left over from the thirties. We may have missed Mame for lunch, though. She would have driven down to Santa Rosa. She said she danced in a club down there."

"Mame? *Danced?*" Lord, she kept spinning his head around.

"Didn't you know?" Alys glanced at him in surprise. "Mame traveled for a year as a professional dancer— you know, the sixties go-go kind of stuff in clubs? They're scattered all along Route 66. I think that's how she made her way back to Springfield after her husband shipped out to Vietnam."

Astounded, he didn't know what to say. The aunt he knew had always been a bit of a loose cannon, but she'd never swerved in her dedication to him and his brothers. He'd never seen her drink alcohol or smoke a cigarette, never heard her curse. *"A go-go dancer?"*

She laughed, and Elliot could swear the sun peered

out from behind the heavy clouds for just a moment to see who had made the joyful noise.

"What's the matter, Elliot? Doesn't the world conform to your specifications?" She sat forward to watch the dancing sparkles from the blackened sky. "There's so much out there to be admired; why put a limit on your expectations?"

The car fishtailed on a curve, and Elliot slowed down to concentrate on the road while Alys checked on Lucia. He scanned the highway ahead. The sides of the pavement were disappearing in the blowing snow. He downshifted and slowed some more. Beulah had a huge engine and could take these hills without a hitch. He just didn't trust the visibility or the ice.

The snow fell harder, hitting in hard pellets, blending the air and sky in a blanket of gray. No headlights illuminated the dangerous curves ahead. The Caddy's lights created triangles of yellow broken only by the falling snow.

They hit a bump, the car fishtailed again, and the small back tire ran off the road. With a curse, Elliot held the wheel steady, downshifting again and slowing without braking.

"I don't know if we'll make it forty-five miles," he murmured as he regained control of the car. He slowed to a crawl. "We may need to return to the interstate."

Even though he tried to speak calmly, Lucia woke and climbed over the seat to settle into Alys's lap. Alys worked the seat belt around her rather than sending her to the back. Only Purple made a sound. She was meowing kitty curses and cowering on the floorboards. Elliot couldn't see her in the mirror.

"I can call the road department and check on road conditions ahead."

Elliot could see Alys's hand tremble as she reached for the cell phone he kept on the console. He wanted to halt the car and haul her into his arms, but this wasn't the time or place.

"There's no reception," she murmured, returning the phone to its case.

They couldn't say anything more in front of Lucia. The child had settled in Alys's lap and now stared out the front window intently.

"We need to get rid of this car." He was thinking aloud, cursing the road, the car, and the truck who had sent them off their safe route. "We're a bright pink moving target if we turn back to the highway."

"Beulah is Mame's baby," she protested.

"And we don't have another vehicle," he agreed. "Maybe we've lost them."

"Or they're behind us, figuring we'll have to stop in Las Vegas in this weather."

Elliot could hear the businesswoman she must have been behind her curt words. He wanted the dreamy, laughing gamine back, but for right now, he'd accept her shrewd depiction of the situation.

"Check the map. Where else can we go? I don't want to travel much farther north in this weather."

She scanned the map and shook her head. "If you don't want to go north, all we can do is drive to Las Vegas or back to I-40."

They needed to eat, fill up the car, and buy a tire. This was the most bizarre experience of his life, but adrenaline had roused primitive instincts that demanded he protect Alys and Lucia, at whatever cost.

No amount of logic could convince him to leave them with the police and go after Mame. Of course, logic had gone out the window the moment Alys had walked into his life.

Another fifteen minutes of crawling down the road, and Lucia made a demanding noise, tugged on her seat belt, and leaned forward, pointing at something on the side of the road. He scanned the horizon for whatever was bothering the child.

"Slow down, Elliot." Alys tilted her head, trying to read the sign ahead.

"Looks like a gate." Whatever had been painted on the ranch sign dangling from the metal post over the driveway had worn away. The countryside sprawled out around them in undulating hills and scrub disguised by cloud and snowfall. Another half hour and they could be in town—if they didn't slide off a mountain.

Lucia bounced up and down and pointed eagerly, looking hopefully from him to Alys and back at the gate.

"Do you know this place?" Alys asked the child.

Lucia nodded and pointed again.

Elliot carefully downshifted and braked in front of the turnoff. If a dirt road lay beneath the layer of icy snow, he couldn't see it. Judging by the absence of scrub along the hill just past the posts, it was possible pickups used it, but it didn't look any safer than the dilemma awaiting them ahead. "I'm thinking being stranded in the middle of a cow pasture in a snowstorm is not a wise idea."

"There's a mailbox." Alys pointed out a tilted post with a rusted box hanging on by one nail. "Lucia lived in Amarillo and she's going to Albuquerque. Chances are good she has relatives in between. This may even be a reservation, for all we know."

Lucia nodded eagerly. *"Bisabuelo."*

Alys caught Elliot's gaze. Lucia had spoken.

"Remember that in Spanish?" she murmured.

"Abuelo is grandfather. Great-grandfather?" Against his better judgment, Elliot gave in to the will of the two women in his care, even if one was a half-pint who'd spoken only one word. He knew this wasn't the reservation where they were supposed to take the child, but it was better than nothing. He hoped.

The weather was bad. They had mysterious thugs trying to drive them off the road. And they were driving a target the color of Pepto-Bismol. Driving into a cow pasture couldn't be much worse.

❧ NINETEEN ❧

Alys leaned forward to scan the horizon as Beulah lurched down the ruts of the dirt road. She prayed they were still on the right track. She doubted if the road would be easy to see in good weather. How did people live without grass or neatly fenced fields or some attempt to mark the boundaries of civilization? "I see smoke."

"With our luck, it's a volcano. Or Old Faithful." White-knuckled, Elliot gripped the steering wheel tighter, easing the old car over ruts and rocks disguised by blowing ice and snow and sand.

"I don't think we're that far off the route." She tried to keep amusement in her voice, but it was difficult. She'd persuaded him to this insane side trip because a five-year-old thought she knew where they were. What were the chances?

But Lucia had actually spoken. She didn't want to terrify her into silence again. Sometimes, miracles happened. *Positive energy, Alys.* Maybe they could find out what this was all about.

"I think it's a ranch house." Relief colored Elliot's voice. "Now, if no one shoots at us . . ."

Lucia glanced out the windshield, murmured *"Bis-*

abuelo" once again, then buried her face in Alys's shoulder. This time, her little body seemed to relax. Alys wished she'd never have to let her go. *Dangerous,* her mind screamed.

"It's going to be all right. I can feel it." Thinking positive meant believing Lucia would be safe here, and not fretting that she'd never have a child of her own to hold. She would shed these maternal instincts once she had a life and career. "Look, there are trucks and cars in the drive. There are people here. And Lucia isn't frightened. Maybe there's a phone."

Thinking positive also meant not worrying that Elliot would have a heart attack while they were stranded out here in the middle of nowhere. She cast him a surreptitious look. He seemed tense but fine.

She wasn't so certain *she* was fine after watching him in action. She had badly underestimated the good doctor. She'd thought him a slightly cranky teddy bear she could cuddle and enjoy for a little while. Now that she knew what he was capable of, she had to adjust her whole view of him.

He'd acted swiftly, thoroughly, and deliberately, endangering life and limb in the process. He'd made a life-and-death decision right there in the middle of the road, and he'd come out the winner. He'd been terrifying. And wonderful.

"I'll leave the car running and go to the door." Elliot parked the Caddy behind an ancient pickup missing its cargo gate.

That sounded eminently practical and more like the world as she knew it. But before she could relax, Lucia pulled loose of the seat belt, leaned over to open the door, and ran after Elliot. Well, so much for practical.

She wasn't even wearing a coat! None of them were. She'd had no idea climates and weather could change so rapidly. Well, this was how one learned.

Turning off the car and pulling the key from the ignition, Alys climbed out and opened the trunk while Elliot and Lucia ran to the ranch house. She'd packed sweaters. She didn't think they'd fit Elliot or Lucia, though. At least she knew how to be prepared for the unexpected. She just needed to learn to prepare for everyone else as well—for now, until she was alone again.

Finding a short-waisted, short-sleeved cardigan for Lucia and a cable-knit pullover for herself, Alys shut the trunk, fished around inside the Caddy until she found Purple, and hurried up the path toward the house. A rectangle of yellow light opened through the gloom, but she couldn't see past Elliot to the occupant. She heard Lucia's squeal of delight, though. They'd come to the right place.

After a brief exchange with whoever opened the door, Elliot turned to wait for her to catch up, and Alys imagined she saw relief and something softer in his features as he held out his hand to her. Obviously, her positive thoughts had inflated to ridiculous proportions, but she wouldn't pop her balloon right now. She let him wrap his arm around her and haul her inside as if he had every right to do so. Purple clawed to be free, but she was afraid to let her go.

To Alys's shock, Lucia was chattering in a rapid spate of English, Spanish, and some other language, obviously reciting everything that had happened to her in the entire five years of her life. Very little of the tale was immediately coherent, but the elderly gentleman crouching beside her nodded understandingly, holding her as if she were a precious gift.

A woman of an age to be his wife hovered in a doorway, wringing her hands and sending them nervous glances. If Alys had to guess from her limited experience, both were Native American.

"I've apologized for the intrusion and asked for a phone," Elliot whispered against her ear, "but I haven't been able to squeeze a word in edgewise since."

Alys leaned into the comfort of his strength and let his arm tighten around her in almost the same way she cuddled the kitten. She had been shaking half the morning. Right now, she wanted to soak up the pleasure of safety and Lucia's happiness. "I'm warm and there aren't any muggers at the door, so I'm not complaining."

Finally settling Lucia's extended monologue, the elderly gentleman stood up. His thick gray hair had been woven into a long braid. His gnarled brown features expressed neither curiosity nor welcome. He merely nodded at their presence and gestured at Lucia.

"My great-granddaughter tells me you have saved her from *villanos,* as she calls them. We offer you our humble hospitality in return." He turned to the woman in the doorway. "Kaya, do we have coffee?"

With a nod, she turned back to the kitchen.

"We do not mean to intrude upon your hospitality, but the weather is dangerous. Like I said, we need a phone so we can call for road conditions ahead. May we use yours?" Elliot asked.

"No phone. Please excuse my bad manners. I am Sam Wolf, Lucia's maternal great-grandfather. Kaya is my wife. We will not talk of what brought you here just yet." He indicated the child hanging on to his knee and his every word.

"I'm Elliot Roth, and this is Alys Seagraves. I'm not certain I can even explain what we're doing here."

"The gods work in mysterious ways. Come, warm yourself by the fire."

Thrown so far into a different world she may as well have dropped from a tornado, Alys stayed at Elliot's side and took everything in. She thought maybe she knew how Lucia had felt when left in their care. What could she say when her whole world had turned inside out?

She drank steaming chicory coffee in front of an ancient fireplace in a kitchen that had come straight out of the early 1900s. A tin sink with a pump faucet, an old-fashioned icebox, and a woodstove were the major appliances. Kaya moved efficiently from one to the other while Sam spoke with shadowy figures out the back door, and Lucia played with Purple in front of the fire.

Hot dishes of food appeared on the old pine table in front of them. Alys followed Elliot's example and dug into them. They weren't sweet or chocolate, but they were delicious. Lucia climbed up on a bench and ladled the food into her mouth in between excited chatter about kittens and snow and her *tía*. Alys thought the child might have also mentioned Mame a time or two, but she was operating on sensory overload and couldn't be certain.

Once Lucia had cleaned her plate, Kaya bundled her off to another room. Purple slept on a rag rug in front of the fire, and Alys wished she could join the kitten. None of them had slept much last night.

Instead, she toyed with the camera from Lucia's backpack. Elliot had retrieved the pack so Lucia had her nightshirt and fresh clothes. The camera still had film in it, and Alys snapped a picture of Purple.

Ice coated the windows, and they could still hear the ping of sleet on the roof. She didn't want to go out again. She wanted to sit here beside Elliot, sipping hot coffee, until it was time for them to go to bed. Together.

So much for her independence. If she desperately needed a warm body to snuggle up to every time the going got rough, she was in trouble.

Sam stomped his boots free of ice on the back porch, then entered and hung his heavy woolen coat over a coat tree. Kaya handed him a mug of coffee as he entered.

"The road is not passable," he announced, settling on the bench where Lucia had sat. "No one can find you now."

"But they can once the weather clears," Elliot added, bringing the problem out in the open now that Lucia wasn't around.

Sam nodded. "Our granddaughter was hit and killed by a car recently, and her husband took his own life shortly after. They do not tell an old man everything, but I hear and I listen. Lucia's paternal grandfather claimed her, and he has the wealth and power to keep her, but Lucia does not belong with a man who bears hatred in his heart. The younger ones have spoken of rescuing her, but they have families of their own. We thank you for saving Lucia from such a man."

"We didn't save her," Alys said, thinking it time all the facts were laid on the table. "Elliot's aunt left her with us with a note saying we were to take her to her family on a reservation in Albuquerque. But bad things kept happening, and we're kind of off the route now."

Sam waited, but Elliot didn't attempt to explain his

aunt. Alys watched him worriedly, terrified he'd strained his health today, but he didn't appear fatigued, just thoughtful.

"The reservation is the safest place for her until the courts rule," Sam agreed. "I have one daughter who chose to live on the reservation after her husband left her, but her children and her sisters and brothers are scattered throughout Texas and New Mexico. My grandchildren, like Lucia's mother, have made lives for themselves all about here. We are not a small family. We can protect our own."

So it wasn't entirely a miracle that they had found a relative of Lucia's, Alys thought sleepily, leaning against Elliot's shoulder. Lucia could have pointed out the residence of any number of relatives anywhere along the route. She had just waited for the right moment and the right one.

"On the reservation, the law is ours," Sam continued. "If Lucia's grandfather calls on the authorities for her return, it is best that she is with my daughter where our laws prevail."

"I don't know how we can take her there if her grandfather is looking for us," Elliot admitted. "Our car is too distinctive. I can't imagine anyone's grandfather driving a semi, but if he is, he can find us too easily."

"Her grandfather owns the trucks. I don't think he drives them anymore." Sam sipped his coffee and thought about that. "His drivers, or even Salvador, won't know of our existence. You are safe here for now."

"But we cannot stay here," Elliot answered. "We must find my aunt and see that she is safe."

"From what Lucia tells me, it sounds as if your aunt is with one of my grandchildren," Sam said dryly. "Lucia's mother asked her sister to be Lucia's guardian. Dulce is very attached to the child. Lucia spoke of her aunt taking her. Two and two usually makes four. Is it possible that they left Lucia with you, thinking to draw Salvador's thugs away from her like a mother quail protects her young?"

"Very possible," Elliot said grimly. "If so, their ploy failed. Someone must have followed them and seen them leave Lucia with us."

"Salvador Mendoza owns a very large trucking company. His drivers travel up and down the highway every day." Sam tapped his fingers against the table in thought. "I am astounded that he even cares enough to look for Lucia."

Kaya refilled their mugs and finally spoke, in loud, heavily accented English. "He does it from spite, because his only son died hating him. He eases his pride by saying we destroyed his son's life, and that we tore up the will his son made appointing him guardian."

Alys had wondered at the woman's silence since Sam seemed so talkative, but she hadn't liked to question another culture. Now she suspected that English was not only Kaya's second language, but that she was hard of hearing. Alys's mother had refused to buy a hearing aid and had often spoken abruptly and loudly like this.

"It does no good to speculate," Alys said, projecting her voice slightly and receiving a nod of affirmation in reply. "First, we must think of Lucia and figure out how to get her to safety."

"Any of her relatives would be suspect," Elliot pointed out.

"My children all have young families," Sam said slowly, appearing reluctant to involve them. "But this is a family matter. I could send one of my men to my grandson—"

"I don't have children," Elliot interrupted. "If you think it is best for Lucia to continue on, it's better if she hides with strangers."

Sam nodded his head thoughtfully. "That is generous of you. I do not know how long it would take to drive Lucia to her uncle in this weather. He lives far off the road, back toward the highway. It would be faster if you could continue on this route, but you will be a target if you continue driving your . . . car," he said, obviously hesitating over describing the pink elephant sitting in his yard. "We must hide it in the barn for now. If we decide to do this, you can take my truck. It is not as pretty, but it is serviceable and unremarkable. It will get you there safely."

Alys covered Elliot's hand with hers and squeezed. "It's less than a day's drive. We have to go in that direction to find Mame."

She thought Elliot far more capable of looking after the child than an old man with slow reflexes, or a younger man who couldn't handle a car as well.

Elliot nodded in agreement. "I'm always inclined to finish what I set out to do."

"Excellent." Sam rose from the table and began giving orders as if he were a general in the field. "You will stay with us tonight. The weather is not fit for man or beast. We have an empty cabin you can use. If anyone is looking for you, they'll be searching the towns and not find you here." Sam headed for the back door to throw out more orders.

"It's not Santa Fe," Elliot whispered against Alys's ear, looking for her approval.

"It's better. Motels all look alike. This is the *real* New Mexico." Happily, Alys held Elliot's hand while they followed Sam out of the house to the one-room cabin near the stock barn.

She assumed it must have been meant to house ranch hands, but it echoed of emptiness when they entered. A quilt-covered feather bed occupied the biggest part of the space. Firewood was stacked on the front porch, ready for the woodstove that filled a corner of the room. A sturdy wooden table bearing a stack of paperbacks, two chairs, an oil lamp, and an old wardrobe completed the interior. Shades of the Old West.

No phone, no electricity, no television. No distraction. Just each other. She was in really deep trouble.

Without saying a word, Elliot followed the older man out to collect their belongings from Beulah, leaving Alys to contemplate the gray day out the window.

Odd, how one little choice led to another and another and before she knew it, she was traveling down a path she'd never considered.

She would be back on track once they reached Albuquerque. One more day couldn't hurt. Or one more night.

⚝ TWENTY ⚝

"Want to go horseback riding?" Elliot asked, returning to the cabin wearing his snow-covered Stetson and carrying bags under both arms.

The sight of Alys curled up on the bed with the oil lamp on the table beside her and reading a paperback as if she'd lived in these primitive conditions all her life shook him into saying the first inane thing that had come to mind. He was being sarcastic, but it didn't seem to faze her.

She smiled as she took in the assorted gear he carried in. "No, thank you. I'm in hibernation mode right now. I'm thinking of not emerging from my cave until the sun comes out."

"I left Purple's cage in the car. I figure here's as good a place as any to leave her, if you like." He dropped one of her suitcases near the wardrobe and his beside it, but he watched Alys in the process.

Her smile disappeared, and her face closed up. "Okay." She buried her nose in the old book.

She didn't want to leave the cat any more than she wanted to leave Lucia, but she was stubbornly sticking to her decision to go it alone, Elliot realized. Under the circumstances, he supposed that was the right choice. He just didn't like it.

"I left the orchid with Sam. I thought it might be warmer in the kitchen. Think we should leave that here, too?" Thanks to Mame, they were carrying around everything but the kitchen sink. They'd be able to set up housekeeping in the Caddy at this rate.

She shrugged and pretended to continue reading. "I can keep it if they don't want it. Plants aren't much trouble."

"Liar." He dropped down on the end of the bed and began removing his boots. "You want the plant and the cat and the kid, and they're all three a lot of trouble."

He had no right to be so certain of someone he'd known less than a week, but Alys was as transparent as glass. Everything she thought and felt showed up in her expressive features or in her actions. The lady had no hidden agendas that he could find—except when she was fooling herself.

The problem here was him.

She kicked her socked foot at his hip, but with no real force. "You're a lot of trouble," she said, echoing his thought. "And I'm not abandoning *you*."

"That's because I have other uses." Boots off, Elliot kneeled on the sagging mattress, propping his arms on either side of her head. "Like this." He leaned over and caught her luscious bottom lip between his teeth and nibbled. She might have won the battle last night by default, but he never gave up without trying.

To his joy, Alys grabbed his arms, dug in her fingers, and responded fervently, with a desperate need to match his own. Then equally fervently, she shoved him away and scanned his face. "Shouldn't you be resting? That's what they told Mame to do. We've had a really bad day."

"And you're not making it better." Elliot rolled over on his back and glared at the cabin ceiling. A tattered spiderweb hung across the far corner near the woodstove chimney.

She was right and he was wrong and he wanted to howl at the unfairness of it. He felt better than he had in years. It was as if a heavy weight had been lifted from his chest. He wanted to take advantage of every minute with Alys that he was granted. He hungered for her in so many ways that he thought he was more likely to die of denial than heart failure.

But he couldn't hurt her by using her like that. She had warned him that she didn't want attachments. He could see how easily she formed them. Had he been a perfect specimen of health, he would have scoffed at her fears and proceeded to show her that she needed him as much as he needed her. But he wasn't. He was the worst possible risk for a woman who had wasted too much of her life nursing an invalid. He gagged at the idea of her standing anxiously over him while he measured his life in doctor's visits, surgeries, and pills.

"All right, then," he said crossly. "What do you want to do? Play charades?"

He couldn't look at her but waited to hear her pronouncement of how they would go on. Resentfully, he rubbed at the fire starting to simmer in his midsection.

Maybe she was right. Maybe he stressed out too much.

She lay still beside him, but after a moment, Elliot thought he heard her stifling a giggle. He crossed his arms over his chest and glared at the ceiling some more. Alys rolled on her side and tickled under his arm.

He resisted twitching but couldn't resist lowering his gaze to her face. "What?" he demanded. "I'm trying to rest here."

"No, you're not. You're shooting holes through the ceiling. The roof is likely to fall on our head any minute now."

He captured her tickling fingers with his arm. She spread her other hand across his chest and rubbed where he'd been rubbing. Her caress was more soothing. "I don't know how to play charades," he told her.

"You don't know how to play. Or rest. Close your eyes."

He shut his eyes, but his body was as tight as a bowstring. If she thought rubbing his chest would relax him, she came from a different planet than his.

She curled up beside him until he couldn't resist putting an arm around her and tucking her head against his shoulder. She hummed happily under her breath and continued her gentle, circular rubbing.

"What is the most restful place you can think of?" she asked.

Her bed. After sex. But he might not ever see that again, so he thumbed through his memories to make her happy. He couldn't remember too many restful ones. Studying late at night? The lab at midnight when there was no one there to bother him?

Mame's kitchen before his brothers woke up? She would warm up a biscuit just for him, and he'd take it out on the porch to watch the sun rise before he set out on his paper route.

Watching Alys play with Purple on a sunny playground. Alys laughing and leaping to pick a leaf off a tree. Alys.

"A fishing boat," he said, giving her the expected response.

She ran her fingers through his hair, stroking his brow. "Imagine the fishing boat bobbing on blue waters, dawn sparkling like diamonds on the water."

He liked that picture if he included Alys in the boat. He could see her turning her face to the sun, lifting her arms to embrace the day. But she would be wearing a swimsuit, and his mind's eyes drifted downward to her breasts, and he wasn't very relaxed anymore.

"Focus on just one small part of the image. Is there a branch dangling over the water? A leaf drifting back and forth? Do you feel the waves bobbing up and down?"

He'd focused all right. He could see her breasts bobbing up and down with the waves. He mentally rearranged his image to lay his head in her lap. But then he had to close his mental eyes, too, or he'd be looking up at her breasts instead of down.

"This isn't working," he complained.

"No, not yet. Give it time. Have you ever been snorkeling? I hear watching the fish float is restful. Would that work?"

"I don't know. I've never been." In some ways, his life had been as limited as hers. He hadn't climbed any mountains, swam any seas. He ought to see what he'd been missing.

"Does your boat have a comfortable seat? Can you tilt it back and feel the sun beating down on your hair?" Her fingers continued their rhythmic stroking.

Focus, Roth. "Okay, I'm leaning back, watching a butterfly over the water." He was lying in her lap, leaning back, smelling that exotic scent she'd worn the night they'd first made love. If there was a butterfly in this picture, he wasn't seeing it, but she didn't have to know his real space.

"Good." She spoke softly, in rhythm with her fingers. "Focus on the butterfly. See the colors on its wings. Are they blue?"

"Red." He pictured the kind of swimsuit Alys might wear. "No, orange, with gold stripes. And black spots."

Amusement laced her voice. "Where does the butterfly land? On a flower? A tree branch? Your finger?"

His lap. Wrong answer. His erection rose against his zipper. If Alys was paying attention, no wonder she was laughing. Elliot fought his rampaging libido back down and tried to picture butterflies and flowers. They weren't working any better than fish.

"Think about a heartbeat," she suggested, massaging his temples.

How the hell was she reaching his temples? He didn't want to think about it. He was thinking about heartbeats—beneath an orange swimsuit with full breasts spilling over the top. "Heartbeat," he murmured agreeably.

"Just close your eyes and listen to the beat. It's slow, in time to the gentle drift of the butterfly wings, up and down."

Up and down—with her breathing. He could feel Alys breathing. He steadied, concentrating on matching his heartbeat to hers. "In and out," he murmured hoarsely. "Up and down."

"Back and forth?" she asked dryly, in not quite the same voice as earlier.

"Yeah, that, too." Grinning, realizing they were on

the same wavelength even when he wasn't telling her where his mind was, he continued picturing heartbeats and bobbing waters. He was beginning to like this boat.

"Relax now. Your little storm is over. No more up and down. Just peace, and a gentle wave, lifting, lowering, rocking ever so slightly. You're completely relaxed. Soft breezes caress your brow. You're warm, satiated."

Kind of hard to be satiated when he had a stiff one poking at his pants, but he liked the warm, soft breezes part. He should take up fishing—in warm waters. Or skinny-dipping. Now, there's an extracurricular activity he could enjoy. He could see Alys running into the waves, laughing, her bare breasts bobbing up and down, up and down.

"If you grin any wider, you'll crack your face."

The massaging fingers slapped his cheeks. Before he could come back from the Hawaiian lagoon and blue waters, agile fingers had his fly unzipped. She was good. She was real good.

She was even better when her lithe tongue stroked his straining erection.

He shouted something incomprehensible and grabbed her hair. Fighting the urge to just lie there and let it happen, Elliot flipped her over on her back, climbed on top, and hungrily attacked her mouth.

Alys instantly went slack, flinging her arms to either side and closing her mouth.

Elliot sat up and stared at her in confusion. "Why the hell did you stop?"

"Because I'm the one in control here." She tucked her hands behind her head and smiled up at him—an evil gamine messing with his mind.

He eyed her skeptically. "You won't be once I get

started." But he'd have to pry off her sweater and sweatshirt, then wiggle her out of her jeans. He didn't want an uncooperative woman.

"We're not getting started until you tell me I'm the one in command," she warned. "We're practicing relaxation techniques, and taking charge is not one of them."

"Yeah it is," he growled, flinging himself back down against the lousy mattress. "I feel a *lot* better when I'm in control."

"You feel a lot better after you've *lost* control," she reminded him. "Think about it, and tell me when you're ready to leave it to me."

She lay there beside him, looking up at the ceiling as if they weren't both raging out of control. Or he was, at least. He didn't think she was as calm as she looked— until she stretched and then consciously set her feet slightly apart, turned her palms upward at her sides, and took several deep breaths. He could swear he saw her visibly relaxing one part at a time, from shoulders down to toes. She had her eyes closed and didn't seem to notice when he leaned over her.

"What the hell are you doing?"

She didn't respond but continued taking even breaths, becoming one with the sagging, soft mattress. She looked so blissful, he was jealous.

He debated fastening his pants again and saying to hell with it. Maybe he could chop a few trees or jog to the highway and back. But he'd have to be a real stupid chump to give up when temptation lay right there at hand, just begging to be taken.

"Okay, you're right. I'm relaxed after I've lost control. But sex is not always available, so you're not teaching me anything useful." He lay back down and didn't look at her. She was probably already asleep.

"But giving up control *before* sex is new, isn't it?" She popped up as if she hadn't become one with the mattress. "Find your fishing boat," she commanded.

"Slave driver." But he did as she said, re-creating the mental image, except this time he gave himself a yacht and he was lying on a big air mattress on the deck.

And in this new picture she was massaging his chest. While kneeling over him.

"You are at one with the boat and the sea and the air," she told him.

He was at one with anything she told him as long as she was removing her jeans and sweater. Elliot peeked to be certain that's what she was doing. He didn't like surprises.

"You're peeking." She shimmied back into the sweater she was in the process of removing.

Elliot closed his eyes. "No I'm not." She'd straddled his legs but she still wore jeans, to his disappointment.

"I am the wind and the sun," she informed him. "You cannot command me. I will shine and make you warm, if you let me. Or I'll freeze you and blow you off course if you insist on taking over. Just lie there and let me take care of you."

He thought taking care of him might be the last thing she needed to be doing, but he could correct her impression another time. Right now, he really, really wanted whatever she thought she was doing. The day had left a bad taste in his mouth and a pain in his heart and he wanted her to make it all go away. If this was how she chose to do it, he could try.

"Very good," she said approvingly when he closed his eyes and attempted to relax.

After that, he just let it happen. He rocked on his yacht in his mind while she removed their clothing and massaged his chest. He sunbathed in her warmth even though the cabin was heated only by an old woodstove. He muffled a shout when her "wind" blew salt water over his arousal and brought him to the brink of climax.

But then she whispered, "I'm here," and sank down on him.

She was as wet and aroused as he was. Elliot grabbed her hips, positioned her where he could do the most good, and pumped into her until she cried out in the same frenetic ecstasy as he achieved.

In the aftermath, she tumbled on top of his chest, her silken hair brushing his chin, and he held her against him, letting their hearts slow to a matching rhythm.

"If I get any more relaxed, this ship will sail off into the sunset without a captain," he murmured.

"Good." Pulling the covers over them, Alys curled at his side, and they sailed off to the land of Nod.

❋ TWENTY-ONE ❋

Alys fastened the center seat belt of the old pickup around Lucia's waist and settled Purple into the child's lap. "Hold on to her, if you can, or we'll have to leave her here," she murmured. "We only have a few more hours to go."

"Yes, ma'am," Lucia piped. "Will we see Dulce?"

Still amazed to hear the child speak, Alys smiled down at her. "I certainly hope so. And your grandmother."

Elliot threw their luggage into the battered truck bed, protected by an old camper top. Purple's cage joined it, but Alys had overruled putting the kitten back there. She let Elliot tie the orchid near the back window, but the cat would be miserable in the cold.

The weather had already warmed up enough to melt the ice of yesterday. Another night of just the two of them in that cabin, and she would never strike out on her own.

Yesterday, Elliot had actually let her take charge. A medical doctor with a national reputation, and he'd listened to her silly relaxation techniques. And they'd worked! He hadn't rubbed his chest once since then. And they'd both slept like babies all night. After napping half the day. Maybe they'd both needed to unwind.

Of course, the kind of unwinding they'd practiced when they weren't sleeping might have a lot to do with it. Elliot had a fertile imagination once he indulged it. After his Hawaiian fantasy with her as a hula dancer and him as a surfing champion, she probably didn't have to ever bother visiting the islands. They'd never compare.

She'd never laughed so hard in her life. Which was why she had to leave him the instant they hit Albuquerque.

Watching him tuck Lucia's red backpack into the camper, Alys heaved a sigh and climbed into the cab. Lucia had her doll and her camera in the seat beside her. Alys hoped that was enough to keep her entertained for the morning. If she thought about the mundane, she wouldn't have to break her heart thinking about leaving all this behind. It wasn't as if she could spend her life riding around in a pickup with someone else's child and Doc Nice, after all. Life went on.

Elliot slid behind the wheel, and they all waved at Sam and Kaya as he backed the truck out of the drive. Sam had ordered one of his hired hands to follow them into Las Vegas to be safe, and the other truck fell in behind them as they rattled up the dirt road to the highway.

"We should check my voice mail once we have cell reception again. If Mame's been trying to reach us, she'll be worrying," Elliot said, hanging on to the bouncing steering wheel.

While Purple roamed from lap to lap and Lucia played with her doll, Alys checked the rearview mirror. The only other vehicle on the empty highway belonged to Sam's hired hand.

Last night had been moments outside of time. Today, they were back in the real world. "Maybe we should be worrying about Mame. Do you think the trucks have been following her? Should we call the police?"

"I want to talk to Mame first," he said grimly. "I think we might be missing a few details."

Knowing his aunt, he could very well be right. She didn't want to think Mame had actually *kidnapped* Lucia. She'd rather believe Lucia had been rescued. The authorities might not agree.

On the outskirts of the small New Mexican town of Las Vegas, Sam's employee beeped his horn and pulled into a parking lot. They waved farewell, and Alys checked the cell phone Elliot had slid into the slot where a tape player should have been. "We have reception. I don't know how to check your messages."

Kaya had fed them a huge farm breakfast even Elliot had eaten, so they didn't need to stop for food. But traveling with a child and a cat required rest rooms and exercise time. He pulled into a shopping center parking lot, and Alys snapped on Purple's leash while Elliot checked his voice mail.

"It's Mame!" He listened intently to his phone while Alys froze, watching his expression. "She's fine. She expected to meet us last night in Santa Fe. She's worried about us."

Alys waited, her stomach clenching as he frowned, continued listening, then snapped off the phone. "What? What else did she say?"

"She's on her way to Albuquerque." He glanced at Lucia, who watched him almost as intently as Alys. "Your aunt is anxious to see you."

Lucia brightened. "She said we will see great big balloons."

"Yes, lots and lots of them. So let's hurry." He
climbed from the truck and held out his arms for Lucia
and Purple.

Alys climbed down to follow them to a grassy area
where they let the kitten romp. Purple wasn't ecstatic
about the leash. "I don't see any purple cabs," she murmured for Elliot's ears alone, eyeing the parking lot.

"If the crooks are looking for Beulah, we've lost them
this time," he agreed. "I don't see how they can possibly
follow us now. That truck resembles every other truck in
the lot."

Alys glanced around, and he was right. One old
pickup looked like any other. Theirs had a camper on
top, but so did several others, all in the same battered
state of repair. It wouldn't be as comfortable as Beulah,
but it would be safer.

"We might want to keep Lucia out of sight, just in
case," he said in a low voice so the child couldn't hear.
"I'm trying to block the view, but there's only so much I
can do."

She hadn't realized he'd hidden Lucia between a stand
of trees and a Dumpster; anyone casually glancing from
the lot wouldn't know she was there. "We'll have to take
her in to the rest room."

Frowning, Elliot scanned the shops. "Let's take her
into the café instead of the store. I'll carry her and cover
her head with your hat. We're all dark-haired, so she's
not too noticeable, but let's not take chances."

He was behaving as if they had the Mafia after them,
but Alys figured she would do whatever it took not to

experience any more terrifying incidents. She'd wanted to experience life, not die of it.

Wearing his Stetson and boots, Elliot looked like half the other men out here, except tougher and leaner and more aware of his surroundings as he waited outside the rest room while Alys went in with Lucia. Only the kitten on its leash diminished his Clint Eastwood stance.

She was starting to adjust to this tough side of Doc Nice. She supposed truly bookish physicians didn't achieve what Elliot had achieved in such a short time. The man had grit and determination. And a bad heart, she reminded herself.

They emerged from the café with cookies and fruit drinks and returned to the truck. Purple settled on the floorboard to take a nap, and Alys crossed her legs in the seat to accommodate him. Placing her hands palm-up on her knees, she tried to locate her center while Elliot steered the truck out of the lot. Maybe she should change her mantra from *Love is the power that heals* to something involving *peace*. She desperately needed peace for her frantic heart. And they needed a peaceful ride to deliver Lucia to the reservation.

And *love* was a very dangerous topic. It was quite impossible to love someone after just six days, she told herself. But they'd spent those days living in each other's pockets, through stress and sex and beauty. They knew each other's idiosyncrasies by heart, right down to what they preferred to eat and why. It was possible.

It just wasn't probable or very smart to love another man who could check out on her far too soon, leaving her alone again.

For some reason, she had difficulty remembering Elliot was ill. He was too vital.

Deciding if he didn't want to think about his health, neither would she, Alys scanned the view out the windshield. "We really are in the mountains," she exclaimed as they drove onto the interstate.

Elliot hadn't asked her for the Route 66 directions. The time for side trips had passed.

"The colors aren't as spectacular as back East. You should see New England in October." He spoke with calm assurance but continued checking his mirrors as well as the traffic around him. She watched his jaw tense, and her nervous stomach performed a flip-flop.

Alys checked the side mirror. All she could see was interstate traffic. She watched Elliot, but he didn't look at her. "Do you see anything?" she asked, keeping her voice casual while digging around in the map bag she'd hung over the headrest.

"Can't tell for certain. The road's full of semis."

She glanced over her shoulder. It was almost impossible to see clearly through the pickup and camper windows. "Should I drive next?" The interstate signs indicated the Santa Fe exit ahead. She should have thought of driving earlier, but she'd had horrendous fears of attacks on snowy mountain roads and had willingly acknowledged Elliot's expertise.

"No." He didn't offer explanation.

The cell phone rang, and they both looked at it as if it someone had dropped a burning torch in their midst.

Alys grabbed it first. "Hello."

"Alys! Thank goodness. We've been worrying ourselves to death. Where are you? Is everything all right?"

"Mame! We're fine. We're just turning off the road into Santa Fe. Where are you? Can we meet you somewhere?"

Elliot stuck out his hand for the phone, but Alys refused to relinquish it. He needed to concentrate on driving.

"We're in Albuquerque, near Balloon Fiesta Park. I've found Jock. Dulce's frantic about Lucia. Could you put her on?"

Remembering the name from the conversation last night, Alys held the phone to Lucia's ear. "Your aunt wants to speak with you. Say hi."

She could tell Elliot was about to shoot the roof off again, but he had his hands full in the traffic at the bottom of the exit ramp. Mame sounded fine. If he could drive around without doctors and hospitals, so could his aunt.

Lucia listened carefully, brightened, and began to chatter cheerfully in Spanish. When she halted, Alys took the phone back. "Dulce?"

A soft contralto answered. "Yes, Mrs. Seagraves?"

"How is Mame? We're worried sick about her."

"She is resting. I think she is ready to go with you when you arrive. But we think it may be better if you meet us at the reservation."

"Why?" Alys could hear the concern in Dulce's voice, but they hit a patch of static and she couldn't ask more.

"It is not safe here," Dulce was saying when her voice came back in. "There may be . . . bad men looking for us. Mame thinks her friend Jock will take care of her, but I am calling my mother to take me to the reservation. It is not safe for Lucia until we know more. If you could keep her . . ."

"Tell us what's happening so we know what to do," Alys urged.

"We don't know for sure. Lucia's grandfather . . . we

think he has men looking for us. They know our car. We hid it last night . . ." Static drowned out the rest of the sentence. When she came back in again, she was saying, "If anyone recognizes Lucia . . ." More static. ". . . do not bring her just yet."

Alys bit her lip in frustration. The signal was growing weaker. "I think they've seen her," she yelled back. "I think they're following us. We're not—" She glared at the cell phone. "It's dead."

Elliot jerked the phone adapter from the cigarette lighter hole, rummaged around for the lighter, and plugged it in. "The lighter doesn't work. We weren't recharging the phone's batteries. I should have kept it plugged into Beulah."

Lucia swung her head back and forth, her braid flying, taking in every word that they spoke. Alys couldn't scream her frustration or cry her fear. "We don't even know how to reach them."

"Do we need to?"

She hated adding any more worries on his plate, but he had to know all that she did. "Eventually. Mame's with her old boyfriend and thinks all is fine."

"Boyfriend?" Elliot turned to stare.

Alys chose not to share and continued. "Dulce seems less certain. She's calling in her family." She smiled for Lucia's benefit. "Your aunt is planning a party. We need to give her a little time to call everyone."

How much time should they delay? What could Dulce and Mame be planning?

She and Mame had intended to take a walking tour of Santa Fe, but that wouldn't distract a child. Remembering the tourist attractions she'd just read about in the guidebook, she rummaged in the bag for it. "I know, we can see the children's museum! That will give them time to prepare a party."

"I don't think she has any idea what a museum is," Elliot said, checking the side-view mirror and steering into the traffic, evidently dismissing his earlier question for something of greater importance. "I'm going to get us a little turned around while you consult the map."

Alys glanced over her shoulder again, but it was still impossible to see out the back. Frustrated, she consulted the guidebook for an address and the map for a location, as if this were really just a pleasure outing. "The road off the interstate takes us right past the museum."

"Sorry about that." He swung the wheel hard to the right, into a residential neighborhood. "We're taking a side trip first."

She swallowed a gulp of fear and clutched the guidebook. "We need a compass. If we keep going north, we could see the old part of town." She was talking like a tourist while he was driving like a maniac. Denial was the better part of valor, she decided.

"I have an excellent sense of direction. Tell me if you see a good place to eat." With that, he took another quick turn and merged into a busy intersection with a heavy flow of traffic.

He wasn't eating Tums or rubbing his chest. Alys had to take that as a good sign. She had no other choice. Hospitals were out of the question if the bad guys were on their trail again.

❧ TWENTY-TWO ❧

"I'd give anything for my Rover right now," Elliot muttered, swinging the truck into the heavy traffic of a major Santa Fe artery, ignoring the assortment of semis barreling past. "I think I've lost them, but keep an eye out for a car rental agency and somewhere that might have a place to recharge the phone."

That sounded like an excellent idea to Alys. Just precisely what kind of men did Lucia's grandfather have on their trail if Lucia's aunt was afraid of them?

They located a car rental agency first. Telling Lucia to stay seated, Alys hopped down when Elliot climbed out.

"Are we still being followed?" she demanded.

"I don't know for certain. A semi with a purple cab fell in behind us in Las Vegas, but I haven't seen them since we took that little detour. I think we need a faster car, one where we can plug in the phone. I'll charge it up while I'm talking with the agent, and hopefully that will give us enough to check voice mail just in case Mame calls again."

He strode off, in full command of the situation, while Alys shook in her shoes. She cautiously glanced around for a semi, and seeing none, returned to the pickup.

Snapping on Purple's leash, she helped both the cat and Lucia out of the cab.

"Let's see if we can guess which car he'll choose," she told the child, gauging the lot behind the agency to be safer than the street.

Lucia didn't think this a strange occupation, and she happily danced along beside Alys, admiring the bright red of one car and her reflection in a shiny black SUV while Alys checked to see if they could be seen from the street.

She *hated* this. People had almost *killed* them yesterday. Those same people were still out there. Even having some suspicion of why they were being followed didn't ease her terror.

Had yesterday's drivers known Lucia was in the car? Or had they been told to stop them any way they could? Surely they had just been hoping to frighten them into pulling off the road.

Keeping a vigilant eye, Alys could see only a few sprawling shopping centers along this road. She didn't think they were big enough to get lost in. Santa Fe was too broad and open through this stretch. Maybe they needed to find an airport and just fly away.

She kept an eye on Elliot through the rental company's big picture window. He looked relaxed and confident as the clerk completed the paperwork. Would she have thought of renting another car?

No, because she didn't have that kind of money. Maybe Elliot's confidence came from having sufficient funds to pay for whatever he needed.

She tried again to think of a mantra that included "peace," but the only one she could summon under these conditions was *Give peace a chance*. That didn't

cut it. She might as well choose *Give peas a chance*. Or
Give pizza chants. She was getting hysterical again.

Both Lucia and Purple were straining at the bit by the
time Elliot loped out to the lot in search of them.

"I've called the number Sam gave us to tell him where
he can find his truck. The agent is pulling our car
around so we can load it up."

To Alys's surprise Elliot bent over and kissed her—
hard, right there in the lot where everyone could see.

As if he hadn't done anything unusual, he picked
up Lucia, tickled her, and started for the street. Alys
grabbed the kitten and followed, her lips still tingling
from the kiss. That hadn't been a kiss of lust, but one of
affection and appreciation. She could easily get used to
kisses like that. It had been a very long time since a man
had shown her affection, and her lonely heart clung to
the sentiment.

Elliot hadn't rented a shiny new SUV but a nonde-
script white Taurus sedan that barely held their suitcases. She couldn't imagine that it had any of the power
of Beulah, but it would certainly blend into traffic as
well as the old pickup. Better. And it had tinted windows.

"The museum's back through town." Elliot buckled
Lucia into a child's seat and handed her the backpack to
rummage through. "The cell won't charge while the car
is parked, so I'm leaving it plugged in here. We have to
come back this way when we head for the interstate anyway."

"How will we know when they're ready for us in Albuquerque?" Alys murmured, climbing into the front
passenger seat.

"I vote we leave here as soon as we're done in the museum. The way things have been working out, we could probably hide down there as easily as here." Elliot drew his hand through her hair, leaned in the car to kiss her nose, and shut the door.

The day wasn't hot, but Alys felt warm right down to her toes.

Feeling a little safer, she appreciatively sniffed the new-car smell and buckled up, checking on Lucia and the kitten in the backseat. With the cooler weather, Purple should be comfortable if they left her in here for a little while.

Elliot drove out of the lot. She'd quit fighting him for the keys. They would probably never see each other again after today, so the fight seemed pointless. She tried to imagine driving off into the sunset, seeing the sights on her own, but she couldn't quite wrap her mind around it. She had a whole future ahead of her to be alone. She might as well enjoy this moment. Opening the local map, she directed him to the road for the children's museum.

"We won't need that. Watch." Elliot pressed a few buttons on a small monitor fastened to the car's dash.

Alys watched in amazement as a street map appeared and a computerized voice announced, "Proceed to route and turn right."

"I rented a GPS," Elliot said in satisfaction. "Can't live without one."

"It's amazing! I wouldn't need a map anywhere." She studied the tiny computer as it flashed maps and talked them through Santa Fe, back to the highway they'd come in on. "I could be a traveling salesman with one of these!"

Elliot laughed and steered down the street from the

museum to locate a parking place. "You'd have to learn how to lie if you wanted to sell anything."

They filled Purple's water and food dishes and left her to explore the new car. Lucia carried her camera but was persuaded to leave her backpack behind. Alys knew Elliot was memorizing every vehicle around them as they walked through parking lots and alleys to the museum, staying out of sight as much as possible. His alertness frightened her. At the same time, his willingness to look out for them warmed her already mushy heart.

As they wandered through the museum, Alys continued to remind herself that Elliot would be gone tomorrow, that this was only a memory she could store away to bring out in the lonely nights ahead. Perhaps she ought to work in a restaurant in the evenings so she had lots of company and little time to be lonely.

He held her hand while they watched Lucia diligently design her own motif on a loom. She was a bright, active child who sparkled and chatted when she felt safe. The arrival of other children drove her back to watchful silence.

"I can't believe anyone would want to harm her," Alys murmured a while later as Lucia held back to watch a group of rowdy toddlers tumbling over the climbing structure.

"I'm not certain the drivers intend harm. From the sound of it, the old guy just wants his own way and will stoop to anything to get it. His drivers may be a little rough and out of control." Elliot stooped down beside Lucia and showed her how to aim the camera to catch a picture of a rabbit.

Fascinated but subdued, Lucia held his hand as they walked to the next area. *He's good with children,* Alys thought, then shook her head to get the thought out of it again. This was just a break from his usual routine. Driven men were not good with children.

Dead men were even worse with children.

Her mind unexpectedly rejected that equation. Mame had the same heart problem, and she was still living.

Her real problem was a fear of attachments that could so easily be torn apart by circumstances. Her head said she couldn't handle that kind of loss again.

The problem was that her heart knew no fear.

Walking the roundabout road back to the car after leaving the museum, Alys recognized the instant Elliot tensed again. Surreptitiously, she checked over her shoulder, but the sidewalk held numerous pedestrians, and without a purple truck, she didn't know what else to look for.

"Back to the car," he murmured, with a hand at the base of her spine, hurrying her toward a side street before he scooped up Lucia and followed.

Alys checked over her shoulder again. This time, she saw a surly-looking Hispanic man in a soiled baseball cap increasing his pace behind them. Across the street, she noticed an equally untouristy man in denim shirt, with a cell phone at his ear, cutting diagonally across the intersection.

Taking the lead, she dodged behind an office building and through a parking lot, knowing the way back to the car without taking the direct route. With Elliot on her heels, she hurried into a small restaurant, and ignoring the hostess at the door, led the way to the hallway with the rest rooms. These places were tiny and the floor plans obvious. The hallway also contained the exit to the loading alley behind the building. Alys aimed straight for it, not caring if the door set off alarms.

Fortunately, it didn't. Outside again, they raced down the back alley to the parking lot where they'd left the Taurus.

Alys buckled Lucia into the child seat while Elliot started the car. She fastened her seat belt as he pulled into the light traffic on the narrow street outside the historic district. His expression was grim as he hit the gas.

In moments, they were cruising the crowded streets of historic downtown Santa Fe. The narrow lanes were filled with tourists and difficult to negotiate with all the pedestrian closures, but a semi couldn't easily follow them.

Thinking they had to be safe, not wanting to believe those men had actually recognized them, Alys tried to imagine poking through the shops of designer clothes and artwork. She craned her neck to look up in awe at the Palace of the Governors as they drove by. The guidebook claimed it was one of the oldest public buildings in the country.

She might never see these ancient streets again. She'd like to experience them, but not at the cost of Lucia's safety. At least she now knew downtown Santa Fe didn't look like a cowboy Western.

They didn't immediately encounter any semis until they reached the main road. She couldn't always discern the color of the cabs drawing the trailers in front of them, but she thought she spotted a purple one at an intersection.

She was afraid to ask what Elliot saw as he drove around the city in the direction of the car rental company. She just clenched her hands in her lap and watched him dodge in and out of traffic with practiced ease and a determined expression. The little computerized guidance system went crazy trying to return them to the location he'd punched in earlier, then died into a sullen sulk. Alys turned the radio onto a classical station and did her best to generate positive vibes to soothe him.

When another purple cab loomed in the rear window, Elliot took a sharp left turn across traffic and zigzagged down residential side streets. Returning to a main highway, he abruptly bumped the car into a parking lot in a bustling shopping center, parking in between two hulking SUVs. Alys looked at him questioningly.

He snapped off the ignition and reached over the seat for Lucia's backpack. "Lucia has a bug on her somewhere."

"A bug?" Alys asked in alarm, hastily glancing at Lucia for some sight of an ugly flying cockroach. While Elliot rummaged through the backpack, she unfastened her seat belt and reached into the backseat to brush hair off of Lucia's face. The child merely looked surprised, not alarmed.

"A global positioning device, similar to the one we're renting. That's the only way they can keep finding us." He gave up sorting through the contents and dumped them on the seat beside Lucia. Still not seeing anything, he climbed out of the car and began ripping up the backpack.

A woman emerging from a nearby bookstore stared but didn't stop. A train whistled in preparation for leaving a tourist depot down the block.

"The thing on the dash?" Not totally understanding what he was talking about, Alys watched him examine the backpack seams.

"That 'thing' is a computer. There's a device inside it that beams up to a satellite and tracks our location so it can tell us where to turn. If there's one on Lucia, her grandfather would know exactly where she is at all times, just as the satellite knows where the car is and tells us where to turn."

Alys stared at him in disbelief, not knowing whether he'd lost his mind or if he was really serious. "That's ridiculous. Only rich people have things like that. Or cops maybe. Don't they stick them on luxury cars so they can locate them if they're stolen?"

"They can stick them anywhere they damned like. And if Lucia's grandfather owns a trucking company, he likely owns dozens of the devices." Satisfied there wasn't anything on the backpack, Elliot began examining Lucia's toys. "He could be sitting in his kitchen tracking our movements on a monitor, coordinating them with whichever of his drivers are nearby. He's only a phone call away. I might lose the nearest truck, but all Mendoza has to do is pick up the phone and tell the next guy where we are."

The scent of spicy tacos drifted from a nearby restaurant. Lucia hugged the doll Elliot had given her and retreated to a corner of the seat.

Alys couldn't think of any way that a computer could stick to books or dolls. She'd given Lucia a bath, and there hadn't been anything strapped to her body. She'd like to believe it was something mechanical that allowed their routes to be traced, and not coincidence or paranoia, but it seemed too much like a movie script. She'd lived too long in her own narrow world to believe the outside world had gone that crazy.

Just as Elliot searched the last piece of clothing, the same idea occurred to both of them.

"The camera!"

Alys dug the hot pink child's camera out of the console between the front seats and offered it to Elliot. He flipped it open, threw the film cartridge to Alys, and examined the camera's insides. With a curse, he snapped the back closed and glanced around.

The train rumbling out of the depot drew his attention, and his long face lit up as if a thousand-watt bulb had turned on inside his head. With the set expression of a man on a mission, he raced across the shopping center parking lot in the direction of the restaurant and train station, carrying the camera.

Alys watched in astonishment as Elliot jogged through gravel alongside the moving train until he came abreast of an empty open-air sightseeing car. With a powerful swing of his arm, he lobbed the camera onto the flatbed as the train rumbled down the track.

Alys wanted to scream in glee and pump her fists in the air in triumph. He'd done it! He'd thrown the bad guys off course and saved the day. She hoped.

Which meant they might only have a few more hours together.

He wasn't even breathing hard when he jogged back to the car and slid into the driver's seat. With satisfaction, he turned on the ignition and drove straight for the rental agency.

"I can't believe you did that," Alys whispered in awe. Over her shoulder to Lucia, she said, "We'll buy you another camera in Albuquerque. What color would you like?"

"Purple!" Lucia yelled with glee, apparently unfazed by the loss of her toy.

"It's all beginning to make a crazy kind of sense." Elliot checked the rearview mirror and the side streets they passed. "The trouble didn't begin until we picked up Lucia. Mame assumed Mendoza knew what she was driving, so she left Lucia with us, and hoped to lead the trucks on a wild-goose chase. She didn't know about the GPS. She thought they'd follow the Rover."

"Do you think they might be following her anyway? Just to cover all bases?"

Elliot winced and drove a little faster. "I think we'd better find out."

"Before grandpa figures out his thugs are following a train," Alys agreed.

Elliot hit the gas.

≋TWENTY-THREE≋

"Look!" Alys pointed at a group of motorcycles parked at a restaurant on the road leading out of Santa Fe after they'd picked up Elliot's phone. "I think that's the Harley club we met. Stop!"

Elliot glanced at her to see if she was insane, but she was unfastening her seat belt before he'd even applied his foot to the brake, obviously confident that he would follow her request. He wasn't certain he trusted Harley drivers any more than truck drivers right now, and traveling with a woman and child he had to protect, he was operating on paranoia mode. Still, he braked and turned the rental car into the parking lot.

At least Alys was wearing a sweatshirt and not one of her formfitting bodysuits. He really didn't want to have to pop any noses for smart remarks.

She ran ahead while he helped Lucia out of the child's seat, keeping an eye out for purple semis passing by. These roads out here were too sparsely traveled and open for him to feel comfortable.

As he entered the restaurant carrying Lucia, several of the bikers were shouting comments to Alys. The child retreated into her cocoon of silence while she studied the big, loud men, but Elliot was more immediately concerned about Alys. She had slipped into a booth next to a guy with a dragon covering his huge bare bicep and a scarf wrapped around his straggly brown hair. The two of them had their heads bent over a map.

Elliot suffered the unreasonable urge to strangle her, but he couldn't tell if that violence came from jealousy or fear. He didn't have much experience with either. He had been a reasonably fearless sort of guy until he'd taken on the responsibility of safeguarding an irresistible force.

He felt better when Alys saw him and bounced out of the seat to introduce Lucia to the gang, then lingered at his side as if she belonged there.

"Milo says they're about done here and heading for the Albuquerque leg of the trip. They've offered to follow along as insurance." Alys tweaked Lucia's nose and made her smile a little.

"Insurance?" Elliot asked warily, watching grown men with rings in their ears and gang colors on their leather jackets pay at the cashier's desk.

"I don't think I can tolerate one more sideswipe by a semi," she said flatly. "You may thrive on danger, but it scares the . . . heck . . . out of me."

That she saw him as a man who thrived on danger stifled any protest. He didn't believe he was any such thing, but he enjoyed knowing she did. Cautiously, Elliot studied Alys and the situation. She'd blown his mind last night, taught him things about himself he'd never known. He could learn to look at things from her perspective. If traveling with a motorcycle gang made her happy, then so be it. "I'm planning on traveling quickly," he warned.

Alys beamed. "Of course."

Milo, the man with the huge tattoo of a dragon, strolled

over to join them. "I know Mendoza, man. I used to drive for him."

Alys halted his words with a single glance. Taking Lucia from Elliot's arms, she set her down on the floor so the child could admire a red teddy bear on the counter, then stepped out of her hearing.

With a nod of approval, Milo continued in a low voice. "Mendoza used to work with a lot of his drivers before he bought the company. He pays them well and they owe him a lot of loyalty. He hires only the toughest men around. Some of those guys would rob banks if he asked it of them. All he's got to tell them is that you kidnapped his kid, and they'd beat the brains out of anyone between them and her. He didn't get where he is by being crossed."

Elliot squeezed Alys's shoulder at her look of alarm. "Thanks. It's good to know what we're up against."

With a curt nod, Milo strutted over to the counter to pay his bill. A moment later, he carried a curly-haired red teddy bear to Lucia. Lucia looked at it longingly, glanced up to Elliot, and seeing his smile of approval, eagerly grabbed for the toy.

"She belongs with people who love her," Milo said. Without another word of explanation, he swung on the heels of his heavy leather boots and sauntered out of the restaurant, his graying ponytail swinging.

"They're good guys," Alys whispered, catching Elliot's arm and tugging him out the door after them.

It was a damned good thing patience was one of his virtues, Elliot decided, heading back for the car. He now not only had to look after a fey female, an orchid, a kitten, and a five-year-old, but he had to do it with the escort of a dozen Harley-riding geezers while watching out for dangerous semi drivers. Life was a circus—or life since Alys had become a circus. The three-ring kind.

Pulling out of the parking lot with open highway ahead, Elliot wished he was driving something with more power than the Taurus so they could reach Albuquerque before Mendoza's thugs discovered the location of the GPS device. The roar of the motorcycles around them didn't give him the assurance it apparently gave Alys.

When he'd picked up his phone and voice mail, Mame had left only a message giving the room number of the hotel where they had reservations. He wouldn't be happy until he had Mame in the hospital and Lucia safely back with her aunt.

He deliberately blotted out any thought of what would happen between Alys and him then.

Half the motorcycles formed a phalanx in front of them. The other half formed a rear guard. Elliot thought they should have bought balloons and hung them out the window and called it a parade.

He watched a semi with a purple cab roar past and wondered if they could be any more conspicuous.

"The Balloon Fiesta Park is right off the interstate." Retreating to the security of her old-fashioned maps, Alys pored over their directions while Lucia napped in the backseat, hugging her new teddy bear.

Elliot tried to close himself up in the little box he'd created years ago, the one that allowed him to concentrate on the path he'd set for himself. He'd written books, attained a medical degree, become a successful talk-show host, and created effective research groups by shutting out his surroundings and all distractions.

Like a life.

He'd had life in abundance in the last six days, and he was kind of getting used to it. But the walls of his new box required that he see to it that Alys and Lucia and Mame lived long and productive lives—lives that didn't necessarily include him.

But Alys was too flexible to form much of a wall. Even in sweatshirts instead of halter tops, she held the power to distract him just by breathing. He could sense her fear and worry. If he indulged in too much thought, he'd believe he could build on the attraction and affection tentatively binding them.

So he'd rather not think about Alys at all. Don his blinders, focus on one task at a time, and think about anything but Alys.

"We need to take Lucia to the reservation first," he stated carefully.

Elliot was certain Alys cringed. She'd grown as attached to the child as he was, but she didn't argue. Stoically, she returned to poring over their maps. "We'll have to drive all the way through town," she informed him, apparently locating the reservation that Mame had described.

She had spent years learning how to handle loss. Elliot wasn't certain he had her ability to accept it. "No problem," he replied, trying to sound confident. "Our original instructions were to drive to the tribal headquarters. One assumes they have police there and someone who will know how to reach her family."

"Or Sam Wolf may have already found a way to call and tell them to expect her arrival." Alys nodded in approval of his plan. "We'll just hope the other guys are chasing a train into the mountains and won't expect her to be heading this way yet. Or that Milo and his friends scare them off."

"Exactly."

He hated leaving the kid without knowing what terrors lurked around the corner, but he had no authority or expertise in protecting children. One thing at a time, he reminded himself. Get Lucia to safety. Find Mame. Finish book. Do radio show. Get a life.

He could see Alys straining to memorize the sights as they drove the interstate into the city. He'd been in Albuquerque, knew there was far more to it than the commercial districts seen from the highway, but their little vacation had just reached its end. Once he had Mame, Alys would have to explore the old town on her own. He refused to wax sentimental on the fun they could have had exploring it together—or the fun they could have had if she became a permanent part of his life.

She'd had enough of permanence. Hadn't she made that clear when she'd tried to leave him at the hospital? Hospitals and death terrified her, and one way or another, they were all he knew. She needed sunshine and freedom.

But the quick looks Alys darted the sleeping child in back, and the way she tilted her head down so a shiny curtain of hair hid her expression, broke his heart. He longed to give her what she wanted, not take it away.

The motorcycles broke formation in the city traffic, some drifting to left and right, slowing at entrance ramps, guarding against intruders. At least with all the traffic around him, Elliot didn't feel quite as conspicuous. The damned purple semis seemed to be everywhere. Fortunately, none of them slowed to notice the child in the backseat, even if they could see through the tinted windows. Without the pink Cadillac, they were nearly invisible.

On the other side of the city, the countryside returned to sagebrush and rocks, interspersed with billboards for casinos. The reservation where Lucia's family lived wasn't on the GPS, but Mame had written explicit directions. Elliot took the exit indicated and followed the road to a turnoff. The motorcycles halted at the sign pointing toward the tribal lands.

Relieved that they'd arrived safely without encountering any more dangerous big rigs, Elliot halted the car and got out. Milo rolled his bike forward to meet him.

"We'll let you folks go on from here. Don't reckon the natives will appreciate us riding down on them, and they can look out for their own."

Elliot held out his hand and shook Milo's. "If you're heading back into Albuquerque, go over to the balloon park for the lighting. We know some people there. Maybe we can help you snag a balloon ride."

Milo tipped a hand to his forehead. "Will do that. You got a nice lady there. You take care of her or someone else will."

Elliot watched them roar off before returning to the car. Out of habit, he rubbed his chest, but the pain there had nothing to do with heartburn. It had to do with thinking of Alys with anyone else but him.

Unable to contemplate the emptiness her absence would cause, Elliot climbed back into the car. Alys sent him a questioning glance, but he merely turned on the ignition and drove up the road to the reservation.

No purple cabs followed.

"We didn't buy a camera," Alys whispered.

"We'll come back later, after we find Mame," he assured her. He could keep Alys around a little longer that way. He could add "buy camera" to his list of tasks.

Apparently pleased with his answer since it meant they could visit Lucia again, she turned to study the modern structure ahead bearing a sign announcing it as the reservation's headquarters. Elliot sighed in relief that they were taking the child somewhere safe. He didn't know what he'd envisioned, but this hadn't been it.

"Have you ever been here, Lucia?" Alys asked, unfastening her seat belt as Elliot turned off the car.

Wide-eyed, Lucia shook her head negatively.

"Well, they should know how to find your aunt Dulce. Let's go see, okay?" Alys climbed out of the front seat, opened the back door, and held out her arms.

Elliot admired the way she knew precisely what to say to reassure the frightened child. Holding the kitten and her teddy bear, Lucia allowed herself to be lifted from the car and set on her feet outside the strange building.

Elliot figured he was going to miss the cat as well as the kid, but that was another of those things that belonged outside his box. He'd never allowed himself to miss his brothers or Mame or anyplace he called home. They were irrelevant to his purposes.

His purposes might be wavering these days, but his means of achieving them hadn't. Carrying Lucia's backpack, he fell in step behind Alys and Lucia. The child clung to the kitten with one hand and Alys with the other, staring at the official-looking building with fear.

He didn't know what kind of places the kid had been living in lately, but he hoped this one had people who would love her. Elliot prayed Dulce was a responsible caretaker.

The heavy metal door opened and a slender, black-haired young woman flew down the walk, crying Lucia's name and holding out her arms. With a whoop of joy, Lucia ran into them.

"Well, guess that answers one question," Elliot said, coming to a halt beside Alys. He ignored the twinge of his heart at the sight of the two hugging and crying and talking in three languages at once.

"Dulce is young," Alys replied, watching the pair through worried eyes. "But I suppose with a large family they'll have some sort of support."

Had he imagined the wistfulness in her voice? Alys had never expressed any desire for a large family. She'd barely had any family at all. She'd said she wanted to learn to live alone.

He wanted to change her mind, but he didn't dare.

A sturdily built young man approached, and Elliot stepped up to shake his hand while Alys joined Dulce and Lucia.

"I am Tony, Lucia's uncle. The family thanks you for delivering her safely."

"I can't guarantee that she's safe," Elliot warned him, handing over the backpack. "I think we've thrown them off track, but someone has been following us ever since we picked her up."

Tony nodded. "Salvador has been on the phone in a foaming rage. The law has been out looking for her. But we have a court order. There's nothing he can do now except take it to the judge. He had hoped to get her back in his jurisdiction, where he owns the law and we could not touch her."

"I'm glad she's with someone who cares for her." Elliot produced the film he'd taken from the camera. "She had a camera with a satellite-tracking device in it. I threw the camera on a train going north. If her grandfather has any other tricks up his sleeve, I don't know about them."

"Our police have been warned. Now that she is safely here, you should have no more trouble."

He wanted to believe that. He watched Alys speaking excitedly with Dulce, her hands flying in time with her words. He wanted to give Alys some time in Albuquerque, show her the sights. If it hurt this much leaving Lucia behind, to hell with his box. He needed more time outside of it.

"Why would a man who doesn't seem to like Lucia very much go to this much trouble to keep her?" he asked, trying to think of anything but the emotional scene before him.

Tony shrugged. "He hates losing, and he hates giving up what he considers his. Lucia's father was his only son. Maybe he thinks he can raise her to be the person his son wasn't."

Elliot disliked the sound of that. He definitely wanted to come back and check on the child. "I owe her a camera. May we return tomorrow?"

"You and Ms. Seagraves will always be welcome here." Tony held out his hand.

Elliot shook it. One task done. Mame next. One step at a time. Pretty soon he'd be back where he should be. He dropped his arm around Alys's shoulder and gently pulled her away from her animated conversation. "The Balloon Fiesta, remember? The lighting will take place shortly."

Alys hugged Dulce, kissed Lucia, shook Purple's paw,

exchanged hurried phone numbers—using his cell phone for hers—and backed off with tears in her eyes.

Elliot pretended not to see the tears. His heart hurt in too many places as it was. It hurt worse when Lucia waved her little hand and called *adios* after them, even though there was a huge smile on her face.

"What will you do when we find Mame?" Alys whispered as they drove down the road.

He had been putting off thinking about it. "Find Mame" had been his goal for so long that he'd resisted going beyond that particular wall. "Ask her to go home with me."

"And if she won't?"

With a sigh, he answered, "Sit around and keep an eye on her until she's ready to go, I guess. She'll come around eventually."

"What about your deadlines? And the radio show?" She watched him with open curiosity.

"The book and my notes are in my laptop. I can work on it in a hotel room. Don't know about the show. I took the week off for the book tour and was supposed to return on Sunday. May have to call in and ask that they replay an old show. I can't leave her here alone."

"She's with someone," Alys reminded him. "A man named Jock."

"Yeah, well, we'll see about that when we get there." Setting his jaw, Elliot steered into the heavy interstate traffic heading into the city. At least there weren't any purple semis tailing them. Or anyone else, as far as he could tell.

Alys subsided into silence. Out of the corner of his eye he caught her surreptitiously wiping her eyes, but she picked up the map and shook it out and did her best to look interested.

"We'll check on Lucia tomorrow when we deliver the camera," he reassured her. "She'll be fine now that she's with family."

She sent him a watery smile. "I know. I miss Purple. Maybe I should work in a pet store."

"Or a plant store. You still have the orchid." He nodded at the backseat where she'd carefully buckled in the pot so it could get sun without tipping over.

"I need to mist it again. It's horribly dry out here."

"You'll need to work in a day care, a greenhouse, and a pet store to satisfy all your nurturing urges. How are you on skipping sleep?"

She glanced at him warily, crossed her legs in the seat, and sank into the lotus position. A smooth dark curve of hair concealed her face. "Maybe I should be a doctor so I can sit in an office and write books and never see people. Do you get lots of sleep?"

Elliot winced at the direct shot. He supposed it was only fair. He'd been shooting down her dreams all week. "I can help more people with my books than by seeing one person at a time."

"Not necessarily." She shrugged. "From my experience, medicine might treat symptoms, but for true healing, people need human beings to listen to them. Body and soul are all one—until we're dead, at least." She shifted from her yoga position and brushed a short strand of hair from her eyes, but she didn't look at him.

"Chicken soup for the soul," he said scornfully.

"Chocolate truffles for the soul. Chicken soup is good for bodies but my soul craves decadence." She flipped on the radio and began singing about docks and bays.

What had he been thinking? She needed someone arty who could relate to her crazy way of thinking. Maybe a musician who could teach her to sing. Or some New Age guru with crystals around his neck. They had absolutely nothing in common.

Except he enjoyed her company, insane as it might be.

And somehow, she had saved his life just holding his hand.

"I need to call them, Jock." Standing in a sea of boldly colored, rippling nylon, Mame glanced nervously back to the parking lot. She should have learned how to use a cell phone—then bought one.

The burly man tugging the maroon-and-gold nylon across his allotted piece of the field shook his shaggy gray head. "It won't do a bit of good, Mame. They already know that something ain't right. You can't tell them anything different."

"I can tell Elliot about his car." Although, come to think of it, she'd rather not.

"You can tell them when they get here. If you're crewing for me, you need to get to work, hon. Your nephew isn't a dummy. He'll keep his eyes open." Eyeing the layout of the nylon, he returned to the basket to recheck the tie lines. "Set the fan in position. We're ready to roll."

Mame loved the excitement of watching the big balloons fill with air. All around them other crews were in various stages of the process, spreading out the nylon, securing tie lines, switching on the huge fans to start inflation. She'd anticipated this moment for months—this was what living was all about.

But Elliot and Alys could be driving straight into trouble if she didn't warn them.

Dulce had taken dirt roads Salvador's purple trucks couldn't touch. They had thought they'd led him off Lucia's trail, keeping Elliot and Alys safe.

But when they'd arrived in Albuquerque, someone had slashed the tires on the Rover. Whoever had done it was still out there. Jock had called the police, who'd blamed vandals. Mame wasn't quite so certain.

If Salvador's men had followed her, they knew the hotel where she was staying. They'd see Elliot and Alys when they arrived.

She rubbed her chest and searched the crowd in hopes of seeing Elliot's tall frame or Alys's shorter one safely hurrying toward them, and she prayed.

❈TWENTY-FOUR❈

"Why did she choose a hotel way down here by Old Town if the park is out on the north end?" Fighting the remnants of rush-hour traffic and cursing as he missed a turn, Elliot stopped at a traffic light in the narrow, busy streets near the historic district of downtown Albuquerque.

"Because Route 66 runs through here," Alys explained. "And probably because the hotels out there were already booked. The city apparently fills up a year in advance for the festival." She studied her city map, checked the GPS, and spotted the hotel before Elliot did. "Over there. It's nearer the Convention Center than Old Town. I don't think Mame really wanted to revisit the old motels. She's picked the fanciest places she could find."

Turning around at the light, Elliot pulled the unremarkable Taurus up to the hotel door and popped the trunk so the valets could unload it.

Feeling much too scruffy to enter a fancy hotel, Alys brushed a few loose bits of rainbow glitter from her hand-decorated forest-green sweatshirt, glad her black Keds were at least clean, and she hadn't split any seams on her leggings. Had she known she was supposed to be a fashion plate, she would have packed differently.

She'd known they'd booked a Hyatt and hadn't worried about it when she thought she was traveling with Mame. When had she become concerned about how she looked?

The night she'd gone to bed with Elliot. The night she'd come back to the world of the living. In these last years of grief, she'd forgotten that the real world noticed uncombed hair and strange clothes and people who sang to themselves in grocery stores. She'd been living inside herself for too long.

She'd probably driven Elliot crazy this past week. It was a miracle he hadn't left her behind somewhere along the way.

No it wasn't. He liked going to bed with her. He probably figured putting up with her eccentricity was a fair price to pay.

If she had any sense at all, she'd continue to tell herself he was that shallow. Maybe if she thought it often enough, she'd even start to believe it. Except the path to noncommitment required a negative outlook, and who could criticize a man like Elliot?

He stood there patiently on the sidewalk, wearing a fresh blue chambray shirt and the Stetson and cowboy boots she'd made him buy, looking like a movie version of every romance novel she'd ever read, while she dallied with maps and books and an astonishing nosedive in self-esteem.

He didn't look as if he was ashamed to be with her. He looked as if he was contemplating what kind of bed they would share next.

She could live with that. She shouldn't, but she could. For now. Popping out of the front seat with a handful of guidebooks and her purse, she smiled up at him. "How's the heartburn?"

His eyes were grave as he looked down at her. "Your positive vibrations apparently help."

He was teasing of course, but that worked, too. She was enormously nervous for some reason. "Do you think Mame is inside?"

"No, I think she's out at the park. It takes time to set up the balloons. If we hurry, we may get there before dusk when they light them." He caught her elbow and directed her into the magnificent marble lobby with its palm trees and fountains and acres of seating.

Alys wanted to step back in awe and admire, but accustomed to such luxury, Elliot hurried her up to the desk while the valet followed with a luggage rack of their suitcases. Alys understood his hurry. They'd been worrying over Mame for a week. He needed to see his aunt and make certain she was all right.

And then what? Lucia was safe. Mame was out playing and could make up her own mind what she wanted to do about her health. Elliot intended to stay and monitor his aunt. Where did that leave her?

Mame had told her that she had the attitude of a California native. She had enough cash left to go on. Not in this style, perhaps, but by bus or maybe an economy rental car if she bought groceries and didn't eat in restaurants. She had the guidebooks. She wished they'd offer a guide to her future, which was beginning to look terrifyingly empty.

Room card in hand, Elliot caught her elbow and steered her out of her daydream. The valet led them through the maze to the elevators. What on earth had Mame been thinking when she'd booked a luxury hotel?

She'd probably been thinking she'd meet that Jock person here. Whoops. They could be walking in on a lovers' tryst. "Is the room in your name or Mame's?" Alys whispered as the elevator zoomed upward.

"She asked for adjoining rooms after she got here." He raised a questioning eyebrow. "Do you want to share hers or mine?"

That was putting it bluntly. Name that tune. Pick a relationship. Alys wrinkled her nose and shook her head. "Don't get any ideas, but I think Mame has a boyfriend and we ought to leave her alone."

"Right."

His flat reply didn't sound promising, but he had a lot on his mind. Like maybe how to get rid of an eccentric nuisance when he was tired of her?

She thought it had been pretty plain from the start that they'd both be going their separate ways once they found Mame. It was just a matter of logistics after this. She'd have to make certain Mame told her about any tests or operations so she could be there for her. Elliot wasn't responsible for her any longer. And she wasn't responsible for him. She could keep giving him positive vibrations and hope he stayed well enough to look after Mame. Only it would have to be by long distance.

The room they entered wasn't a suite, but it had a bed bigger than some of the rooms they'd shared. She could happily live in a room like this. It had a couch and chair and desk. What more could she ask for?

Elliot knocked on the door into the next room. No one answered. He rattled the knob, but it was locked.

"Just let me hit the bathroom and I'll be ready." Avoiding prolonged looks at that massive mattress, Alys dashed in to use the toilet, then stopped at the vanity to check her hair. She desperately needed a brush. When had she quit using cosmetics? Did she have time to rummage in her suitcase and find a brush and powder?

Elliot had already discarded his hat and traded his boots for expensive leather walking shoes. He wore his jacket over jeans, but the jeans were his only concession to the man she'd known these last few days. He'd be pulling out his computer and cell phone shortly if she didn't hurry.

To her surprise, he was watching the television news.

"There seems to have been a riot at a tourist train depot in the mountains," he said dryly, watching the pictures flash across the screen. "The reports aren't clear, but apparently a number of semis blocked off the depot while the drivers terrorized an entire car of tourists. They've arrested a couple of truckers for unauthorized entry and vandalism."

Openmouthed, Alys stared at the TV, but the announcers had moved on to another story. "You think . . . ?"

"Yeah, I think. Which means Lucia's grandfather knows we've escaped his little net." He glanced at her, but his eyes didn't light with their usual approval.

She uneasily wiggled her shoulders beneath her cheap sweatshirt. "Well, Lucia's safe, so he can't do anything about it. I'm not dressed for this, am I? I can probably find a jacket in my suitcase. Should I look for it?" Alys grabbed her brush from her bag and ran it through her hair.

"I like your elfin look. Come on, let's find the balloon lighting." Not looking at the big bed any more than she did, Elliot held the door for her.

Elfin look? A little stunned by that description when her head had been on a different plane, Alys hurried to keep up with Elliot's long stride down the corridor. "Balloon Glow, that's what the brochure says."

"Fancier name for it. You'll enjoy it." He hit the elevator button.

After consulting with the concierge, Elliot decided to take a taxi rather than attempt parking this late in the day.

Deliberately shutting out all thought except that of fun, she sat forward in the taxi seat to look out the windshield. She'd spent months anticipating Albuquerque and the Balloon Fiesta, and she intended to experience it all. How close would they have to be to see the balloons?

"Have you ever ridden in a balloon?" she asked, spotting one floating toward the mountains in the distance.

"I've crewed with Mame and her friends. It's fun."

Alys stared at him. "You've crewed? You can fly a balloon? When did you find time?"

Amusement softened his chocolate eyes. "I haven't spent my entire life in a library. My brothers and I have all helped Mame with her various interests over the years. We've not flown here, but around St. Louis. The crew doesn't fly the balloon. The pilot does. But my brothers and I all know the mechanics of it."

"Wow!" Following the path of the golden balloon floating toward the sunset, Alys tried to imagine flying one, tried to imagine *Elliot* flying one, and couldn't. "That has to be the perfect way to relax and escape stress."

Elliot laughed aloud. "You have a lot to learn about ballooning."

"It's not competitive," she protested. "You just float along on the breeze and enjoy the scenery."

"It can be highly competitive and highly skilled and a lot of hard work," he corrected. "Mame *races* balloons."

Alys glanced at him in alarm. "She won't be going up there and racing, will she?" She'd had no idea this was what Mame had in mind. She'd thought they'd come to enjoy the sights and get a free balloon ride. While she'd been doing her daydreaming, Mame had been off on her own trip. She should have known that, but she'd been a little self-absorbed. Her alarm heightened. "What if she has another attack when she's up there?"

"*That's* why I'm out here." He took the hand she offered and squeezed.

It would have been nice if he'd told her all this before they left Springfield—but then, she hadn't asked. Maybe she'd taken her self-protective state a shade too far.

The taxi let them out as near to the front gate as possible. While Elliot paid the driver, Alys stared in awe at the enormous balloons slowly inflating across the park. She saw balloons resembling Snoopy and a cat and a beer can, beautifully colored balloons with advertising logos, artistically designed balloons, and ordinary ones in bright yellows and blues and reds. Stripes and patchworks and zigzags filled the enormous blue sky. With the backdrop of mountains, the spectacle was awe-inspiring.

Openly gaping, Alys let Elliot check with attendants for directions. She simply followed him as he wended his way past balloons in various stages of inflation. Some were still lying on the ground while their crews struggled to fill acres of nylon with giant fans. Other crews had turned on their burners and the heating air was unfolding the colorful envelopes and lifting them skyward.

"How will you find her?" she murmured, clinging to Elliot's arm so she could watch the sky rather than where she was walking.

"The only Jock I can remember is Jock Morton. I just checked and if she's crewing with him, he's number fifty-three and is flying for some race-car driver with the colors of maroon and gold. His space should be to the north of the field." He pointed toward the mountains.

Controlled chaos surrounded them. Burners roared, fans blew, people ran to and fro locating equipment, or just kibitzing. But every person seemed to know their duty as they tied guidelines, ran cable, and kept the area clear while the huge balloons drifted upward one by one, grounded only by a network of cables. Other crews still held on to the lightweight wicker baskets, weighing them to the ground while their balloons filled.

"This is better than walking through Candyland," Alys marveled, swiveling to watch a fiercely painted sunset rise over her head.

"It does seem to suit you," he replied with amusement. "I think I see the colors over there. C'mon, let's find Mame."

Bubbling with excitement, Alys located the balloon with the race-car driver's colors and number and ran in that direction.

"Mame!" she cried, spotting a familiar crop of red curls on a tall, slender woman in navy slacks, wearing a maroon nylon jacket against the evening breeze.

Whirling, Mame saw them coming. Running toward them, she held out her arms. Alys thought she looked healthier than she had been in the hospital.

"Thank goodness!" Mame hugged Alys and reached for Elliot, who gave her a grave hug while she chattered excitedly. "I've been worried sick about you. How's Lucia? Did you find Dulce?"

"They're fine, Mame. We just left Lucia in her aunt's hands." Elliot looked up as a burly man with his graying fringe of hair tied back in a short ponytail left his balloon to head their way.

"Elliot, Alys, this is Jock Morton, an old friend of mine. Jock, you've met my nephew and . . ." She tilted her head with a mischievous smile at Alys. "And this is a special friend of ours. You're looking happier than I've seen you in a while, Alys."

"You're looking stronger than I saw you last," she retorted, gazing from Mame to Jock. The two seemed quite comfortable with each other. And very friendly. Jock had draped one muscled arm over Mame's thin shoulders.

He offered his hand to Elliot. "Glad you made it safely. After seeing what they did to your car, we were worried. I've been keeping Mame close, just in case."

"Seeing what who did to what car?" Elliot demanded. "And in case of what?"

Mame grimaced. "Maybe we should explain later. We thought you'd see—"

Holding Mame at his side, Jock overrode her hesitancy. "Someone slashed the Rover's tires out in the lot so she couldn't go back to the hotel. Maybe it was just vandals, but we can't be sure."

Alarmed, Alys glanced at their grim faces, then to the crowds of people around them. She didn't even know who or what to look for. Everyone here was a stranger.

"When, Mame?" Elliot asked with unnerving calm. "Have you called the police?"

"This morning," she said defensively. "It could have been vandals. And of course I called the police."

"Have you seen any purple semi cabs around here?" Elliot demanded.

"I'm not a simpleton, Elliot. Salvador saw the Rover, that's why we left Lucia with you. I'm pretty sure we led him astray after that. But surely he knows that one way or another we would take Lucia to the reservation. He has no reason to follow any of us now that she's safe. It has to be vandals."

Alys felt the tension in Elliot's arm, knew he was working into a major uproar, and she had no power to stop him. She didn't even know what he was planning that needed to be stopped.

"I'm not putting up with one more day of this. You're both going home, where it's safe. I'll call a taxi." Wrapping his big hands around Mame's and Alys's arms, Elliot tugged them in the direction he wanted to go.

Neither of them budged.

"I'm not spending my life living in fear, Elliot," Mame admonished. "I can be mugged by vandals, die of a heart attack, or be run over by a bus tomorrow. Today, I'm with Jock and having the time of my life."

"Salvador's thugs nearly ran us off the road," he roared. "They tore up a train station in the mountains. If they know where we are, they could kill you out of sheer meanness!"

"You can't hide us forever, Elliot," Alys said, not bothering to disengage his hand. "Besides, you're over-reacting. He has no reason to interfere now."

The roar of a dozen motorcycles entering the parking area interrupted any tirade that might have followed. Jock stopped to fasten a guideline that had loosened as the balloon inflated. Watching him, Mame only turned to the noise after Alys and Elliot did.

"Friends of yours?" she asked as the motorcycles ignored parking limitations and scattered wherever the spirit took them. "That one seems to have found you."

Milo propped his bike near the roped-off area, waved in their direction, and instead of removing his helmet and gloves, jogged clumsily toward them.

To Alys's surprise, Elliot started forward to greet him. Not certain this boded well, she hurried to catch up—in time to hear Milo yell, "There's a convoy of Mendoza semis turning off the interstate, barreling in this direction."

His voice was nearly drowned out by the thunder of big rigs speeding down the access road. Alys watched in horror as they began blocking off all available exits.

Around them, everyone halted what they were doing to stare.

Elliot didn't wait to see what they wanted. "Get Mame into the balloon," he shouted to Jock, grabbing Alys as he raced toward the balloon.

Before she knew what he intended, Elliot lifted her into the basket, yelled "Stay down," and began releasing the guide wires.

Lacking horses, the cowboy intended to rescue them with the next best means of transportation.

❄ TWENTY-FIVE ❄

The blast of a shotgun in the crowd was the worst noise Elliot had ever heard, but the image of Mame slowly crumpling to the ground before anyone could reach her nearly stopped his heart.

Losing hope of sending Alys and Mame safely into the air, Elliot dropped the guide wire he was untying and ran to his unconscious aunt. He fell to his knees beside her to ascertain if she was still breathing. Once satisfied she was alive, he practiced Alys's breathing technique to smother his alarm and began a systematic search for bullet wounds.

Bellowing curses, Jock tripped over guide wires and crashed through the gathering mob to reach Mame. People scattered in all directions, some diving for cover, others fleeing for the parking lot.

The balloon crew crushed together in a protective circle around Mame's fallen figure. Behind them, Elliot could hear Milo and his gang hurling curses and shouting threats as they closed in on the man with a shotgun attempting to escape through the crowd.

He didn't even have to look up to know when the shooter's fellow drivers muscled their way through to rescue him. The roar as a melee of flying fists broke out between the bikers and truckers warned of the ensuing brawl.

Despite his concern for Mame's unconscious state, Elliot turned to warn Jock about the loose guide wires. As he started to speak, another terrifying cry rose over the roar of the brawl.

"El-l-lio-o-t!"

He swung in time to see the hot-air-filled maroon balloon starting to rise. No one had turned off the heat. It tugged on the loosened guide ropes—while Alys scrambled to climb over the high wall of the basket.

On the ground lay the woman who had taught Elliot all he knew about life and love.

Behind him, Alys fell back into the basket as the balloon tilted dangerously under the force of its abandoned burners. Another guide wire tore from its mooring with the movement. She'd break her neck if she jumped now.

Elliot's life ripped right down the middle.

In the distance, he could hear the wail of a siren. The fistfight had escalated into pandemonium. No one seemed to notice the balloon except him.

He couldn't let Alys go.

With a shout of warning and a prayer for Mame, he leaped toward the basket rising skyward.

At his abrupt leap, the crew finally woke to the danger. While some stayed to guard Jock and Mame, others raced for the loosened ropes—but with a full head of air, the balloon couldn't be halted.

Catching the gondola's rim, Elliot vaulted inside to turn down the burner.

Too late. The balloon had already gained sufficient momentum. The final wire tore loose of its mooring and the basket lifted skyward.

Thrown off balance by the abrupt jerk to freedom, Alys threw her arms around Elliot and hung on. Elliot circled her shoulders and glanced downward. Jock was with Mame. Ambulance attendants were racing through the crowd with a stretcher. It looked as if Milo was sitting on top of the shotgun-toting truck driver while the rest of the drivers and bikers fought it out.

And he was up here, high above them. With Alys. And with no power whatsoever over what was happening below.

He could turn off the burners and let the balloon down, but it would be risky in that crowd.

Alys was shaking so hard that he had to help her sit down. Ascertaining the direction of the wind and the clear expanse of airway ahead of them, he dropped down beside her and hauled her into his arms. She buried her face in his shoulder and shuddered with the force of her sobs. He wanted to cry with her, but he'd forgotten how.

It helped to let her do it for him. It was as if she were his other half, expressing the fear and sorrow exploding inside his chest. He was terrified he'd lost Mame this time, but holding Alys, knowing she was alive and well and needed him, kept him grounded.

"It's okay, we're safe," he reminded her, cupping her face with his hand, feeling her tears on his fingers. "The ambulance will take Mame to the hospital. We just need to land this thing so we can go after her."

"I can't do it. I can't do this anymore. How do people live like this, loving and losing the ones they love? It's tearing me in two." She wept harder, clinging to his shirt with a fist.

"Mame's a fighter. She'll need your positive vibrations

when we get back." He didn't know what else to tell her. The gentle rising of the balloon rocked them, providing the comfort he could not.

Had he been on the ground, he'd be tearing his hair out, ordering the medics to the duties they already knew, fighting his helplessness in the only way he knew how—with his knowledge. Or maybe chasing in a bloody rage after the villains who had made his life a living hell—when the police could do it far better than he could.

Up here, he could do nothing at all. He could steer the balloon to the nearest flat field, but they had no ground crew racing after them, no one to help them tie the balloon down, no one to pick them up and take them back to town. Eventually, Jock's crew would fight their way through the melee to come after them, but not yet.

For the first time in his life, he had to let go, to let events happen without him. With Alys in his arms, it didn't seem such a bad thing.

Except, of course, he couldn't keep her.

"The sun is setting," he said, working for that yoga-like calm Alys could inspire with one sunny smile.

She wiped her eyes on his shirt and turned her head enough to look into the sky. "Ow." She winced and sat back some more, poking at a hole in her sweatshirt. "My arm hurts."

With a curse, Elliot grabbed her arm, found the charred black holes and the trickle of blood, and jerked the sweatshirt off of her. Under it, she was wearing the knit shirt that was all collar and no shoulders, and he could see the raw, bleeding wounds across the pale skin of her upper arm.

"He must have used pellets. You've been shot." He'd

had years of practice at speaking calmly, even after he'd just swallowed his heart and it lodged in his esophagus.

He tore off his jacket and threw it on the floor. Ripping at his buttons until they skittered across the basket, he pulled off his shirt, shredded the cotton, and folded it into a compress.

"It's just a flesh wound." He hoped. He hadn't dressed a wound in years, and this one had started to bleed copiously.

"Shot?"

To his disbelief, Alys dried her tears to stare with interest at her arm. "Like in the cowboy movies when the hero says it's just a flesh wound and keeps on fighting?"

"Right. Want to fight?" Elliot used the sleeve of his shirt to tie the compress into place. He didn't think she would bleed to death anytime soon, but now that he had a task to accomplish, he set his mind to it. He understood action far better than the emotions rioting through him.

"No, it hurts like heck. I can't imagine riding a horse like this." She winced while he tied it. "This means some of the pellets didn't hit Mame. Maybe the others missed, too?" she asked with hope in her voice.

"We can hope," he told her, so she could keep giving off those positive vibrations. "If they were just pellets, she should be fine. The idiot was probably aiming at the balloon." Which meant Mame could have had a heart attack. Elliot preferred not to think of either alternative.

She poked at the bandage in wonder. "You're good. I think it's stopped bleeding already."

"No major arteries there, but it needs cleaning."

He glanced doubtfully at his makeshift handiwork,

then at her tearstained face watching him with admiration, and he couldn't resist.

Slowly, so she had time to back off, he lowered his mouth to hers.

She didn't back off. She didn't tell him this was entirely inappropriate. She parted her lips for him and responded with the warmth and vibrancy he desperately needed.

Life and love poured into him through the sweet delight of her lips. To prevent her from lifting her injured arm, Elliot cradled Alys in his lap, tasting the salt on her lips and kissing her tears away. She purred when he covered her breast with his palm, and her nipple sprang alive beneath his touch, as alive as he always felt with Alys in his arms.

He wanted this moment to go on forever—sailing freely above the world, holding happiness against his chest.

Alys applied kisses along his jaw, and he leaned back against the basket, soaking up the pleasure, watching the balloon sail into the dusk. Lust might play a part in what he felt right now, but it wasn't lust healing the pain in his lonely heart. Alys's hand splayed across his chest, teasing him into arousal even though they couldn't act on it. He didn't think he'd ever known a better moment in his life.

Life would go on. No matter what was happening down there on the ground, there was always another day after this. If he let it happen, there could be babies to scare him and break his heart, music to get lost in, laughter to enjoy, his brothers to look after.

And Alys to love.

And because he loved her, he couldn't break her heart

and make her cry. She deserved all the love and laughter life had in store for her.

Trying not to crush her too hard, he kissed her with all the passion he possessed, hoping to gather enough strength to let her go.

The heat from Elliot's broad, bare chest warmed her. The heat of his kisses set her on fire. Alys knew instinctively that her response wasn't just animal passion, but she couldn't think about it right now. He held her and caressed her and made the world go away. Almost literally, since they were flying high above it, and she didn't know if they would ever come down.

And didn't care. She could die happily like this, with Elliot's lips on hers, his strong arms holding her anchored against the winds of fate. She trusted him to do what was best for both of them.

Until this moment, she hadn't realized how long she had been standing on her own. She'd been the one Fred had relied on when he got sick. She'd been the one who had arranged her parents' funerals. No one had offered a helping hand until Mame had dragged her back to her feet after she'd collapsed from the burden of it all. And she'd still been alone.

The sheer bliss of letting go, letting someone else brace her against life's buffets, showed her that she didn't have to be alone. That no one should be.

"I think I could fly with you to the moon," she murmured, stroking the bulge of his upper arms and lifting herself into his hungry kiss, unable to clarify her thoughts any better than that.

"To the moon, Alys," he chuckled against her mouth. "Although there are days I think you're already there."

The balloon hit an air bump and jarred them back to the moment, where they needed to be. Alys glanced up and saw the mountains moving closer. In the rosy hues of the setting sun, the red rocks were spectacular. Shadows carved images into the hills, and her heart soared with the birds.

"I suppose I'd better be looking for a safe landing place. Surely they've sent someone after us by now."

Elliot was looking down at her with regret. Alys didn't want to move. She wanted him to make love with her right now. Burned with the desire for it. And knew they might never make love again.

"We need to get back to Mame," she agreed, knowing that's what he needed more than her.

He didn't agree or disagree. He ran his hands through her hair, cupped her face, and kissed her nose in the very un-Elliot-like gesture he'd developed over the past few days. She wanted to explore this new Elliot and all the other Elliots hiding inside him.

He set her away from him and stood up tall against the sky, efficiently pulling on cords and resetting burners and checking gauges she couldn't hope to understand. The sun gleamed off his bronzed, muscular shoulders and dark curls, and she thought if she lived to be a hundred, she'd never forget the sight of Elliot commanding the winds.

She gave him her heart then, to do with as he wished. She wouldn't need it anymore.

"Tell me what to do." She stood beside him, watching the balloon drift lower into the shadows beneath the hills. The world needed men like Elliot. She would always be proud of this week, no matter what the future held. She'd helped him. She knew she had.

"I don't want your wound to open. Just admire the scenery and tell me if you see a car racing in our direction. We could spend a cold night out here if no one comes for us."

Away from Elliot's warmth, she shivered in the cool breeze. He instantly reached for her sweatshirt and helped her pull it back on, easing her injured arm through first so she wouldn't have to lift it. She'd forgotten how comforting it was to have someone caring for her.

Clinging to a rope, she glanced over the side, locating a highway with cars. She searched the shadows closer to the balloon and saw a racing vehicle. "How do we know that isn't Salvador down there?"

"Do they have a flatbed for the balloon?"

"A trailer of some sort," she agreed, watching the car slow to check their position. "There's a small road and lots of cactus."

He snorted. "We'll survive cactus." He pulled the vent cord some more so the balloon descended in the direction she pointed. "If they have a trailer, they're crew. I don't think Salvador would be so considerate."

She didn't want to land. She wanted to sail off into this fantasyland they'd created. But Elliot and Mame needed her right now, and she threw him a big smile to show it would be all right. "Maybe I could be a balloon pilot!"

"That works." His dry tone returned to the familiar as he gauged his distance to the approaching ground.

Alys laughed. She could do this. She could give him laughter and help him through whatever lay ahead. She knew how to make the best of every minute she was given without wondering what the next would hold. She could teach Elliot to do the same.

"I love the way your chin tilts up when you laugh."
He leaned over and kissed her before returning his attention to the controls.

See, she'd done it right, given him what he needed
while hiding her breaking heart.

Minutes later, the slowly deflating balloon bumped
the basket along the rocky ground. Alys watched in awe
as the crew worked in coordination with Elliot, grabbing the wicker to hold it down, rushing to spread a tarp
across the cactus-studded ground, catching guide wires
to pull the balloon toward the tarp while Elliot opened
the valve at the top of the balloon all the way, releasing
the hot air into the cold night.

The magnificent maroon-and-gold envelope slowly
collapsed over the tarp, and the basket stood still.

Before leaping out as she fully expected him to do, Elliot stopped to caress her cheek. "Thank you."

He didn't give her time to ask for what. He jumped
out and held his arms out to her while men yelled and
ran about, pushing the remaining air from the envelope.
As deflated as the balloon, Alys stepped from the gondola, back into the real world.

❊ TWENTY-SIX ❊

"She's stabilized for the moment," Elliot informed the doctor entering Mame's room on night rounds.

Holding Mame's frail hand between hers, Alys watched Elliot pace while the admitting physician checked Mame's vital signs, noted her chart, and with a nod to Elliot, returned to his rounds.

Elliot was in full doctor mode, wearing his sports coat and a black T-shirt someone had given him, checking the IV, reading charts. The nurse didn't dare shoo Alys or Jock out, for fear the formidable Doc Roth would bark at her.

"They've given her medicine to help her sleep. You can't do anything here, Jock." Elliot stopped beside the other man's chair. "Get some rest. You have a race in the morning, don't you?"

Jock looked as if he hadn't slept in a week, although they'd been here only a few hours. Empty Styrofoam coffee cups littered the table beside his chair. His complexion was nearly as gray as his beard, but he'd watched Mame's lined face with care since they'd arrived.

He shook his shaggy head. "The crew can take over without me. I'd feel better if I stayed here. I've been waiting for this woman to come around for a long time. I'll not leave her now."

"Mame needs his positive energy," Alys argued at signs of Elliot rejecting Jock's offer. "Perhaps we ought to assign shifts so someone is with her all the time."

Mame's pellet wounds weren't serious. The damage to her heart from the second attack might be irreparable. Alys had clung to the hard seat of her hospital chair for hours, her knuckles white from the strain of fighting a panic attack. As usual, the hospital environment made it impossible to find her center, until she realized *Elliot* was her center. After that, her hysteria subsided, and she'd fixed on him, letting his energy flow through her and into Mame. She was worried now, but calm.

Elliot glanced at her. His long face was lined with concern, his dark eyes shuttered against the pain of watching Mame lying there so still. Alys knew him well enough to know what he was thinking. It was tough for him to admit that he couldn't change anything by his presence, that Mame had to come around on her own.

He checked his watch. It was past midnight. Alys knew they couldn't do anything at this hour except watch Mame breathe. If Jock was willing to stay, she needed to get Elliot out of here, give him time to rest before whatever tomorrow wrought.

To her relief, Elliot nodded. "That sounds good. Jock, if you can stay until dawn, I'll come back then. I'll ask the nurse to bring some blankets and pillows for you."

The frown on Jock's forehead relaxed, and he stood to shake Elliot's hand. "Mame's spent a lot of years worrying about you boys, waiting until the lot of you were old enough to stand on your own, before changing her life around. I didn't think she ever meant to let go, but I can see the effort was worth it. She raised you right. I'll call the hotel if anything changes."

Exhausted, relieved, and scared, Alys let Elliot take charge. Mame would want her to look after Elliot. If there was any chance he could end up on a hospital bed looking like Mame, she had to prevent it.

On the way out, they stopped to speak with the policeman in the corridor. He looked as weary as Alys felt.

"You won't be able to get a statement from my aunt until tomorrow, I'm sorry," Elliot told the man. "She has to have complete rest. Are Dulce and Lucia safe?"

The cop nodded and tucked his notebook away. "The tribal police were watching out for them. The guys in the semis thought they were rescuing their boss's kidnapped kid. They watch way too many movies and got carried away playing hero. Once they found out the kid was happy and with her family on the reservation, they cooled down. The jerk who shot at the balloon is a hothead with prior convictions for firearm violations, but he wants to apologize. We told him to get a lawyer."

"Did they mention why there was a positioning device in a kid's camera?" Elliot asked, wearily draping his arm over Alys's shoulders.

The cop shrugged. "Mendoza figured her family would come after her sooner or later. He was prepared. His lawyers are already burning up phone lines keeping him out of jail."

Alys clung to the comfort of Elliot's embrace and wondered if she should feel joy that Lucia was safe or feel sorrow that Lucia's grandfather was such a pitiful man. She was too tired to reason it out. Thanking the policeman, staying at Elliot's side, she dragged her feet toward the elevator. She was too exhausted to even feel relief that they were leaving the confines she so dreaded. Her arm throbbed where they'd stitched it in the emergency room. She probably ought to take the painkillers she'd been given, but she'd wanted to stay alert for Mame's sake. And Elliot's.

"Come on, we'll put you to bed. I know you're tired when you're not bouncing." Squeezing her shoulders, Elliot led her downstairs.

To their surprise, several groups waited in the lobby, huddled over coffee or stepping outside the door for a smoke. At their appearance, everyone converged on them with questions about Mame.

Milo and his friends presented Alys with a slightly drooping calla lily for Mame's room. Accepting the plant, she hugged them all.

With black eyes and split lips, looking as rough as the bikers, several of the truck drivers hung back and waited for their turn. Both groups had apparently settled their differences over a few beers, if Alys was any judge of breath, but she didn't know their faces, just their expressions. When one of the truckers tentatively stepped forward and Elliot tried to pull her away, she shook off his protective gesture to meet the man halfway.

"The guys wanted you to know we're real sorry for scaring you like that." He looked guiltily at Alys's wounded arm. "And we're even sorrier about the lady getting hurt. Mackie's kinda nuts, carrying that old shotgun everywhere he goes. It went off half-cocked. The cops have him downtown. None of the rest of us carried weapons. We were just . . . We thought . . ."

"We know." Alys held out her hand to him. "You were looking after Lucia, just as we were. We don't blame you for the confusion."

The driver shook her hand, then glanced warily over her shoulder at Elliot. "You pack a mean right," he said, as if that smoothed the waters. "There was three of us and only one of you at that motel. I don't want to be on your wrong side."

"Did I tell you how Alys can break boards with her bare hands?" Milo interrupted, boastingly. "Look at that tiny thing! You guys didn't stand a chance."

"Karate? You know karate? Hell, if you two ever want to hire out as drivers . . . I don't think Hank is ever gonna live down the way you bluffed him out and got away."

Alys heard Elliot chuckle and relaxed. She sent him a knowing glare over her shoulder, but he just squeezed her shoulder.

Leaving the drivers and bikers to discuss fights they'd shared, she followed Elliot over to the balloon crew waiting anxiously for some word of Mame. They'd known her only a few days, but she was already a friend.

After Elliot reassured them that all was well for the moment, one of the men handed Elliot a ring of keys. "We had the tires replaced. Thought Mame might be needing these."

The Taurus was still at the hotel. The keys must be to the SUV that Mame had stolen from Elliot. Alys watched with sinking heart as Elliot clasped the keys to freedom in his hand.

"Give me the invoice and I'll pay you back," he told them. "I can't thank you enough for looking after my aunt for me."

Alys didn't listen to the exchange of pleasantries after that but drifted to the plate-glass window overlooking the parking lot. Against the black night, all she could see was her reflection. Had she been fooling herself into thinking she'd be needed here?

Elliot came up behind her. She could see the weariness in his reflection, but he merely put his arm around her and steered her toward the parking lot where the crew had said the Rover was located.

They drove to the hotel with only the mechanical voice of the SUV's computer guidance system breaking the silence. Alys watched Elliot's profile in the pale light of passing street lamps. Self-sufficient and contained, he didn't need her help through the empty streets, just as he'd traveled through life alone without her.

He was probably already regretting the bonds they'd shared. She knew what happened between them wasn't her imagination. She *felt* things. And what she was feeling now was scary. She might believe Elliot needed her, but he'd lived on his own for a very long time. He might not hold the same belief.

It wasn't until they were in the hotel elevator that Alys realized they had two rooms at their disposal now. Mame wouldn't need hers.

"I didn't look for Mame's keys," Elliot said, as if hearing her thoughts. "Do I need to go down to the desk and ask for a copy?"

"No." She might not know what she wanted of the future, but she knew what she wanted tonight.

"Good." He sounded relieved as he opened the door to their room.

The king-sized bed beckoned. Alys didn't think she could even manage a shower. Elliot decided the matter for her. Leaning down, he kissed her. When she responded with every ounce of energy left in her, he swept her off her feet and carried her to bed. Jerking back the covers, he lay her fully clothed upon the sheets.

"You need rest," he said gruffly. "You've lost blood."

"Not to mention a year of my life in sheer fright." Not really agreeing with him, Alys lifted her good arm to tug him down with her. "Tonight doesn't count for much in the scheme of things."

Apparently willing to agree, Elliot climbed in beside her. He propped himself up on one arm and leaned over her. Alys traced the scar beside his mouth with her fingertips, then traced his lips. She was terrified of what the future held. She couldn't bear to lose Elliot. She saw so much compassion and knowledge in his eyes—all trapped inside him and looking for a way out.

He kissed her eyelids closed. "You should rest."

"I won't." She slid her palms over the soft cotton of the black T-shirt, then tugged at the sleeves of his jacket.

He shrugged the coat off, lay down, and pulled her into his arms. "I'll hold you until you go to sleep."

"If you think I'll go to sleep like this, you don't know me well." She rested her head on his wide shoulder and slid her hands over his chest and toward his waistband. She knew what he needed, because she needed it, too.

Elliot buried his face in her hair and didn't stop her. "I think I might burst if I don't have you right now," he murmured. "I just didn't want you to think I expected it."

She smiled and worked on his belt buckle. "I know how to say no when I want to. We nearly died today. I think a little life is called for."

Wordlessly, Elliot pulled off her turtleneck and her sweatshirt at the same time. He kissed the curve of her breast over her bra, then unfastened the bra. "Holding you warm and naked reassures me you're alive. If you're tired—"

"I'm not dead yet. I'd have to be not to want you." There, she'd said it. Sort of. He could make of it what he would. She conquered his belt and started on his zipper.

Elliot rolled her over, crushing her wandering hands between them, leaning over to take her nipple into his mouth.

Yes! she screamed inside her head as pleasure coursed through her, feeding her strength. Freeing her trapped hands, she ran them through Elliot's unruly curls.

He tugged her hips free of her jeans and panties. She wiggled them the rest of the way off while he discarded his T-shirt, trousers, and shorts. Knowing each other's desires well, they merged with a primitive cry of need, seeking oblivion and sinking into it with the fierce mating of their bodies.

Coming together, awash with the pleasure of satiation afterward, they collapsed in each other's arms. Alys didn't need the pain medication to relieve the throbbing in her arm. Elliot's proximity eased her and sex had sedated her. She was asleep in minutes.

Elliot stayed awake long after, holding Alys against his chest, stroking her sleek hair, memorizing every moment before the dawn.

He'd always had one focus until now. Alys had taught him how narrow that focus was. Now that he had a wider one, he had to resist the urge to assume what he wanted was right for everyone. He needed to let those he loved make their own decisions. He didn't know if he could change, but he had to try.

The first step would hurt the worst.

* * *

Chilled, Alys sought the warmth of Elliot's body that she'd come to expect beside her. Funny, how a person could get used to the closeness so easily. It was as if she'd spent these last few years frozen in a block of ice, and now she craved heat.

He wasn't where she remembered, but the bed was big. Sleepily, she rolled over the other way, patting the sheets. They were cold.

The exhaustion of yesterday's terror and loss of blood made her groggy. Her arm hurt. She should take an aspirin at least, but her eyes wouldn't open. She dozed off again.

Alys woke to the noise of a vacuum cleaner in the hall outside. Shoot. The maid would be knocking on the door, and she wasn't wearing anything.

She pried open one eyelid. Sunlight gleamed through the crack between the room-darkening curtains. What time was it anyway? Elliot had said something about taking Jock's place at dawn.

She turned over and found the clock. Almost noon! She really had been wiped. She knew the bed was empty before she sat up. Elliot had gone to the hospital without her.

But they had two cars now. She could drive the Taurus over and take a turn at Mame's side. Mame! She needed to check to see how she was doing. Elliot should have called to tell her how Mame was and what the doctors had decided.

The vacuum whined outside the door. Wrapping a sheet around her, Alys stumbled from the bed and looked for the DO NOT DISTURB sign. It wasn't there. Elliot must have hung it out for her, bless his heart.

Okay, next, find hospital number. She splashed some

water in her face, took an aspirin, and dug out the phone book. The hospital listing was half a page long, but she decided on the admissions number and punched it into the phone.

Adjusting the sheet, she waited for an answer, gave Mame's name, and waited for them to transfer the call.

After a brief interval, the clerk returned to the phone. "Mrs. Emerson was transferred out this morning."

Transferred out? Alys frowned, verified they were talking about the same Mrs. Emerson, obtained no further information from the busy clerk, and hung up.

A pocket of terror formed in her heart.

She glanced around the darkened room as she hadn't earlier.

Elliot's suitcase was gone.

In disbelief, she staggered out of the huge bed they'd just shared last night. His suitcase had been right there, neatly fitting on the dresser. The trousers and shirt he'd discarded last night were gone. His toiletries case had vanished from the vanity.

He'd left without her.

Panic raised goose bumps up and down her arms. How could he do that? She was a reasonable person. He could have at least said some kind of polite farewell. She would have understood.

Had Mame taken a turn for the worse?

Frantically, she snapped on a desk light, wondering if she dared try Elliot's cell phone. The thought of getting his voice mail caused a lump in her throat.

A piece of hotel stationery covered in Elliot's precise handwriting waited in the puddle of lamplight, held in place by the orchid she'd left sitting on the windowsill.

Snatching the note from the desk, she read while she

lowered herself into the chair. Her hand began to shake, and angrily she fought back tears.

She wouldn't let him do this to her. She glanced at the car keys lying on the desk. Damn him! That was the same as paying for her services. She wanted to ram them down his throat. The despicable bastard! Who did he think he was, taking charge of the world?

She scanned the note again, trying to find her inner peace so she could read sensibly, without all her fear and anger raging about, knocking her senseless. He was flying Mame into UCLA, to some heart program there. Good. This was productive.

Get a grip, Alys, read slowly.

There was nothing about him. He gave her the name of some friends in California in case she decided to finish the Route 66 trip. She could leave the SUV keys with them. Or if she decided to stay in Albuquerque, she could drop the keys in a mailbox when she didn't need them anymore.

She glanced at the keys again. She'd thought they were the rental car keys. He'd left her *his* keys?

Was he really asking her to return the car to him? Would he still be in L.A. if she drove there?

That was an awful small hook to hang her hopes on. Heart thumping, she read more slowly. Elliot was flying Mame to California. Jock lived in California. Jock was turning in the Taurus and flying home. Beulah would have to stay at Sam's until Mame could get her. If Mame needed surgery, Jock would be there to help out. Elliot still didn't mention his place in the scheme of things. He told her to enjoy her journey.

He just gave her the facts and left her the keys—giving her the freedom to do as she would.

☀ TWENTY-SEVEN ☀

The Range Rover was a far cry from Mame's Cadillac.

Driving the highway, looking down from the high seat onto other cars, experimenting with the guidance system, Alys let the sun beating through the windshield ease the pain of Elliot's absence.

He had set her free. She wasn't entirely certain how to feel about that, but she was about to find out.

She'd stopped at a discount store and bought a pretty lavender camera for Lucia. She'd gone to the tribal reservation to check on her and Dulce. They'd been surrounded by a huge happy family celebrating their return. Dulce had talked of finishing school in Albuquerque. Lucia was delighted with her grandmother. Purple had been stalking field mice. They would be fine now that they were safe and together.

Alys wasn't feeling particularly fine, but she soaked up their positive vibrations and carried them with her. Lucia's family had developed her pictures and given Alys duplicates. One of the photos had been of Elliot. She kept it in her pocket next to her heart until she decided whether to tear it into shreds or treasure it always.

He was trying to save Mame's life. She could relate to

that. She could return the SUV and maybe they would just be friends. Mame could tell her all about Elliot in long chatty phone conversations. He'd still be in the universe somewhere.

He hadn't died.

He was afraid he would.

But Elliot would fight to live. That's what his life had been about—prolonging life. And not just his life, but the lives of many. She could love a man like that. And he would break her heart—again.

Driving across the vast barren plains of New Mexico and Arizona, admiring the sagebrush and mesas and approaching mountains, Alys thought about that. She turned on the radio and sang along with "Staying Alive." She discovered Elliot had a CD collection in the car and popped one of his classical CDs into the player. The car filled with the drama of Tchaikovsky while she took a side road and drove through the Petrified Forest. She didn't see much reason to stop, though. With whom would she discuss the crumbling remains of strange rock trees? There wasn't a soul in sight.

She found an Eagles CD and played "Take It Easy" as she took the old road into Winslow, Arizona. She stopped and had a Big Mac and a shake, but without Elliot here, caring enough to tell her she was ruining her health, they didn't taste quite as good as she'd expected.

The gradual climb of the interstate into the mountains wasn't as dramatic as flying over the mesas of New Mexico in a hot air balloon with Elliot wrapping her in his arms.

"I'm beginning to see a pattern here," she muttered as once more her thoughts turned to Elliot. She programmed the GPS to find the Grand Canyon, deviating from her route. She'd dreamed of crossing the country, free to go where the spirit took her. This was the opportunity of a lifetime, and she was determined to enjoy herself. Bless Elliot for setting her free.

The canyon was huge. She stood on the edge and stared down and decided she'd enjoyed riding horses with Elliot through Palo Duro more than standing alone above this incomprehensible vastness.

She needed people, dammit. Without people, she'd return to that block of ice she'd been after Fred's death. She wasn't made to live alone.

She found a park lodge, ordered a meal in the restaurant, and looked around, wondering how she could find someone to talk to. It was October, and the only families here were ones with small children who demanded all their attention. There were several couples chattering away in foreign languages. No one sat alone, like her. The isolation chilled her.

She chatted with the waitress, then returned to the front desk to ask about a room. From the clerk she learned snow was expected and that the hotel was full. She hadn't dared make reservations for herself, not knowing if she could afford to finish the trip on her own. Thanks to Elliot, the problem of transportation had been reduced to the cost of gas. She had enough money to eat and still see the sights.

She could find another hotel, then drive back to sit in front of the fire at the lodge and watch the snow.

Or she could keep driving—to California, where the sun was shining.

She climbed into the Rover, drove down the road until she found a cheap hotel, and stopped for the night. The room was shabby and lonely but clean and quiet. Exhausted, she slept.

She was up at dawn, heading out before the snow clouds moved in.

Her heart ached as much as her arm. This was what she'd wanted, wasn't it? She'd had all those grandiose dreams of merrily cruising America, seeing the sights she'd only heard about, meeting strangers in strange places.

And she'd done that, with Elliot. He'd made her laugh and cry, showed her the world from his perspective as well as hers, made her feel at home no matter where they traveled. With someone to share her vision, the mountains were higher, the air was clearer, the people more interesting.

On her own, one McDonald's looked like another, one stretch of interstate didn't vary from the last, and even rattlesnake soup tasted like chicken. Strangers were always strangers, gone tomorrow, making no place for her.

Maybe the song was right. Maybe "freedom" was just another word for nothing left to lose.

She drove through mountain and desert in the same day, asked a nearby tourist to take her picture entering California, but she felt none of the euphoria she had earlier. A road sign wasn't the state of California. Singing about "California Girls" didn't make her one.

She'd experienced love and longing and near-death in one week's time. What would she do with the rest of her life?

Using the car's navigational device, she battled rush-hour traffic into Los Angeles, found the stretch of original road on the east side, and turned onto it. She cruised the old route, thinking of Mame driving out here with her new husband, knowing she could lose him to a cruel war, that she had to make her way home alone.

Tears started sliding down Alys's cheeks as she followed the highway into Santa Monica. In between sobs, she drove around until she found a parking spot where she could walk to the beach. The end of the road.

Standing on the pier, watching the sun fall over her first view of the ocean, she literally stopped breathing. Larger than the canyon, so large it reached the horizon and touched the sun, the sea enthralled her, drying up her tears. She sought her center, hoping to absorb the magnificence, hoping to find a sign to direct her.

She smelled the salt, heard seals in the distance, watched gulls circle and dive over the water. Children ran along the water's edge, screaming with delight. A lone surfer caught a cold wave and rode it to shore. People jostled around her. Shops teemed with activity. She could walk into any one of them and ask for a job and live here forever. That's what she'd dreamed about, wasn't it?

The horizon turned apricot and purple. The waves lapped gently. Strange, contorted trees dotted the landscape. Fabulous flowers climbed the walls. She was in a tropical paradise. Elliot and Mame would return to Missouri.

She had come to the end of the road and reached a crossroad.

Her heart lightened as she finally faced the facts. Elliot had done the same thing as Fred—they had both loved her enough to set her free.

Softly, she whispered, "I understand now, Fred. I love you, too. Thank you." Digging the wedding band out of her purse, she kissed it, then flung it far out into the waves.

"It's a routine angioplasty, Mame," Elliot assured her. "They'll insert a tiny tube in the clogged artery, inflate it like a balloon, clear the passage, and you'll be fine again."

Mame nudged her pillows into a more comfortable position and with the regal frown of a queen, glared at the two men in her life. "I am not spending the rest of my life lying about on a couch like some tragic figure in a soap opera. If I'm going to die, I'd rather just do it."

"Mame, I know plenty of guys who've had this done. You'll be spoiling your nephew's kids when they're in college," Jock argued.

"Will I?" Mame lifted her artificially tinted eyebrows at her nephew.

With a twinge of pain at the mention of children he might never have, given what he'd done to Alys, Elliot picked up her chart. "Lying around is the worst thing you can do. Healthy exercise and diet is the prescription after surgery. You scared us all for nothing."

"It wasn't for nothing. It was for Lucia. Tell me about my grandchildren, Elliot. I can call them grandchildren, can't I? It's a trifle awkward to keep calling them my nephew's children. I think you have to have a wife first, don't you?"

"Mame, you aren't pulling me into this argument. First, the surgery. My love life or lack of it isn't relevant. Will you please sign the consent form?"

She regarded him through knowing eyes. "If this is routine surgery, why don't you have it done?"

Elliot slid his pen back in the pocket of his medical coat and ran his hand through his hair. "They'll run tests on me as soon as I know you're on your way to recovery."

Mame beamed and reached for the clipboard with the consent form. "It's about time you decided to live, young man. Now let's hope Alys is smart enough to forgive you for your stupidity."

Taking the form Mame handed back to him, Elliot feared Alys was smart enough to go on without him. She could be enjoying oceans and sunsets and healthy young men who had decades ahead of them, adventurous souls willing to share their years.

As she'd pointed out often enough, he was a determined man capable of getting whatever he went after. He could have persuaded her to stay with him, but not at the cost of her happiness.

If he could keep believing she was laughing somewhere, he'd be fine. He'd lived with a broken heart all his life.

UCLA was an *enormous* place. Sitting in her shoddy—extremely expensive—hotel room, Alys scanned the pages of numbers in the phone book and located another likely one. She should be out looking for a job. She couldn't afford to stay in hotels for long. Her orchid needed a good home. She thought she saw a bud forming along one stalk. Hotel windows weren't sunny enough.

But she had to find Elliot and Mame before she could move on. She needed to know that Mame would recover. She had to know why Elliot didn't answer his cell phone.

Biting a corner of her lip, she dialed still another number. This time, she got the nursing school—and suddenly all the pieces shifted into place.

An hour later, she was on the road again. The motel didn't have bellhops to help her with luggage as the Hilton had, so she'd left her suitcases in the Rover and simply rummaged through them for the best outfit she could find. She hadn't brought any suits with her, but she'd found a pair of gray dress slacks and her all-purpose navy blazer. The silky white blouse with the ruffled V-neck was a little frivolous, but her only other option had been T-shirts and turtlenecks. They might have been suitable for an interview, but she had high hopes of finding Elliot before day's end.

Maybe she should have worn a businesslike turtleneck for Elliot. Would he take her seriously then? She really wasn't a flake, but he'd only had a week to figure that out, and she hadn't helped him much.

Thinking of all the sensible, uniformed nurses hanging on to Doc Nice's every word, Alys chewed her lip and drove a little faster. The weekend was over. He might have flown back to St. Louis to tape his radio show, for all she knew. She had to do this for *her*.

And she was. This was perfect. Ideal. If she didn't have enough money in the insurance account to cover her tuition and couldn't swing any scholarships, she'd work nights. The possibilities were limitless once she had her degree. She might explode with excitement if she thought about it too hard. She'd been blind for so long . . .

But now she saw. Smiling at the muddled line from "Amazing Grace," she followed the navigation system's directions into the parking lot at UCLA's medical facilities. Pure happiness spilled through her at the sight of all the modern buildings. She didn't have the fortitude to be a doctor making life-and-death decisions, but she understood how caring for the spirit healed as much as medicine did. She would be the best nurse the world had ever seen.

Once she had knowledge, she wouldn't be helpless anymore.

Now that she knew the source of her fear, she marched into the antiseptic hospital without an instant of hesitation and asked for the head of nursing, who had agreed to speak with her. She felt just like her old self again—confident and assured—and a lot more mature.

From there, she was sent from office to office, gathering armfuls of information as she went. They showed her options and choices and even other schools, cost packages, and scholarships. With every step, she grew more certain that she could do this. On her own. All she had to do was decide where she wanted to go: here or home. St. Louis had a wonderful nursing school.

With her course firmly established, she asked the staff how to find a heart patient. Within minutes, she'd learned Mame's location and was on her way to still another medical facility. By this time, she was carrying a canvas bag full of brochures. She clung to them as she took the elevator up to Mame's room.

A little over a week ago she had been a shivering wreck taking a similar elevator up to see Mame in a different hospital. If she allowed the panic to creep back in, she could be reduced to that same shivering wreck, but she had a purpose now, one outside herself, and that gave her strength.

She'd been terrified of being left alone again, and she'd let fear control her. But she'd learned from Elliot that knowledge gave her power. She could take command of her life, as he had his.

She ran into Jock drinking coffee in the waiting room. He looked better today, smiling as he recognized her.

"How is Mame?" she asked eagerly.

"She sailed through the operation with flying colors," he boasted proudly. "Mame's a trouper. I should never have let her get away from me all those years ago."

She took a deep breath in relief, letting it flow through her and sink in. After all these days of worrying, it felt good to know that Mame was alive, and with luck would be for many more years. "She had three boys to raise and you had a life to live. It's good you've found each other now. You'll give her reason to stay healthy."

Jock glanced at his coffee cup. "Yeah, I've got to give up this stuff if I want to keep up with her. The doc says she can't have caffeine, and it's probably not good for me either."

"But she can fly balloons when she's well, can't she?"

He beamed. "That she can. And we will. I got a place out here where she can recover. I'm hoping by the time she's well, she'll agree to stay with me."

Alys raised her eyebrows. "What does Elliot have to say about that?"

He grinned. "We ain't told him yet. He's got enough on his mind right now, so we're letting him figure it out for himself. Mame's awake and kicking. Why don't you run back and see her for yourself?"

Alys didn't need to be told twice. Following Jock's directions, she all but raced down the corridor.

"I'm not walking around on that thing like an old lady!" a familiar voice cried from behind a partially closed door. "If I can't walk on my own, I'll lie here and rot in the bed."

Smiling, Alys shoved open the door. Mame stood beside her hospital bed in a long blue robe, her red hair neatly arranged and her makeup adeptly applied. At the sight of Alys, she smiled hugely.

"There you are. Tell this tyrant you'll lend me your arm, and maybe she'll take that repellent walker away."

Throwing her bag of brochures onto a chair, Alys smiled at the nurse, offered her arm to Mame, and kicked the walker aside with her foot. "I want to be just like you when I grow up, Mame."

"You are just like me already. You just don't know it yet." With a glare at the nurse, Mame held her head high and proceeded to walk out of the hospital room, one very careful step at a time. "It's about time you got here. Come along. We've some visiting to do."

"Mrs. Emerson, you can't go any farther than the nurse's desk!" the nurse called after her.

"Do you believe that?" Mame said sotto voce. "They think I'm old."

"Nah, they're following the rules. I don't think any patient is supposed to walk much after an operation. Besides, Jock is waiting out there to take you back to your room. What room am I visiting?"

Mame looked at her through shrewd eyes. "You haven't fainted yet."

"Don't intend to," Alys replied cheerfully. Waving at Jock in the waiting room, she halted at the nurse's desk. "I've chosen my future. Now it remains to be seen where I'll live it."

"If Jock has his way, there will be a big old house sitting empty in Springfield come spring," Mame said as

Jock headed toward them. "Doing things on your own has its place, but it's even better sharing with someone else."

"For people like us, anyway." Alys kissed Mame's papery cheek. "I'm learning that. It may take time to convince others."

"If anyone can, you can. Elliot's down on the next floor. Someone convinced him he's not indestructible."

"He's a stubborn man," Alys warned.

"Show him your wounded wing. He always did like healing injured creatures."

Alys grinned. "He's stubborn, not stupid. I'll be back in a little bit."

Mame cackled. "I don't think so."

Puzzled over Mame's parting remark, Alys ran back to fetch her brochures, and set out for Elliot's room.

In all her phone calls and visiting, she'd already learned the famous Doc Nice had checked himself into the hospital last night.

❈TWENTY-EIGHT❈

The door closed behind the doctor, and Elliot gazed blankly at the private hospital room his money could buy. Where did he go from here?

He had his computer and cell phone in the closet. He'd already called the radio station and told them to run a tape for next Sunday's show as well. His publisher wasn't interested in scheduling another book tour. He still had a deadline to meet, though. There was Mame to think about. And his brothers.

He'd rather think about Alys, but it hurt too much. His friends hadn't called yet. She hadn't delivered the Rover. Where could she be?

Exploring the Grand Canyon? Driving to Mexico? With a free spirit like Alys, who knew? He would have liked to have shown her palm trees and oceans.

A woman laughed down the hall, and he could hear Alys in the laughter. He would be a basket case at this rate. Sitting up, he shrugged into his robe in case a nurse was headed this way. He hated being on the other side of the bed. He could almost understand what Alys and Mame had been telling him about hospitals. The invasive, impersonal routine was daunting, even when he understood the need for it. He liked his privacy.

339

Tying the belt, he swung his legs over the edge of the bed just as the door swung open.

Alys stood there in all her glorious disarray. She carried a jacket over her arm, along with a canvas bag spilling colorful brochures. Her sexy white blouse revealed the glorious curves of her breasts. He'd never seen her wearing such sedate colors, but he liked the way the ruffle of her blouse teased him with glimpses of what he longed to see.

The load on her arm tugged the blouse open wider as she deposited the bag and jacket on a chair. She'd been running her fingers through her hair again, and upturned ends stuck out in strange places. Sleek, mink-colored hair sculpted her cheeks and emphasized her wide eyes as she studied him.

"How do you feel?" she asked anxiously, her gaze darting to the empty IV bag hanging on the far side of the bed, then down to the unblinking monitors on the nightstand, before coming back to study him.

"You're not about to sit on the floor and go into a trance, are you?" he asked warily. He hated being caught in bed, looking less than a hundred percent, but his perverse heart had just begun a rapid tattoo, and he wasn't certain he dared get up just yet. Just the sight of her had that effect on him.

"Not unless I have a reason to," she said pragmatically. "I've decided what I want to be."

Elliot sat back against his pillows, waiting with interest to see where her fascinating mind had taken her this time. "A travel writer who follows balloon festivals?"

To his surprise, she emptied her canvas bag across the covers. Pages of information on nursing careers and education requirements and universities spilled across his legs in a colorful array of slick papers.

"A nurse," she said with satisfaction, pulling the chair to the side of the bed and excitedly poking through the material. "Look. I can get scholarships. And I have enough left from the life insurance for housing."

He didn't know whether to share her obvious happiness or weep that he'd lost her for certain or laugh at the irony of her choosing a profession that took her into the hospitals she hated. He tried to show interest by picking up one of the papers she handed him, but he couldn't tear his gaze from the excitement dancing in her eyes.

"With your brains and persistence, you could be an astronaut and go to the moon if you wanted. Why would you choose a profession that would put you in the hospitals that you hate?"

She beamed. "Because it makes perfect sense. I love people. Mame was right, and so were you. I'm a nurturer, a natural caretaker. It's the cold inhospitable atmosphere of hospitals that I don't like, not medicine or doctors. I can learn what you know about practical science, and apply what I know about the spiritual nature that must be nurtured, and you can live forever!"

Stunned, Elliot just stared. He wasn't certain if he'd heard her right, or understood what he'd heard.

She waved a hand as if to brush away what she'd just said. "I know people don't live forever. I'm accepting that. But you might live longer. I can learn things like CPR and what's healthy for you. You always concentrate on the physical. I could feed you positive vibrations and—"

Elliot grabbed her hands to halt the spill of words be-

fore she said anything she'd regret later. "You don't need
to do all that for me."

The eagerness in her eyes didn't flee, but flickered with
uncertainty. "It's okay if you don't want me around. I
still want to be a nurse. But if you left me because you
didn't want to die on me, then I'm telling you that doesn't
matter. I can handle it. I know what I'm getting into and
I'm prepared."

He wasn't the kind of man who cried, but he pulled
her onto the bed and hugged her against him so she
couldn't see the moisture building in his eyes. She curled
into his arms as if she belonged there, and Elliot thought
he might burst with love and pride. "I'm not going to
die," he told her. "Not yet anyway."

She tilted her head up. "You had a heart attack, just
like Mame."

"And Mame isn't dying anytime soon either, but that's
not what I mean. My heart is fine. There is no sign of
blocked arteries or congestive failure. The doctor says I
have the heart of a college football player. Looking at
my test results, I wouldn't go that far, but I'm conservative."

Laughter crinkled the corners of her eyes, but she still
studied him, searching for the truth. "Then, what happened? The medics said your heart failed."

"You happened. I can't explain it. I may spend a lifetime trying to duplicate the results. Maybe I just had a
raw ulcer and passed out from pain and you cured it.
There are no guarantees that it won't happen again," he
warned as excitement and happiness burned in her eyes.

"But I'll be prepared next time," she crowed, flinging
her arms around his neck and raining kisses across his
cheek.

He was just getting into the soft crush of her breasts against his chest when she suddenly pulled back and stared at him in horror. If he had had a bad heart, it would have faltered right then.

"But then, you don't need me. I've been assuming you left because of Fred, but if you're fine, and you didn't call, and . . ." she stuttered helplessly, backing away. "I've made a fool of myself."

"When has that ever stopped you?" Bursting with laughter and delight, Elliot hauled her into his lap again. "I know it's too soon, and I can't expect you to agree to anything just yet, but I know my own mind. And heart. I love you. You've showed me a whole new world I would have missed if you hadn't come along. I don't want to live without you. Could you give me time to make you see things my way? Do you think you might consider nursing school in St. Louis so we could see each other more often? If not, I could always—"

"Yes!" she cried, flinging her arms around him again, landing in his lap, narrowly missing a vital part of his anatomy that was in a particularly tender state right now. "I love you. I adore you. I want to spend my life with you. I want to show you life isn't just about diet and exercise. I want—"

Flipping her back against the mattress before she could totally unman him, Elliot shut up her nonsense by firmly applying mouth-to-mouth resuscitation. With a twist.

"Marry me," he said, coming up for air, then returning to kiss her again so she couldn't refuse.

She dug her fingers into his hair and wriggled under him to a better position. Elliot immediately dived for the cleft between her breasts, peeling back silk and lace and freeing her nipple. She gasped when he drank there, but he could feel the heat and desire sweep through her. Maybe he could bribe her with sex into saying yes.

She moaned and ran her hands beneath his robe and Elliot was just beginning to wonder if they could do this without anyone walking in on them when Alys suddenly grabbed his shoulders and pushed. She couldn't budge him if he didn't want to be budged, but he was wary enough to stop what he was doing to study her face.

"Why settle for California when I can have the moon?" she replied, then tugged him back down to kiss him.

Elliot thought he might just have become engaged to be married, but he'd ask questions later.

Right now, he preferred to reinforce his future wife's positive vibrations about hospitals. He'd give her something to smile about the next time she walked into one.

❦ EPILOGUE ❦

Alys tucked mistletoe into the greenery of the arched doorway between Mame's front parlor and dining room. The outdoor scent of evergreen permeated the air. Climbing down from the ladder to twirl around and admire all the decorations, she hugged herself. The twelve-foot Christmas tree in the bay window was amazing.

She still couldn't believe this was happening to her. She felt as if she were dancing on air.

A light coating of white covered the lawn outside the window. Ice glittered in the bare maples, a perfect background for the evergreen tree shimmering in red and silver and crystal. Stacked high around the base of the tree and spilling over the perimeter onto the Victorian fireplace were colorful packages tied in gaudy bows.

Wedding gifts they hadn't opened yet.

From the kitchen drifted the aroma of baking cookies and the roar of laughter. Mame and Jock were in full fettle, she thought, smiling to herself, thinking of the love she'd seen between the two of them. She was glad they had come back here for this. Elliot's brothers had returned home for the occasion, and the house was filled to overflowing with life and laughter. She was loving every minute of it. This was what she'd needed, not loneliness. Not even freedom. She needed the ties that bind.

At the sound of feet on the elegant staircase, she glanced toward the foyer, her smile deepening as she waited for the man of her dreams to walk into the room. He'd taped his farewell radio show just yesterday. He'd turned in his manuscript last week. He'd spent these last weeks turning the library and an adjacent bedroom into an office for the practice he intended to build here in Springfield. She'd known he had to emerge from his study sooner or later.

After all, this was their wedding day.

Reaching the bottom of the stairs and seeing her, Elliot grinned and strode across the waxed wood of the front parlor. For the occasion, he wore a silver-gray suit with his usual conservative white shirt—and a red carnation in his lapel.

"You look gorgeous," he said, just before clasping her face between his hands and stopping her protests with a kiss. "I can spot mistletoe from a mile away," he murmured when they came up for air.

"Your brothers were supposed to keep you out of the way until everything was ready," she whispered against his mouth. She'd never have enough of his kisses, even if they both lived a million years.

"My brothers are too busy chowing down on all the goodies in the kitchen to care where I am. So much for my lessons on healthy eating. When does everyone start arriving? There may be no food left."

"The reverend and the rabbi and some of the guests are already here," she admitted. "They're in the kitchen sampling the menu. And I don't think you're supposed to see the bride before the wedding."

"I saw her last night," he teased. "And I wager Jock isn't too far from Mame right now either." Holding her arms, he stepped back to admire her dress. "I want the photographer to get a full-length picture of you so I can put it on my desk and remember the day you wore just one color."

She'd chosen an ankle-length soft rose velvet gown for the occasion, with romantically puffed long sleeves and a soft frill of lace on the cuff and a heart-shaped neckline. She even wore heels so she matched Elliot's height better. For a corsage, she wore a bouquet of small orchids from the plant that Mame had given her. It was thriving in the kitchen window now.

She pulled out the skirt and did a little twirl for his benefit. "You'll only see me in uniforms before long, so enjoy."

"In uniforms and out," he reminded her with a leer. "The bow around your neck was a nice touch last night."

She laughed and almost didn't notice the front doorbell until the noise from the kitchen spilled into the hallway.

Elliot caught her waist and held her. "Do you want to greet the guests or hide upstairs until the appropriate moment?"

"I've done the big wedding before. Unless you have a sudden overwhelming desire for tradition, I'd rather just keep this as we planned, call it a party, and have fun." She studied Elliot's beloved features, willing to accept his decision since this was his first wedding.

"I'm not well acquainted with weddings, parties, or fun, so I'll follow your example," he agreed without protest.

At the shouts of excitement in the foyer, they turned in that direction. The crowd of people milling in the opening, throwing off overcoats, collecting scarves, and passing around hugs, was too thick to penetrate at first glance.

Alys was the one to look beyond the Christmas tree to the yard. "Beulah!" she cried, tugging Elliot forward.

The pink Cadillac gleamed in all her snow-covered glory in the driveway. The front bumper still sagged. Plastic covered the driver's window. The small tire had been replaced, but the back fender appeared dented. She wore a bright green wreath and red bow on her front grill.

"She has a lot of years left in her," Elliot said in awe. "That car may outlive us all."

With a cry of joy, Alys darted from beneath his arm toward the guests gathering in the foyer. "Lucia!"

The child ran into the parlor and flung herself into Alys's waiting arms, chattering animatedly about a deer and chocolates and Santa Claus. Disregarding her rose wedding gown, Alys sat cross-legged on the floor, pulled Lucia into a hug in her lap, and let her rattle. Elliot thought his heart might burst from pure pride and love at the sight. Someday, she'd hold his child like that, here in this room where he'd grown up. This time around, he meant to enjoy the holidays and the small triumphs of living.

While Alys pulled out an album from under the tree to show Lucia photos from their trip, Elliot looked up to see his whole family in the doorway, watching. He caught a look of startlement and appreciation in the eyes of his brothers and hoped that meant they realized what a treasure he was about to bring into the family. They'd not been home long enough to know Alys, but they were quick studies.

Mame beamed with pride and winked at him when she caught his eye. Jock, wearing his best blue suit and a white carnation, draped his arm around Mame's shoulders and led her into the parlor so their guests could spread out. Elliot knew the two of them were ready to return to the warmth of California and the lifestyle they'd found there, but they looked like a couple of kids at Christmas poking through the assorted packages.

Dulce entered with her brother Tony, both of them carrying boxes. Whispering something into Lucia's ear, Alys put her down so the child could hunt for a package under the tree. Then she leaped up to greet their guests. Seeing Elliot lingering behind, she caught his arm and pulled him into the circle of friends.

"This is your life now," she whispered, standing on her toes and kissing his cheek. "These are your friends. Open up and let them in."

With Alys at his side, that was easy. He didn't want to be anywhere else. Not caring if he looked too much of a sap in front of his brothers, he hugged her waist and kissed the top of her head. She radiated all the positive vibrations he needed.

"Sam Wolf sent these," Dulce murmured as the front door blew open to allow in another flurry of guests. She handed the package with a silver bow to Alys. "He sends his gratitude that Lucia's grandfather Mendoza can no longer cause us grief."

"Paying for the damage his drivers caused should have cost him enough. The jail term ought to teach him a little anger management," Elliot said dryly, watching with interest as Alys untied the ribbon. His curiosity was as strong as hers.

When she idled over admiring the gift wrapping, Elliot impatiently tugged the ribbon free from the box.

The top popped open. A pair of jade-green eyes and a silver head peered from beneath the lid.

"A kitten!" Alys exclaimed in delight—just before the creature leaped from the box into the center of the Christmas tree.

While everyone shouted and danced about attempting to untangle the kitten from the tree and the ornaments, Elliot tugged his bride-to-be away from the confusion to whisper in her ear.

"I love you more than there are stars in the sky. You are my life and my heart and my future. But could we please keep the animals out of our bedroom?"

Her laughter chimed like the musical bells the cat had liberated from the tree branches, and Elliot knew he had only to ask and she would give him everything his heart desired. And more.

In return, he would give her the world and the freedom to explore it.

A ray of sunlight broke through the clouds, illuminating the sparkling diamond on Alys's left hand, the one he'd set there to replace the one she'd removed. The gold ring he carried close to his heart burned a hole in his pocket. In a few hours, he'd place it on the ring finger of her left hand.

To the moon together, he'd had engraved upon it.

Read on for a sneak peek at
PATRICIA RICE'S
next historical romance,

Much Ado About Magic

Coming in July 2005
from Signet Eclipse

London, September, 1755

Lady Lucinda Malcolm Pembroke pulled the hood of her gray mantle around her face and hurried down the nearly empty halls of the art gallery ahead of the morning crowd. She didn't halt until she reached a full-length portrait of a laughing gentleman on a galloping white stallion.

Not precisely a gentleman, she supposed, trying to be honest with herself. Romantic fantasies needn't be gentlemen. Looking up, she fell under the spell of the subject's mysterious dark eyes all over again. It was as if he looked just at her and that they shared a wonderful secret. She'd painted the portrait, so she knew the secret: The dashing gentleman didn't exist anywhere except in her imagination.

But that wasn't how rumor had it.

With a sigh, she admired the gentleman's exotically dark complexion, rakish smile, and unsettling eyes. She loved the contrast between his scarred, piratical features and his elegant clothes. She'd deliberately given him a romantic white stallion and painted the innocent background of a family fair to contrast with his aura of danger. Amazingly, the playful setting seemed to suit him.

The man didn't exist. If he had, she would never have embarrassed herself and the subject by entering the oil in the exhibition. She had even signed the painting with just her initials, to avoid any potential harm, except that there were enough people familiar with her style to set rumor rolling. She would never understand why people saw more in her art than she intended.

She couldn't imagine why the Earl of Lansdowne would want to ruin her triumph and this magnificent painting with his scandalous accusation. If he hadn't suffered an apoplexy immediately after seeing the portrait and making his furious allegations, she would demand an apology. She would never paint a *murderer*.

The sound of footsteps warned her that the first arrivals at the gallery were approaching the back hall more quickly than she'd expected, probably heading directly for the scandal of the moment rather than examining the better-known works in the front hall. She had no intention of making a spectacle of herself by appearing in public with the portrait. Looking around, she located a small niche across the hall where she could sit, unobserved.

Her fingers itched for the sketchbook and pencil in her pocket. She'd like to have a drawing of the exhibition for posterity. After this episode, her father wasn't likely to let her enter another oil, and she couldn't blame him. She'd never meant to achieve notoriety. She'd only wanted others to admire the portrait into which she'd poured her heart and soul.

She peered around the corner of the niche as a tall man strode determinedly in her direction, the skirt of his elegant coat rippling about his legs with the strength of his stride. The coat was tailored to fit shoulders and chest wider than that of most gentlemen. The lapels and cut were of precisely this year's fashion, except that the coat was *black*. No gentleman wore black in London, not even for mourning. How very odd.

His neckcloth was a pristine white with just the right amount of starch for crispness, without an inch of foppery. His breeches were of a tawny silk that matched the elaborate embroidery on the coat's lapels and pockets. His long vest matched his breeches and was embroidered with black in a simplicity that caused her to sigh in admiration. More gentlemen should accent their masculinity in this way instead of dressing as peacocks.

But when he was close enough for her to see his face, she gasped in horror and drew back as far into the niche as she could go.

Crossing his arms over his new, correctly tailored and damned expensive clothes, Sir Trevelyan Rochester studied the ridiculous portrait hanging in the Royal Art gallery for the entire world to see. Fury bubbled at the outrage perpetrated on a perfectly respectable piece of canvas that would have been better used in making sails. He dropped his gaze to the artist's signature, *LMP,* and his ire flared anew. The coward hid behind initials.

He'd spent twenty years working his way up from impressed sailor to owner of his own ship, and not one man in those twenty years had dared insult him in such a flagrant manner—not and lived to tell about it anyway. He'd defeated bloodthirsty pirates, captured French privateers, gained his own letter of marque from the King of England himself, only to be humiliated by an unknown artist on the other side of the world who could not possibly know more than rumors of his exploits.

Had it not been for his desire for peace and a home of his own rather than preparing for yet another senseless war with France over the colonies, he would never have walked the streets of London again. Had the artist counted on his not returning to England?

He would make the damned man walk the plank at sword point and dispense with the gossipmongering, scandal-provoking scoundrel as a favor to society. It was the duty of any self-respecting privateer to rid the world of enemies to king and country.

Except he'd resigned his commission and wasn't a privateer any longer, and Mr. LMP had provoked only him and not king or country.

A deep scowl drew his eyebrows together as he studied the details. It was his likeness, all right, unless he had a twin somewhere he didn't know about. Given the propensities of his noble family, that was possible but not likely.

The painting depicted *him*—Sir Trevelyan Rochester, knighted by His Majesty for action beyond the call of duty—riding a prissy white horse adorned with red ribbons on a beach in the midst of what appeared to be a summer fair. Trev assumed Mr. LMP had intended to poke fun by decking him out, a feared privateer, in macaroni attire of fluffy lace jabot and useless cuffs that spilled lace past his fingers. The boots were cuffed and shiny and foolish for riding.

The subject of the portrait was defiantly hatless and wigless. A deep blue riband tied his hair back, and one black strand blew loose to fall across his battle-scarred cheek. Trev had to admit the artist had captured his olive complexion and sharp features with painful accuracy. His mother's mixed Jamaican heritage could not be denied. Brushed with tar, his noble grandfather had called his coloring, just before he'd let the Navy take him to do with as they would.

Still, the painting was hopelessly silly. The man in it managed to look romantically dashing despite a touch of savagery behind his flashing dark eyes. Trev didn't mind that so much, but the contrast between the man and the frivolous white horse was laughable.

No wonder people were talking. Still, he did not see what had sent his cousin's widow into such fits when he'd arrived at her door. He'd spent all his adult years on the other side of the world, and she couldn't know him from Adam, but she had barely given him a minute to introduce himself before slamming the door in his face.

It was James, their old butler, who had sneaked out to explain about the portrait all of London was talking about. The preposterous painting was so well known that word of it had spread even to the rural village in the south of England where his late cousin's family resided. James hadn't had time to explain *why* the portrait was so scandalous. Or perhaps he hadn't known.

Trev hated being the center of scandal before he'd even set foot in England. He'd come home hoping to turn his prize money into a respectable merchant fleet so he could live out his remaining years in the peace of England rather than the perpetual warfare over the West Indies. He wanted the solidity of land beneath his feet for a change. He'd foolishly hoped that his wealth would pave his way despite his mixed heritage and the earl's refusal to acknowledge his legitimacy. If he didn't know better, he'd think his grandfather had planned this humiliation.

He studied the portrait, trying to determine why he'd been slandered and shut out before he could do anything to deserve it.

The painting made him look a fop, he supposed, but he hadn't been in England to sit for it. He could see no reason for alarm, except for the smirch on his masculinity. That could cause difficulty in his search for a wife, but he doubted any sensible woman in his presence would question his virility.

He was about to spin around and stalk out when a whisper from the crowd gathering behind him caught his ear. During years of living by his wits, he'd learned to keep his senses tuned to all about him. He eavesdropped unabashedly.

"They say the earl had an apoplexy right on this spot." The whisper was distinctly feminine and horrified.

Trev crossed his arms and pretended to study the portrait.

"It's a Malcolm prediction, of a certainty," another voice said in awe. "See that boat sinking in the corner? It's the viscount's. The red is quite recognizable. They say he's been missing at sea for months."

Trev ground his molars and waited. Malcolm? The M in LMP stood for Malcolm? He would know the full name of the blackguard who'd put his face upon a wall without permission and made him a laughingstock.

"There could be other red yachts," a male voice said scornfully. "But the man certainly looks a pirate."

"But Rochester hasn't been in England since childhood," the first female voice protested. "How could the artist have painted him so accurately without having seen him?"

"They don't hold fairs on the shore in Sussex," a bored male voice drawled. "It's a hoax."

Trev couldn't agree more. The silly little boat in the painting was hardly noticeable. The grieving widow standing on the rocky shoreline was buried in veils and could be anyone. An artist's ploy, contrasting laughter with grief or some such flummery. His cousin had gone down at sea months ago, so to add his yacht to the background was the artist's deliberate scandalmongering, not foretelling.

Now he understood why his cousin's widow had slammed the door in his face—the portrait showed him laughing as his cousin's yacht sank. He'd have to wring the artist's neck after all. Laurence had been a good, decent man, and his death was no laughing matter.

"The shire held a fair this year," a timid voice countered. "The new Duke of Sommersville sponsored one. That is when the yacht went down."

The crowd murmured more loudly as the conversation picked up in several places at once. "He looks dangerous enough to have murdered his cousin."

Trev snorted. No self-respecting murderer would wear that much lace, he wagered. It would get all bloody.

"Now that the viscount's gone, if the earl dies, Rochester could claim the title," said a female, followed by a horrified, "The man should hang!"

Trev figured neither spectator knew what they were talking about since Laurence had left an infant son as heir and his grandfather had declared him illegitimate. Truth never fazed good gossip, though.

Both comments overrode the more sensible voice that said, "But the man says he just arrived in England, and the viscount died last summer."

"I know Lady Lucinda," a timid female interjected. "She always paints one of her kittens into the landscape. See the orange tabby in the tree? It died of old age in April. That oil was painted last winter, well before the viscount's yacht went down. I saw her working on it."

A gasp of awe escaped the fascinated crowd, and Trev gritted his teeth at this nonsense.

"If The Prophetess painted it, then it must be true," said another woman. "She painted Pelham in his grave before he died."

"She painted my mother walking across Westminster Bridge before it was finished."

"Lady Roxbury fainted when she saw The Prophetess in the park—painting Roxbury with a woman that wasn't her and children that weren't theirs."

"You know his mistress is bearing his child," someone else murmured.

The whispers grew riper and louder, but Trev disregarded all the gossip except the relevant—a woman artist! Rocked by the enormity of such perfidiousness, he had only one thought in mind—to locate this attention-seeking *Prophetess* who had painted him as his cousin's murderer and throttle her until she admitted to all London that the painting was a hoax. Furious, he swirled around to cut a path through the crowd.

Confronted with the man in the portrait come to life before their eyes, the crowd recoiled in horror.

Feeling as murderous as they believed him, Trev stalked off without looking right or left.

Pillow Talk